Courtship
in the
Regency
BALLROOM

Annie Burrows

MILLS
BOON

Mills & Boon, an imprint of Harlequin (UK) Limited,
Eton House, 18-24 Paradise Road, Richmond, Surrey TW9 1SR

COURTSHIP IN THE REGENCY BALLROOM
© Harlequin Enterprises II B.V./S.à.r.l 2014

His Cinderella Bride © Annie Burrows 2007
Devilish Lord, Mysterious Miss © Annie Burrows 2009

ISBN: 978 0 263 90679 0

052-0114

Printed and bound
by CPI Group (UK) Ltd, Croydon, CR0 4YY

Annie Burrows has been making up stories for her own amusement since she first went to school. As soon as she got the hang of using a pencil she began to write them down. Her love of books meant she had to do a degree in English literature. And her love of writing meant she could never take on a job where she didn't have time to jot down notes when inspiration for a new plot struck her. She still wants the heroines of her stories to wear beautiful floaty dresses and triumph over all that life can throw at them. But when she got married she discovered that finding a hero is an essential ingredient to arriving at 'happy ever after'.

In The Regency Ballroom Collection

His Cinderella Bride

To Aidan, my own hero,
for always believing in me.

I wouldn't have been able
to do this without you

Chapter One

Lady Hester Cuerden did not wait for anyone to answer the kitchen door of Beckforth's vicarage. After thumping on it with her clenched fist a couple of times, she just pushed it open and marched straight in.

Caught in the act of hiding a book under her skirts, Emily Dean, the vicar's daughter, looked up from her chair beside the fire in guilty shock. Her eyes widened when she realised that Hester was visibly trembling.

'Whatever is the matter?' she asked, forgetting to conceal the worthless novel from her closest friend as she got to her feet.

Hester pulled off her gloves as she headed for the warmth of the kitchen fire. 'C...cold...' she said through chattering teeth. 'And w...wet...'

'And absolutely filthy!' Emily grabbed Hester's gloves before they had a chance to contaminate the freshly scrubbed deal table on which she had been about to deposit them, and ran with them instead to the sink in the adjacent scullery.

With numbed white fingers, Hester fumbled the buttons of her overcoat undone. Emily came back in time to see her drape it over the back of the chair she had just vacated and stretch her hands out towards the fire.

'Where's your bonnet?' Emily asked as Hester tucked a wayward coil of her distinctive vibrant auburn hair behind her ear. 'You came out in this weather without one?'

'Of course not,' Hester said. 'I was prepared for any eventuality when I set out. I had a bonnet, and a shawl wrapped over it to keep the wind off, and a basket full of provisions over my arm. You want to know where they all are now? In the bottom of a ditch, that's where.'

Emily blinked at the circle of greenish slime that was dripping on to the flagged floor from the uneven hem of Hester's skirt.

'The only eventuality for which I was not prepared,' Hester continued through gritted teeth, 'was that I should step out of the lodge gates at the exact same moment when his Lordship, the high and mighty Marquis of Lensborough, happened to be rounding the bend in the lane at breakneck speed. That reckless, foul-mouthed…' she struggled to find an epithet black enough to express her wrath, coming up eventually with 'Marquis!' as though it were the lowest form of insult she knew '…was going too fast to stop, and clearly deemed it imprudent to take evasive action. He might have injured his horses, mightn't he, if he had veered towards the ditch, or scratched the paintwork of his shiny curricle against the park wall if he had tried to swerve the other way. Do you know what he chose to do instead?' She continued before Emily even had a chance to draw breath. 'He swore at me for flinging myself under his horses' hooves. I've never heard such language.'

Emily found it hard to believe anyone was capable of exhibiting such callous behaviour. 'Didn't he make any attempt to stop?'

'I was too busy diving into the ditch myself to notice.' Hester shifted from one foot to another, drawing Emily's notice to the greenish sludge that was oozing out between the uppers and the soles of her ancient walking boots.

'You must get those boots off at once,' Emily said, promptly dropping to her knees so that she could untie the sodden laces.

'They're done for,' she pronounced as the mud-clogged sole peeled away in her hand as she tugged one boot from Hester's foot.

Hester shivered violently, then sank abruptly on to Emily's chair. 'At least I'm not,' she said, passing a shaky hand across her mud-streaked face. Her mind had been so preoccupied by the news that had sent her scurrying from the house as soon as she could slip away unnoticed, that she hadn't paused to check for traffic before stepping out into the rutted lane. She didn't know what had made her glance up. She certainly hadn't heard the curricle approaching over the noise of the wind that was buffeting her ears.

Seeing a vehicle bearing down on her had been a shock. Far more shocking was the look of blistering fury that emanated from the driver's night-dark eyes. It had pinned her, for a split second, to the spot, until the unbelievable sound of his foul language triggered her indignation, and from somewhere deep inside the instinct for self-preservation had kicked in.

'I honestly believe if I was not such a good swimmer…oh, not that there was much water in the ditch, I don't mean I would have drowned,' she explained at Emily's puzzled look. 'And that was half-frozen. Just slushy enough to cushion my fall…no…I mean that it was all those hours I spent diving into the tarn at Holme Top that gave me the expertise to dive out of the way before his Lordship had the chance to crush me.'

'Don't make it sound as if he did it on purpose, Hester,' Emily reproved. 'Just because you decided not to like the man before even meeting him.'

It was all very well for Emily to take the moral high ground, but she hadn't had all her plans overturned by the arrogant, cold-blooded…lecher! For the past three weeks, ever since he had written to inform her uncle Thomas of the date he was going to visit, and decide which one of her cousins was going to have the dubious honour of becoming his wife, the household had been rather like an ant hill after a mischievous boy has poked a stick into it. Her aunt and cousins had embarked on a shopping spree for clothes that had her uncle practically tearing his hair out at the prospect of the bills, leaving her to placate staff who were already braced for a family house party that included her imperious aunt Valeria the very same week. There was no putting off a marquis. Telling him that the date was inconvenient and could he please come another time, or saying that no, there wasn't sufficient room to accommodate the friend who had been spending Christmas with him. Oh, no. She'd simply had to devise a way of squeezing them into a house already crammed to the bursting point with assorted guests, their servants and horses.

She smiled a little maliciously to herself. Just wait till he tried to get to sleep in the rooms in the North Wing that she had persuaded her uncle to open up for his sole use. On learning from her aunt Susan that the marquis, whom she had met on several occasions, was a tall man, she had taken great delight in having the so-called Queen's bed made up for him in the abandoned Tudor apartments. His legs would overhang the end of it by miles if he tried to stretch out flat. If he did manage to doze, propped up against the mound of pillows she'd provided, the noise from the uncarpeted servants' attics directly above him would be sure to disturb him. If he lasted the full week he'd declared he intended to stay, she would be surprised. A man of his wealth was used to the finest of everything. He had only to snap his fingers and whatever he wanted was handed to him on a plate. Naturally she hadn't needed to meet him to decide that she loathed him.

'You haven't heard the worst of it yet.' Hester's hazel eyes glowed almost amber with the heat of her indignation. 'While

I was struggling to climb out of the ditch, his groom sauntered over to tell me off for frightening his lordship's horses and perhaps even costing him the race.'

'No.' Emily sat back on her heels, suitably appalled.

'Yes. And do you know what he was doing? Backing his team up so that they blocked the gateway. So that his friend had no chance of overtaking him. When he saw his groom trying to help me, he told him to stop wasting time and get back to where he belonged.'

Hester neatly omitted to tell Emily that at the time the marquis called his groom to heel, she was physically attacking the man. She had the volatile temper to match her red hair, and when the groom had implied his master's horses were of far more value than a mere woman, she had seen red. She had only intended to slap the man's face, and wipe off the impudent grin he'd been wearing since the moment he had come upon her, sprawled face down in the mud at the lip of the ditch she'd just clambered out of, her skirts tangled round her knees. He'd dodged her slap, laughing, and she'd snapped. Forgetting she was a lady, that he was merely a servant, that she was on a public highway for anyone to see, she had launched herself at him, pummelling his chest with her clenched fists, kicking at his shins with her disintegrating boots.

It had taken his lordship's exasperated voice to cut through her humiliated rage and bring herself back to a sense of what she owed her station in life. Hitching up her dripping skirts and battening down her temper, she had squelched across the lane to confront the author of her disaster.

'Just what do you think you are about?' she had demanded. 'Taking a blind bend at that speed—you might have killed somebody. A child might have been playing in the roadway. A farm cart might have been going down into the village.'

'But they weren't.' He lifted his left eyebrow a fraction. 'Let us stick to the facts of the case.'

'The facts,' she spat, justifiably incensed by the brusque tone that accompanied his irritated expression, 'are that I had to take such drastic action to save my skin that everything I had in that basket is now crushed at the bottom of that ditch.'

His only response was to sit a little straighter while he ran his eyes swiftly over her. 'Not to mention the loss of your bonnet, the ruination of your stockings...'

Hester had gasped, feeling her face grow hot. The fact she wore no bonnet was obvious, since the wind was whipping her hair round her face, but when had he been able to catch so much as a glimpse of her torn stockings? She had tried to tuck some of her hair behind her ears, suddenly acutely aware of the picture she must present, but her movements had been jerky with embarrassment. The bulky, muddy cuff of her coat had flapped against her cheek and she knew that, in trying to tidy herself up, she had only succeeded in daubing her face with muck. While she had prayed for the road to open up and swallow her, so that she would not have to endure another second of the Marquis of Lensborough's coldly withering gaze, his groom had gone off into fresh gales of laughter at her expense.

'God give me strength,' she heard the marquis sigh as his mouth twisted in disgust.

How dare he! How dare he look down his nose at her as though she were something he wished to scrape off the sole of his glossy Hessians. She glared at the offending footwear for a second. He probably gloated that his valet could achieve a shine he could see his arrogant face in. And what if those tightly fitted buckskins, that multi-caped driving coat and the supple gloves cost more than her uncle spent on his own daughters' clothes in a year? His manners and morals were straight from the gutter. She didn't care what anyone else thought of his reasons for coming to The Holme. He was despicable through and through.

She hadn't bothered to disguise her disdain, and he hadn't liked it. When their eyes finally met, hers flashing with contempt and his black with fury, he had gripped the handle of his whip and sworn at her yet again.

Who knew how long the stand-off might have lasted if they had not both turned at the sound of a second vehicle approaching?

'And then he just whipped up his t...team,' Hester told Emily through teeth that were still chattering with a combination of cold, and shock, and temper, 'and t...took off without so much as a backward glance.'

'You need to get out of that dress,' was Emily's measured response. 'I will lend you one of mine.'

Emily followed Hester up the stairs with a dishcloth in her hand, mopping up the footprints and puddles as they went.

'He is so addicted to sporting pursuits, and gambling, that he cannot even spare the time to find himself a wife in the usual way,' Hester grumbled as she climbed out of her wet dress and petticoats. 'He gets his mother to write round to anyone with a couple of spare daughters and a pedigree worthy of being mingled with the Challinor blood line—' her stockings hit the floor of Emily's bedroom with a resounding slap '—just as if he were selecting a brood mare.' Emily handed her a towel.

'And then informing my uncle that he would come and look my cousins over, in a letter so lacking in feeling it could have been referring to a visit to Tattersalls,' she huffed as she vigorously rubbed her legs dry.

'You make it sound far worse than it really is. Men of his class routinely contract marriages arranged by their families. And your aunt and his mother have corresponded for years. Julia is Lady Challinor's goddaughter, isn't she? She must have thought she would suit him, and he has only agreed to come and meet her to see if he thinks so too.'

'But it isn't only Julia, is it?' The damp towel went the same way as the ruined stockings. 'You cannot have forgotten that awful letter his mother wrote suggesting he may as well look Phoebe over while he is here? In case he finds a very young girl, whose opinion is not yet fixed, might be more easily moulded to the position she would fill. Moulded! As though she were a thing of clay, a puppet for him to play with. Not a real person at all.' Her voice was barely above a whisper as she concluded, 'Em, she's barely sixteen. I cannot condone a man of his age and experience forcing a girl so young to his bidding, simply because he has not so far been able to find what he wants from a wife elsewhere.'

Emily handed her a pair of clean stockings. 'Neither of your cousins object to the prospect of marrying a marquis, though, do they? And he could not have come visiting if either your uncle or aunt had indicated he was not welcome.'

Hester sighed, one stockinged foot curling over her cold, bare toes, remembering how her cousins had waltzed each other round the parlour, giddy with glee on the day her aunt received the letter confirming his intent to make one of them his wife.

'I think that is the worst aspect of the case. They are willing to sell themselves to this heartless, horrible man simply because of his stupendous wealth and the position he occupies in society. By the end of this week, one of my poor cousins will have given herself into the keeping of a virtual stranger, a man cold enough to take a wife on his mother's recommendation, sight unseen, heartless enough to run a defenceless female off the road and despicable enough to berate his groom for wasting time going to her help.'

She thrust her other foot into a neatly rolled stocking and jerked it up her leg. 'If I hadn't been only a few yards from the vicarage, and known I could rely on you to provide me with a quick change of clothing, I would have had to go home instead of…'

She bit her lower lip, knowing her friend must disapprove of the way she had intended to spend this afternoon. As she had guessed, Emily laid a hand on her shoulder, before saying gently, 'Perhaps you ought to look on him as a messenger of divine providence then. Sent to deflect you from—'

Hester leaped to her feet, throwing her friend's hand from her shoulder. 'I am not doing anything wrong. Not really.'

'Nevertheless—' Emily's voice was muffled as she rummaged in the bottom of her wardrobe for a spare pair of boots '—you do not want any of your family to know what you are about, do you? Not to mention the fact that your aunt must need you today, with so many guests arriving.'

Hester stamped her feet into the shoes Emily set in front of her. 'I have spent the last few weeks ensuring that everything will run like clockwork. The staff all know exactly what to do, and my aunt will be in her element. Nobody will miss me. They will all be far too busy fussing over the new arrivals.' Then she shrugged. 'I deserve a day off.'

Emily went back to the wardrobe to select a dress suitable for the errand she knew Hester was embarking on. 'It's the talk of the village that the gypsies set up camp in The Lady's Acres last night. Running off to visit them behind your uncle's back is not at all proper and you know it.'

'If I asked his permission, he would not let me go, not today,' Hester cried. 'And it has been a whole year since they were last here.'

Emily sighed. 'You are determined to go?'

'Yes.' Hester raised her chin defiantly, knowing that though Emily disapproved, she would not betray her.

'Then would you consider letting me come with you, so that if anyone were to find out, you can at least say you had a chaperon?'

Hester felt her dark mood dissipate as swiftly as it had descended. 'I would be delighted to have your company, if you are sure? I know Jye can be a bit…'

'Scary?' Emily shivered.

'I was going to say unpredictable, but, yes, I know he scares you. That is why I would never have asked this favour of you. And the meeting today is not likely to go smoothly, either, now that I've lost the basket of provisions I intended to sweeten him up with.'

'I can run quite fast, you know, if he decides to set his dogs on us.'

Hester laughed. 'And no man is going to stop us from following the dictates of our conscience, be he marquis or gypsy.'

Having washed her face and changed into dry clothing, Hester set out back down the lane, with Emily at her side, to see if she could rescue anything from the ditch before heading off to the gypsy camp. She managed to hook her bonnet from the hawthorn branch that had earlier snagged it so painfully from her head. She could sew new ribbons on to it. The old ones had got a bit threadbare anyway. There was nothing left of the pies, pastries and preserves that had been in the basket but an unappetising reddish mush studded with shards of broken pottery. But a package containing coloured paper and a box of crayons had survived. Triumphantly she wiped the gloss of freezing mud from her spoils with the sleeve of her borrowed coat.

They had not gone far when Emily, who had clearly been turning something over in her mind for quite some time, said, 'Has it occurred to you that it might not have been the marquis himself who ran you off the road? You did say he was bringing a friend with him.'

'Oh, it was him,' Hester breathed. 'He more than matched the description my aunt Susan provided us with.' Her lip curled. 'Of course, she used terms that were meant to make him sound attractive. Saying he had the physique of an accredited Corinthian, besides being tall and distinguished in his bearing.' She snorted in derision. 'The truth is that he is a great brute of a man with shoulders like a coal heaver and a permanent sneer on his face. He has eyes as hard and black as jet. I don't think I have ever seen a man who is so…dark. Like a creature of the night.' She shivered. 'Everything about him was black. His clothes, his hair, even the language he used came straight from the pit. And,' she concluded, 'expressed complete contempt for lesser mortals.'

Em looked thoughtful. 'I suppose he must have thought you were just a simple working woman, though, Hester, since you are dressed for visiting…um…the disadvantaged, and were without a chaperon.'

'Well, that would excuse him, of course!' Hester's pace quickened as her temper seethed, forcing Emily into a trot to keep up with her longer-legged stride. 'In effect, it was all my fault for getting in his way.'

'No, that was not what I meant at all,' Emily panted. 'Only that it might have accounted for his attitude. I am sure he would not treat your cousins with the same—'

'Contempt?' Hester supplied. 'Oh, he might gloss it over with society manners, but that is exactly how he will treat them. Men of his class think of women as playthings at best. Have you forgotten what I told you about the poor women Mrs Parnell takes in?'

Hester had renewed her acquaintance with her former schoolfriend during her short, disastrous Season, and become heavily involved with the refuge she ran for unwed mothers and foundling children. She had found it increasingly hard to mingle, in the evenings, with men who she knew full well were capable of using and discarding women of the lower classes without a qualm. Who would then compound their villainy by duping an innocent girl of their own class into marriage with the intention of squandering their dowries on vice. When any of them had looked her over with the sort of lascivious gleam in their eye that other girls regarded as a form of flattery, she had gone hot all over, and then icy cold, and then begun to tremble so violently that she usually had to flee the room altogether.

'And wives have no legal rights,' she continued. 'A husband can do what he likes with his wife, as he can with any other of his possessions, while she must turn a blind eye to his conduct if she values her own skin. I dread to think of either Julia or Phoebe in the hands of such a brute as Lord Lensborough.'

She dreaded him being in the house at all. He would be looking her cousins over in that speculative way that single men had when considering marriage, polluting the wholesome atmosphere of what should have been an informal family gathering.

'Surely his sense of pride in his family name would prevent him from being downright cruel, though? Even I have heard how high in the instep the Challinors are.'

'On the contrary. Having met him, I fully believe he is so conceited that he doesn't care what anyone else thinks of him. He acts as though the rest of the human race is so far beneath him that he need not pay any heed to what they think, or say.'

Emily reached out and gave Hester's hand a squeeze. 'Don't judge him before you have even got to know him. During the course of this week you will have ample opportunity to observe him, and perhaps find that he had reasons to explain his behaviour this afternoon. It is all too easy to misjudge a person's motives. After all, a person who did not know you as well as I do might well put a most ungenerous interpretation on your own behaviour.'

Hester broke away abruptly, climbed on to the stile that spanned the hedge, and swung her legs over it.

'That is entirely different,' she insisted as she dropped into the meadow on the other side of the hedge and strode, head held high, towards the cluster of brightly painted caravans that were drawn into a semi-circle around an open fire.

She did not look back. She knew Emily would soon realise that she would feel much safer beside her than hesitating timidly on the stile.

Eagerly, she searched among the swarm of ragged children who were tumbling out of the caravans for one very special little girl. Tears sprang to her eyes the moment she saw Lena's copper curls bobbing amidst the sea of black, and it was all she could do not to rush forward, sweep her into her arms and kiss the tip of her freckled little nose. How she had grown.

Emily was so naïve. Men were beastly, even the ones you thought you could trust. The very thought of marrying one of them was akin to enduring the most degrading form of slavery. And as for saying she should observe Lord Lensborough before deciding what his motives were—she knew all too well what motives men had for the way they acted towards women. She had Lena as living proof.

Chapter Two

Lord Jasper Challinor, the fifth Marquis of Lensborough, lounged against the mantelpiece, watching in growing disbelief as the room filled with Sir Thomas Gregory's extended family. They greeted each other with a noisy, informal exuberance that made him shudder with distaste. Nobody gave so much as a passing nod to the rigid etiquette that governed the behaviour of the circles in which he normally moved. No wonder the children were so boisterous. They were running about as if this were a playground, not a drawing room, and nobody saw fit to check them.

On the contrary, Sir Thomas had been quite adamant that he wished to encourage the children to mingle with their elders, that he liked having all the children present at this annual family gathering, and had warned him, in quite a belligerent voice, that they would all be sitting down to dinner that evening, right down to the youngest babe in arms. That had been just before he had introduced him to the nursery maid, in whose arms the babe was being carried.

His mood, which had not been all that sanguine when he set out that morning, had been growing steadily blacker as the day had progressed. It set up a tangible barrier that none of the other guests dared broach, leaving him to stand in haughty isolation beside the fire.

Stephen Farrar, who as an ex-soldier had no qualms about making the most of whatever company he found himself in, detached himself from their hostess, Lady Susan, and came to stand beside him, his face alight with merriment.

'I'm glad you are enjoying yourself,' Lensborough said through clenched teeth.

'I have to admit, the whole day has been vastly entertaining.' Stephen grinned.

Lord Lensborough grimaced. Agreeing to pit his bays against Stephen's showy greys had been an act of monumental folly. Neither of them was familiar with the terrain. That, Stephen had said, was the point. It gave the race an edge. It had almost resulted in tragedy.

And brought Bertram's death horridly close. His brother had never told him what it felt like to look someone in the eye as you robbed them of their life, and now he knew why. That woman's face was indelibly seared into his memory. Was his brother's face seared into the memory of whichever Frenchman had slain him? Or had he too become a casualty of Napoleon's ferocious ambition? He shook his head. At least Bertram had died with a sword in his hand. That woman had nothing with which to defend herself. She had briefly clutched the basket she had been carrying to her chest, as though the wickerwork could shield her from the massed force of several tons of galloping horseflesh. He had vented his horror at his inability to prevent the inevitable in a torrent of abuse, as if she had flung herself in front of his curricle on purpose.

'I don't know why you should be frowning,' Stephen persisted. 'Those two girls are real charmers.' He smiled across the room to where Julia and Phoebe Gregory sat next to each other on one of the sofas that were scattered about the edges of the room, which was little more than a broad corridor connecting various wings of the house to the central Great Hall where they were about to dine.

That was another factor to add to his gloom. Yes, the girls his mother had selected for him were exactly to his taste. Blond and blue eyed and well rounded. Unfortunately, they were no different from any one of a dozen eligible females he might have tossed the handkerchief to in London. Coming to Yorkshire had been a waste of time. If not for Bertram…

He clenched his fists, reminding himself that at least by coming here, he could fulfill the vow he had made to his brother. He had to marry and produce an heir, now that Bertram was gone. He was the last of his line, and it was unthinkable that it should end with him. It was equally unthinkable to make a selection from any of the vultures who had begun to circle round him with avaricious eyes as soon as he donned the black garb that the etiquette of mourning decreed. They were glad Bertram had died, because it meant they had a real chance of fixing their greedy talons in him. Well, he was not going to give any of them the satisfaction of trampling on his brother's memory by making them his marchioness. He had told his mother, when she had reminded him of his obligations to the family, that he didn't care who he married, so long as she had never set her cap at him.

'But you are willing to marry someone?' she had persisted.

'Yes, yes, I know I must.'

'Shall I introduce you to one or two girls who might suit you?'

His mother was clearly keen to get his nursery set up before he changed his mind.

'No,' he had said. 'I am leaving town tomorrow.' He had taken all he could stand. Tours of the Belgian battlefield had become all the rage, and there was a roaring trade going on in the most grisly souvenirs of Wellington's victory. Eventually the only man in London whose company he could tolerate was Captain Fawley, a man who had served in his younger brother's regiment until he had been invalided out after Salamanca, a man he normally only visited out of a rigid sense of duty because his bitterness over the horrific nature of his injuries had left his attitude as twisted and stunted as his body. He was beginning to think, and speak, so very like this bitter man that he had to get right away from people, immerse himself in the business of running his racing stables. 'Write to me at Ely.'

He had been only too glad to leave the matter entirely in his mother's hands, knowing that she had a network of acquaintances among England's noble families that stretched as far from London as it was possible to go. If there was a woman who matched his requirements in a wife, his mother would know where to find her. Someone who would be content to bear his name and his children, he had stipulated, and not expect him to dance attendance on her. He could just about tolerate having a wife who was well bred enough to know she must never attempt to interfere with his lifestyle.

His faith in her had soon borne fruit. Not long after Stephen, a man he had first met in Captain Fawley's gloomily shuttered rooms, had run him to ground at Ely, she had written to inform him that her goddaughter, Julia Gregory, was available and willing. If he did not like her, she had a younger sister who was reputedly very pretty as well. The family was large, she had added. Lady Susan had given her husband two male heirs, as well as four daughters, and was still in robust health. He understood the implication that if he married one of her daughters, they were more than likely to provide him with a clutch of healthy offspring. They were not wealthy, but she felt bold enough to put their names forward, because he had not stipulated that having a dowry was of much relevance. Their main attraction must be that they were unknown, and as such would infuriate all the ambitious women he wished to put firmly in their place. He had smiled ruefully at his mother's complete understanding of his unspoken wishes, and decided he might as well marry one of the Gregory girls, if they would have him.

Of course they would have him, she had written in reply. They were too poor to have romantic notions about marriage. An offer from a man of his wealth would seem like a godsend. They would take him on any terms he cared to name. Since she knew he was spending Christmas at Stanthorne, the hunting box he kept near York, she suggested he get over to Beckforth, which was less than a day's drive away, and clinch the deal. That way, he could marry before the Season got under way.

'I like their mother too,' Stephen said, causing Lord Lensborough to eye him in frank disbelief. Lady Susan had come bouncing down the front steps to greet him when he had arrived that afternoon, her arms outstretched as though she meant to embrace him. Stephen had found it hard not to laugh as the insular Lord Lensborough recoiled from such a vulgar display of enthusiasm. 'No, really. Almost as much as I like Sir Thomas.'

Lord Lensborough scowled. The reception he had received from Sir Thomas had been as different as it was possible to be from his wife's. When the butler had first brought them down to this room to await dinner, Sir Thomas had positively glowered at them as they went to join him by the roaring fire. When he had asked them if they had any complaints to make about their rooms, he was almost sure the man expected to hear a whole litany of them.

Lord Lensborough had been taken aback when the butler had led them into what appeared to be a disused wing of the house. Although, looking around the room now at the Gregory family's lack of decorum, he could appreciate the man's explanation that Hester, whom he had assumed was the housekeeper, hoped the apartments would afford him some privacy. Stephen had replied that he liked the fact that their shared sitting room overlooked the stables, and appreciated the information that a fire would always be kept alight in case they wanted to retreat there.

'It is a very cosy set-up,' he had said generously.

Lord Lensborough had not been able to draw any comfort from that fire. No sooner had he sunk into one of the squashy leather chairs drawn up before it and stretched out his feet to the flames, than an image of a shivering woman in soaking clothes, reproach in her moss-green eyes, had pricked at his conscience. He ought not to have left her standing in the lane like that. But he had been so infuriated by his groom's callous disregard of her plight, that he had decided his only recourse, if he was not to dismiss the man from his job on the spot, was to remove him from the scene and let his anger cool. He was sure he could trace the woman later. How many red-haired shrews could a village the size of Beckforth contain, after all? Leaping from the armchair, he had summoned his valet and instructed him to begin the search. He gave the man enough money for the woman to buy several changes of decent clothing to replace the ones she had been wearing, and something over to compensate for her distress. He was absolutely not the sort of person who thought nothing of running a member of the lower orders off the road whilst in pursuit of a sporting wager.

'Aye…' Sir Thomas nodded '…Hester assured me it would be once we got the chimneys swept. My sister always lays claim to the blue room when she comes, and short of turning her out…'

Lord Lensborough wondered why they had not simply requested he come at a different time, if they already had a house full of guests, none of whom he particularly wished to meet. He had not been able to keep the irritation from his voice when he had said, 'I hope we have not caused you inconvenience, Sir Thomas.'

Sir Thomas had snorted. 'Nay, for it is not me that sees to

the running of the household. Hester is the one who has had all the extra work. And you may as well know right now that I do not intend to alter any of my plans for this week because you have invited yourself into my home. My lord, I made up my mind that you would not inconvenience me, do you see? You have come to find out what my girls are like, you say. Well, we are not sophisticated folk, and you won't find me trying to impress you by pretending otherwise. You must take us as you find us.'

'Do I take it,' Lord Lensborough had replied, his voice at its most glacial, 'that you do not approve of my intention to marry one of your daughters?'

His host had shrugged. ''Twould make no difference if I did—their silly hearts are set on it.'

While he was still reeling from this insult, Sir Thomas had cocked his head and observed, 'Though you are somewhat younger than I was led to believe. How old are you, exactly?'

'Eight and twenty.'

'Quite fit, too, by the looks of you.' Sir Thomas had run his eye over Lord Lensborough's physique with obvious approval. No need for padding in his coat to make his shoulders look broad. His lordship's shoulders were broad, the stomach beneath the neat, plain waistcoat was flat, and the muscularity of his thighs and calves was clearly delineated by the snug fit of formal knee breeches and black silk stockings.

'Oh, don't poker up like that.' Sir Thomas had matched Lord Lensborough's affronted frown with one of his own. 'If you are going to be my son-in-law, then you'll have to get used to my blunt speaking. I ain't the sort of chap to smile in your face and speak ill behind your back. You'll always know exactly where you stand with me.'

'And where, precisely, is that, sir?'

'How the devil would I know? I've only just clapped eyes on you.'

While Stephen had nearly choked with the effort of keeping a straight face, Sir Thomas had walked away, and only returned sporadically, to introduce the various members of his family as they made their way into the enormous reception room.

'It looks to me,' Stephen remarked, 'as though this week is going to be an educational experience for you, Lensborough.'

'I can certainly confess that I have never come across anything quite like the Gregory family en masse,' he replied grimly.

'The house adds a certain piquancy to the affair too, does it not? It could have been designed for the purpose, all those unexpected alcoves and staircases, passages leading to odd forgotten rooms where nobody goes any more.'

'In some of which we are being forced to sleep. Did you smell the mildew in the corridors? The Holme is a rabbit warren—each successive generation since the Norman conquest seems to have tacked on whatever additions were currently in vogue with no thought to overall harmony—'

'Oh, come. You could not wish for a more fortunate place to go courting two pretty girls at the same time.'

Lord Lensborough glowered at the two pretty girls in question. They were sitting on the sofa, hand in hand, regarding him with identical rapt expressions on their otherwise vacuous faces, dressed in a tasteless combination of low decolletage and explosions of ruffles that could only have come from a provincial dressmaker. He would have to write to his mother and ask her to invite whichever chit became his betrothed to stay with her in Brook Street for a week or two before introducing her into society. It was one thing plucking an unknown damsel from obscurity. Quite another to look as though he had no taste.

Not that either of them would object to purchasing an entire new wardrobe. Look at them, simpering and giggling behind their hands. They could not disguise their excitement at the prospect of landing such a magnificent catch. Never mind that on arrival he had been so shaken by the near accident outside their gates that their mother's twitterings had provoked several quite brusque rejoinders from him. They had not cared. Their eyes had glowed as they looked him over, seeing nothing but the jewels and carriages they hoped he was going to buy them. They had overlooked his manners altogether.

He could not help contrasting their mercenary appreciation with the queenly disdain shown by that woman in the lane. That freckle-faced beggar maid had not cared what his rank was. His behaviour had been wanting, and she was not afraid to tell him so. She had nothing to lose by speaking her mind, since she had nothing he could take from her. Except her life.

A chill swept the length of his spine. He had gone over and over their encounter, and the devil of it was he could not remember if he had uttered a single word to express his regret. His valet would, of course, be making apologies on his behalf when he found the woman, but that was not quite the same. He wanted to see that reproachful gaze soften, those moss-green eyes glow with pleasure instead of glazing with fear. He had never seen eyes quite like hers. They had seemed huge in that white little face, changing from dull mossy green when she was afraid, to glowing amber when she had been angry. He did not want, he admitted to himself, to carry that image of a terrified white face for ever in his conscience. She would haunt him, if he did not take care. Already, her image was more real, in his imagination, than the other occupants of the room he was standing in. He could see her now, glaring at him from the shadows at the corners of the room, her body pathetically thin beneath the shapeless gown she wore, that wild red hair framing her sharp, pale features.

Dear God! He could see her standing in the shadows in a shapeless gown with a frown on her face. He reached blindly behind him for the mantel to steady himself as the floor seemed to pitch beneath his feet. What was a beggar woman doing in his host's home?

'We'll be able to go in to dinner now Hester's here,' Sir Thomas said, strolling to Lord Lensborough's side. 'Can't think what can have kept her,' he added wryly, drawing a watch from his waistcoat pocket ostentatiously. The red-haired woman, catching the pointed gesture, flushed and hung her head.

'Hester.' Sir Thomas raised his voice to make himself heard above the general hubbub. 'When you have a minute.' He beckoned to her.

The sound of Sir Thomas calling her name alerted every single child in the room to her presence. As one, they surged in her direction and broke about her knees in a wave of exuberance that she met by dropping down to their level and embracing as many of them as she could get her arms around.

Sir Thomas sighed. 'I do apologise, my lord. I am afraid Hester is so fond of children she tends to forget little things like good manners when they enter the equation. You will be pleased to hear, I am sure, that after this evening, when they will all sit at table with us—' he glared to make his point '—Hester will make sure they are all kept out of your way. She always organises the children's entertainment when they come to stay, and as such she is a special favourite with them all.'

'Hester?' Lensborough repeated, his initial shock at seeing her turning to an icy rage that quickened his breathing. She was not a beggar woman, but a member of his host's staff. This was the Hester who had organised a suite of rooms for him and Stephen in the farthest flung, most dilapidated corner of the house. The same woman about whom he had been fretting all day, who would never have been in any danger if she had stayed within doors attending to her duties. Worst of all, she must have known exactly who he was when she had flared across the lane, hair streaming behind her like a rocket's tail, spitting fire and brimstone.

Sir Thomas uttered an exclamation of impatience when it became clear that Hester intended to stay exactly where she was, soundly kissing every single child that vied for her attention, instead of obeying his summons.

Lord Lensborough's eyes narrowed as a mulish look replaced her unfeigned pleasure in the children when Sir Thomas pulled her to her feet and propelled her across the room in his direction. He drew himself up to his full height. The man intended to introduce her to him! Though why should that surprise him—he had not scrupled to introduce him to the nursery maid who had charge of his year-old grandson. A low growl of anger began to build in his throat as the pair came to a halt not a foot in front of him, Sir Thomas looking belligerent, and the woman, Hester, the housekeeper, glaring defiantly straight ahead.

Hester's face felt as if it was on fire. She had tried to slide unobtrusively into the room, hoping that nobody would notice her late arrival. Time had slipped away from her once she had entered the gypsy camp. Jye had been surly, but he hadn't ordered her to leave. Before she knew it, it was growing dusk, and she'd had to run all the way back, with time only to splash her hands and face in cold water, and pull on the first clean dress that came to hand. She'd been aghast when she'd looked in the mirror and seen the state of her hair. It looked just as if she had been swimming in mud before letting a hurricane blow it dry, which was pretty much what had happened. There was no time to wash it. All she could do was hack the worst of the matted clumps out with her nail scissors, then pin the cleaner bits on the top of her head in the hopes that nobody would notice the damage. She'd flown down the stairs, skidding to a halt with her hand on the handle of the salon door. She'd eased her way into the room with pounding heart and ragged breath, only to come face to face with Lord Lensborough. She hadn't been prepared for the paralysing effect that coal-black glare would have on her. She had been banking on the hope he would not even recognise her. After all, he had barely glanced at her earlier, so preoccupied had he been with the welfare of his horses and winning his stupid race.

But there was no doubt he had recognised her. He had started in disbelief, his nostrils flaring as if he had just smelled something very unpleasant, and then his eyes had narrowed, impaling her with a malevolence that declared he did not think she had the right to breathe the same air that he did.

She dropped to the floor, weak kneed, immersing herself in a healing tide of affection. And then Uncle Thomas had dragged her from behind her human shield, and force-marched her across the floor. Why was he insisting on this formal introduction? She had told him over and over again that she would much rather keep busy, behind the scenes, and leave the socialising to her cousins. She had hoped, using this excuse, she would be able to avoid the dratted man for the entire duration of the visit. She felt as though her uncle had betrayed her by forcing this introduction, particularly after the way their earlier, explosive encounter in the lane had gone.

'Lord Lensborough, my niece, Lady Hester Cuerden,' Sir Thomas said, releasing her elbow.

So he really was Lord Lensborough. Hadn't she told Em that this black-haired, black-tempered man was the cold-hearted beast who was coming to pick one of her cousins like a pasha looking over slaves on the auction block? She resisted the urge to back away from the spot where her uncle had forced her to stand, though she felt acute distaste at being so close to the brute. It would be too much like a surrender.

'Your niece?' he echoed, in a tone that gave Hester a glimmer of satisfaction. He was thoroughly disconcerted. Hah—it could not be often that one of his victims rose up and confronted him with the vileness of his behaviour in a polite drawing room.

Lord Lensborough's frown intensified. She was not the housekeeper either, but a member of the family. Yet, *Lady* Hester? When she had hauled herself out of the ditch, he had discounted the possibility she could be anyone of importance, despite her well-modulated accent, since her clothes had been so truly awful. No lady would go abroad dressed like a tramp. Even one in straitened circumstances would make some attempt to put together an outfit that flattered her, wouldn't she? He ran his affronted gaze over the sludge-coloured gown that hung from her slender frame like so much mildewed sacking, finally coming to rest on the crown of her head, which she was presenting to him, since her own gaze was fixed firmly on the carpet before his feet. There were little truncated spikes of green amidst the copper curls. He could only surmise that rather than taking time to wash the ditch water out of her hair and make herself presentable for her uncle's guests, she had flung on the first thing that came to hand, snipped off all the evidence of her afternoon's escapade that she could see, then shoved a random assortment of combs into those wild tresses to fix the bulk of it on the top of her head.

'I thought you were the housekeeper,' he grated.

Her head jerked up. For a second they looked straight into each other's eyes, his contemptuous look heating her own anger to flash point.

'And that excuses it all, does it?' she snapped.

Feeling her uncle stir uncomfortably, she clamped her teeth on the rest of the home truths she would dearly love to spit at the vile marquis. She had no wish to embarrass her family by letting rip before they had even sat down to dinner. She contented herself by glaring at the tie pin that was directly in her line of vision. Her lip curled when she noted it was not a diamond, or a ruby, but only a semi-precious tiger's eye. Provincial nobodies only rated the wearing of semi-precious jewels, even though he was one of the wealthiest men in

England. His whole attitude demonstrated the contempt in which he held his prospective brides, from the curt tone of the letters he had written, right down to the tie pin he chose to stick in his cravat.

'Ah, well,' her uncle broke into the protracted silence that simmered between them, 'Hester is of invaluable help to her aunt in the running of the house, especially when we have such a large influx of guests.'

'I believe we have you to thank for arranging a most charming suite of rooms for us, Lady Hester,' Stephen added gallantly.

To Lord Lensborough's astonishment, Sir Thomas gave Lady Hester a hefty shove, which propelled her some three feet to her left, so that she was standing directly in front of Stephen Farrar while he made the introduction.

He continued to glare at her. She was angry with him, still. She had been clenching and unclenching her fists as though she would like to throw a punch at him. He conceded that she had some justification for that anger, considering he had subjected her to a couple of doses of language no well-born lady should ever have to hear, but he would never forgive her for snubbing him like this.

'It is a pleasure to meet you,' Stephen began, reaching out to take her hand. It was the opening gambit to the charm offensive he invariably launched against the fair sex, no matter what their age or condition.

Lady Hester whipped her hand behind her back before he could grasp it, never mind raise it to his lips, stepping back so abruptly she would have stumbled had not one of her cousins, Sir Thomas's oldest married daughter, Henrietta, chosen that moment to drape her arm about her waist.

'Come and sit by me, Hester darling,' the heavily pregnant woman cooed. 'You will excuse me, gentlemen? We have so much to talk about. Barny is cutting another tooth, you know.'

While the woman bore Lady Hester away in a flurry of silk

skirts, Sir Thomas glared from Stephen to Lord Lensborough as though challenging them to make any comment on the extraordinary rudeness of his niece.

'Odd kick to her gallop,' he eventually conceded. 'But for all that, she's worth her weight in gold.' He cleared his throat and changed the subject. 'Well, now we're all here, we can go in to dinner. You will escort my sister, Lady Valeria Moulton, of course, since she is the highest-ranking female present,' he said to Lord Lensborough, turning to beckon the venerable lady to his side.

Stephen took the opportunity to murmur into his ear. 'This just keeps getting better and better. We're staying in a decaying labyrinth, populated by a family of genuine eccentrics—and to think I was afraid I was going to be bored while you clinched this very sensible match you claim to have arranged.'

'And I never dreamed,' Lensborough growled in retaliation, 'to see a female back off in horror when confronted by one of your waistcoats.'

'Ah, no. You have that quite wrong.' Stephen ran a hand over the cherry-striped silk. 'It was coming face to face with a genuine marquis that did for Lady Hester. She began to shake the minute she set foot in the room and you raised your left eyebrow at her.'

The Great Hall, to which the entire assembly then trooped, was, according to Lady Moulton, the Saxon thane's hall around which successive generations of Gregorys had built their home. It certainly looked as though it could have been around before the Norman invasion. The exposed roof beams of what reminded him forcefully of a barn were black with age, the stone flags were uneven, and the massive oak door looked as though it could withstand an invading army. Mullioned windows were flanked by dented suits of armour, and he couldn't help noticing that every single child that sat down at the refectory-style table was gazing round eyed at the impressive array of antiquated weaponry, from broad swords to chipped battle axes, which hung upon the walls.

Lady Moulton guided him to a seat near the head of the table, rather closer to the fire than he would have liked. In the event, he need not have worried about being excessively hot. Though the fire was large enough to roast an ox whole, and had probably done so on numerous occasions, the heat that emanated from it was tempered by the vast quantities of freezing air whistling in through cracked window panes and gaps under the doors. The faded banners that hung from the minstrel's gallery fairly fluttered in the ensuing breeze.

Both Julia and Phoebe, who were seated opposite him, one on either side of Stephen, broke out in rashes of extremely unattractive goose pimples. Even he, in his silk shirt and coat of superfine, was grateful for the warming effect of the fragrant onion soup that comprised the first course. As footmen cleared the bowls away, he grudgingly revised his opinion of Lady Hester's gown. Seated as she was at the far end of the table, among the children and nursery maids, it now looked like an eminently practical choice, given the arctic conditions that must prevail so far from the ox-roasting furnace. While he watched, she absentmindedly hitched a toning green woollen shawl around her shoulders, knotting the ends around a waist that appeared hardly thicker than his thigh.

'Marvellous with children,' Lady Moulton commented, noting the direction of his gaze. 'Which makes it such a shame.'

'A shame? What do you mean?' For the first time since being partnered with the voluble dowager, he felt mildly interested in what she was saying.

'Why, that she is so unlikely ever to have any of her own, of course.' She addressed him as though he were a simpleton.

He quirked one eyebrow the merest fraction, which was all the encouragement Lady Moulton needed to elaborate. Once the footmen had loaded the board with a variety of roast meats, raised pies and seasonal vegetables, she continued, 'You must have wondered about her when she was introduced to you and your charming young friend. Nobody could help wonder at such behaviour.' She clucked her tongue as he helped her to a slice of raised mutton pie. 'Always the same around unattached gentlemen. Crippled by shyness. Her Season was a disaster, of course.'

He dropped his knife into a dish of bechamel sauce. Shy? That hoyden was not shy. She had erupted from that ditch, her hair like so much molten lava, screaming abuse at the hapless groom he had sent to help her while he single-handedly calmed his nervously plunging horses by forcing them into a maneouvre that distracted them from their stress at having a woman dive between their legs while they had been galloping flat out. He had never seen a woman exhibit such fury. It was anger that had made her quiver in silence before him in the saloon. Anger, and bad manners.

'She came out the same season as Sir Thomas's oldest girl, my niece Henrietta.' Lady Moulton waved her fork in the direction of the pregnant lady. 'To save expense, you know. Henrietta became Mrs. Davenport—' she indicated the ruddy-cheeked young man sitting beside her '—but Hester disgraced herself...' She leaned towards him, lowering her voice. 'Ran out of Lady Jesborough's ball in floods of tears, with everyone laughing at her. She stayed on in London, but very much in the background. Got involved in—' Lady Moulton shuddered '—charitable works. Since she has come back to Yorkshire she has made herself useful to her aunt Susan, I can vouch for that. But she will never return to London in search of a husband. Poor girl.'

Poor girl, my foot! Lady Hester was clearly one of those creatures that hang on the fringes of even the best of families, a poor relation. It all added up. The shabby clothes she wore, her role as a sort of unpaid housekeeper—for all that she had a title, she relied on the generosity of her aunt and uncle. And how did she repay them? When they brought her out, even though she could not fund a Season for herself, she had wasted the opportunity by throwing temper tantrums. Just as she abused their trust today by wandering about the countryside when she should have been attending to the comfort of her family's guests.

'You are frowning at her, my lord,' Lady Moulton observed. 'I do hope her odd manners have not put you off her cousins. They do not have the same failings, I promise you.'

No, he mused, flicking an idle glance in their direction, causing them both to dimple hopefully. Though it was highly unlikely they would ever become leaders of fashion, he was confident his mother could make either of them presentable with minimal effort.

Lady Hester, on the other hand, would never be presentable. Socially she was a disaster, was ungrateful to the family that had taken her in. He shrugged. No point in dwelling on a female he would be unlikely to see much of this week. Sir Thomas had stressed that it was only this one night, the first night of the house party, that egalitarian principles held sway. He turned to glare at her, just as she was shooting him a withering look. Face reddening, she turned to cut up a portion of the veal for a golden-haired moppet who was sitting beside her.

As he reflected with satisfaction that, come the morrow, servants, poor relations and children would be kept well out of sight, in the background where they belonged, a freckle-faced boy on her other side piped up, 'Tell us about the pike, Aunt Hetty.'

'Oh, dear,' said Lady Moulton, reaching for her wine glass.

'Yes, the pike, the pike,' two more boys began to chant, bouncing up and down on the bench.

Lady Hester looked to her uncle, who raised his glass to signal his permission for the telling of the tale.

'Well,' she began, 'there was once a man at arms, who served Sir Mortimer Gregory, in fourteen hundred and eighty-five…'

Lady Moulton turned to Sir Thomas. 'Must we have these gory tales while we are eating, Tom? It quite puts me off my food.'

Perhaps she heard the complaint, for Lady Hester lowered her voice, causing the children to crane eagerly towards her, their little bottoms lifting from the bench in determination to catch every single word.

'Family history, Valeria,' Sir Thomas barked. 'The young ones should know that the weapons hung about these walls are not merely for show. Every last one of 'em has seen action, my lord.' He turned to address Lord Lensborough. 'The Gregorys have been landowners in these parts through troublesome times. Had to defend our home and our womenfolk against a host of threats, rebels and traitors, and down through all the centuries—'

'Never fought on the wrong side!' Half a dozen voices from along the table chorused, raising their glasses towards Sir Thomas, who laughed in response to their teasing. Hester's sibilant murmuring was drowned out by a collective groan of gleeful horror from the children. The tale of the pike had evidently come to its conclusion.

The golden-haired moppet crawled into Lady Hester's lap, her blue eyes wide. As she curled an arm protectively about her, Lord Lensborough found himself saying, 'Do you think it appropriate to scare such a young child with tales of that nature?'

He had not heard one word of the story, but from what others had told him, he judged it was as inappropriate as all the rest of her behaviour.

An uneasy silence descended upon the gathered diners

when Lady Hester turned and met his accusing stare with narrowed eyes.

'A girl is never too young,' she declared, 'to be taught what vile creatures men can be.'

Chapter Three

When the ladies and children withdrew, Lord Lensborough sank into gloomy introspection over his port.

Captain Fawley, a man who never minced his words, had told him to his face that he was a fool to be offended by the hunting instinct of single females who scented that, with Bertram dead, he would have to find a wife swiftly to secure the succession.

'Women are mercenaries, Lensborough. The same shrinking violets that shudder at the sight of my face would steel themselves to smile upon a hunchbacked dwarf if he had money, leave alone a title. You are deluding yourself if you think you will ever find one who ain't.'

It was depressing to accept that if he were to treat the Gregory females to the sort of language he had vented on the prickly Lady Hester, they would still fawn over him for the sake of getting their greedy little hands on his title. They were the same as all the rest. It appeared to be his destiny to marry a woman he could not respect.

He tossed back the rest of his port, reflecting that however much a man might kick against his fate, he was powerless to alter the final outcome. All he could do was bear himself with dignity.

So far today, he had not done so. His reckless mood had almost resulted in a woman being killed. True, she was not a pleasant woman, but he ought not to have let her make him forget he was a gentleman. When he had thought she was a beggar maid he had determined to ease her want with generous financial compensation. Now that he knew she was gently born, did he owe her any less?

Her position was one of dependence. Life for a poor relation could be well-nigh intolerable. She was vulnerable, and men of his station routinely abused such. Whatever she may have done, he needed to make her understand he was not of that fraternity. In short, he would have to make some form of apology, and it rankled.

There was precious little respite, Hester found, from the malign influence of the Marquis of Lensborough in the drawing room with the ladies. He was the prime topic of conversation, at the forefront of everyone's thoughts. Even her own, she reluctantly admitted.

She had been all too painfully aware of his gaze boring malevolently into her throughout dinner, even though she managed to maintain a cheerful demeanour for the sake of the children.

He had sat at the head of the table, garbed head to toe in unrelieved black like some great carrion crow, waiting to pick over the shredded remains of her dignity.

She shuddered, trying to shake off such a fanciful notion. The marquis could not possibly know where she had been, or with whom, that afternoon. He disapproved of her, that was all, and why should he not? She had given him enough cause to despise her without him knowing the whole truth. Hadn't she been out, unchaperoned? Hadn't she physically assaulted his groom and shrieked at him like a fishwife?

Still, she huffed, he had never inquired how she was, never

mind who she was. And he had the nerve to look down his nose at her?

She forced herself to smile and look interested as Henrietta chattered merrily away. How she wished she had the courage to flout convention and tell him to his face what a blackguard he was. But of course she hadn't. Besides, she had to consider the repercussions. Firstly, she would make herself look like a hysterical ill-bred creature, while he, no doubt, would remain in full control. Perhaps just raising that left eyebrow in disdain, but that would be all.

Secondly, her aunt and cousins had already made up their minds to welcome him into the family, so eventually she would have to deal with him as a cousin by marriage. She had no wish to be barred from any of his homes. If he was as bad as she guessed, whichever of her cousins married him would soon find herself in need of moral support and she fully intended to provide it.

'Of course, I can tell you don't like him.'

Hester forced herself to pay attention. Henrietta could only be referring to Lord Lensborough.

'No, I do not.'

Henrietta rapped her wrist playfully with her fan. 'I shan't take any notice of that. You have disliked every eligible male you have ever been introduced to. In fact, during our come-out, I used to think some of them quite terrified you.'

'Some of them did,' Hester admitted. 'Most of their mothers did too.'

'Oh, weren't some of the patronesses dragons?' Henrietta agreed with feeling. 'And so cruel about your looks, as if there is anything wrong with having freckles and red hair. I do wish you could have found some nice, kind man who could have restored your confidence. You are not unattractive, you know, when you forget to be shy. If only you could have refrained from blushing quite so much, or stammering whenever a man asked you to dance.'

'Or managed to control the trembling so that I could have got through a dance without tripping over my feet, I know. But I could not. And I would rather not hark back to that particular episode in my life. Altogether too painful. Besides, I am happy living here with your mama and papa. I don't feel I am missing anything by not being married. In fact, on the whole, I would much rather stay single for the remainder of my days.'

'You won't let your shyness with them keep you away from us this week though, will you? Peter and I, and the children, would all be sorry if you hid yourself away altogether.'

'I cannot even if I would.' Hester sighed. 'Your mama has strictly forbidden me to skulk, and your papa has backed her up.'

'Quite right too.'

The door opened and the first of the gentlemen began to saunter into the drawing room. Phoebe and Julia scurried to the piano, hastily arranging the music they had been practising for this evening's entertainment.

'Oh, my. They're doing it,' Henrietta squealed, stuffing a handkerchief to her mouth.

'Who is doing what?'

'Lord Lensborough and Mr Farrar.' Henrietta leaned closer and lowered her voice. 'Harry told me how they are known for entering fashionable drawing rooms arm in arm, just as they are doing now, and of the stir it creates among the ladies present.'

Hester cast a withering look at her cousin Harry Moulton, who, as usual, had slouched to a chair at the farthest end of the room from where his rather faded-looking wife was sitting.

'They call them Mars and Apollo,' Henrietta continued. 'The one broodingly dark, and the other sublimely fair, and both possessed of immense fortunes. Harry says the combined effect is such that he has known ladies to faint dead away.'

That was exactly the sort of tall story Harry would tell the impressionable Henrietta. Hester's lip curled as she looked from one to the other as they lounged in the doorway, gazing complacently upon the assembled company. The arrogant black-hearted peer and the self-satisfied golden dandy.

She turned her head away abruptly as Lord Lensborough's hard black gaze came to rest upon her.

'Oh, my,' Henrietta breathed. 'Lord Lensborough is looking straight at you. With such a peculiar expression on his face. As if you've displeased him…oh, I expect it was the way you answered him back at the dinner table. You know, you really should not have spoken so sharply—whatever possessed you?'

'I couldn't seem to help myself,' Hester confessed. 'He just…'

Henrietta collapsed against her in a fit of giggles as Hester struggled for a reasonable explanation.

'He brings out the worst in you—my, you really don't like him, do you?'

Lord Lensborough gritted his teeth as he strolled towards the vacant seat beside his hostess. The ensuing conversation with Lady Susan hardly exercised his mind at all, leaving him free to wonder what Hester had just said, after looking at him with her lip curled so contemptuously, to make her companion collapse with laughter.

He managed to commend the accuracy of Julia's playing, and compliment the sweet tenor of Phoebe's singing voice whilst reflecting with annoyance that, while they were doing their utmost to impress him, it was their red-headed cousin that was uppermost in his mind. So intense was his irritation with her that he began to feel as if he was bound to her by some invisible chain. Whenever she moved, she yanked on that chain, drawing his attention to whatever she was doing. And she was always on the move, flitting from one group of chairs to another, seeing to the needs of the guests while their hostess lounged indolently beside him.

He took a deep, calming breath, taking himself to task. Wasn't it a guiding principle for any horseman to get over heavy ground as lightly as possible? The woman was impossible, ill mannered, shrewish, all that was true. But it behooved him as a gentleman to apologise for his own part in their unfortunate first meeting. He would explain that he had initiated proceedings to reimburse her for her losses. Then it was up to her whether to accept a truce or continue hostilities.

When Sir Thomas called for some card games, Hester went to a side table and began to rummage through its drawers. Lensborough took the opportunity to get the thing over with, crossing the room in half a dozen purposeful strides.

He cleared his throat. She jumped, as if truly startled to find him standing so close behind her. For some reason the gesture seemed like the height of impertinence. Women usually fell over themselves to attract his attention. How dare she be impervious to him, when he was gratingly aware of her every move?

'Do you mean to stand there glowering at me all night, or is there something specific you wished to say?'

Hester's head was still bowed over the packs of cards she was laying out on the table top.

A smile tugged at the corner of his lip. She might keep her head averted, but she was as aware of him as he was of her.

'Vixen,' he murmured, reassured. 'You just cannot help yourself, can you? I suppose it is on account of your red hair.'

It was not a true red, though. Standing this close, in flickering candlelight, he could see strands amidst the copper that were almost black. The effect was of flames flickering over hot coals. The fire was spreading to her cheeks, too, a tide of heat sweeping down her neck. She turned suddenly, glaring directly up into his face.

'I...you...' she stammered, her fists clenching and un-clenching in pure frustration. Hadn't he already done enough? Sworn at her, abandoned her in her sopping clothes at the side of the roadside, and lastly provoking her to retaliating, in the most unladylike manner, to his jibe at the dining table, causing the shocked eyes of her entire family to turn in her direction. It hadn't helped that Phoebe had promptly dissolved in a fit of the giggles, drawing a scathing glance for her own lack of self-control.

'We must talk, you and I,' he purred. 'This matter between us needs to be addressed.'

They had nothing to talk about. Every time they got anywhere near each other disaster struck. She could not see that changing when everything about him infuriated her. The only way to avoid further clashes was to stay as far from him as possible.

She took a hasty step backward, preparing to dodge away. 'I would far rather we simply not speak of it again.'

'I can well believe that,' he drawled. 'However, I, at least, feel the need to explain my lapse of good manners.'

She gasped. How dare he imply her manners needed explaining? Even if they did, it was certainly not his place to say so.

She stepped smartly to one side, intending to get right away from him. He mirrored her movement so that they remained in the same relative position. He was determined that she should understand the cause of the language he had subjected her ears to, at least.

'The way you were dressed, the fact you were on a public highway unescorted, led me to believe you were—'

'A woman of no account,' she flashed, her eyes blazing. 'Yes, I had already come to that conclusion for myself.' She drew herself up to her full height. 'I suppose you are one of those imbeciles who think that if a lady of good birth goes visiting the poor she should do so in a carriage, attended by footmen, flaunting her wealth in the face of their poverty and making everyone ten times more wretched in the process.'

Visiting the poor? So that was what she had been doing. Didn't she consider herself poor? He raised one eyebrow, considering the possibility. In relation to some people, no, she probably was not. He pursed his lips. He would have to be doubly careful how he handled the next part of what he wished to say to her, then. That telling remark showed exactly how she felt about being the recipient of charity herself. He would try to make light of it.

'At least I can call my valet off, now I have found out your true identity.'

'Your valet?'

'Yes. I had him scouring the countryside for a woman fitting your description so that I could reimburse you for the clothes that got spoiled when you…ah…fell into the ditch.'

First he sent his groom to see to her, now his valet. 'Do you always get your servants to do your dirty work for you, my lord?' She thought of the letters. 'Or your mother? You odious, pompous… Do you think your money can buy anything, or anyone?'

'That's enough, Hester.' Sir Thomas appeared at Lord Lensborough's elbow. He had been so involved in his altercation with Lady Hester, the rest of the occupants of the room might as well not have been there. 'We are all still waiting for the cards.'

All her wrath evaporated, leaving only a quivering lower lip to show where it had been. As the light of battle faded from her eyes they reverted to that dull, indeterminate hue between brown and green that he had first supposed them.

'Sorry, Uncle Thomas. I was…' she faltered. 'That is, Lord Lensborough…'

'Yes, I could see what was going on over here.' Sir Thomas's voice was grim. 'Go on, girl, off you run. Your aunts Susan and Valeria are waiting for their game of whist.'

She scooped up the packs of cards and dodged round both men in her haste to get away.

Lord Lensborough eyed Sir Thomas with new respect for dousing that violent temper with only a few firm words.

'My lord, I hope you will not take what I am about to say amiss, but I really think it would be better if you were to stay away from my niece.'

'I beg your pardon?'

'I need hardly remind you that it was my daughters you came here to look over, not her.'

Did the man think he was a complete imbecile to even consider that hoyden as a fitting wife for a man in his position? She was so far from being suitable, the very suggestion was an insult.

'If you think I was attempting to flirt with that person, you are very much mistaken. I was merely trying to reassure myself she came to no serious hurt this afternoon, and to assure her I would make good any damage her clothing may have sustained when...'

'When what?'

Lord Lensborough hastily explained, 'Your niece took a tumble into a ditch this afternoon, and I happened to witness the accident, that is all, sir.'

'A ditch? On the lane you drove up... Dear God, she wasn't carrying a basket, was she? I can see by your expression she was.'

Dear heaven, was the woman in the habit of stealing from the kitchens in her misguided zeal to help those she considered even worse off than she was? His mouth thinned. He had not meant to give away the fact that she had been neglecting her duty to her aunt. He had just been so determined to correct the ludicrous misapprehension that he had been flirting with her that for perhaps the first time in his life he had spoken without taking thought of the consequences.

Sir Thomas stormed across the room, bending to murmur words in Lady Hester's ears that had her turning first red, then deathly white. And when he straightened up, Hester leapt to her feet and fled from the room, turning just one look of reproach in his direction before she closed the door behind her.

It was hardly his fault she had been sent from the room. Sir Thomas must have known her behaviour was beyond what was acceptable. He should never have introduced her to him if he did not wish him to converse with her. Poor relations ought to be kept out of sight, especially ones who did not know how to behave themselves.

And how dare Sir Thomas forbid him, Jasper Challinor, fifth Marquis of Lensborough, from talking to any female he wished? It was the height of impertinence.

He would take pains to demonstrate that no man had any right to so much as comment on his actions. He was going to make a point of seeking that woman out at every opportunity and, if nothing else, wringing a damned apology out of her.

Chapter Four

Lord Lensborough strode down to the stable yard at first light with a sense of having endured a night of unmitigated torture. The bed, his temper, the troupe of clog dancers who'd been practising in the room above his all night, had all conspired to rob him of sleep.

After a few nights, he'd grow accustomed to sleeping in a semi-recumbent position, or exhaustion would inure his feet to dangling off the edge of a bed that only a midget could stretch out on in comfort. He could even deal with the clog dancers by stuffing cotton wool in his ears.

Which only left his temper. And he had a nasty suspicion that was not going to improve until he'd left The Holme, and one infuriating red-haired shrew, far behind.

No sooner had his thoughts bent in her direction, than Lady Hester trotted into the yard on a pretty little grey mare. He shook his head in disbelief. Not only were there not many people who could beat him down to the stables in the morning, he had the peculiar feeling that he had summoned her up, like a genie from a magic lamp, exactly as he'd done the night before.

Grudgingly, he admired her splendid seat. Then noted, as she bent forward and patted her mount's neck, that her cheeks were flushed, and her eyes sparkled with pleasure almost like a woman who had just made love. No, he corrected himself, annoyed that such a comparison had sprung to mind in relation to Lady Hester. She looked just like she had done when she had been surrounded by the children last night, until she had seen him and all the animation had drained from her face.

Her clothing was in better condition than the frightful rags he had seen her in before, though. The bottle-green habit fitted her like a glove, outlining a figure that, though it was slender, was not totally without womanly curves. The jacket hugged a surprisingly full pair of high, firm breasts. As she slid from her mount, her skirts snagged briefly on the pommel and he caught a tantalising glimpse of a booted ankle. Rooted to the spot, he had sudden, total recall of endlessly long legs, encased in torn black stockings, splayed out as she lay face down in the mud.

He frowned at the inappropriate image that had lodged in his mind, forcing his eyes to return to her face. They widened at the sight of a garland of paper flowers decorating her riding hat. What could have prompted her to adopt such a touch of whimsy to what was otherwise quite an austere outfit? Was she, in defiance of her hopeless state, the kind of girl who rode through the morning mists, dreaming of a prince on a black charger riding to sweep her away from her life of drudgery and dependence? Who would place a coronet among those vibrant curls, deck her swanlike neck with jewels, and murmur the sort of flattery she would never hear from a real flesh-and-blood male? The notion amused him.

He could certainly understand her very evident pleasure in having been out on such a fresh, clear morning, whatever had prompted it. There was nothing like having the world to yourself before the business of the day crowded in.

As she smoothed down her skirts his eyes followed her gloves' progress over the contours of her hips. Having been privy to a breathtaking display of her athleticism the day before, he just knew that little posterior would be firm and muscular.

She looked up, catching his very masculine appreciation of her feminine attributes, her whole body tensing as the colour leached from her face. He frowned, feeling truly sorry that her antipathy for him had the power to destroy her pleasure in a pursuit that was so dear to his own heart. With a sigh, he began to cross the yard. All his anger towards her had achieved so far was to deprive him of sleep. It was time to call a truce.

He would use their mutual love of riding as a means of extending an olive branch.

'Good morning, my lady. I see you enjoyed your ride.'

'Yes.' Her tone was guarded, her eyes wary. He supposed he ought not to be surprised she was gearing up to do battle after the way their previous encounters had gone.

'I am very fond of riding myself.'

'At this hour? I assumed you would lay abed till noon like most gentlemen of fashion.'

'Ah, but I am not a gentleman of fashion. And when I am in the country I keep country hours.'

'But I don't suppose you ride every morning.'

'Ah, but I do.'

'Before breakfast?' She rapped the side of her boot with her riding crop in vexation.

He nodded. 'I never breakfast until after my morning ride.'

'Bother,' was all she answered.

The smile this response produced died on his lips as Hester suddenly shrank back against the stable wall, guilt written all over her face. He whirled round, following the direction of her horrified stare, to see Sir Thomas and his ruddy-cheeked son-in-law enter the yard. Sir Thomas was glaring from one to the other of them as if he could not decide which of them he was most annoyed with.

Lord Lensborough's hackles rose. The man had every right to deal with his own niece as he saw fit, but did he think that he should meekly obey his dictum to avoid her company?

Sir Thomas raised his crop as he approached Hester, and for one awful moment he thought the man was going to strike her with it. Instead, he used it to point at the paper garland on her riding hat and growled, 'I suppose I do not need to ask where you have been.'

Lady Hester's hand fluttered up to her hat in an unconscious gesture of self-defense.

'No, Uncle.' She lifted her chin defiantly.

'Peter,' Sir Thomas barked.

His son-in-law jumped at the sound of his name.

'Perhaps you would be so good as to show his lordship around the stables, and, if he wishes to ride out, accompany him round the estates in my stead. I am going to be occupied with other matters for a while.'

While Hester hung her head, Lord Lensborough leaned against an open stable door, folding his arms across his chest.

'I had no idea you were such an early riser, my lord,' Sir Thomas addressed him with forced politeness.

'Neither had I, Uncle. Truly,' Hester blurted, raising her head. For some reason, that statement caused amusement to flicker across her uncle's face.

'That I can well believe.' He chuckled, before turning to Lord Lensborough and remarking, 'Harry mentioned last night that you keep extensive stables, my lord. He spends a lot of time in London, does my nephew, and seems to regard you as a regular Corinthian.'

Lensborough dipped his head in acknowledgment of an accolade he often received, though on this occasion he recognised it for the attempt it was to divert attention from Hester.

Peter ambled forward. 'I'm a keen rider myself,' he began, 'though not up to your standard, I warrant. But I would be honoured to show you around the place. There are some good gallops to be had up towards the moors.'

'A word of warning, Peter,' Sir Thomas interjected. 'Keep well away from The Lady's Acres—the ground is not fit. And as for you—' he rounded on Lady Hester, jerking his thumb over his shoulder '—my study. Now.'

Sir Thomas turned and strode out of the yard and Lady Hester, to Lord Lensborough's surprise, meekly followed him.

Her dejected demeanour wrung a pang of sympathy from him. Perhaps her punishment might be less severe if he were to explain to her uncle that their meeting had been accidental.

But then a groom brought his hunter, Comet, to the mounting block, and good sense reasserted itself. It really was none of his business, and he could not deny that the girl needed disciplining. Her behaviour was atrocious. And as for Sir Thomas thinking there was the remotest possibility he might respond to any advances she might make towards him... Why, he could not find a less suitable candidate to become his marchioness if he scoured the known world.

Lady Hester was hopeless, he thought, swinging into the saddle. If any man was ever foolhardy enough to contemplate marrying her, he would find his hands full with the battle to curb her wilful nature, and no guarantee of eventual victory. He'd wager the taming of Lady Hester would be a well-nigh impossible task.

Julia and Phoebe, on the other hand, were exactly what he'd told his mother to find. Plump and pretty, and willing to be content with such crumbs of his attention as he chose to throw their way. How could Sir Thomas seriously think Lady Hester could compete with them?

It was a pity that he could not work up more enthusiasm for either of Sir Thomas's daughters. But then he had never expected marriage to be anything other than a duty to be got through with as little unpleasantness as possible. That was why he had been adamant that he required a wife who would not cavil at his keeping a mistress. He would need some compensation for the tedium of doing his duty to the family by getting heirs from a woman who only saw him as a means of social advancement.

He reined in his impatience with Peter, who was leading him through the park at a sedate trot when what he was aching for was a seriously hard gallop.

So little did Julia interest him that he could not remember having attended her come-out ball, though his mother had insisted he had, as a favour to her goddaughter. But then he routinely attended several such events in the course of an evening during the Season, and they all merged into a vague oneness in his memory. Not that there was anything amiss with his memory. He could name every winner of every race meeting he had attended at Newmarket that same spring.

His mother had indicated that Phoebe would enjoy being introduced to society as an engaged woman, but he thought it would be rather unfair to rob her of the fun girls seemed to take in attracting a bevy of suitors. And she would have plenty, she was so pretty. He had to make it look as though he was giving her serious consideration, however. She looked at him with such awe he suspected it would crush her if he dismissed her out of hand.

Finally, Peter urged his mount into a canter, and Lord Lensborough dug his heels into Comet's flanks. The stallion shot forward like an arrow in flight, and the blood began to sing through his veins as they gathered speed. This was what he had been waiting for.

His breath caught in his throat as the wild notion that marriage to Hester would feel something like this—a wild gallop over unknown terrain, never knowing if your mount was going to put its foot into a rabbit hole and toss you over his head. Julia or Phoebe would never exercise him beyond a brisk trot.

He laughed aloud as he let his stallion have his head. Wasn't that the whole point of coming to The Holme in the first place—to pluck some damsel from obscurity and flaunt her in the mercenary faces of the harpies who had been pursuing him so relentlessly? Lady Hester would be even more of a slap in the face to them all than her prettier, more accomplished cousins. Above all, he had wanted a woman who had never set her cap at him. Well, that was Hester all right. While her cousins had fluttered and flattered, she had spoken her mind, and given as good as she got on every occasion their paths crossed. Even the way she walked showed that she was totally resigned to her spinster state. When she was not creeping about like a cowed little girl, she strode about with a purposeful air, almost mannish in her bearing. Never did she adopt that seductive little sway to the hips that females employed to entice a man's eye.

Why not? the thundering hooves seemed to echo. Why not? Why not?

Marrying such a harridan would be disastrous. So what? He had never expected his marriage to be anything other than a farce, after all.

They crested a brow, and momentarily he admired the rolling vista opening up below him. His plan had been to find a woman who would be content to remain for the most part on one of his estates and breed his heirs. He had thought to pick a woman too complaisant to interfere with his life in London, or his interests in his racing stables. But Hester— well, she was so socially inept she would not want to spend much time in London, if the account of her disastrous Season was anything to go by.

And in her case, boredom would not be an issue. On the contrary, getting heirs by her was likely to be a tempestuous affair—a vision flashed into his mind of her fists raining blows onto Pattison's chest—if he could teach her to channel all that passion and energy more productively, he might even think about putting off his mistress altogether. Lush curves were not all that a man sought from his bedfellow.

He might do it. He really might do it.

Both men slowed their horses to a walk, their breathing laboured, their faces flushed with exertion. He turned in his saddle towards Peter.

'Can you satisfy my curiosity with regard to Lady Hester? Am I right in assuming she performs the duty of unpaid house-keeper for her aunt?'

'Ah, in a manner of speaking. That is, shouldn't say so, but dare say you've noticed already. My mother-in-law gets flustered very easily. Not sure how she would cope with us all descending on her like this if Hester wasn't here to help out, but Hester loves that sort of work, you know. Brilliant organiser. According to my wife, she loves planning things down to the last little detail.'

He had already deduced that Lady Gregory could not be the brain behind the smooth running of her establishment. So, Lady Hester would not shine at *ton*nish parties, but then he did not care overmuch for them anyway. She could certainly cater to the needs of guests he might invite to any one of his estates for hunting, say, or a shooting party.

'And she organises the most marvellous games for the children, treasure hunts and what have you. They all love coming to stay here.'

Yes, they did. A smile curved his lips at the thought of her rapport with children. He had never voiced his hope that he could find a wife with strong maternal instincts. But that was what he wanted. A woman who would not regard presenting her husband with an heir as a chore to be endured, nor regard successive children as expendable spares. His smile faded. It would hardly matter in the long run if his wife and he came to detest each other. If he could only provide his children with a mother who would want to be with them, who would lavish affection on them as his own mother so conspicuously had not. She had not even shed a tear, so far as he knew, for Bertram, so little did she care for anything but the fashionable world.

Lady Gregory would be livid if he chose her gauche, neglected niece over one of her pampered daughters. And as for Sir Thomas... His lips curved into a malicious smile. It would almost be worth marrying Hester simply for the joy of putting that jumped-up country squire in his place.

He would have to conduct his campaign with care, though. He wouldn't put it past Sir Thomas to prevent his access to Lady Hester altogether if he got wind of his intentions.

His smile widened. From what he had already learned of Lady Hester, he would warrant she would revel in a clandestine courtship. Her propensity for sneaking off when she ought to be about her duties, her very desperation to escape the confines of her existence, would soon drive her into his arms in spite of the poor start they had made, if only he could somehow alert her to his intent.

As they turned their mounts towards The Holme, he discovered that he no longer felt depressed at the prospect of matrimony. On the contrary, he was looking forward to the many challenges it represented.

Sir Thomas tossed his riding crop on to the cluttered desk, raising a cloud of snuff.

'How could you, Hester?' He turned to stare out of the window, his hands clasped behind his back as she slunk into the room and softly closed the door. 'I was prepared to let it go yesterday, especially when I learned his lordship saw you. I did not want to add insult to injury by reminding you what a foolish risk you took. However did you think you would get away with sneaking off like that?'

Hester sighed wearily and lowered herself into the chair

that faced his desk. 'I didn't think anyone would miss me with all the excitement his lordship's arrival had stirred up. I thought the servants would assume I was above stairs with the family, and that the family would assume I was below stairs tending to household matters. Indeed, if his lordship had kept his mouth shut, nobody would have been any the wiser.'

'Then I am glad he did.' He turned, bracing himself upon the desk, his fingers splayed. 'I knew the temptation would be great. As soon as Baines came and told me the gypsies were camping on your land, I knew how much you would want to go down there and see Lena. And before we get into that old argument about whether or not they poach game from my coverts while they denude yours, I must insist you consider the possible repercussions of your clandestine visits to Jye's caravan.'

'I was careful—both times.'

'Yet the marquis almost discovered what you were about both times,' her uncle snapped. 'Yesterday, as I said, your visit was understandable, given that they have been away a full year, and your heart is so deeply involved. But to go down there again this morning... And there is no point in denying the gypsy camp is where you have been. I can tell from the artwork adorning your hat.'

She fingered the paper flowers ruefully. How ironic it was that a gift given with affection had betrayed her.

She sighed. 'Truly, Uncle, I never dreamed Lord Lensborough would be up and in the stable yard so early.'

'No...he is not what your aunt led me to believe he would be at all. In fact, the more I learn about him, the more I think...' He shook his head. 'Did you know he breeds racehorses? But we are straying from the point again. The point is, if anyone should see you hobnobbing with gypsies, the fat will be well and truly in the fire.'

'But nobody will see me. And even if they did, what could they possibly suspect, other than that I am a bit eccentric for wanting to help children that most would shun. They will only see me teaching a group of children to read and write.'

'Hester, anyone with eyes in his head will take one look at Lena's pale, freckled skin and see that she is not a pure-blood Romany. Then they will look at you beside her, and wonder why her hair and eyes are exactly the same colour as your own.'

Hester wound a tendril of burnished chestnut round her gloved finger guiltily.

'How do you know how closely she has grown to resemble me?'

'Because,' he admitted with a rueful smile, 'I went down there myself yesterday to take a look at her too.'

Hester's eyes filled with tears. For all Sir Thomas's anger when he found out about the liaison of gentry with gypsy, for all his refusal to allow the offspring of that illicit coupling to be reared in his home as Hester had once begged him to do, he could not quite quench all feelings for the little girl, Lena, his great-niece.

'Well, then...' Hope flared, only to be abruptly extinguished by her uncle's next words.

'Hester, we cannot undo the past, but I will not permit another's sins to threaten the welfare of my own daughters. Julia and Phoebe are both insistent they want a match with their marquis, and believe me, a man of his stamp will not take kindly to the scandal we have sitting—literally, as it happens this week—on our doorstep.'

He added briskly, after Hester had brooded over his words in silence for some minutes, 'Besides, consider the sensibilities of your aunts, Lady Susan and Lady Moulton. You must see how upset finding out about Lena would make them? So far we have managed to keep her existence secret from all but our two selves. I would like it to stay that way. I particularly do not wish any scandal to break this week, while my own girls' futures hang in the balance.'

Hester sighed. 'You are right, Uncle Thomas. I have been abominably selfish. It is just that the few hours I can snatch with her are so precious. And I want so much for her to be able to read and write, to have at least a rudimentary education. She has already been denied so much.'

'I know, I know. But, do you think it wise, now that she is older, and more noticing, to put her in the way of guessing she is different from the other gypsy children? It would not be fair to raise her expectations, or make her dissatisfied with her lot.'

'Oh, you need not worry on that score.' Hester gave a wry laugh. 'Jye will never permit me access to her alone, or give her any special treatment. If I want her to read, it will be because she is one of a class with all the others. In fact...' she frowned '...she is quite a poor scholar. She sits in class with the others, but does not pay much attention. I suppose you have already guessed it was she who made me this garland.' She sighed. 'From the paper she was supposed to be practising her letters on.' The little imp had given her such a cheeky grin when she tacked the crown round the brim of her hat at the end of the lesson, that she had not had the heart to scold her. But if she were not permitted to even try to teach her...

Her uncle came round the desk with a handkerchief in his hand as silent tears began to trickle down her cheeks.

'It is better she never knows about her origins. Jye was wise to insist on that when he agreed to raise her himself.'

'It is so hard, Uncle—' her breath caught '—for her to be only a few fields away and not go to her.' She drew in another ragged breath. 'Not to be able to sit her on my knee and hold her while she tells me what adventures have befallen her since last we met.'

Her uncle pounced on her statement. 'Then you do agree. Until our guests have left, you will stay away?'

'Yes.' The single word was an admission of complete surrender. 'I know you are right. I have no wish to upset anyone else with what is, after all, purely my own affair.'

She blew her nose and rose shakily to her feet. 'I should be about my work. I have wasted enough time.'

Sir Thomas heaved a great sigh. 'Oh, Hester, my girl, no female should have to bear the burdens you have borne. Especially not at the age you were when…'

Hester stood with her hand poised on the doorknob, her head averted, bracing herself for what he would say next. She was immensely relieved when he only cleared his throat noisily, before turning abruptly to glare at the frost-ravaged shrubs that huddled round the lawn outside his window.

Chapter Five

B y the time Lord Lensborough had eaten his breakfast, he
had begun to have second thoughts. Out on the moors, with
the cold wind whipping his cheeks, and his horse pounding
the frozen ground beneath him, the idea of considering
marriage to a shrew had possessed a certain kind of logic to
it. A crazy, defiant sort of logic.

Determined to put her from his mind, he spent a pleasant
afternoon strolling through the shrubbery with the two blond
beauties, and Stephen to act as chaperon. It was only when
he went to change for dinner that he realised he could not
remember a single thing either one of them had said. Discarding his ruined neckcloth, he frowned at his reflection in the
mirror. He had no trouble remembering every scathing word
Lady Hester had ever flung at him, nor every minute expression that flitted across her sharp-featured little face.

It was galling in the extreme when he was aware of the very
second she entered the saloon where they gathered before
dinner. Though there were no children to herald her arrival,
all his senses went on the alert. He did not need to watch her
progress round the edges of the room. He could feel her de-

termination not to come within forty feet of him. Her relief, when she gained the sofa on which her cousin Henrietta was sitting, was just as palpable. And just as irritating.

In one swift, penetrating glance, he absorbed the fact that the dress she wore was as outmoded as the greenish thing she had donned the night before, being long sleeved, high necked and made for somebody several sizes larger than she. At least the bronze colour toned in with the lighter shades in her hair. It was a great pity she did not dress that hair in a more becoming style. With a little effort, it could become her crowning glory. The shade was truly unique. Only an unimaginative fool would dismiss it as merely red. It was elemental flame. A man could warm his hands on it on a cold night.

He gave up. There were many highly sensible reasons why he should not marry her. And he might not, in the end. But she was as eligible, in many ways, as his host's daughters, and he could not deny that he was becoming increasingly intrigued by her.

And so, as soon as was possible after he had finished a very excellent dinner, the menu of which, the butler confirmed, Lady Hester had devised, he made a point of seeking out her company in the withdrawing room. As he paused on the threshold, her cousin Henrietta happened to make a comment that made her throw back her head and laugh.

The result was astonishing. It was as if the rough outer shell of an oyster had been prised open to reveal the pearl glistening within. With her head tilted slightly back, her eyes half-closed and her lips parted, revealing evenly spaced white teeth, Lord Lensborough saw that Lady Hester had the potential to be a quite remarkably attractive woman. If she would only laugh more often, displaying just that mischievous tilt to her head, even the freckles that sprinkled her little tip-tilted nose were not such a disadvantage as all that—they showed character, that she was a woman who would pursue activities out of doors whether they spoiled her complexion or not.

Or if she would only wear the sort of clothes that flattered her willowy frame, he smiled to himself. It was not as if the other two girls would impress the *ton* without the benefit of his mother's tuition. All three needed to learn how to dress. She could as well make Lady Hester presentable as Julia or Phoebe. On that score they were all even.

While he was musing, she made her way to a quiet corner and took out some knitting. He pursued her.

'May I join you?' he inquired, pulling a chair up to the table on which her work bag lay open.

She started, though her eyes never left the work that was growing visibly as her nimble fingers made the needles fly. She was fashioning a tiny garment out of wool, a sock or a glove, he could not tell which. It seemed typical of what he had gleaned of her character so far, that she spent her evenings making something that was going to be of use to someone, rather than waste it on some decorative embroidery.

'I don't suppose I can stop you,' she murmured.

'No…' he leaned back and crossed one leg indolently over the other '…nor can anyone else.'

She shot him a mutinous look at that, just one, but it heartened him.

'Not completely cowed, then,' he drawled. 'I am glad that whatever punishment your uncle decreed this morning has not managed to quench your indomitable spirit altogether.'

Bewildered, she frowned. He did not like her, nothing about her, least of all what he drily referred to as her spirit. She cast about as to what he might mean, and after a moment could only suppose that he took delight in tormenting her. That contrary to what he said, he was glad to think her uncle might have punished her, since it was what he was itching to do himself. Anger swept her confusion away. Before she could stop herself, she snapped, 'What possible concern is it of yours? What do you want?'

'Why, to get to know you better, of course. I have already discovered that you like riding, that you are as competent in that as you appear to be at everything else you attempt.'

If she had felt confused before, this last statement sent her mind reeling. Why would he want to get to know her better? He was here to decide whether he was going to marry Phoebe or Julia. She was nothing to him. Less than nothing—he had made that all too clear when he had driven away leaving her soaked and freezing. His sneering, scowling looks spoke more clearly than his words did. She darted a look at him from under her sooty eyelashes. A faint smile hovered about his lips.

He was enjoying this, like a cat playing with a mouse; he would toy with her for a while, before swatting her with one of his great paws. She looked down at the hand that lay in his lap, relaxed now, resting on the silk fabric that clothed a muscular thigh. Resentment swept through her.

'Well, thanks to you I will not be doing any more riding while you are staying at The Holme.' She glared at him. 'I suppose that makes you glad.'

Amusement faded from his face. So. Her uncle had withdrawn the use of a horse, because he feared that their mutual love of riding might throw them together. His breathing quickened. No wonder she was looking daggers at him. She had few enough pleasures in her life, and unwittingly he had been the cause of her losing one—and what it must have cost her. He could not imagine what it must feel like to be unable to get out on horseback whenever the fancy took him. At least when she was his wife, she would have access to some of the finest mounts in the country—aye, and she would probably be able to manage a fair proportion of them too. A smile tugged at the corner of his lips as he thought of how her face would light up when he showed her round the stables at Ely.

'Yes,' Hester hissed as she saw, and misinterpreted, his slow smile of anticipation, 'I thought you would be pleased to know you can now go to the stables without fear of running into me. I would so hate for you to be put out…bother.' She sighed, returning her attention to her knitting. 'Now you have made me drop a stitch. I will have to start this row all over again.'

Lord Lensborough was disconcerted that she had misconstrued his smile so badly. Of course, she could not have known what direction his thoughts were taking. He would have to make sure there were no more misunderstandings of that nature. The poor girl was upset enough about losing her riding privileges without thinking he was gloating. Her fingers were shaking quite badly.

'Leave off that knitting and talk to me instead,' he urged her, leaning forward and laying one hand over her trembling ones.

She jerked them away, her whole body rigid. Yes, she was right, he must move with extreme caution lest her uncle suspect he had begun to consider her in earnest, and contrive to remove her from his sphere altogether. He withdrew his hand, picking up instead a stray hank of wool that lay on the table between them.

'Talk…' Her voice had become quite husky. A tide of red swept from her cheeks, down her neck, to disappear into the tantalisingly concealing folds of her voluminous gown. 'What about? What can we possibly have to talk about? Please go back to Julia and Phoebe and leave me be.'

'No. Not yet.' The tone of his voice was implacable. 'I have a fancy to discuss politics, and I don't think either of them have any political views one way or another.'

'Well, neither do I,' she exclaimed. 'At least, none that a man like you would respect.'

Her eyes sought out her aunt, and her expression was such a speaking mixture of fear and guilt that he shifted his chair slightly, blocking the woman from Hester's view.

'I shouldn't be the least bit surprised if I found your views novel, though. They might amuse me. Come, tell me what you thought about Wellington's crushing defeat of Napoleon.'

Hester didn't even pause to take a breath. To speak of amusement, and war, in the same sentence! She had known he was callous, but not to the extent of regarding men suffering and dying as a topic for amusing conversation.

Her wool fell to the ground and rolled unheeded across the polished parquet as she struggled to find words that were adequate to express the depth of her disdain for such a man.

'I suppose you regarded Waterloo as a glorious victory,' she hissed. 'I suppose you admired Wellington's determination to stop Napoleon at any cost.'

'And you didn't?' He leaned forward, suddenly arrested by the notion that if her feelings ran counter to his own on this, he was going to be bitterly disappointed.

'I think it was wicked of him to send so many men to their deaths. I don't think there was anything glorious about the grief of the widows and orphans left behind. Nothing noble about the conditions those who survived were forced to endure when they returned home, crippled fighting for their country, unable to work. And I think it monstrous that the government does nothing to help them.'

By God, Captain Fawley could do with meeting Lady Hester Cuerden. She was the perfect antidote to all the shrinking society damsels that had done the man's self-esteem so much damage. She would see beneath the scars, to the man, and whether she liked him or no, it would have nothing to do with the way he looked.

'And you think the government should…?'

She turned her face to his, puzzled by something in his voice that sounded like genuine interest. 'Provide relief, of course. Those men died, or were wounded, fighting for their country. Their country should now help them in return. Men like you…'

Her voice died away in her throat. His face was less than two feet from hers, his eyes fixed on hers with an expression that was so like admiration that for a moment she forgot what she had been about to say. His eyes, she noted, were not black at all, but dark brown, flecked with amber. Almost exactly like the patterns on the tiger's-eye pin he was wearing in his neckcloth again.

'Men like me…what?' he prompted in a voice so gentle that suddenly he did not seem like the Marquis of Lensborough at all.

She swallowed, but found it impossible to break eye contact. And she resented that. What business had she noticing that his eyes were a fascinatingly unusual colour? His heart was still black.

'You should pass a law. It's no good saying such men are a menace and try to sweep them off the streets. If they are menacing, it is only because they were trained to be menacing by their drill sergeants. It was their ferocity that ensured our freedoms, wasn't it?'

'I cannot pass such a law, if I would. It takes more than the word of one man to get a law through parliament.'

'Even a marquis?' she jeered. Then, flushing, she lowered her head, aware of muted conversations going on all around her. The rest of her family was managing to engage in the sort of polite conversation fit for a drawing room. Why couldn't she turn aside his barbs with some innocuous remark? Why did his proximity rob her of the ability to keep a civil tongue in her head? Lord Lensborough seemed able to reduce her to the point where all she wanted to do was slap his rugged, arrogant face.

She heard him sigh, and waited for his reproof. When it did not come, she felt even more in the wrong, which only served to make her angrier at herself. And at him.

'You could do something if you wanted to, a man of your

influence. Why, any charity would be glad of your patronage. People would queue up to make donations if they thought that by doing so they could curry favour with you.'

'A charity,' he mused. 'A trust.'

A trust, in his brother's name, to bring relief to the dependents of his regiment. What a fitting memorial that would be. He could not imagine why he had not thought of such a thing before.

It had taken this woman to inspire him, this remarkable woman who did not think or act like anybody else.

'My brother fell at Waterloo,' he confided quietly.

Hester's hand flew to her mouth, her eyes filling with mortified tears as she looked up into his grave countenance.

'Oh, I am so sorry. I spoke without thinking. I did not mean to wound you…at least I did, but I would never have said quite what I said if I had known of your own loss.'

Lord Lensborough searched her face intently. There was a remorse there that showed she knew she had touched upon a pain that nobody else had even guessed might lie concealed beneath his impenetrable façade. Hardly anybody so much as suspected there was anything but the façade.

Determined to alleviate her distress, he explained, 'Bertram looked on battle as an adventure. He died doing what he loved, what he believed in.'

To finally acknowledge this truth, out loud, was like healing balm pouring over his aching soul. Much of his grief, he suddenly realised, had stemmed from regarding his brother's death as a sinful waste. He went to grasp her hands for a second time, feeling an irresistible urge to raise them to his lips in gratitude.

She snatched them away, shrinking back into her chair as a shadow fell over them both.

'Uncle Thomas,' she squeaked.

'I saw you drop your wool, Hester.' His voice was barely more than a growl. Lord Lensborough turned and saw that the man had painstakingly rolled the wool into a neat ball and was holding it out to his trembling niece. 'Is anything amiss?'

Lord Lensborough's hackles rose. 'Nothing is amiss here, sir. We were discussing Waterloo, and Lady Hester was making some very helpful suggestions about what might be done for the relief of war widows.'

Sir Thomas did not even bother to turn his head in Lord Lensborough's direction. He pointedly addressed his next remark to Lady Hester.

'My dear girl, you have no need to stay here if you do not wish to. You may retire to your rooms whenever you please.'

Without a word, Lady Hester leapt to her feet and quit her chair, scattering her knitting in all directions as she fled without so much as one backward glance. Lord Lensborough rose to his feet somewhat more slowly, his glare boring into Sir Thomas's back as he followed his niece at a steady pace from the room.

'Hester,' Sir Thomas called out as she began her headlong flight up the stairs.

She turned, forcing a tremulous smile to her lips.

Sir Thomas looked up at her, frowning. 'You know, my dear, if that fellow makes you uncomfortable, you need not suffer his manners.'

'But my aunt wishes us all to—'

'Bow and scrape to him. I know.' He made a dismissive gesture with his hand. 'You gave us all fair warning that you objected to his coming here, and that you wanted nothing to do with him. I should have listened. My girls must put up with his overbearing ways, since they are set on marrying the fellow, but for my part you may tell him to go to the devil if you wish.'

Hester's smile faded altogether. 'Oh, Uncle Thomas, I have already said the most terrible, unforgivable things to him. Now I know you will not disapprove, I think it would be as well to keep out of his way. In fact, I rather think Julia and Phoebe would do better if I kept out of sight. I appear to annoy him almost as much as he annoys me. I really do not set out to provoke him, Uncle Thomas.'

'I know, I know, it's like a red rag to a bull. The atmosphere would certainly be less fraught if you were kept apart. We are all holding our breath, waiting for the next explosion to take place.' He smiled. 'Why don't you go back to Em's after church tomorrow, and have the afternoon to yourself?'

Hester came down one step. 'Will Aunt Susan be able to manage without me? Dinner tomorrow is quite elaborate, and I had planned on a treasure hunt for the children.'

'I am sure any domestic crises can await your return. Nor will it harm the children to remain in the charge of their nurses for one afternoon.'

Hester looked more relaxed immediately. 'About dinner,' she began hesitantly.

'No need to put in an appearance unless you want to. Have a tray up in your rooms, if you like. If you want a gossip with Henrietta about Barny's progress, or whatever else it is you two girls find to talk about, you could always invite her to one of those midnight feasts you used to have when you were schoolgirls.'

Hester shook her head. 'Uncle Thomas, those midnight feasts were supposed to be secret.'

'With everyone who was invited to them having to traipse through the servants' hall to get to your staircase?' he asked. 'Stealing biscuits and jugs of lemonade from the kitchen on the way?'

Hester felt a warm surge of affection for her uncle, for his forbearance with her prickly insistence on maintaining the complete privacy of her rooms. Nobody went into them without an express invitation, not even a maid to clean.

She had felt at a loss when she first came to live at The

Holme after her parents had died during an epidemic of typhus. They had been so demonstrably affectionate, and her uncle was rather gruff. But when she had removed up to the attics he had supported her decision, as though he sensed she needed some territory she could still call her very own. She did. Her rooms were her sanctuary.

'I will give it serious consideration, Uncle Thomas. Em always manages to talk me into a more reasonable frame of mind. And entertaining my own chosen guests, in my own rooms, will certainly be preferable to being downstairs with him prowling about the place like a caged tiger.'

What a relief. No need to dread any more confrontations with the insufferable Lord Lensborough. She went up to her rooms in a more cheerful frame of mind than she had experienced for weeks.

Chapter Six

'Of all the dull days that we've spent in this Godforsaken hole,' Lord Lensborough drawled late the following evening as he tossed back his second brandy, 'Sunday has to rank as the dullest.'

'Oh, I don't know,' Stephen countered, stretching his legs out towards the fire, which crackled cheerfully in the grate of their shared sitting room. 'I got a great deal of amusement from attending church this morning.'

Lord Lensborough shot him a look of loathing.

'Julia informed me over dinner,' he remarked, barely able to keep a straight face, 'that the congregation has not been so large since the pig-face lady passed through this district on her way to the fair at Scarborough. People attended from several adjoining parishes in the hopes of catching a glimpse of a genuine marquis.'

'If you think I enjoy being trotted out like some specimen at a freak show…'

'And then, of course, we must not forget the treat of coming across the divine Miss Dean, the lovely Emily.' Stephen raised his glass in tribute.

'Good God.' Lord Lensborough's eyes narrowed as he saw

the lustful expression on his friend's face. 'You are contemplating setting up a flirtation with the vicar's daughter.'

'Well, as you yourself pointed out, what else is there to do in this neck of the woods? You have appropriated every single female within these four walls, although…' He stared abstractedly into his brandy glass for a few seconds, before continuing, 'I feel obliged to warn you that you are not likely to be successful if you decide on Cinderella.' Stephen had so nicknamed Hester on account of her station in the house, her marked shabbiness in contrast with the two girls who were vying for the marriage prize, who were sisters, though not hers, nor the least bit ugly.

'What? Why not?'

'Well, for one thing, you are no maiden's version of Prince Charming. You have no charm whatsoever.'

Lord Lensborough snorted in derision. 'I do not turn on the charm in order to seduce innocents into my bed, if that is what you mean. I have never had any taste for that sort of game.' Then, running with the metaphor Stephen had begun, he said, 'However, there is a certain appeal in making the attempt to rescue Cinders from her life of drudgery. Her wicked stepmother—'

'Fuddled aunt,' Stephen corrected him.

'—would not even let Cinders out for meals today. She took them on a tray in her rooms.' He neatly omitted to mention that only a few days previously he had believed that was exactly where the poor relation should take her meals. 'Attic rooms, no less, which can only be reached by going through the servants' quarters.'

Stephen raised an eyebrow and grinned at his friend. 'You have been busy. Where did you come by all this information?'

'My valet,' he said. 'And when she wasn't shut away up there today, she was banished to the vicarage in Beckforth on the pretext of visiting Miss Dean, who is purported to be her dearest friend in the neighbourhood.'

'There. I told you I should flirt with the lovely Emily. It will help your own suit no end if we were to take to visiting the vicarage together.'

'I have no need of your help.'

'No, you are beyond help. But it will amuse me no end watching you make a cake of yourself. I shall always treasure the moment when Cinderella rated you below the value of her knitting. I should think everyone in the drawing room heard her berate you for making her drop a stitch.'

'She has a temper.' He shrugged. 'And we got off on the wrong foot, that is all. There was a misunderstanding.'

He frowned. He never had really made a decent apology for his awful behaviour during their first encounter. She might still harbour some resentment, but the prospect of the lifestyle he was offering would more than make amends for all that.

'And of course her uncle has repeatedly warned her to keep away from me. He wants me for his own daughters. So she has not dared think of me in the light of a suitor. She is naturally on edge whenever I pay her a little attention in case her family think she is putting herself forward. Once I manage to declare myself, and promise her that I will prevent her family from exacting retribution, you will see a marked difference in her attitude towards me.'

'You think so?'

'I know so. What woman would not go instantly into raptures upon receiving a marriage proposal from a marquis?'

Immediately after breakfast the next morning, Hester tied her hair out of the way with a brightly embroidered cotton scarf, rounded up the children, and took them up to the long gallery for a game of indoor cricket.

It was not long into the game when she gave thanks that

all the breakables had been removed, for Harry, her twelve-year-old cousin, younger brother to Julia and Phoebe, had a powerful swing.

She leapt as high as she could in an effort to catch the tennis ball he had just struck, but was not surprised when her fingers closed on empty air. What did surprise her was his cry of, 'Oh, well caught, sir,' and the smattering of spontaneous applause that rippled among the other players.

As Harry dutifully lowered the tennis racquet he was using to guard the upturned coal scuttle which was his wicket, Lady Hester turned to see which one of the fathers had taken the unprecedented step of visiting his offspring, rather than the stables, so early in the morning.

But it was Lord Lensborough who was striding towards them, tossing the ball and catching it nonchalantly in one hand as he came.

'That means you are in bat now, sir, by our rules,' Harry cheerfully explained while Hester's jaw dropped.

Lord Lensborough in bat. Not if I can help it, thought Hester, snapping her mouth closed firmly.

'Make your bow to his lordship, children,' she commanded her charges, sinking into a dutiful curtsy herself. She felt a spurt of satisfaction when his brows drew down in an expression of displeasure. He was no fool, she had to give him that. He had picked up her unspoken message that he was unwelcome.

'You appear to have lost your way, my lord,' she said, keeping her eyes fixed on the ball once he came to a halt only a few feet from her. 'My cousins are waiting for you in the library.' The long, strong fingers tightened perceptibly around the ball.

'What you are doing looks far more interesting.'

Hester detected a hint of a threat in his tone. She took a step back. He took one forward.

'I have observed,' he said in a voice pitched so low that nobody but she could hear it, 'that the most interesting things seem to occur wherever you are. Do not banish me to the library just yet. It is a sentence too harsh, even for you, to condemn me to the tedium of your cousins' conversation.'

Hester gasped. Whatever could he mean? A scion of society would not really wish to spend time with a woman who dived into ditches, indulged in fisticuffs with his groom, spat insults at him at every available opportunity, never mind a pack of grubby children.

'You will find no conversation at all here, my lord. We are simply playing a children's game.'

'I already know that it will give me more amusement than being closeted with your hen-witted aunt.'

'My aunt is not…' Hester's head flew up as she launched into a defence of her aunt, only to falter at the twin hurdles of her aunt's lack of intelligence, and the amused twinkle she encountered in those tiger-striped eyes. Still, to insult Aunt Susan while the children stood within hearing distance…

'You have not seen my aunt at her best,' Hester hissed between clenched teeth, taking a step nearer to prevent the children overhearing. 'She is a little flustered at present, since we have a house full of guests.'

'From what I have observed,' his lordship cut in ruthlessly, 'she does little more than sit on a sofa, issuing a plethora of contradictory orders while you run yourself ragged making sure the house runs smoothly in spite of her.'

Hester clenched her teeth on the riposte she would dearly love to have given him in defence of her aunt. Was that what he was about? Taunting her, baiting her till she could not help lashing out at him? So that she would feel, as she had done after blundering into the facts of his painful bereavement, that she deserved to have her tongue cut out? Better to change the subject altogether than end up looking like a heartless shrew yet again.

'Please, sir, may we have our ball back? The children grow impatient to continue their game.'

'But I am in bat,' he countered.

'Oh, no, you're not.' She glared up at him, promptly forgetting all her resolutions to keep an even temper in his presence. 'You shouldn't even be here. You are supposed to be in the library.'

'I think not.' His voice dropped to little more than a growl, so threatening it sent a shiver sliding the length of Hester's spine. She couldn't believe she had just more or less given him an order. Lord Lensborough took orders from nobody.

She clasped her hands together before her, an unconsciously defensive gesture, and glanced nervously over her shoulder at the children.

Lord Lensborough sighed, following the direction of her gaze. Any one of these children could report back to its parent that, instead of playing with them, Lady Hester had been flirting with him. On his account she had already had her riding privileges withdrawn, and been painfully reminded of her lowly station by being forced to take her meals out of sight of the other house guests.

This was not going at all the way he had planned. His attempt to keep things lighthearted had only succeeded in confusing her, and making her nervous. All he could now do was make the whole episode appear as innocent as possible.

'Just stop arguing with me for once, madam, and explain the rules,' he growled.

'Th...the rules...' she stuttered, backing away from him.

'The rules are brilliant,' Harry cheerfully asserted, stomping over to where they stood and handing the battered tennis racquet over to Lord Lensborough. 'One man in bat, defending his wicket...' he gestured towards the coal scuttle '...the rest fielding. To ensure fair play, Aunt Hetty has devised a system of handicaps. The bigger and stronger you are, the more handicaps you have.'

Lord Lensborough nodded, taking in the range of ages of

the assembled children. The youngest involved in the game, the little blond moppet who had crawled on to Lady Hester's lap during that first supper in the Great Hall, looked to be scarce more than a toddler. 'That does seem fair,' he agreed. Glancing at Lady Hester, he couldn't resist asking, 'What is the handicap imposed on Lady Hester?'

'Oh, she's a female,' Harry blithely returned.

'He means,' Hester put in, seeing the mocking twist to Lord Lensborough's lips, 'that my movements are sufficiently hampered by wearing skirts to render me handicapped. I should point out, though, that any catch I make only counts as an "out" if I use my left hand, and the ball has not bounced off any other surface.'

Lord Lensborough's lips twitched, remembering the determined leap she had been performing the very moment he had entered the gallery. 'Dare I ask what my handicap might be?'

The children had abandoned their strategic fielding positions to gather around the tall, imposing stranger who had suddenly given their game a whole new dimension by deigning to join in.

'You can only bat with your left hand,' Harry decreed. 'The other will have to be tied behind your back.' There was a general murmur of agreement.

'Not much of a handicap to a sportsman like his lordship, I shouldn't have thought,' Lady Hester objected. 'There should be more than that.'

So…she knew him for a sportsman. Not so indifferent as she would like to have everyone believe.

'How about blindfolding him?' the freckle-faced boy suggested.

'Capital idea, George,' Harry agreed. Before he had time to react one way or the other, the children were urging him to the coal-scuttle wicket, holding up a variety of scarves and neckcloths with which to bind him.

'Can I not just keep my right hand in my pocket?' he laughingly protested.

But the children were insistent, and it was amidst much hilarity that Hester took hold of his wrist and pushed it behind his back.

His arm was heavy for her to manoeuvre into position, though he was making no attempt to resist. It was muscle, she knew, not fat, that made his upper arm so bulky beneath his coat sleeve. He was an all-round sportsman. Harry Moulton had told Henrietta that, besides breeding and training racehorses, Lord Lensborough boxed regularly at Gentleman Jackson's, and fenced in an exclusive academy off St James's Street. He was in superb fighting condition. It felt strange to be moving his arm wheresoever she pleased, when he could have swatted her off like a pesky fly if he so wished.

She had to reach right round his waist, lifting his coat tails to secure the bindings in place. She wondered that she dare take such liberties with his person. By the time she reached up on tiptoe to fasten a silk scarf about his face, her fingers were trembling so much she could scarce get the knot tied. Handling his bulky physique like this made her excruciatingly aware of his leashed strength. This must be what it felt like to take a tiger by the tail.

Her breath was warm on the back of his neck. Her fingers were trembling. The silk kept slipping down his face as she fumbled with the knot, and she had to reach around repeatedly to hold it in place over his eyes. When she did so, the whole length of her body was pressed up against his back. Did she know what she was doing to him? Dear God, he hoped not.

It had been bad enough when she'd passed her arms round his waist, securing his arm behind his back. A lurid fantasy of her binding his limbs to a brass bedstead had flashed into his mind. Now, with the entire length of her against the length of him, the fantasy took flight. He could almost feel those supple fingers exploring his helplessly bound body, her long limbs tangling with his. The heat that had inevitably built between them whenever they came together had so far only resulted in conflict. But if they ever channelled that heat into gaining mutual satisfaction... His pulse rate rocketed.

There was no question about his choice of wife any more. All the determined flaunting of her full-bosomed cousins had left him unmoved, but her innocent fumblings, the warmth of her sweet breath on the nape of his neck, had induced erotic images so powerful he could barely keep his body in check.

Finally, thankfully, the sweet torture came to an end, and Harry warned him he was about to bowl.

Exactly how was he supposed to defend his wicket when he could not see the ball coming? His only chance was to wave his racquet wildly before his legs, in the hope that a lucky swipe would keep him safe. A slight jolt up his arm, and the cheers of the children informed him that he had made such a lucky strike. There was a shriek of delighted laughter, quickly followed by the voices of Hester and Harry in unison, shouting, 'Out!' When he pushed the blindfold from his eyes with the thumb of his free hand, he saw that the curly-haired moppet had the ball clutched tightly in both her hands.

'She caught me out?'

'Indeed she did,' Hester chortled. Lord Lensborough had looked so determined in his defence of his wicket, so dumbfounded to have been bested by such a tiny child. A girl at that.

'Remarkable.' He eyed the grinning child, who was skipping up to him, with something like awe.

'Oh, she did not catch it in the regular way, sir,' Harry promptly explained. 'It rolled straight at her. All she had to do was scoop it up.'

Ah, yes, Hester's rules ensured that every single child had a chance to enjoy the game equally. Gravely, he surrendered his bat to the moppet, and turned towards Lady Hester with a slow smile. He could have shrugged out of the restraints had he so wished, but the prospect of having her trembling fingers working over the length of his body was too great a temptation to resist.

'My lady…'

Before he could even ask Hester to untie him, she was walking away, towards the butler, who had just entered the gallery.

'Your presence is requested in the library. You have visitors,' Fisher explained.

Lord Lensborough's mood took an abrupt nosedive. He was not even permitted to enjoy her company when surrounded by the most effective chaperons of all, innocent children. He ripped the scarf from his face, and freed his arm from the bindings about his waist.

'But I promised the children until eleven,' Hester protested, watching the shredded neckcloths flutter to the floor.

'I will stay and supervise until then,' Lord Lensborough grated. 'Harry can apprise me of the rules.'

'You? No, better not. They can return to the nursery. Some of the little ones are due for a drink and a nap.'

'Why not?' It would do her no good if he escorted her down to the library. For them to enter together—what a hornet's nest that would stir up. 'It is my turn to bowl. You would not deny me that experience? Or rob the children of their amusement? Do you think I am incapable of minding a handful of children for ten minutes?'

'N…no, of course not.'

Her perplexed frown made him smile in a grim fashion.

'Capital,' Harry yelled with glee, scooping up the discarded silk scarf. 'I can't wait to see you bowl blindfolded!'

Hester closed the door to the gallery on the amazing sight of the autocrat surrendering his dignity to a grubby twelve-

year-old schoolboy, and wondered if Em had been in the right.
Perhaps she had misjudged him from the very beginning.

She had been appalled at the clinical tone of the letter his
mother had written to her aunt regarding his need to produce
an heir. But that was just it. He had not written it. And he really
seemed to like children. Perhaps he would be…not an indul-
gent father—no, she could not imagine that. He would be
stern, rearing his offspring to know their duty. She shrugged.
That was no bad thing. Julia or Phoebe would be most indul-
gent mothers; he would provide a balance that would prevent
the children from becoming spoiled.

As for his quip about the most interesting things happening where she was—perhaps he had not meant it as an insult.
Perhaps it was his roundabout way of trying to mend fences
between them, to brush off their unfortunate habit of ending
every discussion or encounter they entered with argument. It
had already occurred to her that, since they would be related
by marriage, she must strive to keep her poor opinion of him
well shackled. Perhaps his own code of honour demanded that
no matter what his feeling for her might be, he would owe it
to his future wife to make some attempt to be on easy terms
with all her family.

Her pace slowed as her brain whirled. That might account
for it—an outright apology was, after all, too much to expect
from a man like him. She snorted in a most unladylike fashion.
Apologise? That would be tantamount to admitting he was
less than perfect. He was far too arrogant to ever make the
kind of apology that would satisfy her. She reached the bottom
of the stairs and drifted along the passageway that led to the
wing of the house where the library was situated.

She supposed she could hardly expect him to be anything
other than exceedingly conceited and self-satisfied when he
must have had people fawning over him his entire life. His
rank alone made him a target for toadeaters, and his almost

obscene wealth meant he only had to snap his fingers, and people fell over themselves to supply whatever he wanted.

So why was it getting so hard to hold to her belief he was wicked through and through?

Because he was demolishing her prejudices one by one, that's why. He genuinely liked children. He couldn't be so natural with them if he didn't.

And she had jumped to the wrong conclusion about the way he dressed. He was not expressing contempt for his humble surroundings. His clothes were cut for freedom of movement because of his active lifestyle. And they were black because he was in mourning.

It was only as she was opening the library door that she realised she had been so distracted by Lord Lensborough that she had completely forgotten to ask Fisher who her visitor was. The butler had stayed in the long gallery so that he could guide his lordship to the library when the game ended.

Her aunt was sitting on one side of the fire, her embroidery frame set up before her, with Julia and Phoebe on a sofa opposite her. In the window embrasure, Mr Farrar lounged with a newspaper spread open upon his lap, and beside him stood Emily Dean.

'Em.' Hester made towards her, hands outstretched in welcome. The day before, Em had expressed her wish to come and inspect the marquis at close quarters, so that she would feel better equipped to join Hester in dissecting his failings. They had agreed that she would use the pretext of returning the laundered clothes Hester had left at the vicarage, and, indeed, there was a brown paper parcel in her hand.

Em smiled. 'I have quite a surprise for you. You will never guess who turned up, quite unexpectedly last night, for a short stay at the vicarage.'

'Well, then, tell me.'

'Better yet, turn round, and you will see me for yourself.'

A cold fist seemed to close around Hester's heart at the sound of the voice she had not heard since she was thirteen.

'Lionel Snelgrove?'

She whirled round to face him as he stepped out of the shadows to the right of the door, grinning. Bold as brass. That knowing, challenging, lopsided grin.

She drew herself upright, reminding herself that she was a grown woman now, and the room was full of people—everything was different this time.

'Aren't you glad to see me, Hetty?' He laughed a little raggedly, running his fingers through his thick tawny hair. 'Everyone else is thrilled to have me back.'

But then nobody else knew him like she did, did they? Her eyes narrowed. He was taller than she remembered, his body that of a man now, not a gangly schoolboy. As if his thoughts mirrored her own, he added, 'You've certainly grown—don't know if I would have recognised you if I'd come across you in the street.'

His eyes raked her frame. 'Last time I saw you, you were just a skinny little carrotty-topped thing, romping about the meadows after your brother and me, and now...' before she could stop him he had seized her hand and pressed it to his loathsome, thick lips '...I can scarce credit what a beauty you have become.'

She snatched her hand away, wiping the back of it down her skirts.

He laughed. 'Come, Hester, don't pretend to be shy of me. You were never shy of me before—why, we were almost like brother and sister when last I was here. In fact...' he leaned even closer to her, his voice taking on a conspiratorial edge '...you really were a very naughty little girl at times. If I were to recount some of the mischief you and I used to get up to...'

Somewhere in the distance, through the roaring in her ears, she heard Em's voice saying, 'Stop it, Lionel. Hester cannot help her colouring, and if she was carrotty haired and a bit of a tomboy when she was little, it is not at all gentlemanly to remind her of it.'

'No, indeed,' Lionel purred, completely unabashed by the public reproof, 'but now her hair is—what I can see of it—a shade that puts one in mind of a forest in autumn. Such a pity to hide it away under that funny little scarf. Wherever did you get it, Hetty?' He gave her a look loaded with meaning. 'It looks exactly the sort of thing a gypsy would wear.'

He knows, she thought. Then, in despair, of course he knows. He and Gerard were so close, there was no way he could have kept the secret from him. And he is warning me that if I do not play along with him, he is quite capable of spilling the whole thing, in the drawing room, in front of my aunt, and my cousins, and…she spun round…

'Lord Lensborough,' she moaned. He was standing in the doorway, not three feet from her. How much had he heard? Why couldn't he have stayed with the children a few more minutes? Trust him to turn up just when she particularly wished him elsewhere.

'Come and sit by me, Hetty.' Lionel was standing far too close. His breath was hot on her cheek as he murmured in her ear, 'I think you will agree, we have a great deal to discuss.'

She could not make her legs move. Her head swam, her stomach churned. Wildly she looked about for a means of escape.

Em was clutching the parcel tight between her hands, looking from one to the other with a helplessly puzzled expression on her face. Her aunt was bent over her embroidery, oblivious to the undercurrents. Julia and Phoebe, no help from that quarter. The minute Lord Lensborough entered a room neither of them could concentrate on anything but impressing him. Mr Farrar? The fashion plate? He was about as much use as paper stirrups.

There was nothing for it. On this occasion she had no choice but to go apart with Lionel Snelgrove, and listen to whatever deal he had come to put to her. Sensing her defeat, he smiled, his nostrils flaring as if he relished the scent of her fear.

He did. She shuddered. She knew of old that he thrived on it.

Lord Lensborough watched her wilting before his astonished gaze. He had heard enough, through the open door as he had approached the library, to know that this fellow was purposely unsettling Lady Hester. Her face was white, her lips were white, and she was trembling from head to toe as if she was on the verge of a faint.

He recalled all the things he had been told about her in a jumbled rush. He had not believed that her Season had been disastrous because she was shy, having been on the receiving end of her temper, but could she really be as shy as everyone had told him? Could a woman have two such opposite traits of character existing side by side?

Yet why not? He had known many horses just like that. Trembling and sweating nervously when the halter went over their head, then kicking out wildly in an attempt to break free. Just like a wild colt, she responded to a man's approach by either shying or kicking up her heels in a display of defiance.

His eyes narrowed. Whatever this revelation might mean for him he would consider at his leisure. For now, all that mattered was that she was in dire need of rescue. This oaf was bullying her, delighting in reducing her to a mass of quivering nerves. He had met fellows who broke their horses in that way—the fools. The end result was a mount that was not worth riding. For the thrill of mastering, breaking another creature's spirit, they destroyed all that was fine and admirable.

Well, not while he was here to prevent it. He would not stand by and see a man mistreat a horse, let alone the woman he intended to marry.

He took a calming breath, reminding himself this was a

drawing room, not a boxing ring. The method would have to be different, but as far as he was concerned, the gloves were off.

'Snelgrove, did I hear your name was?' He held out a hand, forcing the man into either ignoring his overture, or re-linquishing his grip on Lady Hester's elbow. 'I am Lens-borough. I dare say you have heard of me.'

After the briefest of hesitations, the man let go of Lady Hester to shake his hand. 'Friend of the family, are you?'

There was an awkward pause. Hester still did not appear to have the ability to move as yet, let alone frame a coherent introduction.

'Mr Snelgrove is a distant relative of mine,' Miss Dean supplied. 'He arrived unexpectedly last night.'

On a repairing lease, no doubt, Lord Lensborough thought, taking in the waxy countenance and bloodshot eyes that betokened a life of dissipation. 'Do you stay long in the district?' he inquired, taking a pace into the room. In order to continue the conversation, Snelgrove had to turn away from Lady Hester slightly.

'As long as necessary, my lord. It all depends.'

To his relief, he saw a tide of angry colour rush into Lady Hester's face, her fists clenching at her sides when Snelgrove glanced her way, grinning.

'I have many old friends in this area, with whom I wish to renew…links. Lady Hester's brother was a very dear friend of mine, and I used to run tame in this house during school vacations. Sadly I have not been able to return since the funeral, but now that I am here I had hoped to make up for that omission.'

'You lost a brother, too, Lady Hester?' Lord Lensborough's voice was gentle.

Hester managed to open her mouth, but no sound came out. How could he sound so sympathetic when she had ridden roughshod over his own grief?

'Alas, he died about six years ago,' Lady Gregory piped up. 'A terrible tragedy.' She looked nervously at Lord Lensborough, then meaningfully at Hester as she went on, 'We never speak of it…it is too upsetting.'

He looked at Hester, whose face was pale as milk yet again. 'Forgive me, Lady Hester, for intruding on your grief.' He spun towards Mr Snelgrove abruptly, turning his back to her.

'You know the area well, I take it, since you spent so much time here in your youth?' He began to stroll towards the window, indicating the vast empty moorlands with a sweep of his arm. Snelgrove trailed in his wake reluctantly. He clearly did not wish to move away from Hester, but nor did he dare to defy a marquis in mid-flow.

'Yes, I do, my lord.'

'And you ride.' He paused by the window, hands clasped together behind his back. 'I would very much like to explore the locality. What I have seen of it is quite intriguing. Perhaps you would care to act as my guide? I have brought a couple of my hunters with me, and so far I fear they have not had much exercise.'

Snelgrove was hooked. There was not a man who'd ever placed a bet on a horse who had not heard of the Marquis of Lensborough's stables. He would not pass up the chance to ride one of his own hunters. And then, he thought with contempt, he would dine out on the story for weeks.

He felt rather than saw Lady Hester move to a chair and sink into it, and sighed with contentment. He had never felt such satisfaction in knowing that his actions had brought comfort to another person, but then, neither had he experienced such a strong urge to protect a female before.

Lady Hester sighed with relief as Lord Lensborough launched into a detailed account of the pedigree of the horses he had brought with him, while Lionel drank it all in. Her lips twisted in bitter humour. Typical that the two men in the world that she loathed the most should hit it off instantly. But she was not about to complain. That coincidence had bought her a temporary reprieve. With any luck, Lord Lensborough would keep droning on about his stables until it was time for Mr Snelgrove to leave. And now that she knew he was in the area... She bit her lower lip. He had dropped enough hints about gypsies to let her know he would blow her cousins' ambitions out of the water if she did not bend to his will. The only way to prevent him from blackmailing her was to keep well out of his sight.

As she glared at Lord Lensborough's back, he half-turned, and ran his eyes over her just once, briefly, as if to ascertain her condition. When she bristled, he nodded, as if satisfied, and turned back to Snelgrove. It all happened so quickly that Hester could not be sure she had not imagined it. If she had not known better, she might have assumed that he was checking up on her, as if he had been sensitive to her distress, and had drawn Lionel away from her, and was keeping him at his side for her benefit.

That could not possibly be. Lord Lensborough notice something that had been hidden from her close family? Absurd. He was far too self-absorbed; she was just so shaken by Lionel's sudden reappearance, her imagination had run away with her. She was seeing Lensborough as her saviour because she had been desperate for one, that was all.

'I am glad to see you two are getting along so well!' Lady Gregory suddenly remarked, her eyes fixed on the two men chatting by the window. 'You must dine with us one evening, Lionel. You, too, Miss Dean, of course. You can walk over from the vicarage together.'

Hester sprang to her feet. All she wanted to do was avoid Lionel and the stupid woman had invited him into her home!

'Oh...' Em caught her eye '...I am sure you cannot want us to intrude upon a family party.'

'Nonsense.' Lady Gregory blithely swept her protestations aside. 'We already have Lord Lensborough and his friend come among us. Another couple at the table can only serve to enliven things. In fact, it would be a very good thing if you were to join us, because then we should have enough couples to get up some dancing. It would be a lovely way to round off the house party. Say Wednesday evening? Lady Moulton's last night with us?'

'Oh, yes, Mama, the very thing,' Julia cried, clapping her hands in delight.

'Come on, Em,' Lionel drawled, prowling over to where she sat, gazing with concern at Hester's obvious distress. 'Don't say no. Your father will be glad for you to have a chance to get out and enjoy yourself for once. He won't thank you for using his infirmity as an excuse to stop at home. Besides, everyone is relying on us to make up the numbers. And I for one will be only too glad of the chance,' he said, looking keenly at Hester, 'to oblige the ladies.'

Lady Gregory followed the direction of his gaze, and a vexed expression flitted across her brow. 'Hester, dear…' her brow cleared '…would you mind having a word with cook right away? I know the invitation is for Wednesday, but these things take time to arrange. You will need to get a room prepared for dancing. Well—' she smiled '—I am sure I do not need to tell you. You know exactly what to do.' She nodded in a satisfied way as an expression of relief washed across Hester's taut features.

This time, in tune with her true state of mind, Lord Lensborough appreciated what Lady Gregory had done. She had given Hester the excuse she badly needed to leave the room without having to speak to Snelgrove again. She was protecting her shy niece.

He recalled, with a chill, the number of times over the past few days various members of her family had sent her from the room on the most paltry of errands when he had been trying to engage her in conversation. Could it possibly be that they had not been bent on thwarting her chances after all, but had been attempting to protect her…from him?

Chapter Seven

'What on earth has come over you, Lensborough?' Stephen enquired on Wednesday evening as he put the finishing touches to his neckcloth. 'If you were to meet a cur like that in town, you would give him the cut direct.'

'You wanted an excuse to visit the vicarage, did you not? I have provided it.' Lord Lensborough had been so determined to prevent Snelgrove from getting anywhere near Hester that he had ridden over to Beckforth vicarage at first light the past two days and kept him hacking round the local countryside till all hours.

He had not repeated his foolish attempt to get her alone and flirt with her either. No. The way to win the trust of any nervous colt was to demonstrate that he posed no threat.

'Since when did you put anyone else's interests before your own?' Stephen scoffed. 'It strikes me you're trying to prevent him from getting at Cinders. I saw the way he drooled over her in the library on Monday.'

'Astute of you.' Lensborough smiled. He was looking forward to this evening's entertainment. Dancing would provide him with a legitimate opportunity to hold her in his arms.

'You're really going to make the poor relation an offer?'

He shrugged. 'Why not? She will suit my purposes as well as either of her cousins.'

Stephen selected a ring, threaded it on to his finger and paused to admire the effect.

'I hate to burst your bubble, Lensborough, but have you not noticed that she doesn't like you?'

'She doesn't dislike me as much as she dislikes Snelgrove,' he pointed out.

'But you cannot want to marry a woman who does not like you.'

'You talk a deal of nonsense at times, Stephen. What has liking to do with marriage? In fact, I would find it tedious to marry a woman who liked me too well.' She was an intelligent woman. Even if she did not like him much, she would certainly like to become a marchioness.

'I have a great deal to offer her,' he reassured himself. 'Instead of acting as unpaid housekeeper to her aunt, she will be mistress of her own establishment. And she will become a mother. She adores children.'

Stephen regarded his fingers steadily for several moments, before remarking, in a voice devoid of all inflection, 'You know I wish you well, Lensborough. But marriage is…well, it lasts a long time. Not like taking a mistress whom you can pay off when you've had enough of her.'

'If you are intending to say anything derogatory about Lady Hester, then I strongly advise you—don't.'

For some reason this outburst brought the smile back to Stephen's face. 'Then I won't,' he said. 'We'll go down to dinner in silence if you like.'

And they did.

'What is the matter, Hester?' Em and Hester were standing by the piano, which had been moved to the Great Hall, sifting through the sheet music while the ladies waited for the gentlemen to join them. Hester had been pleased with the atmosphere the servants had managed to achieve at such short notice. There was fresh greenery everywhere, the pots and containers swathed with every kind of red material they had been able to lay their hands on. They had even resurrected several old-fashioned flambeaux and stuck them in iron wall sconces or the gauntleted hands of the suits of armour.

She had unearthed the primrose-satin ball gown left over from her Season in honour of the occasion, though she had taken the precaution of tacking a fichu into the indecently low-cut bodice. She had even taken pains to make sure all the accessories matched. The cream kid gloves and gold satin slippers she had bought in Bond Street were as good as new, since they had been packed away in tissue paper after only one outing. Mary, the head housemaid, had helped her pin up her hair with a matching set of gold-and-amber combs. The ensemble was not as up to date as her cousins' creations, of course, but then she was not the one trying to attract the notice of a marquis.

'You hardly spoke a word at dinner, and you still seem strained. Is the house party not going well?'

'In some ways,' Hester mused, 'it is going better than I expected. Aunt Valeria is so overwhelmed by Lord Lensborough's magnificence…' she stuck one hand on her hip, flicking an imaginary coat tail out of the way in the process, and looked down her nose at Em, raising one eyebrow in mimicry of Lord Lensborough at his most haughty '…that she hasn't thrown a single tantrum. And Mr Farrar,' she confided, dropping her pose, 'who I at first thought was nothing but a dandy, is in fact doing his level best to put my cousins at ease. Not entirely successfully, I might add.'

'Oho! What has the monstrous marquis done?'

'Oh, hardly anything worth mentioning,' she replied airily. 'Apart from sneering at Phoebe's watercolours and yawning over Julia's embroidery, depressing Aunt Valeria's pretensions and taking up with Lionel Snelgrove so that he does not have to go out riding with my uncle.'

Em giggled. Dinner had been one of the most strained occasions she had ever attended at The Holme, which was normally one of the most informal of venues. Julia and Phoebe, Hester had told her, were becoming increasingly agitated as the allotted week drew to a close and neither felt any nearer knowing which was likely to receive the formal offer. The marquis himself had not spoken a word throughout the entire meal, but sat with his mouth drawn into a line as though he were biting back scathing retorts. He even raised his haughty left eyebrow at Stephen Farrar for repeatedly provoking Phoebe into fits of giggles.

'Has he ever spoken about running you down that first day? Or apologised for just taking off afterwards?'

'Oh, that.' Hester fanned herself with a sheet of music with a languorous air. 'He has quite forgot all about that. I dare say he runs so many women off the road he cannot differentiate between all his victims. When he deigns to speak to me at all, which is not all that often, I promise you, it is on the subject of politics.'

'P...politics? Oh, dear.' Em laughed. 'Does he try that with Julia? Or Phoebe?'

'I wouldn't put it past him.' She glanced at where they stood by the fireside, heads close together in a frantically whispered conversation. 'The one good thing to come from his insufferable attitude was my uncle's decision that I need not be a part of any entertainment that involved him. Except...' she heaved a sigh '...for tonight. Since you and Mr Snelgrove are technically my guests, I may not withdraw until you have gone home.'

Em drew herself up, giving Hester a direct look.

Hester could have kicked herself. 'You know if it were just

you I would gladly put up with…I mean, I would have had a tray in my room and we need not have even…oh, you must know it is Lionel. I do not know what I shall do if he should ask me to dance.'

Impulsively she reached out to clasp her friend's hand. Em patted it, but her tone of voice was brisk.

'Really, Hester. What harm do you think would come from dancing with him in your own home, with all your family about you? I fail to understand how you can march into a gypsy camp and confront that dirty ruffian Jye one minute, then quiver like an aspen leaf at the prospect of taking part in a perfectly civilised pastime with a relative of mine.'

Hester hung her head. 'It is not because he is your relative. It is the way he—' She blushed crimson.

Em pursed her lips. 'I know he is rather a flirt, Hester, but don't you think you are overreacting?' She sat down firmly on the piano stool. 'Now look, the gentlemen are coming in, and the first set will be forming soon. His marquisness will no doubt solicit the hand of one of your cousins, and Mr Farrar the other. The other men will dance with their wives, so Lionel is bound to ask you to stand up with him. And you must.'

Hester blenched.

'Don't be a goose. It is only a dance. You'll feel better once you've got it over with.'

Em's words were prophetic. In moments, Lionel was the only man without a dance partner, and he was bowing over her hand. And standing far closer than she liked. So close that she could feel his body heat through the flimsy barrier of her primrose gown. She backed into the piano, shivers of revulsion coursing through her limbs.

'A pretty show of reluctance,' he teased. 'But you will not refuse me this dance. Another couple is entirely necessary to complete the set.'

With a sudden flash of clarity, Hester saw that when they

got on to the dance floor, Lionel would only be able to touch her hand briefly, when the movements decreed it. He would not at any time be able to stand as close to her as this. She levered herself off the piano, and walked, stiff legged, to join the bottom of the set.

Em struck the first chord, the gentlemen bowed to the ladies, and the dance began.

It seemed to go on for ever.

By the time it was over Hester's head was spinning with the effort of pretending she was unaffected by the taunts he whispered into her ear whenever they drew close enough to converse. Her entire body was trembling from the effort she had expended in taking mincing little steps when all she wanted was to hitch up her skirts and run a mile. The only thing that had prevented her from doing just that was her refusal to let him triumph. She would never let him beat her again!

While everyone else was applauding Em's playing, Lionel sidled up behind her.

'You look delightfully flushed.' His voice oozed down the back of her neck. 'Let us sit the next one out, while you recover your breath. I have something I particularly want to say to you.'

She was ready to drop; she needed to sit down and recover, but not with him.

Before she could collect her wits enough to make some excuse, he had taken her by the elbow, and was steering her towards a shadowy alcove beneath the minstrel's gallery.

And then Lord Lensborough was blocking their path, he was bowing, and through the roaring in her ears she heard him ask if she would do him the honour of being his partner for the next dance.

Hester had never dreamed a day would come when she would seize at the opportunity to dance, let alone with Lord Lensborough, but it had come now with a vengeance.

She could not yet control her voice, but when she tugged her arm from Lionel's grip, decorum decreed he had to relinquish it. She stretched her hand out to Lord Lensborough; wordlessly he took it, and with a profound sense of relief Hester walked back to the dance floor.

'I believe you do not care for dancing any more than I do myself, my lady,' he said softly as they took their places in the new set that was forming. 'Convention demands that we appear tolerably amused, however, lest a shadow be cast over the pleasure others take in the exercise.'

Why had he asked her to dance, then, if he really had noticed she did not enjoy it? Did he take some kind of perverse pleasure in making her uncomfortable?

She glared straight ahead at the tiger's-eye pin that nestled in the deep black folds of his silk cravat. As for taking pains not to cast a damper on others' enjoyment...well, what a plumper! He didn't care if his mood cast a shadow. He'd had the whole household on edge ever since he'd arrived.

'And I shall not be offended if you do not make any attempt to speak to me.'

Well, that she could believe. Whenever they had spoken they had come to cuffs, and for the last two days he had been as much at pains to avoid her as she had been to avoid him.

Then he confounded her by finishing, 'I do not wish to make this more of an ordeal for you than it need be.'

Hester stumbled through the opening sequence in a perplexed silence.

'You are doing well,' he said as he took her raised hand and turned her. 'I have often found myself that going through some dull, repetitive task enables me to restore my composure when I have been sorely tried by some idiot or other.'

Hester gazed up at him in frank astonishment. Was he saying that he had noticed how badly Lionel affected her, and was deliberately trying to help her recover? Could this be the same man who had subjected her to a torrent of oaths, less than a week ago, when she had got in his way?

He gave her a rueful smile. 'I am capable of behaving as I ought, though I have not so far given you reason to believe it.'

Heavens, was he reading her mind now? Before she could respond they moved apart again. But perhaps it was just as well. She could not have framed a fit reply to that remark to save her life.

'At least I have the satisfaction of knowing that dancing with me is preferable to being drawn into a tête-à-tête with that crass suitor of yours.'

Without thinking, she snapped, 'Well, anything would be preferable to that.'

Lord Lensborough let out a bark of surprised laughter, a sound so astonishing that everyone, or so it seemed to Hester, turned and stared. It was the first indication he had given during this visit that a sense of humour might lurk beneath that stern façade.

Hester tilted her face up towards him in surprise, and made the discovery that with those little crinkles at the corners of his eyes, his mouth turned up with genuine, rather than sardonic, humour, all the harshness had melted from his sombre features.

'I beg your pardon,' she apologised, heat flooding her face.

How could she have been so rude? And how could he possibly find her rudeness amusing? She supposed it must have some novelty value to come across a person, especially a female, with so little regard for his rank that they would dare say exactly what they thought.

Did he appreciate the unconventional? Was that why he favoured the tiger's eye, whose swirling bands so exactly matched the varying shades of brown that twinkled in his own eyes, rather than a diamond, or even just a plain gold pin?

He had not responded to her apology before they moved

apart again. Really, it was vexing trying to hold a conversation during a dance. The figures separated them at the most inopportune moments.

'Don't mention it.' He smiled down at her when next they came together. 'I think we both owe each other roughly the same number of apologies now. Shall we just cry quits?'

She nodded as she twirled away, reflecting that perhaps she did not need to pity her cousins. After all, they kept on saying they wanted to get married. And she was beginning to suspect Lord Lensborough might be the kind of husband Uncle Thomas was to her Aunt Susan. Blunt of manner and speech, more used to the society of men and sporting men at that. Yet for all his lack of address in company, his preference for the hunting field over the drawing room, her uncle's rough exterior cloaked a kernel of solid decency.

She was faintly surprised to find that the dance had come to an end, and Lord Lensborough had led her the full length of the room to where his friend Mr Farrar was standing.

'I will leave you in Mr Farrar's capable hands.' She heard the smile in his voice, though she did not see the accompanying warmth in his eyes. She was gazing in perplexity at her hand. He must have held it in his own, all the way across the room, and not for one second had she felt the least bit intimidated by his superior masculine strength.

'I assure you,' he continued, 'you have nothing to fear from him.'

She darted one astonished glance at him before placing her hand on Mr Farrar's coat sleeve and meekly following him into the next set.

She had to concede that Mr Farrar was not so bad either. As soon as he had noticed how uncomfortable his flirtatious manner made her, he had dropped it with her, though he continued paying the most outrageous compliments to Julia and Phoebe.

She wondered why he felt the need to bother with her. In

her experience, men of his and Lord Lensborough's sort got far more enjoyment from making sport of a shy, clumsy creature like her. Yet they were both displaying the same tolerance of her gauche mannerisms as her uncle and her cousin's husband, Peter, did.

She frowned as she watched Lord Lensborough dancing a stately minuet with the ponderously large Henrietta and making her laugh at some comment he had made. She shook her head, thoroughly bemused. Ever since she had fallen foul of Lord Lensborough's single-minded determination to beat Stephen in that race to The Holme, she had written them both off as boors. But now, here was Stephen being kindness itself, and there was the marquis…

And hadn't he just referred to Lionel as an idiot? She had thought when they met in the library Lord Lensborough had found a kindred spirit, and that was why they spent so much time out of doors together. Could it possibly be true that all this time he had been taking steps to shield her from Lionel's unwanted attentions?

At that very moment, as if he was aware she was thinking about him, he turned his head and his eyes locked with hers. For a breath, a heartbeat or two, it was as if there was nobody else in the room. She had never felt anything like it before. The physical distance between them faded to nothing as she connected with him in a way that was beyond rational explanation.

She blinked, determined to free herself from the spell Lord Lensborough's obsidian eyes had cast over her. She stumbled, Mr Farrar gently corrected her false step and the contact with Lord Lensborough was broken. She could hear the music again, the babble of conversation of the other dancers.

'Mama,' Julia trilled when that dance came to its courtly climax, 'would it be improper to have a waltz next?'

Hester felt her hard-won composure shatter. A country dance was bearable when the only contact was brief, confined to the holding of hands, and the gentleman who partnered you was as considerate as Mr Farrar, or his lordship. But a waltz, when a man held the woman in his arms and forced her to submit to every manoeuvre he cared to make? It was a vile public demonstration of male domination over womankind in which she would never participate.

'I see no reason why not.' Impervious to the message Hester's entire body was silently screaming, Lady Susan gave her blessing to the enterprise. 'This is just a private family gathering. There can be no impropriety in it.'

Having caught the horrified expression on Hester's face, Em rose from the piano stool. 'I beg to differ, my lady. Not all present are members of the same family. We have here three single gentlemen quite unrelated to your daughters or your niece.'

'Don't be such a prude, Emily,' Lionel drawled. 'Must I sit out watching, while others enjoy themselves, because of your antiquated notions of propriety?'

'By no means. You could waltz with me, I suppose, since we are cousins of a sort. Lady Hester may take my turn at the piano, since it would be unfair to put her in the position of having to refuse any of the guests in her aunt's house.'

As the two girls crossed the room to swap positions, Lord Lensborough's brow arched in the gesture with which Hester was becoming all too familiar.

'You do not waltz, Lady Hester?'

Throwing him a defiant look, she shook her head. Well, now she would see him in his true colours. He would be bound to sneer—the decency she had thought she could discern beneath that haughty exterior would prove to be nothing more than a mirage after all.

'Well, I see nothing wrong in waltzing either,' Julia declared. 'When I was in London, I waltzed with all manner of gentlemen to whom I am not in the least related.'

'Then you must certainly waltz with me.' Lord Lensborough ceased his contemplation of Lady Hester, and walked to Julia's side. But his voice was gentle as he remarked, 'And we will have the pleasure of hearing Lady Hester play, for the first time during my visit.'

Hester sank down on to the piano stool. Once Stephen had asked Phoebe for the dance, each lady who wished for it had a partner, and Hester struck up a waltz.

Her fingers caressed the keys softly as she followed the printed notes across the page. She was not mistaken, not this time. By upholding her decision to play the piano, Lord Lensborough had enabled her to avoid dancing without looking ridiculous.

Poor Em seemed to be suffering for her generous impulse to rescue her, though. She did not appear to be very good at waltzing. From time to time she heard Lionel mutter an oath as she stepped heavily upon one of his feet, and once, as they passed by her station at the piano, 'Em, I swear you have all the grace of a performing elephant.'

'I never claimed you would enjoy dancing with me,' she retorted. 'You cannot suppose I get a lot of practice at this sort of thing at the vicarage.'

'You will never get much practice, wherever you go. No man would risk dancing with you a second time without the protection of hobnailed boots.'

As his back turned towards Hester, she could have sworn Em winked at her over his shoulder. Stifling the urge to giggle, Hester brought the piece to a conclusion.

The dancers applauded her playing, and negotiated for new partners. Lord Lensborough, having waltzed with one sister, quite properly asked Phoebe for the next one. Hester decided to perform a piece she could play from memory. For some reason she wanted to see how Lord Lensborough behaved with Phoebe, now that her opinion of his character had shifted somewhat.

How strange. He did not appear to be making much attempt at conversation. He looked, if anything, faintly bored. She frowned. Perhaps that tension about his mouth was not indicative of boredom, but something else. When he had danced with her, he had seemed far more relaxed. Even with Henrietta he had been more animated than this. It was only with Phoebe and Julia that he seemed so brooding.

Of course. He was on the verge of taking an irrevocable step, one that would affect his entire future. Though he had initially approached her cousins through a third party, he did now appear to be weighing the pros and cons of each prospective bride most carefully. Perhaps he took his duty to marry far more seriously than she had previously suspected.

As she watched the dancers swirling about the Great Hall, she noted with a frown that Em did not appear to be faring any better with her next partner, Mr Farrar. She had not stepped on his toes; indeed, he had her gliding about the room with a grace that seemed effortless, their steps perfectly matched.

But she was not enjoying herself. Her face was flushed. Knowing her as she did, Hester deduced Em was on the verge of losing her temper. Oh, dear, she hoped Mr Farrar was not teasing her in the manner he adopted with her cousins. They found it endearing, but Em detested flirting almost as much as Hester did. Moreover, she had very strong views about the dandy set, men, she had often stated vehemently, who lavished money on so shallow a thing as their own appearance, when there were families on the verge of starvation begging, unheeded, at their doors.

That waltz ended, but since her young cousins were clamouring for another, and Lady Gregory gave her permission, Hester struck up a third waltz tune.

Lord Lensborough became Em's partner, and to set the seal on Hester's confusion, promptly set about soothing her ruffled feathers, while Lionel managed to coax a smile out of Phoebe, who had come from Lensborough's embrace looking thoroughly downcast.

The waltz, Hester concluded, was a dance that appeared to have the effect of turning everybody's feelings upside down.

Sir Thomas declared that three waltzes on top of a set of energetic country dances was quite enough excitement for one evening, and that it was high time they removed to the drawing room, where light refreshments had been laid out.

Hester automatically began to tidy up the sheet music that was strewn across the piano lid.

It was only when Lionel materialised at her side she realised how careless she had been. With everyone else heading for the exit, she had given him an ideal opportunity to catch her on her own.

'It is no use trying to avoid me, Hetty,' he hissed 'You know full well why I am here. I told you when the time was right I would come back and marry you.'

Marriage? No, not that. She would rather he blackmailed her!

He laid one hand on top of the piano, leaning over her seated form like a vulture hunched over its prey.

'And here you are, still single, waiting for me.'

She fought the urge to cringe away from him, determined not to betray the sickening feeling of helplessness that roiled in her stomach.

'Please move away from me,' she managed to gasp.

Lionel laughed. 'Why, Hetty, if I did not know you better, I would think you did not like me.'

'I don't.' She forced the words between lips that were stiff with outrage. 'And I won't marry you.'

For an instant, as he straightened up abruptly with a curse, Hester feared he was going to strike her. It took a second or two to register that he had responded to the fact that Lord Lensborough was standing not five feet from them, with Em on his arm.

'Miss Dean wishes to go home, Mr Snelgrove.' His voice was icily polite. 'She is not easy about leaving her father too long alone.'

'It is quite a long walk across the park,' she explained, her voice somewhat higher than usual, and far louder than it needed to be. 'Papa will be worried if I return too late.'

Hester realised that the words were not intended so much for her, as Mr Farrar, who was standing behind the couple, looking every bit as furious as Mr Snelgrove.

'Of course,' Lionel replied, bowing stiffly to Hester. He escorted Em from the room, Stephen Farrar trailing moodily along behind them.

It was only once he had gone that reaction set in, and Hester began to tremble violently. She could not have got up and left the piano stool had her life depended on it. Head bowed, she waited till the trembling subsided, and it was not till she looked up that she discovered Lord Lensborough was waiting patiently some few feet away.

'I…' Her face flushed. She felt she owed him some explanation, but he curtailed her, shaking his head and merely holding out his arm with a rueful smile.

'No explanations necessary. Allow me to escort you to the drawing room. You look as if you could do with a refreshing glass of lemonade.'

'Thank you, my lord.' She placed her hand on his arm, and rose shakily to her feet. 'That would be most welcome.'

Lord Lensborough contented himself with walking Hester along the passage to the supper room in sympathetic silence. It would be crass to allude to the exchange he had overheard, unfeeling to talk of anything else as if he was unmindful of her emotional state.

They paused on the threshold, and he watched her face intently as she scanned the occupants of the room, her fingers tightening convulsively on his sleeve.

She looked at Julia and Phoebe, giggling together in a corner, cock-a-hoop because they had each waltzed with their intended. How little it took to set them in alt! There sat Henrietta, gazing up at her husband with foolish, untrammelled devotion, basking in the glow of impending motherhood.

Even her aunt and uncle were locked in a little world of their own, side by side on a sofa, sipping tea from matching china cups.

Never had she felt so excluded, so utterly alone.

She sighed, exhaustion washing over her. She was glad that her family were all too content to probe into her life. If any of them were to guess what lay beneath the carefully maintained mask she wore... She shuddered. Pray God nobody would ever guess the secrets she harboured.

'Will you excuse me, my lord?' She looked full into eyes that once she had thought were dark with menace. They held no fear for her now. He might not want anybody to know it, but Lord Lensborough could be kind.

'I find suddenly that I am very tired. It has been a busy day.'

She needed her sanctuary. She would feel far less lonely up in her attic than down here with people who were oblivious to her lacerated feelings.

Lord Lensborough hesitated for only a fraction of a second before bowing and bidding her goodnight. He was content with the progress he had made tonight. Snelgrove had played right into his hands. Twice the fool had pushed her too far, and she had accepted his offer of help. Before long she would be eating out of his hands.

Chapter Eight

Hester was too worked up to fall asleep for a very long time. And when she did, the nightmare came back.

Even though thick smoke was blinding her, she knew she was in the summerhouse. She could hear the rain thundering on to the roof. The smoke was getting thicker, choking her. She tried to get to the door, but he caught her round the waist and dragged her to the floor, crushing her beneath the weight of his body. The harder she struggled to free herself, the louder he laughed. Then he was grinding her cheek into the rough floorboards with one hand and leaning down to open his breeches with the other. The blackened hem of her muslin gown crumbled to ashes in his hands as the flames licked up her legs. If she couldn't stop him, she would burn to death.

She took as deep a breath as she could, her mouth opening wide.

The sound of her scream, thin and reedy at first, quickly grew to a howl that was loud enough to wake her.

Her heart pounding, she fought free of the blankets that were tangled round her thrashing limbs and rolled from the bed to land on all fours on the floor. Sweat was pouring from her body. Kicking the blankets away, she reached up and grabbed a glass of water from the bedside table, gulping it fast to try to wash the acrid taste of burning flesh from her mouth.

There was no way she was going to lie back down on that bed again tonight. She shook the eiderdown free from the rest of the bedding that littered the floor, wrapped it round her shoulders and padded barefoot from her windowless bedroom. Taking the lighted lantern from her hall table, she went down the stairs to make sure the only door that gave access to her rooms was locked. Then she climbed on to a straight-backed chair and pushed at the latch on the skylight. It was secure. She was safe. Nobody could get in.

Not physically. But her imagination—oh, that was a different matter.

Lionel had come back, and his return had stirred up all the memories she had fought so long and hard to suppress. She padded into her sitting room and stoked up the fire, then settled into the armchair, knowing from bitter experience there was no point in trying to get any more sleep.

That was why she was so grateful she had these attic rooms. Nobody could hear her up here, when she woke screaming. Nobody could see her obsessively checking and rechecking the locks. Nobody would urge her back to bed, when she knew the only way to get any rest was to doze, propped upright in a corner somewhere with a poker in her hand.

She rubbed her creased forehead with two fingers. Fortunately the house party was breaking up tomorrow. Saying farewells and tidying up would provide plenty of activity. By the time night fell again, she would hopefully have worked herself to a state of exhaustion that would ensure she got at least a few hours of deep, dreamless sleep. Hard work had always proved an effective remedy in the past.

But the quieter the house became, as the guests departed one by one, the more vulnerable Hester felt. By early afternoon her nerves were so jittery, she decided her only recourse was to find some work to do in a room where the presence of at least a couple of other people would give her an illusion of security. She knew her cousins would be in the library, discussing how to while away the rest of the day. So she gathered up the books that various guests had left in their rooms to return them to their proper places.

Lord Lensborough and Mr Farrar were there too, but for once she was glad of their presence. Her cousins would concentrate all their conversational efforts on impressing Lord Lensborough. She would have the advantage of company without needing to dredge up a steady flow of chatter herself.

She was doubly glad of their presence when, not long after arriving in the library, Fisher announced that Lionel Snelgrove had come to pay a call.

Why had he come here so soon after she had refused him? Did he think he could make her change her mind? That he could bully her into submission? Well, he could think again! She would not even speak to him.

Seizing a random selection of volumes, she strode to the farthest corner of the room and began to thrust them into any vacant slot she could find.

After making the appropriate greetings, Lionel turned to Lord Lensborough.

'I was a little surprised that you did not ride over this morning, my lord. I trust you are well?'

Hester slammed a copy of *The Monk* into a gap between two improving works penned by Hannah More.

'I thought it might be more appropriate if we were to make up a party including the ladies next time we ventured out.'

Hester's ears pricked up at Lord Lensborough's icily civil tone. Lionel had somehow managed to offend him.

Julia clapped her hands in glee. 'Oh, yes, I should love that, and so would Phoebe. How clever of you to think of it, my lord.' From the corner of her eye, Hester could see her batting her eyelashes at him quite shamelessly. 'Everything always seems so flat after guests leave.'

'And, Lady Hester, perhaps we can persuade you to leave your household duties for one afternoon and join the party?' Lord Lensborough said.

'Yes, do come with us, Hester.' Julia rose from her chair impulsively and crossed the room to stand beside her. Turning to Lord Lensborough, she added, 'Lady Hester is a much better rider than either of us, but then she goes out so much more often.'

'And Lady Hester knows the country even better than I, since I have been so long away.' Lionel added his weight to Lord Lensborough's invitation. 'I am sure she will know of a delightful route we could take, suitable for less experienced riders than us, my lord.'

Lionel had followed like a shadow in Julia's wake, rendering her tactic of making for the far corner of the library quite useless. Still, she had the table between them, and Julia at her side. Taking a volume from the pile, she cleared her throat, saying, 'That will not be possible. Strawberry is stabled over at Lady's Bower. It would take an age to send for her.'

Damn. Lord Lensborough had forgotten that her riding privileges had been withheld because... He frowned—that could not be right. He had assumed that she was being punished for dallying with him, whereas in fact her family were shielding her. Was she so averse to being alone with a gentleman that she would voluntarily have her horse sent to a neighbour's stables?

Apparently, he thought glumly, since he knew Lady's Bower was the manor that Snelgrove had pointed out to him, laughing, because it was so inappropriately named. The eccentric Captain Corcoran, the current tenant, would only employ men, particularly ex-seamen like himself.

'You must all go, though,' she continued. 'I would not like to think of his lordship forgoing his daily ride on my account.'

Damn again. The whole purpose of suggesting this expedition was to make Lady Hester a part of it.

'Oh, come on, Hetty.'

Lord Lensborough bristled at the familiarity with which Snelgrove addressed Lady Hester, at the way he leaned his hands on the table, thrusting his face towards hers. 'A bruising rider like you? You could manage any of the mounts Sir Thomas has in his stables, or even one of his lordship's, if you put your mind to it. Borrow a horse, Hetty, and come out with us. It will be just like old times.'

She flinched. Instantly, Lord Lensborough forgot all about his own desire to spend some time in her company, in the more urgent need to protect her from a situation she would clearly find intolerable.

'Perhaps Lady Hester is a little tired after all the work she has put in over the past weeks for our benefit, and is too polite to say so, Snelgrove.'

Julia put out her hand, taking hold of Hester's. 'Now that his lordship mentions it, you do look dreadfully worn, Hester. I am so sorry, I did not notice before. Are you quite well?'

The fleeting look of gratitude Lady Hester flashed him more than made up for Lord Lensborough's disappointment at her refusal to come out. At last. She had recognised that he was deliberately defending her from Lionel's unwelcome pursuit.

'I admit I do not feel up to racketing about on horseback today.' Hester shamelessly grabbed at the lifeline Lord Lensborough had thrown her. 'And I have been neglecting Em— that is, Miss Dean,' she explained to his lordship, the germ of an idea causing a surge of wild excitement to go winging through her, 'during the past week or so. I may walk across the park to visit with her.'

Lionel shot her a glance loaded with such malevolence that

the words died in her throat. It shook her for a moment, until she realised that, with his back to the rest of the occupants of the room, she alone was able to see it.

Lord Lensborough remarked, 'Let us hope you return refreshed from your visit, my lady. And do you dine with us this evening, now that you are released from your duties towards the nursery party?'

'I…' She frowned, dragging her gaze from Lionel's spiteful countenance. Truth to tell, having a tray alone in her room was the last thing she wanted in her present state of mind. And she no longer felt the need to avoid the marquis. He could be pleasant enough when it occurred to him to bother. She had already come to the conclusion that once he'd made up his mind which of her cousins should have the honour of taking his name, he might even make a fairly kind sort of husband, in an offhand way. He would want the mother of his children to be content in her role, and though she could not imagine him doing anything as vulgar as actually developing a *tendre* for his wife— Abruptly she brought her woolgathering to a halt, and, with flushed cheeks, murmured, 'Yes, my lord, I will.'

She missed the exultant gleam her response brought to his eyes as she hurried from the room. All she could think of was escaping Lionel. If he was here at The Holme, she would be safe to go and fetch Em from the vicarage. Not that she had any intention of staying there, and risking being there when he returned.

Because Lionel had more or less told her where he was going to ride—he planned to revisit their childhood haunts. The tarn where she and Gerard used to swim would offer Julia and Phoebe a gentle enough ride, or perhaps along the course of the beck where they had fished, or through the park to the copse where there were trees they used to climb. In any event, all those destinations lay in the opposite direction from the gypsy camp on The Lady's Acres.

* * *

In no time at all, she was ensconced in Jye's caravan, a mug of hot sweet tea in her hand, her beloved little girl sitting at her feet with her head resting on her knee. Once she had drunk the tea, and the half-dozen or so children who were squashed together on the caravan floor had devoured the macaroons Hester had purloined from the kitchens on her way out, she opened her satchel, and distributed sheets of coloured paper and crayons.

In spite of the fact that the children only had instruction from her, just once a year during the time when they camped in The Lady's Acres, at least a couple of the boys had clearly been putting the intervening months to good use.

'Any advantage we can get over Gorgi,' one of them cheekily remarked, knowing full well that Lady Hester had not a drop of Romany blood in her veins, and so qualified as Gorgi herself, 'is worth a bit of effort. If we can read their writing, when they still can't know our signs and ways, well, we got the edge over 'em, don't we?'

She was on the point of gathering up the primers and rounding off the session, when Jye, who never stayed within hearing when she was playing the part of school ma'am, came clattering up the steps and put his head through the top half of the door.

'Gorgi,' he panted. 'Men. A bunch of them on horseback. Could be trouble, Lady Hetty.'

Their eyes met. Trouble not just for the gypsies, who were prey to all sorts of oppression by suspicious locals, but for her too, if she was found here. She drew herself up, 'I'll come at once, Jye,' she assured him. 'They won't attempt anything while I am here.'

'I'll finish off in here.' Em began to gather up the primers and crayons that were scattered about the floor. Hitching Lena on to her hip, Hester nodded to show she understood

Em's reluctance to show her face. Though people fully expected the vicar's daughter to visit the poor of the parish, most would also feel she ought not to be encouraging a band of rogues and vagabonds to linger in the parish either.

Just as Hester began to clamber down the steps of the caravan, the party on horseback broke through the trees at the perimeter of the tan.

Her breath froze in her lungs as she saw Lord Lensborough, Mr Farrar, Julia…

They were all staring at her in as much stupefaction as she felt herself.

'Hester,' Julia squealed. 'Whatever are you doing here?'

As Hester stiffened in horror, Lena reacted to the threat these strangers represented by winding her arms more tightly about Hester's neck. What was she to say? Her uncle had made her promise that his daughters would never find out about her relationship to the gypsy clan. And now, seeing the expression of utter disgust on Lord Lensborough's face, she could understand why. *Ton*nish people did not mingle with the offscourings of society, nor did they permit their womenfolk to do so. In his eyes she had overstepped the boundaries of propriety so far she could never find a way back.

She wondered briefly why she felt so crushingly disappointed by his reaction.

'I could ask you the same question,' she replied defiantly, giving Lena a reassuring kiss on the cheek so that she would know the anger was not directed at her. When Hester set her down on the ground, Lena grabbed hold of her skirts, clinging to her side, though she kept her eyes trained warily on the intruders. While the other menfolk about the tan slowly began to shift into defensive positions, Jye climbed down from the steps of his own caravan, coming to stand next to Hester, with Lena between them.

'Friends of yours, Lady Hetty?' he asked in a voice that was meant to carry across the frosty air of the clearing, as he stooped to gather Lena's free hand into his own.

'Yes, Jye, but I didn't invite them.' Her eyes came to rest on the malicious smirk on Lionel's face. Of course. He had known she would come straight here given the chance. He had dropped veiled hints from the first that he could make trouble if she did not play along with him. She had resisted him. So now she would pay.

'Those ladies are my cousins,' she explained to Jye and Lena. 'Miss Julia Gregory, and Miss Phoebe Gregory. The gentlemen, Lord Jasper Challinor, Marquis of Lensborough, on the bay gelding, and his friend Mr Stephen Farrar are guests at The Holme. I am sure they mean you no harm.'

'You have left Mr Snelgrove out,' Julia cried. 'It was he who brought us here. He said he had a surprise for us, but I never expected it would be anything like this. This is the surprise, Mr Snelgrove?' she half-turned in her saddle to ask him. 'This quaint little gypsy camp?'

Hester did not bother to wait for his reply. Lena had been tugging at her skirts to get her attention, and as she bent, the little girl whispered, 'Is that the marquis you told us about? The one wot knocked you into a ditch and left you standing there in the road all muddy?'

'Yes, dear,' Hester confessed, ashamed now that she had spoken so heatedly about him that day, less than a week ago. But she had still been angry with him, and she had needed to explain to Jye, and the other gypsy elders, why she had come to them empty-handed. She couldn't have borne it if they had refused her access to Lena.

'But he didn't mean to do it, you know. You don't need to be afraid of him.'

'I ain't afraid,' Lena declared, glowering at the offending horseman. Lady Hetty held one of her hands, and Jye the other, and she had complete confidence that these two could shield her from the wickedest of marquises.

One of the women sashayed across to where the girls sat their docile mounts, and held her hand out, palm upward.

'Tell your fortunes, pretty ladies?' she wheedled.

'Oh, how thrilling,' Julia trilled. 'That is why you brought us down here, isn't it, Mr Snelgrove? To have our palms read by a genuine gypsy fortune teller. How clever of you to think of such a diversion when we confessed how dull we all felt today.'

Phoebe cleared her throat nervously. 'Do you think we ought, Julia? I am not quite sure Papa would like it. Lord Lensborough, what do you think?'

Lord Lensborough could not repeat out loud what he was thinking while Julia and Phoebe, in their innocence, could hear. There stood the woman he had thought he would marry, holding the hand of a little girl with a riot of dull copper curls that exactly matched hers, a sharp little nose spattered with freckles just like hers, while the expression of wary defiance matched that of the sullen, dirty gypsy who held her other hand. His lips curled into a derisive sneer. What a charming family tableau.

This resolved so many of the mysteries surrounding her behaviour. The guilt he had read on her face when he had encountered her in the stable yard, her resentment at his suggestion he ride with her and those flowers she had about her hat, that he had thought so girlishly whimsical—why, they were nothing more than a fanciful token from a penniless lover to his high-born mistress.

That was why her uncle had her horse removed and stabled with a neighbour, to prevent her from succumbing to the temptation of sneaking down here to meet with her gypsy lover and her illegitimate child.

'I think,' he finally managed to growl through clenched teeth, 'that you should do just as you wish.'

How would the deceitful hussy brazen her way out of this situation? Did she think she could look to him for aid now? Let her think again!

'Then I am going to have my fortune told,' Julia declared. 'After all, Hester is already here, so I am sure Papa can have no objection. Why should we not go where she does?'

Jye turned to Hester and gave her a look that his lordship could only interpret as a reaction to their guilty affair having been found out. And Hester's face, as she gazed back at him, was deathly pale.

For all she cared, he might as well not be there—all her attention was on this other man, this dirty ruffian. This... this nobody!

He became dimly aware, through the darkness that seemed to be swirling round him, blotting out everything but the sight of the two guilty lovers, that Snelgrove was leaning over to take hold of Julia's reins so that the silly chit could dismount.

'Come close to the fire, then, pretty lady,' the gypsy woman said, 'and I will see what is writ in your hand.'

Julia giggled. 'Oh, this is so exciting. I had no idea you got up to such larks under the pretext of visiting Em. Have you had your fortune told already?'

'No.' Hester darted forward. 'Nor do I ever wish to.'

'Why not?' Julia's brow wrinkled with perplexity.

'If something good is going to happen to me, I would rather it came as a lovely surprise. And if something bad is to befall me, I would not want to live in permanent dread of its advent.'

Emily chose this moment to emerge from Jye's caravan with the remnants of their ragged pupils and hurry to Hester's side.

'I must side with Lady Hester on this matter, Julia,' she said sharply. 'It would be the height of folly to do such a thing without your father's permission. Does he even know you are here?'

'Well, of course not. We did not even know there were

gypsies camping on The Lady's Acres until Mr Snelgrove brought us, so how could we have told him?'

'I thought as much.' Emily rounded on Mr Snelgrove. 'Why must you always be so intent on stirring up mischief, Lionel? Don't pretend you don't know how Sir Thomas would feel if he were to learn you had brought his girls down here, never mind encouraging them to have their fortunes told.'

'There is absolutely no need for him to know,' Lionel retorted. 'We can guard Hester's little secret as well as you.'

Jye clenched his fists and took an involuntary step towards the sneering horseman. Swiftly, Hester reached out and grabbed at his arm. 'Don't, Jye,' she cried. 'You will only make it worse.'

Flinging herself in front of him, she rounded on Lionel. 'You are very much mistaken if you think I have any secrets from Uncle Thomas. The first thing I shall do when I return home is to tell him exactly what has happened here today. And what passed between us last night.'

Lionel's sneer turned to a furious scowl.

'And if you—' she whirled to face Julia '—have your fortune told I will tell him that also.'

'There is nothing more despicable than a tale bearer,' Lionel sneered.

'N…no…' Julia said, 'Hester is right.' Sadly she took one last look at the gypsy woman, before admitting, 'I knew all along it was not quite the thing, and I know what Papa would say if Hester had to tell him.' She added generously, 'I quite see why she would feel she had to. Thank you, Hester.'

As Julia went back to her horse, the gypsy woman strode towards Hester, and with a ferocious glare, spat contemptuously on the ground at her feet.

'Here.' Stephen Farrar urged his mount forward a little, and tossed a handful of coins to the woman. 'This should make up for losing the wages of your craft.'

'Well, God bless you, sir.' The woman was all smiles again. 'I would wish you luck, but you don't need it. You have the desire of your heart within your grasp.' Seeing his puzzled expression, she cackled, 'At least, all you have to do is reach out, and you could touch it.'

Hester saw a tremor run through his entire frame just before he wheeled his horse towards the edge of the clearing, saying, 'It's frightfully cold out here, Lensborough. Don't you think we ought to be getting the ladies home?'

'Oh, yes, please,' Julia said. 'I should very much like to go home now.'

Silently, Lord Lensborough swung himself down, and with his reins looped over his arm, he bent and cupped his hands to help her remount.

'You should be getting back now, too, Hester.' Emily shook her shoulder gently. 'You look quite white with the cold.'

'If you wish to escort Miss Dean home, Snelgrove,' Lord Lensborough said, 'I will lead Nero back to the stables. She should not have to walk back alone.'

It was a dismissal, and though Snelgrove might have resented his lordship's tone, there was nothing he could do but dismount from his borrowed horse, and surrender the reins. Taking Emily by the arm, he bowed to the entire company, and, casting Hester one last triumphant look, set off across the fields.

'Time to leave, madam.'

Hester ignored Lord Lensborough's peremptory command. Dashing a tear from her cheek with the back of her hand, she knelt in the grass and enveloped Lena in a fierce hug. Lord Lensborough turned away abruptly, muttering under his breath.

'Will you be coming back soon, Lady Hetty?' the child asked, twisting out of her embrace. 'I do like them biscuits.'

Over the top of her head, Hester caught Jye's attention. 'If I can…' she cast her eyes meaningfully towards her cousins as Mr Farrar led them away '…of course I will.'

Jye nodded once in acknowledgment of her unspoken message.

'I'll take good care of her for you, Lady Hetty,' he promised gruffly.

'I know.' She got to her feet, brushing dried bracken and wood ash from her skirt. 'You always have. And you will send me word, won't you, if ever you're in trouble?'

Jye nodded, swinging Lena up on to his broad shoulders, while Hester turned hastily away. She could no longer check the tears that began to roll silently down her cheeks, and, not wanting Lena to see them, she swiftly made for the track that would lead her home, pushing blindly past Lord Lensborough, who stood almost directly in her path.

She had not got far into the copse before she felt a hand tap her roughly on her shoulder.

'Here,' he said curtly, 'take this handkerchief and blow your nose.'

'Thank you,' she replied mechanically, taking it. 'You are very angry with me again, aren't you?'

'Are you surprised?'

'Yes.' She blew her nose. 'Uncle Thomas warned me what to expect, but I had begun to think that you—'

The ferocity with which he uttered a few choice expletives set Hester back to the moment they had first met. This was the real Lord Lensborough: black hearted and black tempered. She had only imagined he was kind and decent.

A feeling of dread washed over her. Might he be so outraged by her impropriety that he would change his mind about marrying one of her cousins? Might they be tainted in his eyes by their very association with her?

'You won't suspend your courtship of my cousins because of this, will you? Neither they, nor my aunt, knew anything about my visits to the tan.'

'Am I to infer from that remark that your uncle did?'

When she nodded, he said, 'By God, this beggars belief.'

Hester reeled. 'How can you be so intolerant?'

'Intolerant? Who could tolerate being so deceived?'

'We did not set out to deceive you…particularly. My uncle just did not want anyone to know. Especially not my cousins, or my aunt. He said it would distress them.'

Lord Lensborough made an odd choking noise.

'So you see, they are entirely innocent. You do believe me, don't you?'

'Oh, yes. Unlike you, your cousins are exactly what they appear to be. A blank slate upon which I may write whatever I wish.'

Hester saw red. 'How just like you to say such a horrid thing. Julia and Phoebe are people with feelings, not blank slates for you to write on.' She clenched her fists. 'And for your information, I don't care how improper you think it is for me to mingle with the raff and scaff of society. I love Lena, and I will never be ashamed of her. If that offends your notion of propriety, then I'm glad. Why would I want an unfeeling, heartless block like you to approve of me?'

He flinched, as though she had struck him. 'We should not keep the horses standing in the cold,' he said, and turned down the track.

He was aware of Hester thrashing through the undergrowth behind him, but he couldn't bear to turn and look at her, not even when he heard a tell-tale sniffle.

How could her uncle permit her access to a lover while she lived under his roof? Or introduce her to his guests as if she were respectable? Did he not care so long as she kept her activities secret from the more innocent females in the family?

All that talk of shyness. He had known from the first it was all humbug. It was guilt that made her awkward around single men. She knew she could never marry a decent man, or encourage one to hope. That was why Sir Thomas had warned him off.

But then why, if he did not want all this to come out, did he not keep her out of sight altogether?

His pace picked up as his mind whirled. The family probably did not have the means to pack her off to some estate deep in the country and forget her. And if her uncle tried to separate her from his other womenfolk, within his house, they would start to ask awkward questions.

So why did she not simply live with her gypsy lover?

That sort of scandal was bound to get out, and his own daughters would be ruined by association.

On the whole, Sir Thomas had followed the only course he could. Ejected the bastard child, and sworn Hester to secrecy to protect the good name of his own daughters.

Though he could never like Lionel Snelgrove, he supposed he had to be grateful that he had forced Hester's secret into the open. It had saved him from committing the ghastly blunder of proposing to a woman who had given birth to a bastard sired by a filthy gypsy. He didn't think he would ever have been able to live that down.

Chapter Nine

'Uncle Thomas, I've ruined everything.' Hester stumbled into the workroom where her uncle was pottering amongst his collection of snuff jars.

'I very much doubt that, my dear,' he said, smiling at her. 'But you are at liberty to confess exactly what mischief you have been up to.'

'I went to see Lena today. I know you asked me not to, but Julia and Phoebe had gone out riding with Lord Lensborough and his friend, so I thought it would be quite safe. I never thought they would ride in that direction.'

'Ah.' Sir Thomas carefully replaced the lid of the jar he'd been inspecting.

'Of course they saw me. And it was just as you said it would be. Lord Lensborough was really, really angry with me. And just when I was beginning to think he was…'

Shakily, Hester sank on to the chair beside her uncle's desk.

'Because you had convinced him of the worth of one sort of charity, he would be sympathetic to other causes?' He shook his head. 'Setting up a trust to honour his brother's memory is a far cry from thinking it acceptable for a well-bred girl to mix freely with vagrants.'

'Yes, and then Julia said it could not be wrong for her to be there since you permitted me. Of course, if she thinks that, then Lord Lensborough will never marry her.'

She got to her feet and laughed a little hysterically. 'All I have achieved by persisting in my visits is to dash my cousins' hopes of a good match.'

'Hester, do try to calm yourself. We do not know that there will be any repercussions.'

'But Lord Lensborough said such horrid things, and I lost my temper and called him names.'

To Hester's surprise, her uncle chuckled. 'Did you though? I should have liked to have seen that.'

'No, Uncle, it was dreadful of me.'

'I hope it may do him good to be called a few names. There are a few names I have been tempted—no, no, let that pass. Did he give you any reason—now think carefully, my dear—any reason at all to justify your wild fears that your deeds have given him an adverse opinion of my girls?'

'No. No, he referred to them as a clean slate.'

'There, you see. It might all blow over. Although, to be frank, I must confess I don't really care if the match with Lord Lensborough goes ahead or not. I just want my girls to be happy. If he is as harsh as you seem to think, then perhaps he is not the man for them.' He turned, frowning. 'Hester, would you do something for me? I know that I have forbidden you to speak to anyone of Lena's true identity. I foolishly hoped we could keep her very existence a secret. But perhaps it might be for the best if Lord Lensborough knew the whole.'

'Everything?'

'Yes. If you tell him how ill you were at the time, how seeing your brother's baby brought the spark back to your eyes…' his own eyes softened with tenderness '…perhaps then he may condone my granting you limited access to your niece, illegitimate though she is. If you tell him I hadn't the heart to ban all contact from all you seemed to have left of your brother—'

'It wasn't like that,' she flared. 'I wanted to right the wrong he'd done. I had thought my brother was a good person, but he used that woman, then abandoned her and the child!'

Sir Thomas held up his hands in a placating gesture. 'He didn't really abandon Lena, though, did he? He died before he even knew of her existence, I dare say.'

'That doesn't make it any less dreadful.'

'No, no.' He sighed. 'What a mess that young scamp left behind.' He shook his head ruefully. 'I know it will be painful for you to speak of it, but…'

'Of course I will tell him, if that is what you want. I would never forgive myself if some action of mine caused any of you grief.' Hester hung her head. 'Do you think it would have been better if I had stayed away from Lena altogether?'

'Who can say? I did what I thought was for the best for all concerned. For you, for Lena herself, for my own girls too, of course. If any harm has been done today, it is my responsibility.' He smiled ruefully. 'Though I could never have foreseen a man like Lord Lensborough stumbling upon your family secret.'

'No.' Her eyes filled with tears. She could never have foreseen just how much impact the marquis would have on her life either.

The atmosphere around the dining table that evening was so oppressive that even Stephen was unable to lift the gloom. Lord Lensborough was in a foul temper, which he took no trouble to conceal. Julia drew his wrath down on her head by making a series of unwise observations, while Phoebe was too nervous to speak at all. Hester was unaware that she was unwittingly fuelling his anger by keeping her head bowed meekly over her plate when he particularly wanted her to feel the full force of his displeasure that she was there at all. Even Lady Gregory, who was not usually sensitive to atmospheres, was relieved when the ladies could withdraw at last.

'What,' she asked, 'has happened to put him in such a fearful temper tonight?'

Julia and Phoebe exchanged glances, and shrugged their shoulders. They'd agreed it would be better all round not to mention their visit to a gypsy camp since it appeared inexplicably to have upset everyone so much.

The only person who seemed his usual self was Sir Thomas. He ate a hearty meal, impervious to the shudders and sighs of his womenfolk, and when they'd left and the covers had been withdrawn, he raised his first glass of port to his lips with a smile.

'Had an interesting day, have you, my lord? I hear you went out riding with my girls over to The Lady's Acres.'

Lord Lensborough's eyes narrowed as Sir Thomas passed the port his way, but he did not rise to the bait.

'Hester told me you were not very pleased when you found her visiting her friends.'

'Naturally I disapproved,' he snapped.

'Really, my lord?' He raised his eyebrows in exaggerated astonishment. 'She was chaperoned by Miss Dean, as she always is when engaged on her charitable work. She has been regularly visiting those folk for the past six years without once coming to any harm. Is there some fact I may have overlooked, perhaps? As the local magistrate, it has become my habit not to form a judgement until I have all the facts clearly presented to me.'

Lord Lensborough's fingers clenched about the stem of his wine glass. This man's barely veiled rebuke was the outside of enough. As he fixed his host with a cold stare that usually had the effect of wilting any opposition, Sir Thomas calmly reached for the nutcrackers.

'Are you quite sure your subsequent treatment of my niece was justified?' he challenged. 'Had you enough facts at your fingertips to warrant giving her such a scolding that she came home to me in tears?'

Stephen winced as the walnut that Sir Thomas held in his hand shattered, sending pieces of shell skittering across the table top.

Of course he was justified. He was still honour bound to marry one of this man's daughters, which meant that he would have to acknowledge their wanton cousin as a relation of his own. Sir Thomas expected a great deal if he hoped he would brush aside an indiscretion he had concealed from the world for six years.

Six years. Lord Lensborough took a gulp of port. Six years ago, Hester would have been about fourteen years old. So young. She could have been scarce thirteen when that child was conceived. Which meant she would have been too young to understand what she was doing. Or—a cold lump seemed to form in his chest—what was being done to her. Could Sir Thomas's leniency stem from the fact he was shielding her from the results of a crime committed against her?

Oh, God. He squeezed his eyes tightly shut for a fraction of a second. Poor Hester. No wonder she was so skittish around men. Although—he regarded his host's untroubled countenance through narrowed eyes—attempting to bring her out into society had still been a mistake. Even if she was not at fault, and they wanted her to be able to lead a relatively normal life, it was quite wrong to attempt to deceive a decent man into marrying her. He downed his glass of port, and poured another.

As he drank it, he began to wonder if that surly gypsy could really be the father of Hester's child after all. Surely, if a gypsy had seduced or raped her, Sir Thomas would not allow them back on his land. He was so belligerently protective of her, he'd be far more likely to see them off with a shotgun.

They must be simply caring for the little girl, so that Hester had an opportunity to see her from time to time as they passed through the district. She'd defiantly proclaimed her love for her child. Sir Thomas must not have had the heart to cut all contact with her completely.

His anger began to bleed away. If he was honest with himself, he had nobody but himself to blame for having come so close to offering for her. Sir Thomas had warned him off on more than one occasion. It had been his own perverse pride that had made him defy those warnings.

'Hester has decided that, since you object so much, she will not go to the camp again while you are here. She does not wish to do anything that might offend you.'

'Offend me?' He felt ashamed. After all she must have been through, she would give up contact with the child she loved so much to avoid giving him offence. He shifted uncomfortably in his chair. 'There is no need for that.'

'Hester thinks there is. And I agree with her. Such visits, now my girls know about them, are bound to raise questions that Hester would much rather not have to answer.'

'I see.' What more could he say?

'Are you quite sure you do not have any more questions you wish to ask concerning *my* guardianship of *my* niece, my lord?' Sir Thomas asked, leaning back in his chair.

'No, sir,' he replied bitterly.

'Hester would like to speak with you further on the matter, though. Since you are about to marry into the family, she feels it only right that you should hear the whole, from her own lips.'

The notion was abhorrent. He had no wish to hear the woman he had thought he would marry relate the details of her downfall.

'I think enough has already been said upon that subject.'

'I disagree.'

Stephen shifted uncomfortably in his chair as the two other

men at the table glared at each other like two prize fighters about to step into the ring.

'You have soundly abused a sensitive young lady entirely without provocation. The least you can do is allow her to state her side of the case, so that the air may be cleared between you.'

The man meant that he owed Hester an apology. Dammit, he was right. Lord Lensborough bowed his head imperceptibly. Whatever her past may have held, he had no excuse for his own behaviour towards her today. Hearing his host say she had gone to him in tears had made him feel like the worst kind of cur. He'd never meant to hurt her.

But his very presence in the house was going to hurt her, from now on. While he remained, she'd told her uncle, she would forgo her visits to her child, lest it offend him.

He hesitated on the threshold of the drawing room, his eyes drawn to where she sat on a chair a little apart from the others, staring broodingly into the fire while her fingers clutched spasmodically at a piece of knitting. And without quite knowing how he'd got there, Lord Lensborough found himself drawing a chair to her side and sitting down.

'I must apologise for my outburst this afternoon.' He kept his voice low, though his tone was urgent. 'My manners were appalling. I had no cause to speak to you so harshly. Will you forgive me?'

She frowned, as if puzzled, then gave her head a little shake. 'There is nothing to forgive. No gentleman could have reacted other than you did. It was all my own fault.' With that, she rose to her feet and left the room, her knitting falling unheeded from her lap to land at Lord Lensborough's feet. When he bent to pick it up, he was unbearably touched to find she had been making a tiny glove.

As soon as he'd come into the room, Julia and Phoebe had

darted to the piano, where they'd snatched up a sheaf of music and dutifully begun to play. The forced cheerfulness of the music grated on his nerves. Never had he been so glad of the arrival of the tea tray, which signalled his chance to return to the sanctuary of his rooms. For once he did not even linger over a brandy in the sitting room he shared with Stephen, but retreated to the isolated purgatory of his bed.

She'd called him a heartless block, but she was wrong. So wrong. He knew he had a heart now, because it was aching.

Before he'd met her he'd had no illusions that his married life would be anything but a duty to be borne. Now bearing it would be doubly hard because he'd had a glimpse of what might have been. With her.

He'd fooled himself with all that talk of rescuing her from drudgery and making her mistress of her own house. From the moment she'd erupted from that ditch, eyes flashing fire, she'd occupied his mind to the exclusion of all else. She was the woman he wanted. With every fibre of his being.

But not only could he not have her, he would have to marry someone else. One of her cousins, God help him. Which meant their paths would always be crossing. At every family gathering.

At his own wedding.

He groaned and rolled off the bed. He would have to walk down the aisle with his bride while she glowered at him from the congregation. How could he bear it?

He took a deep, shuddering breath. It was his duty to marry. Duty was all he had left now that happiness had been denied him. That, and pride. The Challinor pride would not permit him to reveal the depth of his feelings. Pride had held him together when Bertram had died, and it would carry him through this. He would never let anyone suspect that he'd had his heart captured, and broken, by a fallen woman.

He leant his forehead on the cool glass of the window and

gazed out into the darkness. Which sister would he condemn to a lifetime of his resentment for not being Hester?

On the whole, he preferred Phoebe to her sister. As his mother had pointed out, she was so young he would be able to train her to suit his tastes. But was that fair, when he would never be able to love her? Wouldn't he only end by making her as miserable as he felt right now? He liked her too well to wish to do that.

Julia, though, would be content to spend his money whether he liked her or not. His face contorted with bitterness. They would deserve each other.

But how could he bear proposing to Julia while Hester was under the same roof?

He clenched his fists. He would go back to Stanthorne. From there, he would write a suitably formal letter to her father. In fact, he would keep the whole thing on an impersonal, businesslike footing from now on. The lawyers would deal with the settlements. His mother could take the girl to London and give her all the town bronze she pleased. All he would have to do was turn up for the ceremony.

He didn't realise how long he had been agonising over his choice until he saw that the sun was creeping over the horizon. Throwing on some clothes, he marched into Stephen's room and shook his shoulder roughly.

'What?' Stephen sat bolt upright. He might affect the clothing of a dandy, but the years spent as a serving soldier in Captain Fawley's regiment had left him with the ability to come awake in an instant.

'I'm leaving this cursed house,' Lensborough explained. 'I'm going back to Stanthorne. Do you come with me?'

'This is a bit sudden.'

'We've been here a week. That's all I ever agreed to.'

'But—' Stephen frowned '—you haven't proposed to any of the contenders for the title yet.'

'I have decided to write to Sir Thomas from Stanthorne on that subject. So, do you come with me?'

'At this ungodly hour? Couldn't we wait till after breakfast?'

'Absolutely not. I've got to get out of here right now. I will break my fast on the road.'

'Forgive me if I go straight back to sleep, Lensborough.' Stephen lay down and pulled the quilt up to his chin. 'I'm not in the army now and I feel entitled to an unbroken night's sleep, and meals at regular hours in comfortable surroundings.'

'As you wish. I will look for you at Stanthorne later today.'

'You may look.' A muffled voice came from under the quilt. 'I may very well stay here for a while. Or I may return to London. I am not one of your minions, to follow tamely at your heels. I only decided to watch your unorthodox court-ship because I thought it would be a lark. And to be quite frank, over the last day or so, I have begun to find your antics no longer amuse me.'

Chapter Ten

Hester was the last person down for breakfast the following morning. The last of the household to learn that Lord Lensborough had left.

The previous day's events had left her wound as tight as a bowstring. For hours, it had been impossible to sit still, let alone lie down and go to sleep. She had finally fallen into a fitful doze just before dawn, and now felt wearier than before she had gone to bed.

Fortunately everyone else was too preoccupied with his lordship's sudden decision to return to Stanthorne to pay her late arrival much attention. She slipped into her customary seat largely ignored, while her aunt and cousins continued to bombard a somewhat harassed Mr Farrar with a barrage of questions.

And while she could only feel relieved that she would not now have to face confiding the facts surrounding Lena's birth to him, she did deplore the manner of his departure. In his typically high-handed, self-centred, cold-hearted fashion, he had left no word of explanation, abandoning her poor cousins to a welter of speculation.

A letter lay beside her plate. She did not recognise the

handwriting, so the first thing she did after breaking the wafer was to glance at the signature.

Lionel.

Before she even began to scan the bulk of the letter her fingers were trembling. Whatever he had written to her was going to be unpalatable. She had refused to marry him, and he had already given her a taste of the vindictive side to his nature. If he could make further trouble for her, she was quite sure he would.

Dear Hester, it read. *I know you must still be angry with me for my little attempt at revenging myself on you, by revealing the existence of your illegitimate niece. But I could not help myself. It hurt me very deeply to find that although my feelings for you have remained constant, you do not reciprocate them. I lashed out without thinking. I admit it. But now I hope you will believe me when I tell you that whatever you may think of me, you will always be very important to me. And for that reason, I felt I must write and urge you to come to me at the vicarage to discuss a matter pertaining to Lena's welfare. I know she means a great deal to you, and I am begging you to put aside any animosity you may harbour towards me, for her sake. I will be ready to receive you any time after eleven. Lionel.*

'Is it bad news, dear?' her aunt asked.

Hester looked up to find that other conversation had ceased and everyone was looking at her.

'You have gone quite pale.'

'I…' She thrust the letter into her pocket and forced a tremulous smile to her lips. 'It is nothing…really…just…I will have to go to see Em this morning.'

'Would you care for my escort, my lady?' Stephen rose to his feet. 'I should be only too happy to lend you and Miss Dean my assistance, should you require it.'

'Oh, no, Mr Farrar, you cannot abandon us too,' Julia

chided. 'After promising you would teach me to play billiards this morning.'

'How stupid of me to forget.' His smile was tight-lipped. 'I beg your pardon, Lady Hester.'

'Think nothing of it, Mr Farrar.' Hester sighed with relief that Julia had freed her from the necessity of fobbing him off herself. 'Besides, I need to leave almost at once, and you are hardly dressed to go—' She pulled herself up short. She suspected she might have to go back to the tan in spite of her uncle's request she not do so. 'Pray excuse me. I must go and change my own clothes at once.'

'The poor…' her aunt grimaced as she left the room '…always wanting something.'

She hurried back up to her rooms to don the serviceable outfit she kept for just such outings. Glancing out of the window on the way up she'd seen that the massing clouds were brownish with the weight of unshed snow. Remembering the unfortunate mishap of the week before, she secured her battered bonnet to her hair firmly with a steel hat pin before wrapping her thickest woollen shawl round her head and shoulders. As soon as she stepped out of the back door, she was glad she'd put on an extra petticoat, and thick woollen stockings. Nevertheless, by the time she'd reached the lodge gates, her legs felt thoroughly chilled by the wind that whipped through her skirts, and her hands and face were stinging with cold.

She was somewhat surprised to see a plain carriage standing in the lane. Even more surprised when the door of it swung open, and Lionel jumped out.

'You've come,' he said. 'Good. Get in, out of the cold, so we can talk.'

'I thought we were to talk at the vicarage, with Em present,' Hester countered, drawing back.

'Good God, woman, you don't think I'd have gone to all the expense of hiring a carriage if it wasn't an emergency, do you?'

'An emergency?' Hester took a step closer. 'Is Lena hurt?'

'Just get in, and I'll explain on the way.' Hester only hesitated for a fraction of a second more before complying. Lionel was shifting from one foot to the other, rubbing occasionally at his upper arms. His coat was not as thick as hers. It seemed harsh of her to keep him standing in this bitterly cold wind when the carriage would offer some shelter.

As soon as Lionel slammed the door closed behind her, the carriage started up with a lurch, flinging her back on to the squabs with a little shriek.

'Don't be alarmed, Hetty.' Lionel smiled. 'The sooner we get started, the sooner we will get there.'

He moved to the seat beside her and draped a blanket around her shoulders. Then he gave up the hot brick for her feet, shaking his head ruefully when her eyes narrowed with suspicion.

'Get where? Are you taking me to Lena?'

'Well, not exactly,' he admitted, tucking another rug about her knees. 'Here, take a nip of something to warm you, while I explain.'

This was not like Lionel. He didn't really care about making her comfortable. He was up to something.

She looked at the flask he was offering her, saw the expectant gleam in his eyes, and she knew.

He wanted her to drink whatever it was he had in that flask. A chill slid down her spine. If he wanted her to drink it badly enough, he would have no scruples about holding her down and pouring the contents down her throat. After all, he'd done exactly that once before, when she'd been hardly more than a child. The brandy he'd forced on her then had made her sick, fuddled her wits, and left her totally unable to defend herself.

It would be far better to pretend to go along with him than force a fight that she had no hope of winning. So she accepted the flask, held it to her lips and tipped it up, stoppering it with her tongue so that hardly any of the contents went into her mouth. She grimaced involuntarily at the taste. It was definitely brandy, but there was an underlying bitterness that must come from some other ingredient that left the tip of her tongue tingling.

She rubbed the back of her hand across her mouth as she handed the flask back to Lionel. Her pretence at taking a drink must have been convincing, because he slapped the stopper back home and tossed the flask on to the opposite seat with a triumphant smile that sent her heart beating a warning tattoo against her ribs.

To hide her mounting suspicion that he was attempting to get her drunk, or worse, Hester reverted to the questions she had been asking.

'Well?' she snapped. 'Where are we going? What has happened to Lena?'

Lionel leaned back, propping one booted foot against the facing seat. 'I shall answer the second of your questions first. Nothing has happened to Lena.'

'But in your letter, you said—'

'I said I had something to tell you that affects her welfare, I believe. And I do. Hester, you are going to marry me.'

The chill in her spine spread icy fingers round her heart.

'No, I am not.'

'Yes, you are.' He grinned. 'And that does affect Lena's welfare, does it not? For I shall certainly never allow you to see her again. My wife will not mingle with gypsies, I can tell you that.'

'Stop the coach, Lionel.' Hester's voice was breathy with panic. 'I want to go home.'

'No, I am not going to stop the coach. And you are not going home until you agree to marry me.'

'I will never agree to marry you.'

'That is just what I thought.' Lionel flicked a glance at the flask before returning his full attention to her face. 'That is why I decided it was useless to apply to Sir Thomas in the regular way. I would have done, you know. I was quite prepared to court you. But when I realised how much you dislike me, I saw that the doting Sir Thomas would never give his consent. I doubted your doors would even be open to me after the stupid way I gave in to the impulse to hurt you yesterday. Even dear old Reverend Dean implied my presence in his house was no longer welcome. I had to act swiftly to secure you. I am completely rolled up, you see, and some of my creditors are…well…let us say that desperate cases require desperate measures. You are very wealthy. At least, I happen to know that upon your marriage you will be.'

Hester looked out of the window. The coach was bowling along at quite a rate now, but she was beginning to fear staying inside it with Lionel far more than the prospect of sustaining an injury by leaping out. She made a lunge for the door handle, but the blankets Lionel had wrapped round her hampered her movements.

He grasped her round the waist, and, with a wicked laugh, yanked her backwards on to his lap.

'Your wits are getting fuddled already—don't you know you would break your neck if you fell onto the road at the pace we are going?'

With a few deft twists the blanket that he'd draped round her shoulders pinioned her arms to her sides. He flipped her over backwards, arching her spine painfully across his thighs.

'I cannot permit you to injure yourself,' he panted as she kicked and squirmed. 'It would ruin our wedding night.'

He reached across her and groped for the bottle, which was rolling around on the cushions. 'You have clearly not had enough of this to make you docile.'

As Lionel pulled the stopper out with his teeth, Hester's brain whirled. If he succeeded in getting the drugged brandy inside her, she would be completely at his mercy. Frantically she jerked her head from side to side as he brought the flask to her lips. Sticky liquid ran across her cheeks, into her ears, soaking her hair.

'Now, now,' Lionel said as she continued to thrash wildly within the confining blankets. 'We mustn't waste this stuff. It cost me a pretty penny. The first lesson I must teach you as my bride, it seems, is the habit of thrift.'

He grasped her jaws in fingers that felt like steel pincers, using his finger and thumb to pinch her nose closed. She held her lips firmly compressed for as long as she could, but all too soon the inevitable happened. Lack of air sent her senses swimming, and her jaw slackened. Lionel's eyes were almost black with excitement as he forced the bottle between her teeth. Though she choked and spat, a good deal of Lionel's poison slid down her throat as she dragged in a rasping breath. Even when he withdrew the bottle from her mouth, Lionel gave her no quarter. Clamping her jaw tight with a ruthlessly strong grip, he tilted her head back at such a severe angle she feared her neck might snap under the pressure.

The panic that she'd fought to suppress took over. She could do nothing to save herself. He was too strong. Her heart was fluttering like a caged bird beating its wings against the bars and she was panting as if she had been running hard. The carriage seemed to be spinning around her. Darkness pressed in from its corners, dragging her down, down…

Uttering one final whimper of despair, Hester went limp.

She did not know how much time passed before she began to come out of her swoon, but when she managed to drag her eyes half-open, it was to find Lionel's face suspended above hers at a very odd angle. It looked so funny she couldn't repress a giggle. Lionel smiled and then his face disappeared from her field of view.…

Funny, she could have sworn she had been very, very frightened not a minute before, but now all she felt was a dreamy languor. And she was so much more comfortable now that Lionel's knees were not pressing into her spine. She wriggled experimentally, stretching her legs and rolling on to her side, discovering in the process that her arms were no longer bound to her sides by the carriage rug. Sighing peacefully, she pillowed her cheek on her hands.

She wished Lionel would stop talking so she could think. There was something of vital importance she had to work out. She let her heavy eyelids droop. If Lionel thought she was asleep, maybe he would be quiet....

A sudden jolt rocked her body so violently she would have rolled on to the floor if she'd still been lying on her side. Her eyes flew open as a blast of freezing air doused her legs, shocking her fully awake.

Lionel had pulled the window down and was leaning out. They must have arrived then. He had said that he planned to get her inside an inn, and upstairs to a bedroom. She giggled. He thought he was so clever, but he had not managed to force enough of that foul concoction into her to render her completely unconscious. She had only been sliding in and out of dreamy wakefulness and had heard exactly what Lionel planned to do to her. He had been trying to frighten her with all that talk, testing her to see if she was really asleep. No woman could have listened to that graphic catalogue of what the coming night would bring and not try to cover her ears. But she had not had the willpower to bestir her leaden limbs.

She had, however, worked out exactly what she must do to escape him.

It was now or never. While he had his back to her, Hester reached up and yanked out the steel hat pin, then pulled one of the discarded blankets over herself, hiding her hands from view.

She closed her eyes, letting herself go limp while somebody tidied her skirts and lifted her out of the carriage. She was deposited none too gently into what she recognised, by the familiar smell of unwashed linen and stale brandy fumes, was Lionel's arms.

She opened her eyes just a fraction, confirming that they had entered the coach yard of an inn. Snow swirled thickly round them as Lionel battled his way, hampered by the dead weight of her body, towards the golden rectangle of the tavern door.

Her fingers tightened and flexed experimentally round the hat pin. She must not act too hastily, she was going to need help…witnesses.

Lionel had to step sideways over the threshold, putting him ever so slightly off balance. This was the best opportunity she was likely to get. With all the strength she could muster, she jabbed the hat pin through the blanket she was wrapped in, into the nearest part of Lionel's anatomy. He gave a yelp, and just as she'd hoped, dropped her as if—she giggled as she hit the flagged floor—as if someone had stuck a red-hot needle in him.

It was not as easy as she'd thought it would be to get to her feet. The blanket that had been her friend when she'd needed to conceal her weapon was now conspiring with Lionel to keep her his prisoner. By the time she'd fought free of it, he had grabbed the collar of her coat, and it was he who yanked her to her feet.

With no compunction she stabbed wildly at him over her shoulder, feeling immense satisfaction as she felt the pin run into the flesh of his hand.

He cursed, jerking his hand free of both her pin and her collar. She did not stop to look back, but ran headlong down the passage, towards the sound of voices. The passage had looked immeasurably long when she'd scrambled to her feet, so she was bewildered when she reached the door at the end of it after only a few stumbling steps.

There was a blaze of light, a flood of heat, and a sea of masculine faces turning towards her.

Momentum carried her into the room, until she careened into what felt like a brick wall clad in homespun.

'Please help me,' she began. The brick wall sprouted hands, which clamped round her upper arms and set her roughly aside.

'My apologies, gentlemen.' Lionel's hateful drawl came from the doorway behind her. 'I fear my lady friend has imbibed a little too freely on the way here. I was fool enough to offer her a little something to keep out the cold, but you know what her sort are like.'

A whiskered face loomed over her. 'You oughta take more water with it.'

'No,' she protested. 'I never drink. He put something in it.'

The room was filled with crude male laughter at her contradictory statement.

'Why won't you help me?' she pleaded. 'He's trying to abduct me and force me to marry him.'

There was a second of disbelieving silence while the occupants of the tap room glanced from her to Lionel before they began to laugh even harder. She knew what they must be seeing and groaned in despair. Lionel was the picture of unruffled elegance, lounging against the door jamb, while she was staggering about spouting nonsense. She'd even been conned into wearing the simple rough clothes she always wore when visiting the poor. Even Lord Lensborough had taken her for a working woman when he'd come across her in the exact same outfit.

She was suddenly furious that she'd taken such pains to stitch the balding velvet ribbon back on to the damaged bonnet only for it to betray her like this. She should have thrown it away. She tore the offending item from her head, flung it to the floor and stamped on it.

No wonder nobody would listen to her. She was acting like a mad woman. She couldn't seem to help it. It felt as if her mind was stuck on the rim of a huge wheel, bowling along at high speed through a whole cycle of emotions, from abject despair, through uncontrollable anger into a weird sort of detachment where she found everything hysterically funny. She raised her balled fists to her throbbing temples.

'Look out,' someone said. 'She's got some kind of a weapon.'

'She looks the violent type an' all. Just look at all that red hair.'

Inspiration struck her. 'I am,' she said, swinging the fist that still clutched the hat pin in a wide arc on a level with the jeering faces. 'Get out of my way or you'll be sorry.'

A path opened through the sea of male bodies and she plunged through it, towards a door she'd spied on the far side of the tap room. Lionel caught up with her just as she set her hand to the latch. Whirling to face him, she dodged his attempt to disarm her by dropping to a semi-crouching position, ramming the hat pin into the side of his thigh and jerking it out again in one viciously fluid movement.

He leapt back, cursing in disbelief as what started as a tiny, ruby jewel welled and flowed down the seam of his breeches.

'That's one for the hell cat,' somebody yelled. Several other men cheered as she scrabbled the latch up and fell backwards into the room beyond the door.

She spun round, ramming her back to the door to hold it fast since there was no bolt. She rapidly scanned the room for something heavy to wedge against the door, and blinked. She had assumed this was going to be a store room, but it was a private parlour. A fire was blazing in the grate. A large wing chair was pulled up in front of it. An occupied chair. She could see a pair of booted legs stretched out towards the hearth. Good quality boots. The sort of boots that belonged to a gentleman. She had no more illusions about the sort of men that frequented the tap, but surely a gentleman would help her?

'Get out,' the man growled, before she had even given voice to her last desperate hope.

Yet the curt dismissal gave her hope wings.

'Lord Lensborough!' She could not mistake that harsh, gravelly voice. How welcome it sounded to her ears. She did not pause to question what his lordship was doing here. His mere presence gave her hope.

'You will not let me down.'

Hester felt Lionel give the door a tentative push. She braced her back more firmly against it.

'You know nothing of the sort.' His lordship did not deign to so much as turn his head to look at her, never mind do her the courtesy of getting to his feet. Yet she knew instinctively that this rudeness only stemmed from some black humour he happened to be in. Just as she knew that he had not intentionally hurt and humiliated her that day they had first met. In the week he had been at The Holme, she had realised that his brusque manner cloaked a basically honourable nature.

She tried to run to him, only to land in an undignified heap on the hearthrug when her rubbery legs gave out from under her. Grasping at the arm of his chair, she pulled herself to her knees. The look of utter contempt on his face almost made her quail.

'Please…' She had to make one last attempt, even under the withering blast of that scorn. 'Please believe me. Lionel lured me into his carriage and drugged me. He's trying to abduct me.'

His lips twisted into a parody of a smile, but his eyes were cold and hard. He did not believe her either. 'Please…' Her eyes filled with tears.

Then the door flew open, and Lionel came pelting into the parlour. He must have put his shoulder to the door, and, since Hester was no longer holding it shut, there was nothing to check his headlong rush.

His eyes homed in on her where she cowered beside the wing chair.

'Don't think you're going to find anyone who will be sympathetic to your version of events, Hetty.' He limped towards her. 'Just be a good girl, leave this poor gentleman out of it, and come with me before I really lose my temper with you.'

Lionel's words had the effect on Lord Lensborough that Hester's had not. He was out of his chair and across the room in a blur of black worsted, his powerful right fist slamming into his jaw before Lionel even had a chance to recognise his assailant.

Lionel staggered backwards through the still-open door into the arms of a semi-circle of spectators. Several of them cheered again, delighted by the entertainment this impromptu brawl was providing. Lord Lensborough, who enjoyed watching a good mill himself, took the time to acknowledge the applause with a bow, before closing the door on their curiosity.

He turned round just as Hester, white faced, slithered to the floor after an abortive attempt to lift herself on to his chair. Two strides brought him back to her side.

Had she fainted? The ordeal that cur had put her through would have floored a lesser woman. He must loosen her clothing. That was the correct treatment for a faint, was it not? His fingers fumbled at her coat buttons.

Her eyes flew open, her bloodless lips drawing back into a snarl.

'Don't touch me.' Her arm arced back as she prepared to strike him, and it was only as he caught her wrist in a reflexive act of self-defence that he caught sight of the bloodied hat pin.

'What do you take me for, madam?'

For a moment longer she continued to resist his grasp. Then recognition flooded into her strangely blank eyes. 'Lord Lensborough?'

'At your service.'

Her whole body relaxed. She opened her hand and dropped the hat pin into his palm, before closing her eyes and murmuring, 'I'm safe now, then.'

He sat back on his heels, frowning. She was out for the count. Hadn't she been babbling some wild story about being drugged before that cur Snelgrove had barged in? Or was it wild? She had certainly lacked co-ordination, she was confused, her pupils had been tiny pinpricks. Might she have been fighting the effects of being drugged, and now she felt safe, have given up the struggle?

With fingers that were sure of their purpose now, Lord Lensborough removed her coat and gently moved her more fully on to the hearthrug, closer to the fire. He then removed his own jacket and wadded it to make a cushion for her head, finally draping her own coat over her.

How long was she likely to remain in this stupefied state? He had no experience with the aftereffects of any kind of drug, but coffee always helped to sober up a drunk. Getting a hot drink inside her could only be beneficial. Her hands had been icy cold. He called for the landlord.

When Hester next opened her eyes she felt deliciously warm and utterly at peace. A slight sound drew her attention to the occupant of a wing chair, at the foot of which she appeared to be lying.

Lord Lensborough was scowling down at her. What a grouch he was. She smiled at him, remembering. 'You got rid of Lionel.'

He nodded. 'I had the landlord throw him out.'

Hester's smile slipped. 'Naturally.' Nobody had believed her, or heeded her pleas for help, but Lensborough had only to quirk that haughty eyebrow and everyone leaped to do his bidding.

'There is coffee upon the table. I believe it might still be warm. You should try to drink some.'

Coffee sounded good. But when Hester tried to sit up, the room began to spin alarmingly. She had to grasp at the floorboards to stop herself from falling off.

'Here.' A strong arm went round her, a cup was held to her lips. She sipped the fragrant brew gratefully, resting her muzzy head against Lord Lensborough's rock-solid chest in between sips.

'When you first came in,' he murmured into the curls that were tickling his nose, 'I thought for one glorious moment that you had followed me. Even now I know it was no such thing, I cannot help but see the hand of providence in this. We cannot fight fate.'

Hester sighed and settled into a more comfortable position.

'We were meant to be together.' While she had slept he had planned it all out. He did not want to let her go. Why should he let her go? What kind of a future did she have anyway? 'From the first moment I saw you I knew somehow you were my destiny, darling.' He dropped a kiss onto the crown of her head. Her hair was so soft, and it smelled like wood smoke, and something herbal, underpinned by an essence wholly feminine.

'To hell with propriety, and duty. I can't marry anyone else when I want you so much. Come with me to Stanthorne. You will like it there. Or if you don't, I have other estates. You can choose to live wherever you wish. We cannot press on in this weather today, but the landlord says he has a room free. Stay with me, Hester. Be mine. And I will never let anyone hurt you or frighten you again.'

He pressed a finger under her chin so that he could raise her face up and look into her eyes. 'Hester, my heart, what do you say?'

Chapter Eleven

Lord Lensborough cursed as he brushed a crusting of snow from the front of his driving coat. On the curricle seat beside him, Hester bristled.

'If my language offends you,' he snarled, 'you have only yourself to blame. I warned you against setting out in this weather.'

'And I told you there was no need to stir from beside that lovely warm fire yourself, my lord.' Her tone was as arctic as the wind that was driving the powdery snow into drifts against any barrier it encountered. 'Your groom is quite used to attending to errands you do not care for yourself.'

'I thought the whole point of this exercise was to get you back to The Holme without arousing any suspicion about where you have been all day. Servants gossip.'

Lord Lensborough swore again, colourfully, at the memory of Hester's response to his impassioned plea to become his mistress.

She had let forth a gentle snore. He had tilted her head back to find that her eyes were closed. Damn him if the confounded woman hadn't slept through the whole thing.

And he was glad that nobody but himself knew how completely he'd lost his head during those few moments when he'd cradled her in his arms.

He had thought that by leaving The Holme, he could dismiss her from his mind, but the minute she had walked into the room he had known he would fight to the death to defend her. The very thought of her in another man's arms had filled him with such revulsion that he had readily sacrificed everything else he held dear, even down to producing legitimate heirs, for the chance of possessing her himself.

And when she next woke, before he had a chance to say a word, she went rigid, exclaiming indignantly, 'Why are we lying on the floor like this? What do you think you are doing?'

The look of horror on her face was too clear for him to misunderstand. Hester was nowhere near ready to become any man's mistress.

Angry that, but for her stupor, he would have just made a colossal fool of himself, over a termagant who neither particularly liked him, nor was worthy of his regard in any respect, he had snapped back, 'I was trying to get you to drink the coffee. *You* fell asleep on *me*, madam.'

'I beg your pardon.' She had pulled out of his embrace. 'I had no intention—that is…I hate being touched,' she had blurted as she had scrambled unsteadily to her feet.

'At least you have some colour in your cheeks again,' he mocked as she busily dusted down her skirts.

The tension was intolerable. He wanted her out of his sight, out of his reach before he did or said something irrevocable.

'You may have the use of the room I had procured for my own stay,' he said gruffly, getting up and brushing sawdust from his breeches. If there were no other rooms available, God help him, he would sleep in the stables, anywhere to get away from her bewitching influence.

'But I can't stay here.'

'Well, you certainly cannot go anywhere else today.

We're stranded in the middle of a blizzard, in case you hadn't noticed.'

She had gone to look out of the window. 'It's not what I'd call a blizzard.' Her voice had dripped scorn. 'There's just a few tiny, powdery flakes drifting down. The wind will blow them right off the road. I could get through.'

'I fail to see why you wish to risk your health by venturing out at all, not when I have made all the arrangements for your comfort, you ungrateful baggage.'

She'd whipped round and he had braced himself for a retaliatory torrent of abuse. Instead her eyes had been luminous with unshed tears.

'Pray forgive me if I sounded ungrateful, my lord.' She had twisted her hands together at her waist. 'If not for you, if you had not been here...' She had turned pale, and swayed, and stumbled to the table where she had dropped on to the seat like a stone. After drawing a couple of deep breaths, she had been able to continue, though not to look directly at him.

'You may not have considered the repercussions.'

'Repercussions?' He had laughed harshly as he had lowered himself on to a chair opposite her. It was not as if she had a reputation to lose. She had given birth to a child outside wedlock.

She had addressed her next remark to where his hands were loosely linked on the table top. 'Well, firstly, there is my family to consider. If I don't return home tonight, they will imagine some dreadful accident has befallen me.'

'Once the weather has improved, you may return home in comfort and explain it all.'

'Explain it?' She had looked appalled. 'Do you think I would want to repeat out loud...what...?' She had shaken her head vehemently. 'Besides, only imagine what effect the telling would have on them. Uncle Thomas is bound to set straight out into the snow with a horse whip and a pistol, threatening to hound Lionel to the ends of the earth. Aunt

Susan, even if she were spared the details, would go into strong hysterics, which would upset Julia and Phoebe, and frighten poor Harry and George and Jenny. The whole household in an uproar, to what end? I am...' She gulped. 'He didn't...' She shook her head again. 'They would all be so much happier if only I could somehow prevent the story from reaching their ears.

'And then—' she had blushed '—there is your reputation to consider. Only imagine what malicious gossips could make of you spending the night in an inn, on the eve of your betrothal, with a different woman than your intended. And if the word "abduction" ever got thrown into the mix...'

'I don't really care what inferior persons may say about me.'

'No. How well I know that.' Her head flew up then, her eyes flashing emerald fire. 'But Julia and Phoebe could be dreadfully hurt if any whiff of scandal was spread about you and me.'

Her selflessness shamed him. A lump came to his throat. 'I will return you to your family at once,' he'd said, rising to his feet and turning his face from her. Taking refuge in sarcasm, he had added, 'God forbid that Sir Thomas should have to venture outdoors in the snow.'

'We really should not be seen together. I can walk home.'

'Walk!' he had thundered. 'Right back into Snelgrove's waiting arms? You little fool. Do you even realise how far it is to Beckforth from here?'

In a tight little voice she admitted she did not, that she was not altogether sure where 'here' was. When he had told her, she had been horrified.

So here he was, having set out to leave The Holme and escape Hester, now having to drive her back there through a snow storm.

'You were quite correct about the snow,' he observed as he brushed another layer of it from his coat. 'It is not sticking to the road.'

'I'm just as cold as you are, my lord, but I have not been complaining.'

'That is because you want to go back to The Holme. I had hoped I would never have to set foot in the wretched place again.'

Hester hunched her shoulders against his anger, finding it hard to believe that less than an hour ago he had gently held her in his strong embrace, all the while crooning meaningless words of comfort.

Had she only dreamed the whole episode? She had been dizzy and frightened, and desperate for comfort. He had made some remark about how providential it was that he had been there, she had recalled the magnificent moment when his fist had connected with her tormentor's jaw, and then her fuddled brain had supplied the rest.

He had certainly reverted to type as soon as her brain had cleared. He had done nothing but snap and snarl at her ever since.

Not that she could blame him altogether. Her arrival had overset all his plans. And he must be furious that his pampered horses should be out in such foul weather. She felt sorry for the poor beasts herself, but she would have walked if he had not made her fear that Lionel might still be lurking somewhere in the vicinity.

She glanced up at his glowering profile, considering that for all his blustering and cursing, he had comprehensively rescued her, ensuring by his own escort that nobody need ever know what had happened to her today. He would never do anything to intentionally cause her harm, no matter how angry she made him. Deep down, in the heart of him, he was…he was…

She forced herself to stop staring at him, and searched the lane for landmarks instead. He was going to make one of her cousins a sterling husband, was what he was.

Unless seeing her with the gypsies had given him such a disgust of her that he had gone off the match altogether? Was that why he had left so abruptly? Was that what he had meant when he'd said he never wished to set foot in The Holme again?

Oh, she couldn't be responsible for that.

She recognised the bend in the lane where they had first met, and they passed through the lodge gates just as the day dwindled to dusk.

'Stop here.' Hester tugged at his coat sleeve. 'Just by the shrubbery.' Lord Lensborough obediently reined in his team. 'You won't be leaving until I have had a chance to speak with you again, will you? Please? It's very important. There's something I must explain.'

'You need to get out of this weather, madam,' he replied icily.

'I can cut across the park from here and get into the house through the kitchen gardens. Nobody will question where I have been. I told them I was going to the vicarage this morning, so they will assume I have been involved in charitable work with Em.'

At his frown, she defended herself. 'It was not exactly a lie. I truly believed I was going to the vicarage. Lionel wrote and asked me to meet him there, but he was waiting for me in the lane. He knows I always go that way.'

She shivered. Lord Lensborough had lent her his muffler to wrap round her head on the drive home but she bitterly regretted losing her bonnet to rage in the tap room, and her shawl to the floor of Lionel's hired coach. Her ears and parts of her scalp and neck had long since gone completely numb.

But she was home. She searched Lord Lensborough's granite features for several seconds, for the first time in her life understanding why a woman might sometimes feel she wanted to kiss a man's cheek.

'Get indoors,' he gruffly repeated. He looked at her hand where it clung to his sleeve, then at the pleading expression in her eyes, and felt all resistance melt away. He could refuse her nothing.

'I will not leave again without speaking to you first.'

'Oh, thank you,' she breathed, turning to clamber down from the curricle. 'For everything.' He thought he heard her call over her shoulder as she disappeared into the swirling snow.

Two grooms came running when Lord Lensborough pulled into the stable yard. He stayed with them until he was sure his team had all the care the absent Pattison would have given them, so that news of his return reached the house before he did.

Lady Gregory and her daughters fluttered into the hall, plying him with offers of a hot bath, mulled wine and assurances that dinner would be held back until he was ready.

'No problems about laying an extra cover either,' Lady Gregory twittered, 'since Hester will not be dining with us tonight.'

'Why not?' he snapped. A hot meal was exactly what she needed. And a bath, and the mulled wine, and all the cosseting he was getting.

'She sent a message to say she is not well, my lord,' Julia replied as her mother backed away from Lord Lensborough's evident displeasure. 'I expect she will have a tray in her room.'

'You expect?' Did nobody care about her enough to go and help her? She would have been better off staying in the inn. At least there he could have looked after her. Here, he could not even alert anyone to her need. She was utterly alone. 'A tray in her room,' he growled.

'I am sure she intends no disrespect to you, my lord.' To his surprise, it was meek little Phoebe speaking up, not for herself, but for her cousin. 'If she says she is not well, then she is not well.'

That was exactly what he was afraid of. He had been chilled to the marrow by the drive back—Lord knew what effect it must have had on her, on top of everything else she had been through.

He could only hope she had the sense to get herself warm

and dry. He glared round at the Gregory family and his lip curled. On second thoughts, maybe he could understand why she was avoiding them. How could she sit at table, and endure their inane chatter, when every nerve in her body would be strung as tight as a bowstring? He shrugged. 'I dare say you are right.'

He hardly noticed what was set before him at dinner. While he had bathed and changed he had come to a decision. He had been right to think that yielding to emotions, especially where women were concerned, would end in disaster. But for a quirk of fate, he would have taken Hester as his mistress, when the world knew he was as good as engaged to one of her cousins. But he was not going to deal with the emotions he had by running away. On the contrary, for the sake of his pride, he must crucify them. She'd made him promise to stay and listen to what she had to say. Very well, then, let her hear something from him too.

The minute she put in an appearance, he would defy the insidious hold she had over him by going down on one knee, while she watched, and proposing to Julia.

Then, if he could only steer clear of her, and perhaps replace his current mistress with a slender red-head, he might stand a chance of getting this ridiculous infatuation into its proper perspective before his wedding.

Hester knew she had to get warm, so she lit a fire in her sitting room. For some time, it did her precious little good, since she couldn't stop scurrying from one room to another, checking and rechecking the locks on her door and skylights, and weeping with the pain that returning circulation brought to her ears.

Once the pain had abated to a bearable level, she considered eating the soup that Mary had left on a tray outside her door. She'd had nothing but coffee since breakfast, so she supposed she ought to be feeling hungry. Her stomach revolted after she had forced down only a few mouthfuls.

She thrust the chamberpot away from her, rubbing at her forehead, which felt as though someone was pulling a steel band tightly round it. Bone weary, she rested her pounding head against her mattress, her heavy eyelids drooping.

The feel of Lionel's hand sliding up beneath her skirts jolted her awake, and she stumbled to her feet, gasping for breath. She'd had no choice! She'd had to allow his hands, and his mouth, to roam freely without uttering a single protest. She'd had to convince him she was drugged and utterly helpless.

She fell to her knees before the sitting room fire, pounding her thighs with her fists. She'd thought she was being so clever, outwitting him by pretending to sleep right through his leisurely assault. But now hot waves of shame engulfed her.

Worse almost than what he had actually done was the violation of her mind. His whispered words swirled round and round her brain till she could almost feel herself naked, bound and helpless beneath the weight of his body.

She heaped another shovelful of coal on to the fire and pulled her eiderdown round her shoulders. She had felt safe, so safe, when Lord Lensborough had held her in his arms, she thought bitterly. It had been an illusion. Lionel was in her head, and she would never feel clean again. Because she had let him… She should have fought.

She must cling to the memory that Lord Lensborough had fought for her. That he had knocked Lionel down with one mighty blow. He had rescued her. Brought her home.

Had she remembered to lock the door after bringing her tray in? It didn't matter, Lionel could not reach her here, she had to believe that.

But there was a noise of splintering wood, booted feet pounding up the stairs, somebody was trying the door to her bedroom…a man's voice…he was coming in. How had he found her? How had he got in? Well, she would not be so compliant this time. She seized the poker. And though she knew nobody would hear her, that there was nobody to rescue her this time, she threw back her head, drew a deep breath, and screamed.

Lord Lensborough's mood the next morning had not been improved by a sleepless night.

'Is Lady Hester not coming down to breakfast today?' he barked as the meal drew to a close. 'Has anyone any idea what her plans are?'

Sir Thomas leaned back in his chair and regarded his lordship thoughtfully.

'If she is not feeling well, she will probably keep to her rooms,' Julia said.

He flung his napkin on to the table and stalked out of the room, seething with impotent impatience. Damn the woman. Perhaps he should just get the proposal over with and leave.

How could he leave without knowing she was recovering? Besides, he had given her his word.

When Emily Dean came to call he followed her into the morning room and was immensely grateful to her when, in spite of Lady Gregory's insistence that Hester was unlikely to receive visitors, the indomitable girl went up just the same. It was scarce ten minutes before she returned.

'Lady Gregory, I fear that Hester may be quite unwell.'

'You must send for a doctor at once,' Lord Lensborough said.

Julia laughed. 'Nobody sends for a doctor on Hester's behalf unless she specifically requests it.'

'She would simply refuse to see him,' Phoebe added. 'She would lock her door and refuse to come out. She has done it before.'

'Her door is locked,' Em said. 'And she hasn't touched the tray Mary took up this morning. I knocked and shouted, but she did not answer.'

'Oh, dear.' Lady Gregory twisted her handkerchief into a knot. 'I do hope she has not got anything serious. What is to become of Harry if she has brought influenza into the house? Thomas, I have said it and said it, you should not allow her to go visiting the poor so often. The poor are always so unhealthy.'

Lord Lensborough's frayed temper finally snapped.

'Miss Dean, I should appreciate it if you would take me up to Lady Hester's rooms at once. I will soon find out if she needs to see a doctor, and believe me, if she does, I will not take no for an answer.'

'Oh, no, my lord.' Lady Gregory's hands flew to her pink cheeks. 'That would be most improper—besides, she will not allow you in. She allows none of us in.'

'If necessary, I will break down her door.'

Lady Gregory shrieked in alarm, then began to plead with Sir Thomas to do something.

Sir Thomas shrugged, muttering, 'I'd leave the girl be, if that is what she wants.'

It was the last straw. 'When she may be in such need of help that she is unable to ask for it?' Lord Lensborough rounded on Miss Dean. 'Enough time has already been wasted. Take me to her this instant.'

Em hurried from the room with his lordship hard on her heels. The stunned silence that fell was only broken by Sir Thomas, chuckling from behind his newspaper.

The way to Hester's rooms lay through the servants' hall, up the back stairs, through the servants' sleeping quarters and then up another narrow stairway. Em knocked firmly on the door at the top of this stairway, but there was no answer.

'You have already established she isn't answering the door,' Lord Lensborough said grimly. 'Stand aside.'

It took him only a few well-aimed kicks to sever the wood from its hinges.

Lord Lensborough followed Em into a tiny hallway furnished with an umbrella stand, a marble-topped table holding a lantern and a row of pegs on which a couple of coats hung. Above the table, what had initially looked like a window framed with curtains turned out to be a mirror on which a woodland scene had been painted.

Em explained, 'There are no windows up here, my lord. That is one of the reasons nobody else wanted these rooms. Hester put mirrors in to increase light and create the illusion of a view.'

By the slope of the ceiling he guessed they must be directly under the roof leads. His muttered curse frosted in the air even as it left his mouth. How could her family house her in conditions like this? Without windows, it must be unbearably stuffy up here in summer. Winter or summer, Hester knew nothing but discomfort.

Em darted back from the doorway she had disappeared through while he stood still, fists clenched at his sides.

'It looks as though her bed has not been slept in.' Beckoning him to follow, she pushed open a second door that led off the narrow hall. Within he could see the embers of a dying fire. At least she had the means to keep warm. He stepped forward into the room, then froze as a bloodcurdling scream emanated from a shape that was huddled before the fire.

Hester was terrified. He eyed the poker she was brandishing wildly, and dropped to his knees.

'Hester…Hester, don't…' he murmured over and over as he inched forward. 'Hush, now…it's me…it's only me…'

Her wild eyes began to focus on him at last and the poker fell from her hands with a clatter. 'You…how did you…why did you..?'

He was almost within reach. 'Miss Dean brought me up here. We were all worried when you did not come down to breakfast.'

'Breakfast?' She looked beyond him to where Em hovered uncertainly in the doorway. 'Is it day already?'

He reached out and laid his hand on her forehead. She closed her eyes and leaned into his palm. 'You are burning up. You must see a doctor.'

'No.' She backed away, tugging the quilt up to her chin. 'No doctor. I just need to be left alone. Please, leave me alone.' She reached into the coal scuttle and a puzzled look flitted across her face. 'I seem to have run out of coal.'

'There is a warm fire in my room. You insisted on it being kept going all the time. Do you remember?'

'Of course I remember. Do you think I'm an idiot?'

Lord Lensborough smiled. 'Forgive me, but you do seem a trifle confused.'

She passed a shaky hand across her face, smearing a sooty trail through the perspiration.

'Have you eaten anything since you came home?' He kept his voice low, so that Em could not overhear. 'At least tell me you changed out of your wet clothes.'

Hester peered down at herself under the eiderdown, as if unsure. Lord Lensborough saw she still had her coat on.

'That does it,' he snapped, hefting her into his arms and getting to his feet. 'You are coming downstairs to get warm, and out of those wet clothes.'

'I am?' Her hands fluttered across his chest, her restless fingers tangling in the lapels of his coat.

'You are,' he replied firmly as she closed her eyes and burrowed her face into his shoulder.

'Miss Dean,' he barked over his shoulder, 'be so good as to procure a change of clothes for her, and bring it down to my room. Then find someone in this benighted place who can come and tend to her.'

Em obeyed without demur.

'Well, somebody needs to keep an eye on you,' he bit out

before Hester could voice any protest. 'Good God, woman, don't you realise you could have caught a severe chill after driving through that snow yesterday?'

He stepped over the wreckage of her front door and strode down towards the main body of the house. 'Hell, woman, I have no notion of how you should be nursed, or what lingering effects that drug may have on you, let alone whatever other horrors that cur put you through.'

She lifted her head and looked up at him reproachfully. 'You promised nobody need know. You promised you would not tell. I couldn't bear it.' She scrabbled frantically at his waistcoat as he strode resolutely along the maze of upstairs landings. 'Please, I don't want a doctor prodding at me... asking questions.'

Lord Lensborough cursed himself for being so insensitive. Of course she could not cope with a man handling her against her wishes yet, even for the best of reasons.

'Then you must make some effort to take care of yourself,' he bit out savagely. He kicked open the door to his own room and marched across to his bed. 'For God's sake, have you no pride?' He lowered her to sit on the edge of the bed. 'Are you going to let that blackguard win by sliding down into some sort of decline?'

Hester clung to his neck while he deftly unwrapped her eiderdown and set to work on the buttons of her coat. When he knelt down to unlace her boots, she ventured, 'C...could you just say then...if anyone should ask...that I got caught in the snow yesterday and have developed a chill? It is the truth... part of it.'

He tugged off her boots, then looked up at her militantly. 'If I tell them that, do you promise to get well?'

'I will promise to do my best,' she conceded.

He nodded once, and got to his feet. A feeling that was almost like panic swept over her when he turned to leave the room. While he was close, she felt safe. Nobody would dare cross him. He was so fierce, so strong.

'Wait!' she cried, involuntarily stretching her arms out towards his retreating form. As he turned, she guiltily dropped them to her sides. She could not do anything so improper as to beg him to take her in his arms again. But nor could she bear to let him go. Not quite yet.

There must be some way she could persuade him to stay; then it hit her. 'You promised you would not leave until I had told you all about Lena—the little gypsy girl.'

'This is hardly the time.'

'This is the perfect time. While we have a few moments of privacy. Uncle Thomas does not want anyone else to know about her.' She held out her hand to him again, and this time, though he looked none too pleased about it, he returned to her bedside.

'Especially not Julia or Phoebe. I think, if they are old enough to get married, they're old enough to know about that sort of thing, but he says no well-bred lady should, or, if she does, she should pretend she does not.' She was babbling, she knew she was, but at least the stream of words was keeping him close.

'Although naturally I would not want either of them to feel the shock I did when I first saw Lena.'

He sank suddenly into the chair by her bed, grasping the hand she'd held out to him.

'It must have been a shock.' He averted his eyes, his cheeks flushing darkly. 'I can understand that.'

'Yes, for I had thought Gerard was a good person.' She shook her head. 'I still find it hard to believe my own brother could have done such a wicked thing. He could never have married Lena's mother. He just used her.' She shuddered.

'Your brother?' His grip on her hand tightened almost painfully. 'And a gypsy girl?'

'I know.' She lifted her chin. 'And you will likely hear

worse about Gerard too. He died when a bawdy house he was visiting caught fire, you know.'

'Who told you that?' He looked thunderstruck.

'I overheard my uncle discussing it with my cousin Harry. Lord Lensborough, please try to understand why Uncle Thomas let me keep on seeing my little niece. I had been so ill after Gerard died that they had to take me out of school and send me back to The Holme. And even here, I could settle to nothing, speak to no one. I spent so much time hiding in the attics that in the end they let me furnish them and have them for my very own. And then one day, there was this gypsy woman lurking round the stables with a red-haired baby in her arms, asking for my brother.' She fingered her own copper curls. 'She couldn't pass the baby off as her husband's, not with all that red hair, she said, and what was to become of her?'

Lord Lensborough's heart pounded in his chest as the truth finally sank in. The baby was Gerard's by-blow. He closed his eyes, hanging his head in shame. How could he have entertained the foul suspicion that Hester was Lena's mother even for a second?

'I begged Uncle Thomas to let me take the baby from her mother so that I could bring her up myself.' She smiled wryly. 'Don't forget, I was scarce more than a child myself. I had no idea what an outrageous suggestion it was. It just seemed logical. After all, Uncle Thomas had taken me and Gerard in after our parents died. He had quite a task on his hands, persuading me it was impossible. I wept and stormed and raged…' Her voice trailed away as she finally took in the slumped set of Lord Lensborough's shoulders. He did not want to hear any of this. He'd just extricated her from one scandal, and now she was pouring the details of another into his ears. And because he was a gentleman, and had given his word to hear her out, he would sit there and listen while every word could only increase his disgust of her.

She blinked back tears she was surprised to feel stinging her eyes.

'I placed my uncle in a dreadful position, I know I did. Eventually he managed to convince me I could not take a baby from its true mother. He made an arrangement with the gypsy clan. They would make The Lady's Acres a regular stopping point so that I could see Lena and be sure she was thriving. And he gave Jye, whose wife was Lena's mother, money to stop him from casting her off. You know,' she mused, 'I think in his own way he is fond of her. Even after her mother died, he kept right on fostering Lena.

'Perhaps you think my uncle should have forced me to accept Lena was being well provided for,' she put in hastily, beginning to feel unnerved by Lord Lensborough's continued silence, the disdain she could read etched on his averted features. 'But after Gerard died nothing seemed to matter any more, until Lena came into my life, and suddenly I was alive again.'

Oh, yes, he knew that feeling all too well. Hadn't he felt his own life was a hollow shell after his own brother's death? For some while before he'd come to The Holme, and met Hester, he had ceased caring about anything much at all.

'Looking forward to seeing her kept me going through those dark months. I began to eat again, and learn as much as I could about babies so I would know what stages she was going through, even though I could not be with her. I haunted the nursery, for Jenny was only a few months older than Lena.'

And suddenly a shiver raced down his spine at the realisation that he had almost lost her, too. He had been on the verge of proposing to Julia. He had only saved her from Snelgrove's vile schemes by the merest quirk of fate. And then he had offered her a position of his mistress. She would never have forgiven him that insult, if she had heard it.

'Lord Lensborough, please say something. Please tell me you understand.'

He did not know how he found the strength to lift his head and meet her anxious gaze.

Hester quailed as he searched her face as though he had never really seen her before.

But he hadn't let go of her hand. That had to count for something, didn't it?

'I understand you have an impulsive, selfless nature, Lady Hester,' he finally managed to croak, 'that puts the rest of us, with our petty prejudices, to shame.'

She sank back, limp with relief, into the pillows just as Em appeared in the doorway with an armful of fresh clothes.

Lord Lensborough was on his feet at once. 'Take good care of her, Miss Dean,' he barked.

Em pulled a face at the proud set of his back as he strode from the room, but Hester no longer felt any desire to mock his autocratic manner. On the contrary, she felt reassured by the knowledge that he was prowling about the place, keeping her safe.

She was amazed at just how shaky she felt as Em helped strip off her clammy clothes, and bundled her into bed.

'You should try to get some sleep,' Em advised, once she'd extracted a list of Hester's symptoms from her, 'while I go and prepare a draught for your headache.'

Hester shuddered at the prospect of closing her eyes, and enduring the kind of memories that had assailed her all through the night. 'I doubt I will be able to keep it down,' she confessed as a spasm of very real nausea assailed her.

Breathing in deeply, she clenched her teeth and turned her face away from Em's concerned gaze.

The pillows had retained that particular blend of clean linen, spicy shaving soap and an underlying musky maleness that was uniquely Lord Lensborough. It was as though he was there with her. She curled into a ball, burying her face deeper, inhaling the feeling of security that was intrinsically mixed with his scent. With every breath she drew, she felt calmer, as if in breathing his essence, she was becoming infused with his strength.

She sighed. To think she had despised him once, believing him cold and unfeeling. It was true that he did not think romance was an ingredient necessary to marriage. But at least a girl knew he would never give way to lustful impulses should they conflict with his rigid sense of honour. Perhaps that was another reason she felt so safe when he had wrapped his arms round her. He was no threat to her, in any way. He had demonstrated repeatedly that he did not like her, that he disapproved of her manners, her temper and her behaviour. But he was going to marry into her family and that made him a sort of cousin. Or a very protective big brother. An understanding big brother, once you got past that forbidding front he put on.

Satisfied that she had her feelings for him clearly defined, Hester slid into a blessedly dream-free sleep.

It was much later in the afternoon when Lady Gregory came and tapped on the sitting-room door.

'This is all most irregular,' she said, peering into the room over Em's shoulder. 'Lord Lensborough says he wishes to give his room over to Hester's use, until she is better.'

'I think that is a good idea, my lady. Think of all the stairs up to her suite. And she will still be far enough away from the rest of the family to prevent the infection spreading.'

'Well, yes, but where is he to sleep, I should like to know?' Her forehead creased. 'And he will need to change for dinner soon.'

'The other guest rooms must surely all be relatively well aired, since the others have not long departed.'

'The blue room,' Lady Gregory exclaimed. 'I always said Lord Lensborough should have the blue room. Mr Farrar must move into the new wing as well. We can't have him on the other side of that bedroom, can we? Then, Em, dear, you could come to stay. That is, if you would like to help look after Hester? Mary can come and sit with her while you go home and inform your papa. I am sure he will spare you, under the circumstances.'

Amidst all the ensuing bustle, Em did not get a chance to report back to Lord Lensborough, as he had requested she do, until just before the dinner hour, when the entire family were gathering in the salon.

'Lady Hester has slept most of the day,' she told him. 'She still complained of a headache and sore throat on waking, but her fever is not so high. Mary is taking some dinner to her room while I slip back to the vicarage for my things. Lady Gregory wishes me to stay here until she is fully recovered.'

'Will you need any help carrying your things back here?' Mr Farrar inquired. 'I would willingly escort you to the vicarage and back.'

'That is most kind of you,' Lady Gregory answered while Em hesitated. 'I am sure Reverend Dean will ask you to dine over there. That will give Em time to pack.'

While Stephen sauntered to Em's side, she turned to Lord Lensborough, saying, 'Thank you for all you have done for my friend, Lord Lensborough. Your intervention was most timely.'

'Will you need any help nursing her?' Lord Lensborough darted a look at the two sisters, who were sitting side by side on a sofa, their heads close together in whispered conversation. It was taking all his willpower to conceal his disgust for two such selfish, uncaring creatures. Hester had bravely borne so much in silence, and they were so pampered it did not occur to either of them to offer to sit for one hour with her.

Em gave him a long look. 'Lady Gregory is anxious to keep Harry from any risk of infection. He almost died when influenza swept through the village some years ago. And Hester would never forgive herself if she inadvertently caused him any harm.'

He flinched. It appeared he had misjudged the depth of the family's concern about risk of influenza. Perhaps he should bear in mind, too, that they did not know what Hester had really suffered.

'And you, Miss Dean? Do not you fear infection?'

'Oh, I never get ill.' She darted a poisonous look at Mr Farrar before adding, 'Illness is one of those luxuries the poor cannot afford.'

As they left the room, Lord Lensborough spun abruptly towards the window, staring out into the darkened park. Catching sight of Julia's reflection, he sighed. He would have made the poor girl the devil of a husband. Her mother and father were going to be deeply disappointed when he dashed their matrimonial ambitions, but there was no help for it. Hearing that his suspicions about Hester's impurity were groundless had been like the sun breaking through the oppressive cloud that had been hanging over him. He couldn't go back to that grey, dismal misery. He was going to marry Hester.

And be damned to anyone who stood in his way!

Chapter Twelve

'Miss Dean does not think it is the influenza at all,' Lady Gregory informed his lordship over the pudding. 'Just a chill from being out in that snowstorm. She will soon be on the mend, so, you see, there was really no need to send for the doctor after all,' she persisted in the face of Lord Lensborough's implacable ill humour. 'She does so detest having a fuss made.'

'We could go to the village and procure lemons, don't you think, Mama?' Julia glanced towards Lord Lensborough to gauge his response. 'To make her a soothing drink.'

They were still twittering about the best remedies for a chill as they withdrew, leaving Lord Lensborough alone with Sir Thomas.

Seizing the port and pouring himself a generous measure, Lord Lensborough braced himself for the confrontation he was determined to have with his host.

But Sir Thomas forestalled him. 'You do not really wish to marry either of my daughters, do you?'

'No,' he replied, taking a large gulp from his glass.

Sir Thomas pressed on. 'In fact, it seems to be my niece who has caught your eye.'

'I dare say you wish to remind me we had an agreement.'

'Don't be absurd, man. You cannot condemn yourself to a lifetime of regret because you made a pledge regarding girls you had not even met.'

'That is…most generous of you, Sir Thomas.'

'Don't imagine I am doing it for your sake. I am not. I do it for Hester. My girls won't ever have any trouble finding a husband, but Hester is a different kettle of fish.' He grinned. 'To be frank, I don't think she has ever taken to any man the way she has taken to you. When Miss Dean related her reaction to you storming her rooms and hauling her downstairs, well, I wanted to break out the champagne there and then. Nestled into your chest.' He laughed. 'Then permitted you to sit by her bedside, holding her hand. Never thought the day would come. I've seen her looking as though she were about to cast up her accounts when some greasy fortune hunter smarmed round her, or wiping her hand down her skirts when some bold fellow tried to take liberties with it.'

'I beg your pardon…did you say, fortune hunter?'

'Hah!' Sir Thomas slapped the table top. 'You did not even know of it, did you?'

When Lord Lensborough shook his head dumbly, Sir Thomas chortled. 'Oh, this gets better and better.' He stretched out his legs, crossing one ankle over the other. 'Hester is a very wealthy woman, will be even richer on her marriage. You see, her brother made a will in her favour as soon as he became Viscount Vosbey. My younger sister, Hester and Gerard's mother, married very well. Had Gerard ever married and had legitimate children…but of course, he didn't. So on his death, all his estates went to her, since he was the last male of that line, besides the land she already had from her mother, The Lady's Acres, which run adjacent to my own land.'

'The Lady's Acres are hers?'

'Aye, and the manor, Lady's Bower. One of those complicated clauses to do with protecting the females of the Gregory family was set up in feudal times, so that will always be hers, and then any daughter she may have, but the rest of her wealth will go straight into her husband's coffers.'

'But, the way she dresses, the way she acts, as if she is at best an unpaid housekeeper…?'

'Ah, she likes to make herself useful to her aunt, that is true. She has a very giving nature.' He leaned forward, a challenge in his voice. 'If you want a fashionable ornament to dangle from your arm, then, no, Hester is not the woman for you. I told you at the outset she has an odd kick to her gallop. She would never spend her allowance on clothes when I gave it to her, except for a decent riding habit every season. Gave the most part of it to the poor.' Sir Thomas grimaced as he pushed the decanter towards Lord Lensborough. 'Especially those wheedling gypsies. So now I deliberately keep her short of funds. And don't go getting on your high ropes over that, my lord. It is for her own good. Her money is all safely invested for her. Your man of business can investigate her affairs as thoroughly as you wish.'

'You may believe that he will.'

Lord Lensborough refilled his glass with hands that were perceptibly shaking. Now he knew why Snelgrove had tried to abduct her. It was not unrequited passion, but avarice that prompted the man. His hopes for his own happiness began to shift towards an urgent need to protect her from all such villains.

'You need not be afraid she will run up bills with the dress-makers, like some women. Or spend much at all upon herself—she will not even have a personal maid, you know, though she could easily afford one. She says it would be tactless to flaunt her wealth in that manner when I could not hire one for Julia and Phoebe.' He watched with interest as Lord Lensborough downed the vintage port in one gulp.

'You might, on the other hand, have a job preventing her

from giving your entire fortune away to what she deems worthy causes. She will need a firm hand on the reins, I won't deny it. Someone who isn't intimidated by that temper of hers. And I believe you are just the man to do it. You can't imagine how much amusement I have derived from watching the pair of you circle each other all week, trying to suppress the sparks flying between you, and wondering when the next lot of fireworks would go off.' He leaned forward, an earnest expression on his face. 'Now I know you didn't like finding her in that gypsy camp. Probably disapproved of seeing her wandering the lanes alone too. But this is the countryside, she wasn't even off our own estates, come to that. I can assure you she knows better than to go out without a footman in a place like London.'

Lensborough held up his hand. 'I have discussed the reasons for Lady Hester's visits to the gypsies with her myself, and I fully understand *her* motives in that regard.'

Sir Thomas looked rather abashed. 'Dare say I may have been a little too soft with her on that score, but I don't think you will find Jye poses you much of a problem. Don't say he isn't a crafty devil, mind, but if I've managed to keep him on a leash—' His face suddenly fell. 'Provided, of course, you can persuade her to marry you.'

'You think she might refuse?'

It was entirely possible. Stephen had repeatedly warned him that she did not like him. His heart felt as though an iron fist were squeezing it as he recalled the number of times she had shouted at him, glared at him, called him names, or even simply avoided his company altogether by flouncing out of the room.

'Oh, aye. She has these plans, you see. On her twenty-fifth birthday she will gain control of her own funds. I will be powerless to stop her from opening up Vosbey House—that is her London residence, which I have leased out at the moment, just like Lady's Bower—and running it as some kind of an orphanage. Em Dean will go with her to lend her countenance, she says, though I cannot say that makes me any easier. She's worse than Hester. If Em had her way, they would sell all Hester's property and live among the labouring poor of some mill town.'

He sighed dramatically. 'I would much rather she married someone strong enough to check her wild starts, someone who would care for her. Someone she could respect. A man who can be firm, but won't bully her.'

'Sir Thomas...' He edged forward in his chair, his mouth suddenly bone dry '...I would never do anything to hurt her.'

'I knew it.' Sir Thomas looked very smug. 'You have developed a *tendre* for her, in spite of what you perceive to be a long list of failings on her part.'

Lord Lensborough pulled a wry face. Every new fact he learned about Hester turned all his previous assumptions about her upside down. The only constant factor was his total fascination with her.

'I cannot seem to help myself,' he admitted.

'Excellent. Now, the next stage will need very careful handling.' Sir Thomas reached for the decanter to fill his own glass. 'We're going to have to box clever. It is my belief you slipped under her guard because she always thought of you as halfway betrothed to one of my girls. You didn't lay on the flattery with a trowel—well, you saw yourself how she reacted to that dandified friend of yours when he tried it on.'

'You may be sure I will propose in a most rational, businesslike manner, then, pointing out all the advantages of such a match.'

'You will do nothing of the sort!' He pounded the table top so hard the stopper rattled in the neck of the decanter. 'What advantages can there be in marrying you, or any other man? I've told you, she is independently wealthy. She can do exactly

as she pleases in another couple of years and has been looking
forward to it.'

No, he mused, she had never been impressed by his
wealth or rank. If she ever did agree to marry him, it would
have to be because she cared for him. Enough to give up her
independence.

His heart began to beat erratically. He would have to
conquer her. Not the obscenely wealthy Marquis of Lensborough. That cipher, who caused so many female bosoms
to heave with avaricious longing, could never win a woman
like Hester. But could the man, Jasper Challinor?

With a start, he realised Sir Thomas was still speaking.
'...so you must not speak to her about this until I have
sounded her out.'

'I will wait.' He looked at his host with unseeing eyes. 'But
I cannot promise I can do so with any degree of patience.'

'Used to getting your own way, ain't you?'

'Not,' he replied drily, 'since I came into Beckforth.'

'Need to square it with Lady Susan, too.' Sir Thomas's face
fell. 'I don't think she will be pleased to have all her aspirations for our girls dashed like this, but you wouldn't have
made either of 'em happy in the long run.' He forced a smile.
'They're not up to your weight, and so I shall tell her.'

Downing the last of the port, he got to his feet, and, pot
valiant, went to inform his wife.

'Oh. Oh,' she cried when, much later, in the privacy of their
own bedchamber, he finally broke the news. She clasped her
hands to her bosom and tears sprang to her eyes. Sir Thomas
backed towards the bedroom door, deciding he would wait till
she had cried out her initial disappointment before pointing
out that such warm-hearted girls as theirs needed a great deal
of affection if they were to flourish, and his lordship was not
the man to give it.

'Oh,' she cried again, flinging her arm out towards him, 'but this is wonderful, my love. Wonderful!'

'Eh?' His retreat ground to a halt. 'You are not displeased? After all that money and effort you expended getting our girls kitted out to attract him?'

'Oh, how can you be so absurd? None of it will be wasted. They will be able to show off their new gowns when we go to London for Hester's wedding, or, if she is not to be married in London, she will surely invite them to stay with her for the Season. She will introduce them into the best circles, they will meet the most eligible men.'

'You run ahead of yourself, my dear. He has not spoken to Hester yet....'

'Oh.' Her plump white hand flew to her throat. 'She would not be silly enough to refuse him, surely?'

He sat on the edge of the bed. 'You never can tell with Hester.' He frowned. 'It would be just like her to turn him down so as not to dash our girls' hopes in his direction.'

Lady Susan's tears dried up at once. 'I will speak to them, Thomas. And I will explain to Hester how delighted we shall all be for her to find happiness in the matrimonial state.'

'Thank you, my love.' Sir Thomas sighed with relief that yet another obstacle to the match had been so neatly removed. Still, he thought it best to sound Hester out before permitting his lordship to approach her. She had long professed a deep-seated aversion to the very thought of marriage, and it would not do to expose a man of his lordship's influence to the embarrassment of the tactless sort of rejection she was bound to mete out should he have misjudged her feelings towards him.

So, first thing next morning, before the family set off for church, he made his way to the sick room.

'You don't look half so bad as I've been led to expect,' he observed, pulling a chair up to her bedside. 'The way Lord

Lensborough goes on, anyone would think you had been at death's door.'

At the very mention of his name, his niece blushed and lowered her head.

'And as for the way he manhandled you down here…' he scowled, deciding to play devil's advocate to sound out her feelings '…shocking behaviour! You aunt was most upset. I can assure you, there will be no repeat of that performance. Who does he think he is, carrying on like that?'

'Oh, no.' Hester turned imploring eyes upon her uncle. 'Please do not quarrel with him over that. He only meant to help me.'

'Throw his weight about, more like.'

'He cannot help himself. Don't you see? He is so used to people jumping to do his bidding that he believes he can behave exactly as he likes without risk of censure. He may have acted in a very offensive manner, but his motive was kindness.'

'Kindness! That man has not a kind bone in his body. The more I see of him, the less I like the idea of one of my girls marrying such a disagreeable man.'

'Oh, no. No.' She seized her uncle's coat sleeve. 'His manner may be brusque, he may have a bit of a temper, but I am sure he would never ill treat a lady.'

'Not intentionally, perhaps, but…' he sighed heavily, patting her hand '…I have to admit that you may have been right about him all along. It may have been a mistake letting him come here.'

'You surely cannot mean to refuse to give your consent to the match at this stage?' She looked appalled. 'Just because he is a little autocratic—surely you must have seen that beneath that gruff exterior he is every inch a gentleman. What better husband could a girl wish for? He is wealthy enough to indulge Julia's every whim, strong enough to smooth Phoebe's path through anything life may throw in her way. Oh, I know he does not cut a very romantic figure, but who would really want a husband who was for ever sighing and languishing at your feet? No, a sensible, rational man would make a much more competent husband.'

'Sensible and rational is all very well and good, but that temper of his. He can be very harsh.'

'Yes.' She plucked a stray thread from his sleeve. 'He does have a short fuse. But they could soon learn how to avoid setting his back up if they don't want him to shout at them. And he would repay them by doing his utmost to take care of them.'

Sir Thomas nodded, as if considering her declaration of his merits dispassionately. 'In effect, you think with a bit of work he might make a tolerable husband in the end?'

How could she make him see what a truly wonderful man he was about to get for a son-in-law? 'Much better than tolerable. I think that once she had got used to his ways, his wife could consider herself the most fortunate woman in the world.'

'My word, Hester, that is warm praise indeed. I did not know you had come to regard him so highly.'

Hester's cheeks flamed. 'I formed a very silly prejudice against him before I ever met him. Now that I have got to know him…' She looked away, her whole body hot with sudden self-awareness. Though she could not admit to anybody how much she owed to him, her feelings for the man who had rescued her from Lionel Snelgrove's clutches were tantamount, at that precise moment, to hero-worship.

Her uncle was wreathed in smiles when he left, so she supposed she must have reassured him that Lord Lensborough would not be unkind to his precious daughters. She slumped back against the mound of pillows, suddenly exhausted, and inexplicably wretched. Her spirits sank even lower once the stillness of the house told her that everyone had gone to church, and she was entirely alone. As she always would be.

Then, out of nowhere, came the memory of Lord Lensborough's scathing voice, asking if she were really going to sink into a decline over Lionel's attempt to break her.

She sat up straight. She most certainly would not. All anybody knew, thanks to Lord Lensborough's discretion, was that she'd had a head cold. She had to get up and get back to normal life sometime. It might as well be now.

She felt much better for having a thorough wash and getting out of her nightgown and into clean clothes. She grimaced when she sat before the dressing table and caught sight of her hair. It bore silent testimony to every minute of what she had endured over the past couple of days. She really ought to wash it, but since it was Sunday there was nobody in the house to heat the water for her. The thought of standing over the fire, and then lugging buckets upstairs without help was too daunting. Laying aside her silver-backed hairbrush with resignation, she dipped her comb into the ewer, teased out a single section of hair, and patiently set to work on the knots.

She was still sitting there, plying her comb, when Julia bounced into the room.

'Hester,' she squealed, flinging her arms round her shoulders, and planting a kiss on her cheek. 'I am so happy. I had to come straight here to tell you I was never so glad of anything in my life.'

Lord Lensborough must have spoken to her at last. It was strange, but she found that she did not know quite what she wanted to say. She winced as her comb snagged on a particularly stubborn tangle.

'The Reverend Dean's sermon was that inspiring?' she quipped.

Julia collapsed on to the bedside chair in a heap of giggles. 'Don't be silly. I'm talking about your engagement to Lord Lensborough.'

'My what?' The comb slipped through Hester's suddenly nerveless fingers.

'Now, I know you have been thinking of refusing him because you are worried one of us might still be hankering after him. Mama told me. That is why I just had to come and tell you how pleased we will be *not* to have to go through with it.'

'But you—' she met Julia's eyes in the mirror '—you have been, you have to admit it, positively drooling over him ever since he got here.'

Julia met her gaze boldly. 'I admit I have been encouraging his advances. And at first, yes, all I could think about was how splendid it would be to have a rich husband. Even when I found out how bad-tempered he is, I still wanted to prove to Mama and Papa that I could be a dutiful daughter and settle down no matter how I felt about him. Mama really wanted this connection and I…' Her great blue eyes filled with tears. 'Well, she has never really forgiven me for not being able to make up my mind between Captain Fitzpatrick and Lysander Wells. I could easily have married either of them. Whenever I read one of the poems Mr Wells composed for me, I just melted inside, but the moment I glimpsed Captain Fitzpatrick in his regimentals, all other thoughts went out of my head.'

Hester suffered a pang of sympathy for Julia, remembering the scenes there had been when she came home from her Season without a husband. She should have known all along Julia would never marry for money alone. Julia needed affection and approval. Her dogged pursuit of Lord Lensborough had been prompted by a sense of family duty.

'But what about Phoebe? The way she looks at him.'

'Yes. As if he is some sort of god. I thought at first she would like to marry him, but once she confided in me how she could not sleep for fear he might choose her, I had to try to save her from him. She could never have plucked up the courage to refuse him anything, you see? And then what would her life have been like?'

'You are talking about him as if he is some sort of ogre.' Hester snatched up her comb and tugged it through one of the remaining tangles. Couldn't Julia see she was turning her nose up at the opportunity of a lifetime?

Julia giggled again. 'Well, we all know now that you, at least, don't think so. When I overheard Papa whispering to Mama in church that you had fallen for him, it was as if all our prayers had been answered.'

Hester sighed with relief. It was all just a misunderstanding. She could soon straighten it out. 'Julia, I said some things to reassure your father this morning, but it was all to do with one of you marrying him. He has not even considered me.'

'Of course he has, silly. He asked Papa for your hand last night.'

He couldn't have done. 'But your father did not agree…'

'Of course he did.'

No! How could he have done such a thing without consulting her? It was the worst form of betrayal, knowing how she felt about marriage.

'He could not…' Or could he? To spare his own daughters from a distasteful marriage, of course he could sacrifice his niece. He would not even feel guilty now, not after what she had said to him before church.

'It is absurd.' What on earth could have possessed Lord Lensborough? He had made no secret of the extent of his dislike for her. Even after rescuing her from Lionel, he had roundly abused her all the way home.

A cold hand seemed to clutch at her heart. It was because of what she had said at the inn. She had warned him what gossips could make of the escapade. So he had decided to put paid to any potential for gossip by marrying her.

'Not at all.' Julia got up and hugged her. 'And the best of

it is, Mama says once you are married, she will permit me to go back to London, so that you can put me in the way of finding a really good husband. One that I can love. A kind, gentle, handsome man who will not look down his nose at me.'

Julia performed a pirouette in the doorway before, presumably, dancing away to her own room, leaving Hester feeling as if all the air had been knocked from her lungs. She gripped the edge of the dressing table, shutting her eyes as the room spun crazily about her.

Marriage. She gulped. To think she had inhaled his scent from the pillows of his bed, imagining she could trust him. That she had found a champion to protect her from all that. When all along he had decided…

She opened her eyes and turned to glare at the bed they had both slept in. Not at the same time, not yet, but once he got that ring on her finger…

Sweat broke out on her brow. A shiver ran down her spine. Their naked limbs would tangle together. There would be sweating, and grunting, and pain, and humiliation. All that Lionel had threatened would become reality. Falling to her knees, she scrabbled under the bed, yanking out the chamberpot only just in the nick of time.

Once her stomach was well and truly empty, she dragged the quilt from the bed and crawled with it to the sitting-room hearth. Her very bones felt chilled, though sweat was pouring from every pore in her skin.

'Oh.' Hester had not heard the knock on the door. 'I thought you were better?'

Hester turned dull eyes to where her aunt hovered nervously on the threshold.

'I tried to get up,' she murmured, wondering where all the optimism, the energy she had felt earlier, had gone. 'I was sick.'

Her aunt sidled into the room and perched on the edge of a chair by the door. 'Well, my dear, I only came to congratulate you on securing such a wonderful match. I do hope—that is, I know you have said a great many things against marriage in the past, but it is the natural state for a woman, having a man look after her, and bearing his children.'

Hester clenched her teeth against another wave of nausea. Most women, yes. But not her. She could not bear the idea of what she would have to endure, at the hands of a man who did not like her, in order to become a mother.

'Now, Hester, I hope you are going to be a good girl. You won't do anything silly like turning him down, will you? This connection would be so beneficial. Only think what his patronage would mean to Harry and George.'

A sense of utter defeat washed over her. Every single one of her family was ranged against her.

'I know this is not a love match, but is that not all to the good? For you, I mean. I know how you dislike it when men go all romantical over you.' She inched her chair a little closer to where Hester slumped on the hearth rug.

'I have noticed that you are not as shy with him as you are with other men. Why, you danced with him quite competently. And you talk to him in a way my girls cannot. About reform, and issues, and all those things they are not the least bit interested in. And horses. That is why he prefers you, I expect. That, and the fact that you are better connected, and have a substantial dowry.'

'Aunt Susan!' she gasped. Hadn't she always said he had come here to pick a brood mare to his stud?

For once, her aunt interpreted her horrified response with complete accuracy. She glanced at the bed. 'I am sure he will be a perfect gentleman in that respect.' She flushed, and got to her feet. 'Perhaps you should keep to your room for another day. You are not in looks yet. When your face has got some colour back, your nose will not look quite so red in contrast.' Before Hester could utter another word, her aunt had left the room.

It was all very well for her aunt to presume he would be a gentleman. She had not seen the murderous light in his eyes before he had floored Lionel with a single, deadly accurate punch. She hadn't been hefted into those powerful arms as if she weighed no more than a feather.

She curled up as small as she could under the quilt, grinding her forehead into the rug. She could not go through with it. Not even to secure her family's future. She had decided years ago not to marry, and her physical reaction now to the prospect of it only went to prove she had made the right decision. She must refuse him. Politely but firmly. That was all she had to do. Say no.

She sat up as a great weight seemed to roll off her shoulders. Once she had refused him, she would have to weather her family's disappointment. It would be uncomfortable, but not impossible.

As for Lord Lensborough, he would simply... She frowned. What would he do when she spurned him? A smile crooked one corner of her mouth. It would not occur to him that any woman would be crazy enough to turn him down. He regarded himself as such a catch.

Her smile faded. How stupid Julia and Phoebe were not to see his finer qualities just because he was a little gruff at times. If they had only seen him in action, the way he had flown across the room to her defence.

But, if she turned him down, and then he asked them, it would be a terrible blow to his pride to be refused three times in a row. She twirled a tendril of hair round and round her finger.

She could not expose him to such shabby treatment, not when she was so deeply in his debt. It was not an exaggeration to say she owed him her life. If he had not rescued her, Lionel would have hauled her up the stairs and raped her. And she would not have survived the ordeal. Lionel had said that afterwards she would have no choice but to marry him, but he did not know her as well as he thought he did. She could not have lived with the shame of such utter defeat. Nor would she have allowed him to get his hands on her money by tamely taking vows. She would have found a way.

She got to her knees, then her feet, and forced herself to look at the bed. She owed Lord Lensborough so much. Could she really be base enough to refuse the one thing he asked of her? Could she strike such a blow to his pride after he had gone to such lengths to preserve hers?

She clung to the bedpost for support. It was not as if he would require all that much of her. All she had to do was appear content. And provide him with children.

She sprang from the bed as if it had burned her, strode across to the window and looked out into the stable yard. Once she was pregnant, she could tell him to take a mistress. He must have had one before. Probably scores of them. She was sure he would be understanding, and discreet. He would leave her alone, and go to another woman when he wanted that sort of sport.

The certainty that he would agree to such an arrangement perversely caused her to burst into tears.

The next morning, although she did not feel any happier about getting engaged to Lord Lensborough, she felt desperate to face him and get the thing settled. Her first strategy, of avoiding the moment as long as she could, was only stringing her nerves into ever tighter knots. Several times, she got as far as walking across the sitting room and placing her hand on the door knob.

It was mid-morning when Em came in, carrying a tray of tea and scones. She had gone home to the vicarage when it had become clear Hester was not seriously ill, and Hester felt as if she had not seen her for years.

'Em. How glad I am to see you,' she breathed as her friend put the tray down on a low table.

Em eyed her coldly. 'Really?' She leaned forward to pour the tea. 'I believe I must congratulate you.'

'Oh.' Hester realised that her marriage would scotch all the plans they had made for living together once she came into her fortune. 'I suppose you are very disappointed.'

'No. Hurt. I thought we were friends. I had thought you would have confided in me. To hear of your engagement from Phoebe, and not your own lips, was such a shock.'

'It was rather a shock when I heard of my engagement from Julia, let me tell you.'

Em looked at Hester keenly. 'Never tell me the marquis offered for you, and your uncle accepted on your behalf?'

'That is about the size of it. And I cannot in all conscience wriggle out of the match. But, oh, Em, this means we will never be able to set up home together, as we planned.'

With a sniff, Em handed Hester a cup of tea. 'Don't give that another thought. They were only foolish dreams of girls who considered themselves too poor, or too awkward, to ever get a husband. It is high time we grew up, and faced reality.'

'Then you are not disappointed in me, for not making a stand against this marriage? I did think of it.'

'Of course not. If I were to get an offer from a man with half Lord Lensborough's looks, or the tithe of his wealth, I would accept without a thought for how it would affect you. It is all very well to fool ourselves that we could have devoted ourselves to good works, rather than pandering to the whims of some selfish tyrannical male, but the truth is, marriage is the only option a girl has if she is to remain respectable.'

She slammed her cup down into its saucer. 'Oh, how I wish we did not have to be dependent on men for everything.' She frowned. 'Well, it is no use repining. Life is the way it is, and we must make the best of it. You must make the best of it. Just think, once you are married to your marquis, you will have many opportunities to do good. He is a man of influence, and you will mix with the sort of people who can make the changes we have always yearned for. You can be a force for good in this land.'

'I don't think I could. I don't have your courage. Living quietly, and being involved in charitable works in my own neighbourhood, is one thing, expressing my opinions to a government minister, or a peer of the realm, quite another.'

Em gave a knowing smile. 'Not at first, perhaps. But once you gained confidence, or even if you lost your temper with one of 'em...'

Hester groaned. 'Oh, and I would too. Why does the wretched man think I would be a suitable wife for him? He just wants a woman who will stay in the background and dutifully breed heirs. Oh, Em, I find the prospect so demeaning. Aunt says motherhood is the natural state for a woman, but when I think of the way he picked me, simply because of my pedigree, like some brood mare.'

'I think we should take a walk down to the stables, then.'

'What? Why?'

'You are very pale. You have been cooped up indoors for too long. And if you think he would treat you like he treats his horses, we really should go and take a look at them.'

For a moment Hester stared at her friend open mouthed, then, at the sight of the mischievous twinkle in her eyes, she began to laugh. 'Em! You are incorrigible.'

'No, quite practical really.' She smiled. 'You can tell much about a man from the way he treats his cattle and his servants. Grooms are notorious for speaking their minds. If you find any cause to fear he is truly a cruel man, you must cry off.'

'Not cry off. He has not actually spoken to me yet.'

'Then you are not legally bound. Your family may regard it as a foregone conclusion, but you have the right to refuse him.'

Hester shifted guiltily in her chair. Having considered the

matter carefully, Hester did not feel she had any rights at all. Only a whole string of obligations.

They decided Em ought to be the one to pump Pattison for information. Since Hester had come to blows with him the last time they had met, she would be unlikely to glean anything helpful from him herself.

Nor did Em, apart from an impression that the man served his master with doglike devotion.

Hester plucked up considerably on discovering Strawberry back in her stall. She was beginning to feel almost like her normal self, when Em tugged urgently at her coat sleeve and nodded meaningfully in the direction of the house. She turned to see Lord Lensborough striding across the yard towards her, Mr Farrar strolling languidly some paces behind.

This was it. His intent frown could only indicate he meant to speak to her now. In a panic, she groped for Em's hand, only to find her friend had melted away into the shadows.

She stared wide eyed at the tall, muscular figure that bore down on her, while she sagged against a half-open stable door. He was wealthy enough, handsome enough, to have any woman he wanted. How disappointed he must be that Lionel had forced him into a situation so awkward that his only recourse was to take on this skinny, awkward, bad-tempered little nobody with red hair and a strong desire to remain single. Although... Her head drooped in misery. He had been planning a loveless marriage. She would serve his purposes as well as another.

He did not stop till he stood right in front of her, so close she could see the toe tips of his immaculately glossed boots only inches from her own.

'I am glad to see you so much recovered, Lady Hester.' The rich warmth of his voice reverberated through her spine. 'I might have known the first thing you would do would be to come down to the stables and welcome your mare back from her exile. She's a fine animal.' He reached round her to pat Strawberry's neck.

Hester cringed. Was he now, for the first time in their acquaintance, going to make small talk?

'Can't you stop beating about the bush and just get on with it,' she snapped.

She felt him go still. 'You are aware that I wish to speak to you on a personal matter?'

'Oh, for heaven's sake—' she kicked her heel against the stable door '—it could hardly be more impersonal. You and my uncle have decided everything between you. I only wonder you bother dragging me into it now, as if I had a choice.'

'Of course you have a choice. If the idea of marrying me is so repugnant to you, I shall naturally withdraw my suit.'

'No.' She seized his coat sleeve as he made to withdraw. 'You mustn't do that.' She turned her pale face up to his. She could not expose him to the humiliation of three rejections. 'It would be dreadful. They...' She dropped her head. She could not bear to think how hurt he would be. 'Of course I am going to marry you.'

Lord Lensborough raised his hand to stroke the bowed head, but she jerked it away before he could make contact. 'I'm going back to my room now,' she muttered. 'I don't feel very well again, all of a sudden.'

'Hester, no.' He seized her by the shoulders as she turned away, spinning her back to face him. 'This is not how I wanted it to be. Please.'

Angrily she shook herself free. Of course this was not how he wanted it to be. Did he think she didn't know he did not wish to marry her any more than she wished to marry him? 'Look, let's just agree not to see any more of each other than we have to. You and my uncle and the lawyers can do all the talking that needs doing. I...' She risked a glance up at him. He looked furious. She supposed this reaction could hardly be more acceptable to a man of his pride than an outright refusal. She had to try to make things easier for him.

'I just need some time to adjust,' she said as gently as she could. 'The notion of marrying you came as a complete surprise. And after the last few days...' She felt her cheeks growing hot. 'It has all been a bit much.'

Lord Lensborough ground his teeth as she fled back to the house. It was too much, she was right. He should never have allowed Sir Thomas to interfere. He should have gone to her himself and laid his heart at her feet. Told her he would do his utmost to make her happy. Instead, somebody else had backed her into a corner with heaven alone knew what threats. No wonder she had lashed out at him.

He strode to the man's study and burst straight in without knocking.

'Well?' Sir Thomas looked up from his snuff jar expectantly. 'Have you asked her? What did she say?'

'I did not get the chance to propose in form, sir.' His voice was laced with bitterness. 'She seemed to feel she had been presented with a fait accompli.'

'But did she say she would marry you?'

'I've already told you, she said she had no choice.'

'Well, there you go, my boy. Congratulations!' Sir Thomas rounded his desk and seized Lord Lensborough's hand. 'Surely you know Hester well enough by now to realise that if she really did not wish to marry you, she would have told you to your face? Nobody can make her do anything she does not want to.'

A memory of a wild-eyed hoyden with a bloodied hat pin clutched in her fist came to Lord Lensborough's mind. She would certainly have resisted Snelgrove to the death. He looked down into Sir Thomas's smiling face and realised the man was shaking his hand.

He was right. Hester had the spirit to defy anyone. Even

him. With a slow smile he returned the pressure of Sir Thomas's hand.

Breaking Hester to bridle, as her uncle put it, was going to cost him blood, sweat and probably tears. But even if she never grew to return the half of what he felt for her, it would still be worth it. For whether she acknowledged it or not, she needed him. Needed him to protect her from fortune-hunting villains like Snelgrove, and her own harebrained scheme of living with Miss Dean, which could only bring her the sort of notoriety she would surely come to detest.

His smile took on an intensity that was almost cruel. He'd given her one chance to slip the halter and she had not taken it. He was not going to give her another. She belonged to him.

Chapter Thirteen

Hester stared blankly at the ornate emerald-and-topaz ring that Lord Lensborough had just slipped on to her finger, while her family cheered and clapped.

'It is a Challinor heirloom,' he murmured, still clasping her hand. 'But if you do not care for it, I can have the stones reset to a more modern design.'

She pulled her hand free and looked away. He sounded as though he was bestowing a great honour on her, but she could only see this ring as a symbol of her imminent subjugation.

Sir Thomas began pouring everyone the champagne he had laid in for the occasion. Even Phoebe was given half a glass, since he had expected it might have been her own engagement they were celebrating.

And they were celebrating. Everyone at whom she darted a glance was smiling. Telling herself she had done the right thing by them all, Hester threw back her champagne and held out her glass for a refill.

'I should like it very much if we could all ride out together at least once before we leave for London,' she heard Lord Lensborough say from his position slightly behind her.

'Capital plan,' Sir Thomas answered, when all Hester could

do was gaze into her glass at the bubbles rising to the surface and disappearing in a salvo of silent little explosions.

'When do you plan to leave?' her aunt Susan asked.

'Within the next day or so. My mother is expecting me to bring my fiancée to her in Brook Street, as you know, in plenty of time to shop for her trousseau before the wedding.' He turned to Hester. 'Will it take you very long to ready yourself for the journey?'

She was too busy getting Owen to refill her glass to realise a question had been asked her.

'And the wedding will still be held at St George's Chapel?' Aunt Susan hastened to fill the awkward silence while Lord Lensborough watched Hester through narrowed eyes.

'If that is what Lady Hester wishes.'

'I take it,' she ploughed on, 'you will extend the same terms in regard to purchasing the trousseau?'

'Absolutely. My wife will have a position to fill in society. It is essential that she look the part. She will need a complete new wardrobe. Not,' he added hastily, recalling Sir Thomas's warning about Hester's attitude to clothes, 'that I expect her to look like a fashion plate, but there is a certain standard that provincial dressmakers never quite seem to reach.'

Hester made a sound that was rather like a strangled cough. When she thought of all the time her cousins had spent on shopping trips to Harrogate, only for the object of all the effort to sneer at the skills of provincial dressmakers. Giggles began to fizz through her bloodstream and burst from her parted lips.

Lord Lensborough removed the empty champagne glass from her hand and said, in a frigidly polite voice, 'Perhaps you would like to retire to your rooms now.'

He might as well have said, 'Madam, you have had too much to drink.' Perhaps she had. She had lost count of the number of refills the obliging Owen had supplied. But since all she wanted to do was escape this farcical celebration of her sale into a lifetime of bondage, she ignored his domineering tone, and simply flounced out of the room.

She wished she had discovered the benefits of champagne earlier in her life, she thought muzzily when she woke next morning. She had fallen quickly into a deep sleep, even though, as she raised herself on her elbows and looked about the room, the door to her suite of attic rooms still lay in splinters across the landing.

A glass of water dealt with her parched throat and rather thick tongue, and she went into her sitting room to warm some clothes before her fire.

Her fire. She halted in front of it, remembering now how, only a few minutes after she gained her rooms the night before, Mary had come puffing up the stairs with a bucket of coal to make it up. On Lord Lensborough's instructions.

She dipped a flannel into her washbasin and rubbed it over her face. How had he known she would seek out her place of refuge, fearing the time when she would have to quit it for ever, when she hadn't known she meant to herself?

She dried herself, shivering. After only a few more days she would be embarking on a whole new life, one in which she would have to rely on Lord Lensborough for everything. Julia and Phoebe may have crowed over what they termed her conquest, but she couldn't look on it like that. She felt like a human sacrifice. They were going to take her to London, dress her up, parade her in public and lay her out on a marriage bed, all to satisfy his lordship's demand for an heir.

She got a surge of rebellious pleasure in tossing the hideous engagement ring into her sandalwood jewel casket when she discovered it was too bulky to wear with her close-fitting riding gloves. Lord Lensborough might think he owned her, but she would make sure there would always be some little corner of her life she could call her own.

It was with head held high and eyes snapping defiance that she met him in the stable yard.

His amused 'good morning' was like oil being poured on to a fire.

'Is it?' She ignored his offer of a boost, stepping instead on to the mounting block.

'I think so,' he said, swinging himself into his own saddle. 'The perfect morning for a good gallop.'

Hester hooked her knee over the pommel and adjusted her skirts. There would be no gallops in London. No escaping to the stables when her spirits were low. Riding in London was a ponderous, decorous affair, requiring messages being sent to the mews, grooms providing chaperonage, sedate trots along designated bridle ways, constant interruptions by persons wishing to have conversations. And without her dear Strawberry to ride, how could she tolerate even that? Shooting his lordship one defiant look, Hester dug her heels into Strawberry's flank, and, bending low over her neck, left the yard at the gallop.

With a bark of laughter, Lord Lensborough plunged after her. His bay stallion soon caught up with her shorter-legged mare, and as they thundered neck and neck through the park, they began to leave the rest of their party farther and farther behind.

A quick sideways glance was enough to tell Hester that he was enjoying this. His coal-black eyes glowed with the pleasure of holding his straining mount level with her own, though the powerful beast wanted to lead. Her mouth twisted in a smug smile. His lordship would not look so pleased with himself when he saw where she was taking him.

This might be her last chance to see Lena. Ever. He'd claimed to understand her motives for stooping to mix with society's outcasts, but she couldn't assume he would permit her to continue doing so once she was his wife. He would soon have the power to curtail her movements. But he was not going to stop her bidding farewell to her niece, and explaining to Jye that she was getting married and leaving the area. The sooner he understood she was no milk-and-water miss whose conformity to society's expectations he could take for granted, the better it would be for him.

She cleared the last hedge that separated her uncle's lands from her own and swung Strawberry's head round to canter along the bank of the stream that watered the tan.

'What a spurting little mare you have there,' Lord Lensborough said as he pulled up beside her. 'Do you wish to take her to London with you? Though, of course, we will not be able to enjoy a decent gallop like this.'

Hester barely heard him. The clearing where the gypsies had been camping was empty. Only a few mounds of ash and patches of flattened, yellowing grass showed where they had been.

She became conscious of Lord Lensborough's hand laid over hers where she gripped the reins. 'I am so sorry,' he said. 'They have gone, and you never had a chance to say goodbye to the little girl.'

She whipped round to glare at him. 'As if you care! If you had your way, I would never see her again.' It was what Lionel had said. What husband would want his wife to consort with gypsies, let alone own to a relationship with one?

'But you will see her again, with or without my permission, won't you?' The ghost of a smile hovered about his lips.

'Yes.' Her whole body quivered with defiance as she flung her reply back at him.

His smile broadened. 'Then all I can do is request the same terms you agreed with your uncle.'

She gaped at him stupidly. 'T…terms?'

'Yes, that you keep your visits discreet, and do nothing to raise Lena's expectations unfairly.' He leaned over and, with one finger, lifted her chin to close her mouth. 'Do you think I am such a tyrant that I would forbid you something that means so much to you?'

The gentleness in his voice and touch was Hester's undoing. Great fat tears began to roll down her cheeks.

'I…I am sorry,' she hiccuped. It was unfair to take her anger out on him. It wasn't his fault she could not bear the thought of intimacy with a man. It wasn't his fault that Lena had disappeared, or that there was no way of knowing when she would see her again. None of it was his fault, yet he was going to be saddled with her and all her problems. The more she tried to gulp back the tears, the faster they flowed, till she gave up, sagged over Strawberry's neck, and just sobbed into her mane.

She felt strong arms go about her waist, and Lord Lensborough was dragging her out of the saddle, her feet were on solid ground, and he was cradling her against his chest. He rocked her while she wept, her hands hanging limp at her sides. When there were no more tears left, she just leaned into him, letting his strong arms cocoon her, while she breathed in the familiar scent of his clothes, the scent that had become inextricably linked in her mind with security. After a while it occurred to her that if this was any other man she would want to pull away. Instead of which, she had an almost overwhelming urge to undo his coat and burrow as closely into his big, strong body as she could get. The urge confused her, alarmed her. With a little gasp, she stepped back, and gazed incredulously into his face.

He loosened his hold as soon as she made to move away. His only indication that he was reluctant to let her go completely was in the fact that he kept his hands resting lightly round her waist.

But he would. If she commanded him to release her, he would. Her breath caught at the realisation that she could wield power over this great, strong man. For some bizarre reason, that knowledge made her want him to keep his hands exactly where they were.

'Are you ready to talk now?' He frowned. 'That was the whole purpose of engineering this time alone with you, after all. When your family are about they seem to do all the talking for you.'

'What do you want me to say?'

She could not bear the concern she read in his eyes, and focused instead on the stitching around the top buttonhole of his coat. 'You must know that I have not been capable of stringing two sentences together since you rescued me from Lionel. I cannot get it out of my mind, no matter how hard I try.'

Her hands ventured up the front of his chest, her fingers finding a home amongst the many capes at his shoulders. 'I cannot eat, or sleep, and then I find I have somehow become engaged to you…and now this…' She gestured towards the abandoned camp. 'This was the last straw.'

'At least becoming engaged to me was not the last straw.' He laughed, but it was a hollow laugh. She had hurt him.

'I'm sorry.' Her eyes filled with tears at the thought she had caused him pain. 'So sorry,' she repeated.

'What have you to be sorry for?' Gently he drew his thumb across her cheek, brushing a tear from her face.

'I never thought I would get married,' she tried to explain. 'And I don't think my reaction can have been very flattering to a man of your pride.'

'Ouch.' He pretended to wince. 'But you did not refuse. I gain comfort from that. You must feel there is something about me that raises me above the level of other men.'

'No, that's just it. You generally make me so angry I forget to be shy, that is all. I don't think I have ever really thought of you as a man at all.'

She gasped after the words had left her lips. What was it

about Lord Lensborough that made her blurt out the first thing that came into her head?

'No red-blooded male can take that sort of insult to his masculinity without instantly having to prove himself, my dear,' he growled.

The hand that had been caressing her cheek slid round to the nape of her neck. He meant to kiss her. Dear heaven, and she had goaded him into it. Her heart began to pound wildly as he slowly lowered his head towards hers.

She could stop him.

She could step smartly away, or turn her cheek, or tell him to stop, or even give vent to her mounting panic by slapping his arrogant face.

Or—she swallowed—she could try to get accustomed to the sort of things he would require of her once they were married. Steeling herself for the first touch of his mouth on hers, she clung on to his coat for dear life, and closed her eyes.

No, that was no good. The only way she could get through this was to keep her eyes fixed on his, and reassure herself that this was Lord Lensborough. The man who had rescued her. The man she had begun to trust.

She felt the warmth of his breath as he sighed. His arm snaked about her waist, drawing her closer to him. It was absurd, but as soon as she felt his arm round her, she relaxed. With his arms about her, she could face anything.

Then his lips were on hers.

And it was not so bad. Just Lord Lensborough, very close to her, that was all. He only applied a very gentle pressure on her mouth, tentatively tasting her. She sighed with relief. She had been an idiot to think he would roughly force his tongue between her teeth. Even her aunt had told her he would be a gentleman in this respect. Was this what she meant? That there was a different way of going about things than Lionel had led her to believe?

Then his mouth was not on hers any more. Instead, he was raining dozens of kisses on her nose, her cheek, along the line of her jaw. Kisses so light they were like butterfly wings skimming all over her face.

'Hester.' His voice was hoarse. A tremor ran through his big, powerful frame. 'I want to kiss every single one of your freckles.'

Her freckles? The laugh died on her lips as he drew her closer and kissed her mouth again. He held her so tightly that even through their clothes she could feel his arousal. He pushed his hips against her stomach, making her every bit as aware of his jutting masculinity as Lionel had ever done, and yet she was not afraid. On the contrary, the pressure of his mouth on hers, coupled with the security of having his arms wrapped tightly round her, was a bit like the sensation of floating in the tarn on a hot summer's day. She was surrounded by the alien element of his masculinity, yet her burgeoning trust in the man buoyed her up. A pleasant languor began to glide through her limbs.

She could bask in Lord Lensborough's kisses. Lionel's had made her feel as if she were drowning.

When he probed gently with his tongue, she responded by granting him the entry he sought, secure in the knowledge that she could refuse. Eventually, with a shuddering sigh, he pulled away, leaving her breathless and dazed that she had not even found that deeply intrusive kiss unpleasant. She had even fleetingly wondered, when his tongue had stroked the roof of her mouth, what it might be like to taste him in turn.

'Come.' His voice harsh, Lord Lensborough turned abruptly away as she touched her hand to her lips in wonder.

When he went to sit on one of the logs left round the ashes of a camp fire, Hester wondered what she could have done to put that scowl on his face. Feeling suddenly very vulnerable without the warmth of his arm about her waist, she followed him as if tugged by an invisible leash.

When she sat next to him, he jerked his leg away from the

brush of her skirts. Her heart sank. She knew she had done something wrong.

She hung her head to hide her burning cheeks. From the very first, Lionel had accused her of leading him on, of teasing him, though she had no idea she was doing so. Perhaps something about the way she kissed had made Lord Lensborough draw the same conclusion.

'After that,' she heard Lord Lensborough say, 'I think you should use my given name, don't you?'

And in the coach, she had lain there, permitting him all sorts of liberties. Had she only been fooling herself that she had to keep still, to lull him into a false sense of security?

'It is Jasper.'

Had she secretly enjoyed some of it? Was that why she had the nightmares? Not because she hated it, but because of guilt that deep down, so deep that she could not admit it openly, that sort of treatment was what she wanted?

Lord Lensborough sighed heavily. 'If there is anything about the arrangements that have been made you dislike, you have only to say, and they can be changed. I know you are shy—your aunt explained that you found your Season difficult. If you cannot face being paraded before the *ton*, we could just have a private ceremony somewhere, without fuss.'

She had to force herself to attend to what Lord Lensborough was asking.

This wedding was all about what others wished. She knew that his mother, Lady Augusta Challinor, wished to host a grand society event. From what Julia had said about her formidable godmother, it would be foolish to set her back up by declaring she would rather be married from The Holme, with Em's elderly father presiding over the ceremony. Besides, she knew how much her cousins and aunt were looking forward to going to London and mixing in circles they'd not previously had access to.

'I don't have strong feelings about it. I told you I never thought I would get married. I only hope your mother will not be too disappointed in me. I do not shine in company.'

'Hester…' he plucked her clenched fist from her lap and kissed her knuckles '…how could she be disappointed in you? You have persuaded me into matrimony, and will give her grandchildren. With a little grooming you will soon outshine society's accredited beauties.'

She snatched her hand away, sickened by the juxtaposition of the word applied to horses with the reminder that her primary function was to bear children. To think she had almost been seduced by his practised kisses, charmed by his honeyed words, when he had never raised his mind above the level of animals rutting in the field!

He frowned. 'Isn't there any way I can make this easier for you, Hester? Would it help to have a friend to stand with you? Shall we invite Miss Dean to come with us to London to act as your companion?'

Her resentment coiled and subsided. It was hard to keep her guard up against a man who kept on thinking of the very thing she would have wished for herself. He had even guessed she would like Strawberry with her before she'd mentioned it.

She wanted to go home. She needed to unravel her tangled thoughts in private, away from this irritating man who would keep turning her preconceived notions about him upside down. Who made her feel both safe, yet trapped, wanton and ashamed, and resentful and grateful all at the same time.

She leaped to her feet and strode away to capture Strawberry's trailing reins.

'We should not leave the horses standing in this cold.'

Lord Lensborough rose somewhat unsteadily to his feet. He had kissed her and she had melted. Oh, she had soon withdrawn into her customarily defensive position, poised to strike, but for a few glorious moments she had been his.

And look at her now, all fingers and thumbs as she tried to untangle the reins. Coming up behind her, he couldn't resist catching her round her tiny little waist and throwing her up into the saddle. She uttered a little shriek of surprise, but she did not spit venom at him.

No—she averted her head, trying to disguise her blushes by carefully arranging the skirts of her habit. Chuckling, he strode over to where Nero was nosing hopefully at a patch of frost-blackened grass.

She was shy, just as everyone had warned him. But he'd just proved that a passionate nature simmered beneath that prickly shell, just waiting for the right man to bring it to the boil.

He was not surprised when she became extremely busy over the next two days. She was afraid of being alone with him, thinking he might try to kiss her again.

Not that she was afraid of him, he was sure, but of her own response to him. He was more certain of it every time she blushed and looked away on the occasions they had to be in the same room. How hard it must be for her to admit she'd enjoyed kissing him, especially to herself. She had vowed she would never marry, and now here she was, darting puzzled little looks at him whenever she thought he was not aware of her.

But he would not gloat over clearing this first hurdle. He was not stupid enough to bruise her pride by pushing for further intimacies just to prove that he could. He laughed at himself. Who was he trying to fool? He dare not take Hester into his arms until they were safely wed. The longing that had ripped through him when she had melted into his embrace had shocked him with its intensity. He had never felt the slightest desire to experiment with al fresco sex before, but one kiss from Hester and it had been all he could do not to fling her to the ground and slake his raging need in her deliciously quivering body. He'd had to break off before he'd lost control.

* * *

His self-control was sorely tried when they finally set out, and they had to spend all day cooped up together. Stephen Farrar, who had decided he might as well make the most of Lord Lensborough's luxurious travelling coach to return to the metropolis, and Emily Dean were hopeless chaperons. They were so intent on quarrelling with each other, that the others might as well not have existed. By the end of the very first stage to London, his frustrating awareness of Hester, coupled with the constant bickering, left Lord Lensborough thunderously ill tempered.

The evening meal, though excellently prepared, was eaten in an atmosphere that was poisonous with simmering tension. So he ought not to have been surprised when Hester woke up at about two in the morning having a nightmare.

Her screams were so piercing they had him vaulting out of bed, across the landing and into her room without even a token thought to the propriety of what he was doing. They had several other occupants of the upper floor peering blearily out to see what was causing the commotion as well.

As soon as he burst through the door, she gave one inarticulate cry, and crossing the room, flung herself into his arms.

'What is it?' he urged, clasping her trembling form to his heart. She was damp with sweat, and the warm womanly scent of her filled his nostrils with every breath he took. He gritted his teeth. Nothing separated them but two flimsy articles of cotton nightwear.

'What happened?'

'N…nightmare.'

'Is that all?' He sighed with relief. The bed was stripped bare, the sheets and blankets scattered about the floor as though a fight had taken place.

'All?' She went rigid in his arms. For a terrible moment he thought it might be because she had noticed how rigid a certain part of his own anatomy had become.

'It t…took all my resolve to undress and lie in that b…bed,' she hiccupped, tears streaming down her face. 'And every time I closed my eyes I remembered what he said he was going t…to do to me once he got me into b…bed, and I kept telling myself it was not that inn, b…but I kept hearing v…voices drifting up from the t…tap room and smell…I could smell…' She stamped her bare foot in exasperation. 'All inns smell the same,' she wailed.

'Oh, sweetheart, I'm so sorry.' He pulled her as close as he dared and rocked her. 'I understand, but you're safe now. I will never permit anyone to hurt you or frighten you again.'

She wriggled closer, till every inch of her was plastered against every inch of him. Oh, Lord, how long would it be before she registered what their closeness was doing to his body?

'When I'm awake I know that,' she sniffed into his chest. 'But when I go to sleep, it all looms up and I can't push it away. I try, I really do, to fight him, but he's always too strong…too strong.' She began to sob quietly.

Behind him, he heard a delicate cough.

'Um, Lord Lensborough? Do you really think you should be in here like this?' Em's voice dripped acid.

'Hester had a nightmare. I am comforting her.'

'A nightmare.' A nightmare, the echo rolled down the corridor, the explanation satisfying the curiosity of the other wakened guests.

'Must we always have an audience every time we stop at an inn?' Lord Lensborough strode to the door, shutting it firmly on Em and anyone else who might still be lingering. Hester trotted after him, her hands scrabbling at his nightshirt.

'Don't go,' she begged. 'Don't leave me alone.'

He turned, gripped her shoulders and looked into her eyes. 'Hush, now,' he murmured, dropping a kiss on the crown of her tousled head. 'You know I cannot stay for more than a few more minutes. It is quite scandalous of me to be in here at all.'

'I don't care.' Hester wrapped her arms tightly round his waist. 'I won't be able to sleep again unless you hold me.'

He reached behind his back and grasped her wrists, peeling her off him with grim determination. 'You don't know what you are saying. I know you were frightened, but believe me, this is not the answer.'

He pushed her away from him before he lost his resolve. The invitation to stay, innocent though it was, was well nigh irresistible to a man in his condition. But if he did stay, she would soon discover he was little better than Snelgrove.

'Go, then.' She wrapped her arms about herself, and looked down at her bare toes.

'Hester,' he groaned. 'I—'

'Just get out,' she screamed.

She stalked to the door and opened it for him, her eyes still glued to her feet. Lord Lensborough went cold. She had finally realised what was going on under his nightshirt. She was disgusted with him. He'd said she could trust him, but his body had betrayed her. There was nothing he could say in his defence. When she most needed him to be kind and protective, he'd reacted to her with unbridled lust.

Defeated, he turned and left her room, flinching as he heard the sound of her dragging something heavy across the floor to wedge against the door she had slammed on him.

She emerged for breakfast the next morning with dark shadows under her eyes. She could not look him in the face. She accepted his hand into and out of the carriage, but withdrew it as swiftly as she could.

Lensborough cursed himself. In one unguarded moment he had undone all the progress he had made with her. She no longer trusted him.

She grew more withdrawn and brittle looking the nearer they drew to London, and he did not know how to undo the damage he had done. There was never an opportunity to speak frankly. She made absolutely certain they were never alone.

At least, he thought as they finally drew up outside his mother's Brook Street mansion, she had not broken off the engagement. He had a few weeks' grace before the wedding in which he could try to win back some of the trust his lust had so brutally shattered.

And she did look shattered. There was a blankness in her eyes when he presented her to his mother that made him uneasy. She did not even seem to register the coolness of his mother's reception. Swaying on her feet, she just mumbled, 'I wish to go to my room.'

'Yes, I think you better had,' Lady Augusta snapped. 'Clothilde!' A maid, who had clearly been expecting the summons, appeared and whisked her away.

Lady Augusta rounded on her son.

'Have you completely lost your senses? When you wrote and told me you had chosen Lady Hester Cuerden above her cousins, I assumed she must have improved since my last sight of her. But she has not. She is hopeless. Completely hopeless. You will be a laughing stock.'

'She is just tired after the journey, that is all. When she has recovered, you will see.'

'Tired? A lady of quality may look tired. That…that creature you brought in looked bedraggled.' She flung herself into an overstuffed chair. 'And how can she have got into such a state after a journey of only four days in a well sprung coach? May I remind you, you went into Yorkshire in search of healthy breeding stock? She looks as if a puff of wind would knock her over.'

Lord Lensborough was tight lipped as he replied, 'She has only recently recovered from an illness. She is not usually invalidish. The journey was…' The journey must have been torture for her. Why had he not considered how she might react to staying in one inn after another, little more than a week after Lionel's attempt to carry her off to one? He had planned his journey with more thought to his horses than he had to her. He had teams sent ahead to hostelries where he knew they would be well stabled, when he could as easily have arranged for them to stay at the houses of acquaintances on the way. Too late to think of that now. The damage was done.

'She always did have die-away airs,' his mother continued. 'And she blushes. She has no address whatever. I've even seen her run out of a ballroom in floods of tears, with everyone laughing at her.'

His frown deepened, but his mother went right on cataloguing Hester's deficiencies. 'And as for her complexion!'

'I like her freckles. And I do not care if she is not a social success.' He had promised he would not divulge anything about Lionel's attempted abduction. All he could do now was throw his mother off the scent. 'Wasn't the whole point of the exercise to choose a woman who would be the most offensive to all the other aspirants?'

His mother looked at him keenly. 'That's all very well, but this will be the mother of your children.'

'Hester adores children, and they respond to her admirably. I have observed her within her family circle, which you have not. She is, besides, an excellent housekeeper and an outstanding horsewoman. We shall do very well in our private life.' He bowed stiffly, then made for the door. 'I will be calling tomorrow to take her for a drive in the park. Good day.'

But the following day, when Lord Lensborough returned, he found the entire household in an uproar. In spite, his mother complained, of being shown to the very best guest room, at some time during the night Hester had left the comfort of her bed and disappeared.

'The servants searched the house from top to bottom. And where do you think we found her?'

Lord Lensborough had a pretty good idea.

'The upstairs maid found her curled up in the upstairs linen closet.'

'Not in the attics?' he ventured with a wry smile.

His mother frowned. 'The linen closet is part of the attics, yes. I just said so. As if that makes a difference.'

'And where is she now?'

'We put her in the nursery and locked the door. The doctor is with her now.'

'You put her in the nursery?' There were bars on the nursery window. His voice was dangerously quiet as he pointed out, 'She does not like doctors, Mother.'

'Doctor Fothergill has an excellent reputation for dealing with nervous complaints.'

'Are you trying to imply that Hester is some kind of lunatic?'

'Well, what else am I to think? She turns up on the doorstep in a daze, wanders about the house in the dead of night, frightening the servants by hiding in linen closets.'

'I entrusted her to your care.' Lord Lensborough spoke to his mother in a tone she had never heard before. The fury that blazed from his eyes blasted Lady Augusta's self-assurance to ashes. Pale and trembling, she dropped into the nearest chair. 'Be damned to propriety,' he swore as he stalked from the room. 'I'm taking her back with me to Challinor House.'

She jumped as the door slammed behind him, wondering if she had ever really known her son.

Chapter Fourteen

Lord Lensborough took the stairs to the nursery two at a time and went straight in without knocking.

Though the door he'd flung open bounced back off the nursery wall with a crash, the figure laid out upon the cot remained ominously still.

'What the hell have you done to her?'

Lord Lensborough stalked across the room, his eyes boring into the tall, frock-coated man who was hovering over Hester's prone body like a vulture.

'You must be the unfortunate fiancé, Lord Lensborough?' The doctor's smile of sympathy made his lordship want to smash his fist right into his mouth. A movement to one side made him aware for the first time that Hester had not been left utterly at the doctor's mercy. Em advanced on him, her fists clenched.

'I will never let you put her away in an asylum, you... you...monster!' Her eyes snapped with a fury as intense as his own. 'I will fight this injustice to the last breath in my body.'

He rounded on the doctor. 'Asylum? You have the audacity to suggest Lady Hester should be locked away?'

The doctor assumed an expression of oily condescension.

'In matters of this nature, a period of quiet, away from the hurly burly, can often effect a marked improvement.'

'Miss Dean,' Lensborough growled without removing his eyes from the doctor, 'kindly remove yourself from this room. What I am about to say to this quack will not be fit for your ears.'

Hearing the doctor referred to in terms she believed he fully deserved cooled Em's antagonism towards Lord Lensborough by several degrees. 'You will not let him sway your judgement?'

'This fool? As if I could take anything he said seriously.'

'I fully endorse your decision to remove the young lady from the room, my lord,' Doctor Fothergill remarked calmly as Em stalked from the room. 'Our discussion will touch on matters that are not fit for innocent ears.'

'What do you mean by that?'

'I have not reached my decision to recommend complete isolation for the patient lightly, my lord. Her mind is deeply agitated. Lady Challinor, your good lady mother, informed me that she has always been highly strung. Possibly the excitement of the impending nuptials with such an august person as yourself—'

'You are both making a lot of fuss over nothing.' There was no way he was going to betray Hester's confidence by relating what had happened to her to an oily specimen like this. 'She had a nightmare, went to fetch a glass of water, and, in a half-waking state, lost her way in a strange house. She had a suite of rooms at the very top of the house where she grew up.'

The doctor raised a hand and, in a condescending tone, said, 'Alas, if that were only all there was to the case. But you see, I had a lengthy chat with the patient. Although she was reluctant to confide in me at first.'

Lord Lensborough clenched his fists. Hester hated doctors, yet this man had clearly been foisted on her, then badgered her into saying heaven knew what.

'I have a way with ailments of this type.' The doctor gave a deprecating little laugh. 'It was not long before she came to regard me as a confidant. It is rather the same with Catholic persons, who unload their guilt on a father confessor.'

'Hester is not guilty of anything.'

'No, no, absolutely not. Given the nature of her sickness, I deemed it vital to establish that she is...' he lowered his tone, as if to prevent anyone else from overhearing '...*virgo intacta.*'

Lord Lensborough was not conscious of crossing the room. The next thing he knew, he had the doctor by the throat.

'My lord. Calm yourself.' Dr. Fothergill wheezed as his face turned slowly purple. 'The examination was all above board, after she was sedated...maid in attendance...entirely professional...'

He flung the doctor's body from him as though his very touch was a contaminant. 'Professional? You subject my betrothed to an intimate examination without my permission and you call that professional? I will see you ruined for this.'

The doctor's fingers were trembling as he straightened his cravat. 'I think not, my lord. The delusions she suffers from were of such a vile and explicit nature that I had no option but to see if there could be any substance to them. You would not wish to marry a woman who had really undergone the kind of experiences she was raving about.'

'Get out.'

'I assure you...'

'No! I assure you. If you do not remove your sorry carcass from this house immediately, I will throw you out. Through the window if necessary.'

The doctor walked calmly from the room. There was no point in arguing with clients as wealthy and influential as the marquis. If he wished to take a lunatic to wife, it was entirely his own business. He had been warned. He would just make sure the bill for this morning's consultation was a hefty one.

Lord Lensborough stood looking down at Hester for a few minutes in silence as he wrestled with his conscience.

'I'm sorry, sweetheart,' he said as he went to the fireplace and tugged the bell pull to summon her maid. 'I should not have left you here alone.'

He crouched down at her bedside, brushing a tendril of copper from her waxy forehead. 'I will take you back to Challinor House and we will be married by special licence.'

'Oh, no, you won't.' Em had crept back into the room unseen as soon as the doctor had vacated it. Like a lioness guarding her cub, she stalked across the floor.

'Hester is not going anywhere unless she wants to. You are not going to bundle her up like a parcel while she is insensible and stash her away in your house.'

'Miss Dean, I only wish to care for her.'

'She might not want you to care for her after this. She may not wish to marry you at all, let alone in some private ceremony as if you are ashamed of her.'

He bowed his head. Em was only voicing the fear he had been harbouring since that night he had gone to her room in the inn.

'You are right.'

'What?'

'I will wait until she wakes, and lay my case before her. I will abide by her decision. Whatever she decides.'

'Oh.' Deprived of fighting her corner, Em looked rather deflated.

A scratching at the door heralded the arrival of Clothilde, closely followed by his mother. He dismissed the maid. He had only intended to ask her to pack Hester's belongings, and accompany her mistress to Challinor House to attend to her needs.

He sent Em to fetch some tea for his mother with whom, he said darkly, he wished to have a private word.

'I entrusted her to your care,' he accused her as soon as they were alone. 'And what happens? You found her in distress, in need of help, and you inflicted some bully of a doctor on her, who wrings a confession from her of an event so painful she swore me to secrecy. He then proceeds to drug her and submit her to the most intrusive and inappropriate of examinations.' He got to his feet. 'I should have known you would be incapable of showing compassion. You have never cared for anything except appearances. Did you even weep for Bertram?'

Lady Augusta gasped, and groped her way blindly into a chair.

'What can you mean?' She ignored the hurtful, personal remarks, homing in instead on something that had shaken her almost as much. 'What event?'

He eyed her with distaste. 'Hester was forcibly abducted by a fortune hunter who thought to subdue her into marriage with threats of rape. He drugged her, and carried her to an inn where he planned to commit the crime. By a fortunate coincidence I happened to be there when they arrived, and was able to rescue her. Can you wonder that she has suffered nightmares since then? That she found the journey here almost unbearable? I will never forget her screams that first night when she woke and found herself in an inn, with memories of his threats crowding in on her.'

His mother's hand stole to her throat. 'If you were there, then it must have only happened…'

'Little more than a week ago. It is all still horribly fresh in her mind.'

'I had no idea.'

'Of course you didn't. Do you think she wanted such a tale noised abroad?'

'No.' She straightened and looked her son full in the face. 'No lady of quality would ever speak of it. No lady would recover her equilibrium all at once either. I accept that.'

His fury was replaced by a look of bitterness. 'It is a great pity your attitude has made it necessary for me to break Hester's confidence.'

She did not blink. 'It will go no further.'

He sat on a chair beside the narrow cot and took hold of Hester's limp hand. 'I will stay with her until she wakes.'

His mother fidgeted.

'I know it is improper, but after all she has gone through it is imperative I am the first person she sees when she wakes up. Do you understand?'

She said yes, but she did not fully understand what had come over her son until somewhat later that day.

It was about three in the afternoon when Hester stirred and opened her eyes, and Lady Augusta happened to be taking her turn to chaperon the couple. So she was the one privileged to witness the expression on her son's face when Hester smiled sweetly up at him and raised a hand to his cheek.

He was clearly afraid, yet hopeful. His breathing grew laboured and there was a sheen of moisture in his eyes. Lady Augusta stuffed a handkerchief to her mouth to stifle a sob.

Her son was in love!

She could never have foreseen this. She had always thought Jasper was the image of his cold, arrogant father, the man who had trampled on all her girlish dreams. She had thought it would be better for his future wife to go into the type of marriage he seemed to want with her eyes open. Someone as lowly as Julia Gregory, who would have felt the meteoric rise in her fortune and status sufficient compensation for being tied to a man who would hardly notice she existed. And she had the advantage of coming from a large and loving family, who would have made sure she never suffered the agonies of loneliness she had known as the fourth marchioness.

But if Jasper loved Hester—well, it changed everything.

She took a long look at her future daughter-in-law. She was nothing like the type of women with whom he usually conducted his *affaires*. She had no address, or dress sense. It would be a challenge, but she would do whatever it took to bring the girl up to snuff. She was not going to stand back and see the poor chit ripped to shreds by society's tabbies. Nor would she permit her to make a fool of herself, and, by extension, her son. With a decisive nod, she got up and quietly left the room.

Oblivious to anything but the fact that Hester was gazing up at him, Lord Lensborough drew her hand to his mouth and placed a kiss in her palm.

'How are you feeling?' His heart was pounding in his chest. She did not look as if she hated him. She had reached out to him. And she hadn't flinched when, desperate for one last contact, he had kissed the dear hand that she had laid against his jaw.

'Thirsty,' she croaked.

He splashed some water into a glass without letting go of her hand. When she tried to take the glass from him with an unsteady hand, he took the opportunity to slide his arm under her shoulders and hold it to her lips.

'You are trembling,' he said gruffly. 'You don't want to spill it.'

'So stupid of me,' she murmured, after taking a couple of sips. 'I feel so utterly exhausted.' She rested her head against his upper arm. It wasn't long before he realised that she was silent because she had gone back to sleep. Loath to break physical contact, he hitched his hip on to the edge of the bed, drawing her up against him till her head nestled more comfortably into the crook of his shoulder. From this position he had the advantage of being able to drop kisses into her hair.

All too soon, as far as he was concerned, she began to stir again. He braced himself for her reaction when she found he was as good as in bed with her, and her clad only in—he swallowed—that same damn nightdress she'd worn in the inn. It must have been extremely modest when it was new, but repeated washing and wearing had rendered it well-nigh transparent. It was no good—now she was waking, he would have to remove himself to the chair.

But when he began to inch away, Hester slid her arms round his waist.

'Please stay,' she whimpered. 'I don't want to wake up from this dream just yet.'

'Darling Hester, this is not a dream.' He tilted her sleep-flushed face to his by hooking one finger under her jaw. 'You are in my mother's house. Do you remember? She sent for a doctor.'

The rosiness deepened, as awareness of reality dawned. Then she frowned. 'If I am really in Brook Street, why are you here in bed with me? Why is there no chaperon with us?'

Startled, Lord Lensborough looked round the room and realised that for the first time that day, they had indeed been left utterly alone. He felt his own face grow hot as he swung his feet off the bed and removed to the bedside chair.

'I…' He cleared his throat. 'Can you ever forgive me?'

'Why?' Her eyes narrowed, though she made no move to hitch the covers up. 'What has happened?'

He tore his eyes away from the tantalising view of her rosy-peaked breasts thrusting against the filmy nightdress. 'The, er, doctor…' He couldn't bear to tell her what the doctor had done while she lay unconscious. It was almost exactly the scenario Snelgrove had planned for her. He tugged at his cravat. 'I want you in Challinor House where I can take care of you myself. I want to get a special licence and marry you tomorrow.'

'Tomorrow? But won't your mother be terribly upset? She has a lavish wedding planned.'

'I don't care. It is your welfare that concerns me.'

'You think I cannot cope with it. That I will let you down.' Her voice was flat. 'You are probably right.'

'You let *me* down?'

She plucked at the rumpled sheet that had slid to her waist when Lord Lensborough had pulled her into a reclining position, supported by his chest. 'I am so sorry for the way I behaved during the journey, and for being so silly when I got here. Please don't cancel all your mother's plans because of that. I'm fine here. Now I have had a good night's sleep, I will be able to be sensible, I promise. I won't embarrass you like this again.'

'Embarrassed? I wasn't...well...'

'Yes, you were. You were very kind in trying to hide it, but I could tell. I caused a scene in the inn.'

He shut his eyes in pain. She had detected his embarrassment, but not the source of it. How could he explain without making the whole sorry mess ten times worse?

She continued, 'I did my best not to have another nightmare.' Her eyes were luminous with unshed tears. 'I just dozed in a chair. I find that I'm less prone to nightmares if I'm sitting up. But I grew so tired, I daren't even let myself nod off in the coach, because, well, that was all part of it. Lionel...' She hung her head. 'I tried to make him think I was deeply asleep so that he wouldn't force me to drink any more, which meant I had to lie still on the seat with my eyes closed no matter what he did.' She swallowed, but before he could think what to say, she plunged on, 'I was so afraid that if I had another nightmare I might not be able to stop myself from running straight to your room and into your arms, and creating a real scandal. You see—' she looked at him directly '—I don't know how it is, but when you put your arms round me I feel as if nothing can hurt me. It was all I could think of, that time you came to my room.'

With a groan, he scooped her out of bed, blankets and all, and dragged her on to his lap.

'I didn't fully understand how difficult this has been for you.' He wrapped his arms tightly round her, while she...oh, heaven…she wound her arms round his neck and clung to him. 'Forgive me, Hester,' he breathed into her cheek. 'Say you forgive me for putting you through such torture.'

'Jasper,' she whispered against his neck. 'There is nothing to forgive. If not for you…'

'No, when you got here.' He gritted his teeth. 'That damned doctor.'

'Oh—' she shrugged '—him. He was just the same as all the others. Didn't believe a word I said. But then—' she laughed bitterly '—who would believe such an outrageous tale? You didn't. The men in the tap room didn't. You all just saw a wild-eyed woman raving hysterically about drugs and abduction. Then, of course, the doctor couldn't quite picture you as the hero coming to the rescue in the nick of time.'

'I? I didn't believe you? When was that?'

'I seem to recall, though my memory is a little hazy, of grovelling at your feet begging for help, and you looking at me as though I was a nasty smell getting up your nose. It wasn't until Lionel actually walked into the room that…' She shrugged. 'Is it so surprising that the doctor wanted to confine me in an asylum?'

'How can I ever make it up to you?' He felt like a worm. It was true. He had let her down in so many ways, assumed so many falsehoods regarding her morals. How could he ever make the half of it up to her? Even the half she knew about?

When he dared to look into her eyes, they were sparkling with mischief. 'Taking me for a ride…no…a gallop in the park might be a good place to start.'

'Galloping in the park is frowned on.'

'So, I should think, is cuddling your betrothed in her bedroom when she is in her nightgown.'

When he immediately made as if to release her, she clung to him still harder. 'No, please. I don't care if it is improper. Don't let me go. Not yet, please!'

She burrowed her face in his neck so she would not have to see if he disapproved. 'I can go through with all that you expect of me. Dressing up, and letting people stare at me and whispering about me and this wedding.' She shivered. 'I can even stay in that dreadful room with windows to a balcony that anyone could climb on to if they had half a mind, if sometimes you will just hold me like this.'

He stayed silent, though his breathing grew ragged. 'Are you disgusted with me?' she whispered. 'Is it wrong of me to want this?'

Lord Lensborough smoothed his hand over her hair, kissing the furrows on her forehead.

'You are such an innocent, Hester. You are just seeking comfort from me, aren't you?'

'Of course.' She looked up, bewildered.

He shifted slightly, thanking heaven that the wadded bedding tangled round her lower body prevented her from feeling his reaction to having her pressed so closely to him. He made a decision.

'Then how can it be wrong? You have been through so much, it is little enough to ask of me, that I hold you close, now and again. Once we are married,' he pointed out, 'you will have the right to draw comfort from my arms whenever you want.'

She sighed, a thoughtful expression on her face. It was something of a revelation to consider there might be anything positive about the married state. She could ask him to cuddle her like this whenever she wished. It might perhaps even go some way towards making up for the unpleasant duty he would expect her to endure beneath him in his bed.

When, much later, he managed to prise himself away with the intention of going home for the night, he found Stephen Farrar kicking his heels in one of the reception rooms.

'How is she?' Stephen was wearing riding clothes, and

Lord Lensborough recalled that he had arranged to go out with him much earlier in the day.

'Have you been here all day, my friend?'

Stephen shrugged one elegant shoulder. 'I had nothing better to do. Miss Dean has been keeping me company.'

Em scowled at him over her shoulder from the desk where she was writing what appeared to be a letter.

'I do apologise. I forgot our engagement to ride, in the light of, er…' He paused. 'And I am leaving now.'

'Then it is time I left too.' Stephen made his way to the desk and made quite a production of taking his leave of Miss Dean, insisting on kissing her hand several times in spite of her attempts to avoid the salutation.

'Must you persist,' Lord Lensborough said as they strolled along Brook Street, 'in tormenting Lady Hester's friend?'

'It is my only option,' he replied bitterly, 'since she despises me so heartily. She thinks I am a social butterfly, a parasite on the back of the honest working man, a useless ornament dangling from the bloated belly of an oppressive system, besides being a heartless womaniser, flitting from one frail blossom to the next, tossing them aside when I have drained them of their nectar.' He flung back his head and laughed. 'Yet the verbal duels I fight with Miss Dean make me feel alive in a way I have not done since I had to sell out of the regiment.'

Lord Lensborough eyed him keenly. 'Are you telling me you care for her?'

'What would be the point? She hates me and all I stand for. You have the devil's own luck,' Stephen said moodily. 'You snap your fingers and the woman you want falls at your feet. All Em can do, when I try to tell her how beautiful she is, is to draw herself up to her full height and spit fire at me.'

Lord Lensborough smiled reminiscently. 'The challenge to your manhood,' he said softly, 'is well-nigh irresistible, isn't it? To conquer a woman who is fully aware of all your faults, rather than having to evade the honeyed trap of harpies who just want to get their hands on your money.'

Stephen laughed. 'Perhaps you could give me some pointers.'

Lord Lensborough clapped his friend on the shoulder. Having finally discovered the perfect woman himself, he now believed every man had the right to experience the same satisfaction. 'You need a strategy,' he agreed. 'A plan so devious that she is left with no option but to surrender. Shall we discuss it over dinner at Challinor House?'

Chapter Fifteen

Hester knocked timidly on Lady Augusta's bedroom door, wondering how on earth she was going to face the dragon in her own lair.

She had been unkind enough to reduce Julia to tears at a rout party. Heaven knew how far she would go in the privacy of her own home. She would not cry, though. She was made of sterner stuff than Julia Gregory. Taking a deep breath, she lifted her chin and marched in.

'Hah!' Lady Augusta reared up from a bank of lace pillows and clapped her hands. 'That's the look you should cultivate. Go and look at yourself in the mirror, quick, before you lose it, that's right. You look every inch a marchioness with that haughty tilt to your chin.'

The opening salvo was so unexpected, Hester found herself meekly going to a cheval glass and examining her reflection.

'Now come and sit beside me.'

Bemused, Hester sat on the chair beside Lady Augusta's bed.

'A pity you favour your father in looks, rather than your mother, but you have potential.'

Hester forgot to feel offended by Lady Augusta's frankness. 'You knew my mother?'

'Oh, yes. *She* had a deal of backbone. She would never have let the tabbies rip at her the way you did during your Season. Why didn't you stick up for yourself?'

'I was afraid of losing my temper and offending someone, which might have blighted Henrietta's chances of a good match.'

'You can learn to turn aside insults without losing your temper.' She took a sip from her cup of chocolate. 'Your aunt was a fool to pitchfork you into society without schooling you how to survive.'

When Hester bristled, she added, 'Yes, I know she's a dear, but she's completely hen-witted. She should have told you that, if you once let them see a vulnerable spot they will not hesitate to tear you wide open.'

Hester swallowed. 'That's horrible. How can people take pleasure in being cruel to one another?'

Lady Augusta stared at her. 'Are you saying you would not enjoy giving some encroaching person a sharp set-down?'

'Not if it would hurt them.'

She sighed. 'I don't suppose you could refrain from blushing whenever some buck flirts with you?'

She groaned as Hester went red at the very idea of flirting. 'It is not so much what they say,' she defended herself. 'More the way they look at me.'

'Ah. Undressing you with their eyes.'

'Exactly.' Hester shifted uncomfortably in the chair as she admitted, 'All I can think about is escaping somewhere and covering myself up.'

'So why did you wear all those low-necked gowns?'

Hester shuddered. 'They were the fashion that year.'

'Well, this year, you will be a leader of fashion. You must choose styles you feel comfortable in, so that you can have the confidence to hold your head up in public. Others will ape whatever style you promote. In fact…' she tapped her chin with her index finger as she ran her eyes over Hester from top to toe and back '…I wouldn't be a bit surprised if red hair becomes all the rage, and silly ingenues begin to fake freckles with make-up.'

She set her cup down in its saucer with a click. 'We are not going to try to disguise any of your deficiencies, or apologise for them. You are the Marquis of Lensborough's choice, and his taste is impeccable. I will back you up, girl. If anyone tries to imply you lack in any way at all, you must look at them as you looked at me when you came in here. That should shrink their pretensions. And as for the men, why, just remember you are not some unprotected chit any more. If they offend you, they offend Lord Lensborough. No man has the right to look at you sideways now.'

Hester closed her eyes, savouring the vision of Lionel stretched out on the tavern floor, blood streaming from his nose.

'Now, what should you like to do today?' Hester came back to the present with a start. 'We cannot begin to do the rounds of people who matter until you're armed with a better wardrobe, naturally, so I should like to get you to my modiste as soon as you feel fit enough.'

Hester gave Lady Augusta a direct look. 'You are being so…' She sighed. 'That is, I thought you did not like me.'

'Let us say…' Lady Augusta smiled a secretive smile '…that now I know how things stand, I am looking forward to the challenge of launching you. I always have played to win with whatever cards fate has dealt me.'

Hester suddenly felt stifled. Lady Augusta was going to enjoy forcing people to accept her, but she did not know how she was going to endure being a pawn in her game. She had to get outside.

'I should like to call on some friends today, if you have no objection,' she said.

'Oh? Anybody I know?'

'I doubt it.' Hester briefly explained her connection to Mrs Parnell, and the nature of her work.

'Interesting.' Lady Augusta chewed on a roll slathered in honey, looking pensive. 'Charitable work...' She flapped a lace handkerchief at Hester as if shooing away a fly. 'Well, run along with you. I need to set wheels in motion if we are going to pull this off. Make sure you take your companion *and* one of the footmen. My carriage is at your disposal this morning. Wipe that mulish look off your face. Lensborough's betrothed does not walk anywhere.'

Hester had opened her mouth to protest, but decided it was pointless to attempt resistance over such a trifling matter. Having Lady Augusta on her side was daunting, but it would be worse to offend her, and have her revert to the frosty hostility she had demonstrated when she'd first arrived.

By the time she returned to the house in Brook Street later in the day, she was in a much healthier frame of mind. How could she grumble about her circumstances when there were women facing complete destitution not half a mile from her door?

Jasper had called while she was out, leaving a message to say he would take her riding early the next morning, if she felt up to it.

She bounced out of bed the next morning while it was still dark to pull on her riding habit. Escaping from the stultifying atmosphere of Brook Street to ride in the park with Jasper, even if they could only trot sedately side by side, sounded like a slice of heaven.

Clothilde came to tell her his lordship had arrived, and Hester dashed downstairs. Jasper had brought a sweet little bay mare for Em to ride while they were in town, and she had Strawberry.

'Good morning, Lady Hester, Miss Dean.' Stephen Farrar touched his crop to the brim of his hat as they came out of the front door.

Jasper pulled alongside her as soon as she was in the saddle. 'How are you?' he said quietly, leaning into her so that the others had little chance of overhearing.

'Glad to be on horseback, my...I...I mean, Jasper.'

He looked around at the cold and gloomy street with a grimace.

'It is a great pity we have to rise this early, but it's the only way to get a decent ride in London. If you want a gallop.'

'If?'

His stony face relaxed into a smile. 'It's the only way to start the day, isn't it? I feel heartily sorry for the fashionable folk who keep to their beds and only emerge when the park is crowded.'

The gatekeeper at the Grosvenor Gate Lodge tipped his hat as they went through, and they urged their horses into a trot. The only sounds were of the beat of hooves on turf, and the occasional protest of a bird they roused as they cantered beneath its misty roost. It was almost like being in the country.

Lord Lensborough led Hester to an open swathe of grass, she dug her heels into Strawberry's flank, and for a few minutes, she left all her cares behind in an exhilarating burst of speed.

When they reined in, in a little copse, Em and Stephen were nowhere to be seen.

Lord Lensborough laughed. 'We have lost our chaperons.'

'Should we go back and look for them?'

'Not yet.' He placed his hand on Strawberry's bridle when she would have turned. 'This may be our only chance to indulge in private conversation.'

'Is there something you particularly wished to say?'

'Yes. My offer to cancel my mother's plans and have a private ceremony still stands. We can put it about that I insisted on observing strict mourning for my brother.' It was hard to read the expression on his face, since it was shadowed by the overhanging branches. The only thing Hester knew was that it was unpleasantly dank under the trees. She shivered.

He was trying to put it kindly, but the truth was he thought she was not up to the rigours of a large society wedding. He had seen her stumbling her way through a private family ball. How would she cope in a glittering salon crowded with upward of three hundred people?

She manoeuvred Strawberry out into the open. 'Your mother is looking forward to hosting the event of the season. I do not wish to disappoint her, just when she seems to be thawing towards me.'

'And what of your wishes? I am trying…'

Hester flung up her head. Didn't he know that if he cancelled the showy wedding, everyone would know it was because he was ashamed of letting her out in public? So, he regretted the chivalrous impulse that made him propose to her instead of her cousins. She had never wanted to marry anyone at all.

'You know very well my wishes have nothing to do with this. Let your mother enjoy herself, then at least someone will get something out of this farce.'

Hester's heart was pounding as she waited for his response. He had never hesitated to roundly curse her before whenever she stepped out of line. She was staggered when he merely enquired politely how she planned to spend the rest of her day.

Darting him one nervous look, she told him, 'Your mother is taking me to her modiste.'

He looked at her quizzically. 'You make it sound like some form of punishment.'

'It will be.' She flung her chin up. 'I hate being measured and fussed and prodded about.'

After a slight pause, he said, 'I confess, I spend as little time as possible under the tailor's hands myself.'

She looked at the elegant cut of his coat, running her eyes down the length of his snugly fitting breeches to his immaculate boots, and quirked her brow at him.

'Ah, riding clothes.' He was smiling now. 'That is a different matter entirely.' He ran his eyes over her own outfit, and as he took his time perusing every detail, from the feather that drooped over the brim of her hat, to the well-worn gloves that she had brought from Yorkshire, Hester felt herself deflating.

'I won't mind if you do not shine in society, you do understand that, don't you?' His tone was clipped.

Hester understood only too well. No amount of expensive clothing was going to make her halfway presentable. He expected her to be a complete disaster. She bit her lower lip.

'I don't normally spend a lot of time in London anyway,' he continued. 'My life revolves around the racing calendar. Luckily I have estates convenient for all the major fixtures and I roam between them like a gypsy.' He swore. 'Hester, I'm sorry, that was a tactless thing to say.'

She smiled sadly. There was no tactful way to inform your bride that you were going to stash her away from the public glare so that she could not show you up.

'Do you wish me to…live like a gypsy? Or would you rather I settled in one of your many homes?'

He wanted her to be with him. He wanted to show her his racing stud, to be at his side cheering on the winners they would train together. But would she want to be dragged all over the countryside? He did not want to exert undue pressure on her.

'You must make your own choice, of course.'

Hester nodded. He didn't really care what she did, as long as she didn't curtail his activities. She was surprised at how much this hurt, but she was determined to show him she could be reasonable. She leaned forward and patted Strawberry's neck. 'So long as I have Strawberry to ride, I will cope with whatever you require of me.'

Jasper frowned. This outing was not going at all to plan. He had wanted to reassure her that he would not ride roughshod over her feelings any more. All he appeared to have done was remind her that he had virtually forced her into marriage when she had vowed all her life to remain single. He had then further offended her with that oblique reference to her illegitimate niece—he was at point non plus.

'We had better find our chaperons before they do each other serious harm.' He sighed, turning back to the bridle way.

Tears sprang to Hester's eyes when she registered the stiff set of his back as he trotted away. She had, after her initial flare of temper, told him she would go along with whatever he would prefer, but it had not been enough. She could hardly blame him. She had behaved extremely badly from the first moment they met, and he must be heartily sick of her tantrums.

Wiping her cheek with the back of her hand, she trotted after him. She did not want him to think ill of her. After all he had done for her, rescuing her from Lionel, she wanted to be able at the very least to—she gulped back a sob—prove that she would never let him down.

It was only this determination to earn his approval that kept Hester calm through the session at Madame Pichot's later that day. The modiste was delighted with Lady Augusta's pronouncement that Hester was going to pioneer an entirely new look, and had immediately begun to circle her, eyes narrowed, pulling at her arms and pinching at her waist. While Hester preserved a stoic silence, Lady Augusta and Madame Pichot between them settled it all.

'We've had enough of ostentatious display, don't you think? Hester must look different, chaste.'

'Ah, like the goddess Diana, perhaps?' Madame Pichot draped a length of shot silk over her shoulders, and twisted her hair off her face. 'A variation on the classical theme—the gown will drape like so, disguising the bony shoulders. And with that hair, all her gowns must be bronze and gold, never white. She will stand out from all the other young ladies. Perhaps greens for the evenings to bring out the eyes.'

She then sat mute while a skilful *friseur* suppressed her unruly mane with plaits of bronze velvet. 'Always bind it close to the head, like so,' he instructed Clothilde, who would have to recreate the look each day. 'So that the delicate bones of the face will no longer be overshadowed. And the length of it, ah, we will leave these magnificent tresses to cascade down her back.'

It took Clothilde well over an hour each morning to maintain the glossily pomaded ringlets to Lady Augusta's satisfaction, but if that was what it took to look the part for Jasper, then she would endure it. She was determined not to let him down by the way she looked or the way she behaved.

Hester was amazed at the amount of accessories Lady Augusta informed her she needed to convince the *ton* that she was fit to marry Jasper. They spent a large part of every day purchasing hats, gloves, boots and slippers in shades to match each gown that came from the modiste, not to mention numerous lengths of corded hair ribbon, petticoats, stockings and fans.

And then people began to return to London. Word quickly got about that the Marquis of Lensborough had become engaged, during a Christmas house party, to a complete unknown, and her drawing room filled with morning callers.

'I must say,' she observed one afternoon to Em, as they were unwrapping the latest delivery from the milliners, 'that there are far more people about with a social conscience than when I last came to London. So many people have invited me to attend fund-raising ventures.'

Em sniggered. 'Naturally, people will go to any lengths to be able to say they rub shoulders with a marchioness, even so far as to pretend an interest in the poor.'

'Oh, surely not.'

'Don't be so naïve. People want position in this world far more than they regard their ultimate station in the next.'

Hester lowered her new green shako-style bonnet back into its delicate shroud of tissue paper sadly. Why hadn't she seen it? She had been quick enough to inform Jasper that people would curry favour with him by supporting a charity he fronted. She sighed. It was so hard to think that she now inhabited the same lofty sphere as he.

'And then, of course, the way Lady Augusta makes out you are some kind of a saint. How you don't have a mercenary bone in your body, and how pleased she is that her son has found such a *worthy* woman to share his life, how you are simply *dedicated* to good works.'

In mock-anger, Hester flung a pair of gloves at her friend.

'I expect she only said it as a riposte to someone foolish enough to make a disparaging remark about my appearance.'

'Now you come to mention it, I do seem to remember her launching her paean of praise by saying that a girl who will become mother to the next marquis needs to be a deal more than a mere adornment on her husband's arm. That it was un-doubtedly your ingrained virtue that captivated her son.'

'What an absolute plumper. Jasper has never been capti-vated by anything about me at all.' She laughed, but even she could hear how forced her laughter sounded.

Far from being captivated, it seemed that the more he saw of her, the less he liked what he saw. Oh, he was never unkind enough to speak harshly to her. It was just that he had taken to looking at her, whenever their paths crossed in public, as if he was poised to leap into action should she misbehave.

Even when they did manage to snatch a few minutes of conversation, during their early morning rides, he kept to im-personal topics such as horses, or the need for reform, or his progress with setting up a fund for dependents of Bertram's regiment. The more he opened his mind to her, the more she admired him, and the more despondent she grew. What could a man as fine as this possibly find to admire in a girl like her?

Conversely, Lady Augusta was all sweetness and light to her, particularly once she agreed to leave all the wedding arrangements in her hands, whilst simultaneously breathing fire over anyone foolhardy enough to voice any criticism of her future daughter-in-law whatever. Moreover, she plied Hester with all sorts of little tips to get her through the sort of situations that had been her downfall during her Season. She must never hang her head. Instead, if a person began to make her uncomfortable, she must look just beyond their shoulder, as if there was something or someone of greater interest standing just behind them. And employ the tight little smile she spent hours practising in front of a mirror, to signify she was bored.

'You are a success!' Lady Augusta eventually declared. It was true that wherever she went, people went into raptures about Lord Lensborough's refreshingly different betrothed. The adulation should have made her happy, but it couldn't. Not when Jasper was growing more remote from her with every day that passed.

'In time for the first ball of the Season.' Lady Augusta patted her cheek fondly as she swept into the nursery, where Hester had elected to stay after that first, disastrous, sleepless night in Brook Street.

'Now, don't worry. The ball to celebrate your marriage will still be the event of the Season. There is no harm in permitting the Countess of Walton to open it. The Earl is not a person I wish to offend, since his half-brother is a particular friend of Jasper's. Besides, there is no point in making matters worse for his poor little French bride by upstaging her. Turn around.'

Hester meekly twirled, the fluid silk of her apple green gown billowing to reveal a pair of sandals that were a delicate tracery of the softest ivory kid. Though her arms were bare from the shoulders, she did not feel exposed, since a pair of emerald-studded clasps fixed the softly pleated drapes that sheathed her entire torso.

'Charming. You look as though you had stepped down from the Elgin Marbles and come to life.' Lady Augusta beamed at her. 'Now, don't forget, when a gentleman asks you to dance, you must appear to consult me. If you do not like him, you will give me the signal.'

Hester pulled at one of the struts of her fan with her left hand.

'That's it. Then I will know to shake my head. Provided, of course, that he is not one of the very few gentlemen you may not risk offending. Then you must employ the other weapons in your armoury.'

The smile, and the vacant stare. Hester stood a little straighter. A few people might conclude she was haughty, but Lady Augusta had said haughtiness was a trait that no member of the *ton* would decry. And nobody could unsettle her by attempting to peer down her cleavage, since she was covered from the neck down. She might be able to get through this night without making a fool of herself, and letting Jasper down, after all.

After Lady Augusta left to finish her own *toilette*, Hester went to see how soon Em would be ready.

Em was examining herself in a full-length mirror with a critical eye. The pale blue of her gown, combined with her almost flaxen-blond hair, would have given an angelic quality to her looks, were it not for the scowl that darkened her features.

'You should not have wasted your money on clothes for me, Hester,' she said with some asperity when she saw Hester's reflection join hers.

'What else can I spend it on? Jasper insists on paying all my bills. It is the least I can do to see you get a pretty gown or two out of this trip to London.'

'It is a pretty gown, isn't it?' Em ran her hand lovingly over the watered silk. 'But the money could have been better spent on the poor.' She half-turned, in order to better admire her demi-train, which was liberally sprinkled with sequins.

Hester sighed as she compared their two reflections. She felt like a ginger beanpole beside Em's curvaceous blond beauty. 'I wouldn't care how much money I spent on a gown if, when Jasper saw me in it, he thought I looked pretty.'

'I know what you mean.' Em sighed. Then, colouring slightly, she added, 'That is, I cannot help noticing that your feelings towards him have undergone quite a reversal.'

Hester agreed. 'I am quite reconciled to the prospect of marrying him now.'

'Oh, but surely..?' She gave Hester a strange look. 'Never mind. We had better go down. Lady Augusta must be champing at the bit by now.'

They had arranged to meet Lord Lensborough at Walton House. As they passed along the receiving line, Hester scanned the crowd eagerly for the first glimpse of his craggy profile. He always stood out amongst the glittering crowds in his stark black clothes.

Ah! There he was. Talking with a somewhat shorter man who... Hester gasped and her step faltered when the man turned to take a drink from a passing waiter. Though a heavy fringe hung over his brows, it could not conceal the way his left eyelid drooped into the ravages of what might once have been a handsome face.

'My dear.' Hester became aware that Jasper was observing her reaction to his companion. Her heart sank. His face might have been carved in granite, so devoid of welcome was it.

She made her curtsy, dipping her head to hide her disappointment. Why couldn't she quash the foolish hope that would keep on bubbling up, only to burst at the reality of Jasper's indifference to her? Dimly she was aware of being introduced to his acquaintance, Captain Fawley.

Hester forgot all about her own stupid hopes when she saw

that the hand that protruded from Captain Fawley's left sleeve was made of wood. His face twisted into a lop-sided grimace. 'Don't expect me to ask you to dance.' He rapped his left leg through the pantaloons he was wearing. 'Haven't learned how with this peg, yet.'

'I don't care for dancing, to tell you the truth.' Hester smiled at him. 'In fact, I would be grateful if you would engage to sit one out with me later on.' She held out her dance card and hinted, 'I particularly dislike the waltz.'

'Then consider yourself rescued from it.' His smile was genuine as he marked her card.

'That was well done,' Jasper murmured, taking her by the elbow and steering her through the crowd. 'If more women were as gracious as you, Fawley might not have sunk into the state he got in last summer.'

Hester felt as if her heart had grown wings. She had finally done something he approved of. So flustered was she that she did not notice he was steering her on to the dance floor until he said, 'I know you do not care for the waltz, but perhaps you would make an exception just this once?'

His arm snaked round her waist, and Hester was so happy that it didn't occur to her to object. Even when the music started, and Jasper began to move her about the floor, her euphoric state did not diminish. And before much longer, she realised that for the first time in her life she was truly dancing. She did not have to force her feet to mark time with the orchestra. There was no sense of being compelled to do something against her will. The two of them were moving as though they were one. She didn't want the music to end. She wanted to carry on dancing, held secure in Jasper's arms, until she dropped to the ground from sheer exhaustion. Nor did she want Jasper to let her go even then. She never wanted him to let her go. She wanted him to fold her closer, to crush her against his chest.

She looked up, startled, to find the music had stopped, and Jasper was frowning down at her.

'Was it so bad?' He took her arm, and calm as you please, escorted her to the chairs that ringed the dance floor.

'No.' Her voice was dull with disappointment that it was over, and Jasper had emerged completely unaffected. 'Not so bad at all.'

She sat beside Lady Augusta during the next set, to give herself time to pull herself together. And reflect. Dancing could be enjoyable when your partner was someone you trusted. What she had always hated, even more than the physical contact, had been the feeling of being in another person's power while they were propelling her about the room. Why didn't other women feel like that? Em certainly did not look as though she felt under Mr Farrar's power as he twirled her round. The look of lofty contempt on her face suggested that though she had agreed to dance with him, she was not, and never would be, any man's plaything.

At last it was supper time. Several couples took their loaded plates into the dimly lit conservatory, which lay beyond the dining room, but Jasper sat her beside Lady Augusta, and began to quiz her about the conversation she'd had with Captain Fawley during the second waltz.

She quartered a glazed cherry pastry with her fork and wondered how difficult it would be to detach Lord Lensborough from his mother, and lure him into the conservatory. Other couples were taking advantage of the secluded benches dotted amongst the thick foliage. How hard would it be to get him to put his arms about her again if she could persuade him to take her in there? Perhaps even to kiss her?

She stared glumly at her plate. Impossible. He had only kissed her that once to seal their betrothal. She watched Jasper dig his spoon into a dish of gooseberry fool. If he had wanted to kiss her again, he'd had plenty of opportunity. They went riding every morning, and invariably lost their chaperons, and all he did was talk about politics. It was not, she thought as he licked a dab of creamy dessert from his lips, that the kiss had been all that delicious. It was just that if he kissed her, then she would know that he liked her, and was not just tolerating her for the sake of his rigid sense of honour.

'Um, excuse me.' Hester tore her fascinated gaze from Jasper's mouth, to see Em hovering at the table.

'Would you mind coming with me to the ladies' withdrawing room for a moment?'

Hester leapt to her feet. She had to get away from Jasper, right now, before she yielded to the temptation to attempt something scandalous. Helping Em repair a torn flounce, or whatever it was her friend wanted from her, was exactly what she needed to be doing.

To Hester's surprise, Em did not make for the stairs, but darted instead into one of the rooms that led off the long corridor that led back to the ballroom. Once she had made sure nobody else was inside, she locked the door behind them and began to pace the floor, wringing her hands.

'Em? Whatever is the matter?'

She stopped pacing, and drew herself to her full height. 'I kissed Stephen. Or at least, he kissed me.'

'In the conservatory?' Hester found herself saying wistfully.

Em resumed her pacing. 'Yes. But he started it. I only kissed him back. And I slapped his face first, I promise you.'

'Well, of course you did.' Hester sank on to a sofa. 'You hate him.'

'No, I don't! I love him,' she wailed. 'I fell in love with him the first minute I clapped eyes on his smug, arrogant face.'

'But you quarrel with him...all the time.'

'Of course I do. Do you think I should have fallen at his feet the first time he asked me to go to bed with him? Laid my heart bare for him to trample on? He would have amused himself with me while he was staying at The Holme and left me without a backward glance.'

'Oh, Em, that's dreadful.'

'He can't now, though.' Em laughed, though her eyes were dark with pain. 'After I slapped him, he said he'd had enough of my temper. He called me a vixen, and held my arms behind my back so I couldn't hit him again. And then he *really* kissed me.' She swayed slightly. 'And soon I was kissing him back, and somehow we ended up flat out on a bench with him on top of me. Then Countess Walton and Captain Fawley walked in on us. I could see them over Stephen's shoulder, but I couldn't make him stop. Captain Fawley yanked him off me.'

'Goodness.' Hester was glad she had not done any luring into the conservatory after all, if that was how it ended.

'And then...' Em covered her face with her hands '...Stephen said there was no need to make a fuss, because we had just got engaged and got a bit carried away.'

'Engaged?'

Em looked up at her, her eyes gleaming with defiance. 'He's got to marry me now. He said so in front of witnesses. I'm not going to let him go.' Her face puckered. 'He must hate me. Whatever shall I do?'

If Stephen had only been toying with Em all along, the marriage was doomed. For one partner to love, hopelessly yearning for the other to love her back—a cold hand seemed to clutch at her heart. She was prophesying her own future. Jasper would never do more than tolerate her, while she... She gasped. Why had she never seen it before? She loved him!

When had that happened? She looked back over the weeks since she had met him. When hadn't he been at the forefront of her mind, goading her into all kinds of absurd behaviour? How could she have denied having such strong feelings for him?

Em's quiet sobbing brought Hester back to the present. 'I

think the best thing would be to go home.' She pulled a hand-kerchief from her reticule and handed it to Em. 'If you stay here, I will go and find Jasper.'

Em nodded, and Hester stepped into the corridor in a daze. When had she surrendered her own will so completely into his? At one time she would have taken charge of the situation herself. Now, all she could do was blindly run to him.

She could hear music. The dancing must have started again. She turned towards the ballroom, but before she had gone more than a few paces, someone came out of another of the side rooms, clapped his hand over her mouth, flung his arm round her waist, and pulled her backwards through the open door.

He smelled of stale brandy, and cigar fumes and sweat. Nausea roiled in her stomach as she recognised her assailant and she kicked out at his shins, wishing she was wearing boots rather than these stupid ineffectual little sandals.

Lionel turned her about effortlessly, using the weight of his body to pin her against the wall, his booted feet sliding between hers and spreading her legs apart.

'Now, now,' he taunted her. 'That's no way to greet such a dear…' he kissed her cheek '…close…' he pressed his lips against her neck '…friend.' He nudged the shoulder of her gown to one side and ran his tongue along her collarbone.

She went mad, writhing and twisting, but she could not break his hold.

'Don't you know your struggles only make me more excited?' Lionel gasped, pushing her legs farther apart. Hester froze when he ground his hips against her stomach, letting her feel exactly how excited he was.

'That's better. Much better.' His voice was guttural. 'Remember the promise I made you all those years ago? That I would come back and finish it?' He pushed his hips against her again.

Hester began to jerk violently. She knew it was useless. Lionel was much too strong, but she would fight him to the last breath in her body.

His arm tightened about her waist, making it hard to breathe, while the hand he held over her mouth crushed her lips into her teeth. Her head started to swim.

Suddenly, he eased the pressure, though he kept his hand over her mouth.

'That's not what I came for, Hetty. Much as I would like to, it won't get me what I need. And what's that, I hear you ask? Or you would ask if I let you speak. Would you like permission to speak, Hetty? If you can be a good girl, I could take my hand away from your mouth. Of course, you know what will happen if you scream, or try to escape, don't you?' He made a fist, running his knuckles over her cheek and down, down, over her left breast till it came to rest on her midriff. He ground it in, hard enough to show what he meant, though not hard enough to leave a bruise.

He took his hand off her mouth. She could taste blood. And she felt as if she was covered with a layer of slime. Her very lungs felt tainted from breathing in the smell of him. Her heart was hammering and her legs—dear heaven, she could still feel the imprint of his knees between hers.

He held her now only by the malice in his eyes. She dare not look away. Lord knew what he planned to do next. She had to be ready, she had to.

'Remember I could have just taken you, up against that wall, and put a stop to your fine marriage.' He wagged his index finger in her face. 'I only stopped because it suits me to let him have you. You are too much of a handful for me long term.' He leered.

'So what do you want? What is the point of this?' Hester managed to find her voice, though it was so hoarse she didn't sound like herself.

'Money. I need money. I told you that.' He looked annoyed. 'And you are going to give it to me.'

'Why should I?'

Lionel's eyes narrowed. 'To prevent me from telling everyone that, far from being a paragon of virtue, you are quite a dirty little slut. There are several gentlemen who would be delighted to hear that the fastidious Lord Lensborough has been made a laughing stock by a seasoned little temptress.'

Hester felt the blood drain from her face. 'I'm not…you can't…'

'Oh, but you are. And I can. Remember the summer house, Hetty?' When she whimpered, he said, 'Yes, I can see that you do. And the other times? What price Lord Lensborough's ignorance, Hetty? Shall we say, five thousand pounds to begin with?'

'I don't have that kind of money. And even if I did…'

'Oh, I can wait till you are married. It's only a week or so to the wedding now, isn't it? Just enough time for you to think of a way to wheedle it out of his lordship. Or persuade him to let you have control of your own funds. Your money, his money, I'm not fussy. So long as I get it.'

Hester sagged against the wall. 'I'll be in touch,' he flung at her as he left the room.

She sank to the floor, in the dark. Why had she ever believed she was safe? Lionel would stop at nothing to get what he wanted. He never had, and he never would. He would bleed her white.

And Jasper—she buried her face in her hands. If he found out… She whimpered with pain as she bit down on her already bruised lower lip. He would be disgusted with her. But that was not the worst part. Once her secret was out, he would look like a fool. Lady Augusta was parading her as a model of chastity, when all the time she was…

Blindly she groped her way to the door. The first thing she had to do was find him and tell him, not about this, but about

Em. They must get home, and then, in the solitude of the little room with bars on the windows, she would have to come up with a plan to save Jasper.

Chapter Sixteen

Although Jasper explained that Stephen had only forced the compromising situation on Em because he had fallen for her hard, and was finding it impossible to breach her defences, Hester seethed with resentment every time she caught a glimpse of her friend's strained features.

Why had he not just courted her honourably from the first? No. That was far too straightforward for a man. He had told her he wanted to sleep with her, making it impossible for Em to trust anything he said or did afterwards.

The carriage stopped, the footman opened the door and let down the steps, and Em shot into the house like a rabbit bolting down its hole.

Jasper helped Hester alight with rather more decorum, and smiled down at her.

'I think you are going to be occupied for some time helping Miss Dean accept the inevitable.'

Hester gazed up at him, knowing only his ignorance could keep that look of amused tolerance on his features. He would never smile at her like that again. Casting caution to the winds, she flung her arms round his waist and buried her face in his neckcloth. At once, though they were standing at the foot of the steps in full view of the coachman and several interested footmen, Jasper put his own arms about her.

She breathed in the scent of him, committing every muscular inch of him that pressed against her to memory, knowing this must be the last time she could savour the illusion of safety she had found in the solidity of his body.

For she could not marry him now. She could not in all conscience take his money and use it to buy Lionel's silence. Nor could she endure facing Jasper's contempt when the truth came out, loving him as she did. It would kill her.

Looking up into his dear, rugged features, she wondered if she dare ask for one last parting kiss. But as she searched his face, trying to garner the courage to snatch one last memory to take with her into the bleak future she must face without him, he groaned, 'I cannot take much more of this.'

And swooped, kissing her with all the ardour she craved. Hester opened her mouth, eagerly drinking in all of him, her own tongue tangling with his, her fingers clawing at the silk of his waistcoat as she tried to merge her whole being with his.

It was Jasper who drew back, shuddering.

'You must go inside now.' His voice was harsh, his breathing ragged. Firmly, he took her wrists and put her away from him. She was trembling. Her legs felt boneless. Her breasts ached to press up against the solid wall of his chest. Her back was cold now he had withdrawn his arms.

She was going to be cold and aching for ever. Aching for what she could never have.

Stifling a sob, she tore her hands out of his and pelted up the steps before she gave in to the mad desire to cling to him, to beg him to never let her go.

She dared not look back. She drove herself up the stairs and along the corridor to Em's room, where she heard herself telling her friend what she had just learned of Stephen's feelings, watching as tears of anguish turned to tears of joy.

At least some good had come from this visit to London. Em and Stephen had been able to sort out their misunderstandings. She shut the door of the nursery behind Clothilde some time later, battling a sense of envy that there was no barrier to their happiness. They loved each other.

She reached into the bottom drawer of the wardrobe for the bag she used to keep her knitting materials, and tipped the half-finished projects that were in it back into the drawer.

While Clothilde had helped her prepare for bed, she had accepted there was only one avenue open to her. Since she would never give in to blackmail, nor marry a man who despised her, she must return to her Uncle Thomas and fling herself on his mercy. He would help her find a way through this unholy mess.

She packed a few items necessary for overnight stops into the work bag and tied the lip shut. Then she sat on the edge of the low cot, balancing an upturned tray on her knees as a makeshift writing desk, tugged off her engagement ring and penned two letters.

I cannot marry you after all, she wrote to Jasper, then hesitated. There was nothing else she could bring herself to tell him. *I am sorry*, she finished, and wrapped the page round his ring. He would understand, in time, when Lionel realised she was not going to part with a penny, and unleashed his venom. The whole of London would know. But she would be far away, and would not have to suffer Jasper's contempt in person.

She addressed the second letter to Em. This one was much easier to write. She knew Em would not feel able to stay under Lady Augusta's roof once Hester had fled, so she gave her written authority to approach her man of business in the city, and take possession of the keys of Vosbey House. It was fully staffed, since the Gregorys had intended to stay there for Hester's wedding, and Stephen would look after her.

Now all she had to do was find her way back to Yorkshire.

The prospect would have terrified her if the alternative, staying and facing the music, was not so much worse.

Gripping her work bag tightly, she squared her shoulders and marched down the corridor to the back stairs.

Some two hours later, Evans knocked firmly on Lord Lensborough's chamber door.

'I am sorry, my lord, but there is a young lady who is most insistent…'

'Oh, for heaven's sake, get up!'

Lord Lensborough sat up, and blinked as Em marched into his room, advanced on his bed, and, to his valet's shock, snatched up his dressing gown and tossed it to him.

'I will, of course, if you will remove yourself from my room. I would hate to think what Stephen would say were he to find you here—'

'Oh, stop blathering, do,' she interrupted. 'I will wait downstairs, of course, but in the meantime, you had better read this.'

She flung a small packet on to the bed and stormed out.

A chill stole round his heart when he opened the packet, and his ring fell on to the quilt. He wasted no time in joining Em in the library.

'Well, what did she say? Why has she done it?' Em snatched the crumpled note from Jasper's nerveless fingers. 'Well, there's less in this than there was in mine.' She looked up at him. 'What are we going to do?'

Jasper gripped her shoulders and shook her. 'Don't you have any idea where she may have gone?'

'No.' Em shook her head. 'None.'

At that moment, Lensborough's butler opened the door and Stephen strode in.

'You.' He glared at Em, then at Jasper, who hastily removed his hands from her shoulders. 'What are you doing here? At this hour? With Lensborough in his dressing gown?'

'Oh, take a damper.' She shoved Hester's note into his chest. 'At least he went home to his own bed.' Her eyes raked his dishevelled appearance. He was still wearing evening dress, but his normally elegantly styled hair was now tousled, as though someone had spent hours running their fingers through it.

'Read the note, Stephen.' Jasper's voice was harsh, his face grim. 'It is from Hester. She's flown the coop.'

'Why?' Stephen scanned the note, unable to disguise his relief that Em had a valid excuse for being in Jasper's rooms, in his arms.

Jasper stared moodily down at his slippers. 'I should have seen it coming. She never wanted to marry me in the first place. I backed her into a corner. And ever since we've been in London my mother has manipulated her for her own spiteful ends. I only wonder she has put up with it all as long as she has.'

'You mean, you're going to let her go?'

Jasper straightened up. 'Never.'

'Has she much of a head start? Em, do you know where she has gone?'

'She can't have left more than a couple of hours ago. I couldn't get to sleep, you see, after…' Em's face went bright pink, and she risked a shy smile at Stephen.

He crossed the room, taking her hands in his, saying, 'Nor me, but go on.'

'I thought I would make myself some hot milk. I didn't want to wake the maid. And on the way past Hester's room, I saw a light under the door. I wondered if she might like a drink to help her sleep, too, so I went in, found both notes, and came straight here.'

'The content of Miss Dean's note suggests she intended leaving London altogether,' Jasper added.

'Then I'll go straight to the coaching offices and see what

information I can gather, while you get some clothes on and prepare for the chase.' Stephen grinned.

He was back before Jasper had finished the coffee and rolls his butler insisted he take 'to set him up for his early morning ride.'

'Found her trail. First place I looked. She got on the High Flyer, bound for Edinburgh, that left the Saracen's Head at eight o'clock.'

Jasper frowned. 'She's going back to Yorkshire.' What kind of state could she be in to put herself through the ordeal of travelling on the stage, alone, when the journey south had all but killed her?

'Come on, man.' Stephen clapped him on the shoulder. 'We can catch her before she even gets to Baldock on a pair of your horses.'

'And then what?' He tossed his napkin on to the table. 'Shall I drag her out of the coach in the yard? Or accost her in the public coffee room and demand an explanation? For the entertainment of every idle loafer within hearing?'

Hester would show no discretion when it came to defending herself, no matter who might be watching. 'She won't come quietly, believe me.' He only hoped she had not armed herself with a hat pin before leaving his mother's house. 'This is going to be nothing short of a forced abduction. And I give you fair warning, she can fight like a wildcat when she is cornered. Are you sure you want to come with me?'

Stephen's eyes lit up. 'This is going to be the biggest scandal to hit the *ton* this Season. Shouldn't wonder if it will be talked about for years. The merciless marquis abducting his reluctant bride. Wouldn't miss it for the world.'

'Isn't there any way you could keep it quiet?' Em laid her hand on Stephen's forearm. 'It's all very well for you to laugh, but Hester will never be able to hold her head up in public again.'

'Oh, all right.' He chucked her under her chin. 'We'll disguise ourselves as highwaymen and hold up the coach on Finchley Common. Kidnap her.'

'How will that help?'

'Because she is travelling under an assumed name.' He grinned. 'Emily Dean. So, as long as you show your face somewhere in public today, when the news of the kidnap of a girl called Emily from the Edinburgh stage gets out, nobody will connect it with any one of us.'

'Oh, but surely…' She turned towards Lord Lensborough, thinking he would never demean himself by sinking to such a course of action. But he was already on his feet.

'Nero and Jupiter are already saddled and waiting in the mews. Miss Dean, a footman will escort you home. You will tell my mother exactly what has happened so far. We must get Hester back to London before anyone finds out she has gone. Put it about that she is not receiving callers—come up with some excuse.'

'Nobody will be surprised to find Brook Street in an uproar today—' Em grinned '—not after what Stephen did at the ball last night.'

'Glad to be of service.' Stephen laughed.

Travelling on the public stage was a far cry from the luxury Hester had found in Jasper's coach, but she did not feel in the least bit nervous. Only cold. Cold to the marrow. She wondered that being squashed between a fat lady and a thin one did not have the effect of warming her, but only made her uncomfortable.

Every jab from the thin woman's elbows as they bounced over a pothole reminded her forcibly of some aspect of the life she had forfeited. How she would have enjoyed seeing how Jasper ran his racing stables. How she would have liked being mistress of the many houses he owned, and being patroness of the various charities that had sought her. Of how she had stood poised on the threshold of unlooked-for happiness, only to have the door slammed in her face.

Most of all, she would regret never becoming a mother. She had always loved children, even the raggedy urchins who swarmed round her in the tan, attempting to pick her pockets. She had dreaded submitting to the procedure by which she would have become a mother, but with Jasper… She heaved a sigh. Would it really have been so bad? If she could have persuaded him to keep his arms about her while he went about it, if she could have focused on his face… She shook her head. It was useless to speculate on that now. She would never have her own children, and that was that. She would never meet another man like Jasper. And nobody else could ever tempt her to consider matrimony again.

Man's nature being what it was, however, there would never be a lack of unwanted, neglected children on whom she could lavish her time and money. She would just have to—

A shot rang out and the coach juddered to a halt, flinging the thin lady into the lap of an American gentleman sitting opposite.

'Stand and deliver!' a hoarse voice rang out.

The thin lady screamed.

'Never fear,' the American drawled, putting her firmly back into her seat and reaching under his own for a case from which he took a pair of wicked-looking pistols. 'I never travel anywhere without these.'

'Are they loaded?' Hester asked.

'And primed,' he said with pride.

'Then kindly stop waving them about,' she snapped. 'Especially not in my direction.'

As if having her hopes dashed was not bad enough, Hester was now trapped in a coach with a maniac who was as likely to blow her head off as get a bullet anywhere near the highwaymen, who were most probably ex-soldiers with years of experience with firearms. She leaned across the fat woman and pulled the window down.

'…just high spirits,' she heard the coachman shout. 'But you gents have had your little bit of fun, so move out of my way. I have a schedule to keep.'

'And for the last time, I tell you to make your passengers get out so that we may rob them.'

Hester stiffened. The robber's voice sounded familiar. But it couldn't be. She stuck her head out of the window.

'Any fool can see you're not on the High Toby,' she heard the coachman say. 'Just look at those horses. Too distinctive by half. Plain, neat, nondescript bays is what you should have used, nor you shouldn't be waving silver-mounted Mantons in my face neither. Horse pistols is what real villains use.'

'Enough. I admit we may not have got all the details right, but we are in deadly earnest. I have reason to suspect there is a lady on that coach who must return to London with me at once.'

Hester shrank back into her seat. It was Jasper! And, by the sound of it, in a towering rage.

'Like that, is it?' She could still hear the argument drifting in through the open window. 'Well, what I say is, if the lady's come to her senses, and wants to go home, good luck to her. I've seen enough innocent country girls lured up to Lunnon and ruined by the likes of you.'

The American eyed Hester's reaction with glee. 'Never fear,' he repeated, 'I'll shoot the villain before he can lay a finger on you,' and thrust the pistols out of the window.

'He's not a villain,' Hester shouted, scrambling to her feet. 'He's my betrothed. Don't shoot him, don't shoot him.' Knocking the pistols to the floor, Hester flung herself out of the carriage.

'It's all right, coachman,' she shouted. 'I will go with him.'

The moment her feet hit the ground, Jasper wheeled his horse in her direction. His eyes glittering through the slits in the mask that covered his face, he leaned down and scooped her off the road and on to the saddle in front of him.

The thin lady tossed her bag out behind her, while the American shut the door with an audible snigger.

With a laugh, Stephen moved out of the road and the coach lumbered off, passengers craning their necks to watch as the so-called highwaymen cantered into the cover of the trees with their prize.

'I'll leave you two love-birds to sort out your differences, then.' Stephen saluted, and turned Jupiter back in the direction of London.

Jasper kept Nero facing into the trees, riding until they were well away from the main road before stopping in a small clearing.

'You got me out of the coach,' Hester said, 'because I did not want anyone shot. But you cannot make me go back to London with you.'

Hester flinched at the raw fury that blazed from his eyes as he pulled down the mask.

'All right, I suppose you could carry me back to London, but you c…cannot force me to marry you.'

'You think not?'

Something thrilled through her at the sensual menace she detected in those three quietly spoken words. He could do to her exactly what Lionel had threatened. Her pulse rate soared, yet part of her brain registered that she did not feel the slightest bit of the sick terror that Lionel inspired.

'Jasper,' she gasped, seizing the lapels of his coat. She felt as if she was drowning in the black depths of his eyes. She couldn't get her breath.

His mouth swooped down to capture hers, and pain lanced through her. She could never be his. She must not let him think she would yield. With a despairing cry, she wrenched her head round so that his kiss landed on her cheek.

With a feral growl, Jasper swung himself out of the saddle, pulling her down into his arms where he rained a barrage of scalding kisses on her cheeks, her ears, her neck; however she turned her head, he managed to brand some area of exposed skin with the heat of his passion.

Hester whimpered. If he carried on like this much longer, she would not be able to keep her arms rigidly at her sides. She clenched her fists on the almost overwhelming need to cling to him.

He pulled away from her so abruptly that she staggered back against the tree beneath which they stood. Her legs gave out from under her and she sank down into the leaf mould that littered the floor of the copse as he turned away from her.

'I thought,' he growled as he attached Nero's reins to a hazel bush, 'that you had overcome your aversion to me.'

'I had...I did...I...' Looking at the stiff set of his back, she knew she had wounded his pride. She couldn't bear it. None of this was his fault.

'I...love you!'

He whirled round, his fury redoubled. 'So much that you refuse to marry me. You shrink away from my kisses, when last night...' He took a faltering step towards her. 'Did I frighten you last night? Was I too ardent? Is that why you bolted?'

She shook her head. She couldn't let him think he was in any way to blame, but to tell him the awful truth... She buried her face in her hands. This was going to destroy her, but he had to hear it from her own lips. She owed him that much.

'You have done nothing wrong. It is me. That is, it is Lionel...'

'Has he been bothering you again? When? Why didn't you tell me?'

'Last night.' She lifted her face from her raised knees. 'Somehow he got into Walton House. He found me...he...'

Jasper closed the space between them in two powerful

strides and crouched down beside her. He wanted to take her in his arms and soothe her distress, for she was quivering from head to toe, but was afraid more manhandling would only add to it.

'He said that if I did not pay him five thousand pounds he would make sure everybody knows that I am not the paragon of virtue your mother proclaims you are going to marry. You would be a laughing stock. I could not let him do that to you.'

Jasper relaxed. She had been more concerned for his reputation than her own when Lionel had attempted to abduct her. Even now she seemed to think what happened that day could somehow damage him.

'I rescued you before he could carry through on his threats, Hester. Nothing happened. If he starts spreading rumours about that day, he will ruin only himself and make me look like a romantic hero.'

'This isn't about that.' Her voice was flat, her eyes bleak. 'It is about before.'

'Before?' A dreadful chill slithered down Jasper's spine.

'When we were children. He was a schoolfriend of Gerard's, and a relative of Em's, so he had the run of The Holme and the village during vacations. He was a horrid little boy. The sort who thought it great fun to drop beetles down the back of my dress or tip me out of the boat into the thickest patch of pond slime.'

Her eyes seemed huge in her pale face, and curiously blank as she continued, 'Gerard wouldn't listen when I complained. Said there was nothing more despicable than a tale bearer. Said he wouldn't let me go out with them if I did not try to get along with his friend. And since Lionel never did anything untoward when anyone was watching, it was always my word against his. So we waged our secret war out of Gerard's sight. The last time he came to stay, they were about seventeen, and I was just thirteen. He...' she gulped

'…he changed his tactics that summer. Instead of dropping beetles down my dress and pulling my hair, he would grab me when I least expected it, and kiss me. Horrible, wet, slimy kisses.' She shuddered at the memory. 'And Gerard…well, I hardly saw him at all. Most nights he would sneak out of the house after dark and go to the tavern, then lie abed till late nursing a sore head. One night I crept into Lionel's room and put a jar of slugs and snails that I had spent the afternoon collecting into his bed. All the wet, slimy repulsive things…'

Revulsion was coursing through Jasper's veins as Hester's tale unfolded, but he dare not interrupt. It was already costing her dearly to speak of her unhappiness.

'He came to my room. He was in his nightshirt and furious and drunk. I was pleased at how angry I'd made him. He said he wasn't going to spend the night picking snails out of his sheets. He said I must do it. I laughed and said make me. He swore, and yanked the covers off my bed. I grabbed them and we fought for a bit. I didn't scream. This was between us, nobody else, just the way it had always been.

'Suddenly he stopped. He was kneeling over me. And he said I could do what I liked, but he was sleeping right there, on clean sheets. And he just flopped down, and shut his eyes, and started to snore. Went out like a light. And I, well, it was my bed, and there was plenty of room, and I didn't see why I should give it up, so I just pulled up the covers and went to sleep myself.

'It's no use telling me I shouldn't have done it. I know that now. The point is, I didn't know it then. At school, we often got in together when it was really cold, and I had no notion of the difference between sharing a bed with another school-girl, and a young man.'

Jasper clenched his fists. She might not have known, but Lionel, at that age, most certainly did. Being drunk was no excuse. He had committed an unforgivable offence against his friend's innocent little sister.

'During the night we somehow curled up together. When I woke, I had my back to him and his arms were round me. It felt—I'm so sorry, Jasper—it was nice.' Her face was bright red, but she lifted her chin defiantly.

'My parents used to cuddle me when I was little, but since their death, nobody had held me. It felt like that. I felt warm, and cherished.'

Her voice turned bitter. 'Until he woke up. Then it changed. His hands were everywhere. He said now I was growing into a woman, I was getting woman's desires. He said I was a whore in the making and that my brother would be ashamed of me if he ever heard how I'd lured him into my bed. That one day I would get what I deserved.

'I was confused by his words, but they made me feel ashamed, and dirty. I knew I had done something wrong, but I didn't understand what it was.'

Jasper couldn't keep silent any longer. 'It wasn't your fault. You were an innocent. The wrong was all his.'

She held up her hand for him to be silent, and though it took an immense effort, he closed his mouth on the comfort he longed to give her.

'Then one day I got caught out in a storm and ran for shelter to the summer house. Though why, I shall never know. He said it was because I knew he was there, that I wanted him to see me in clothes so wet they were transparent, that I was a tease.' She shook her head, clearly still bewildered by her clever abuser's arguments.

'How could I have known he was there? I thought he was with Gerard, but then, why didn't I just go home? I couldn't have got any wetter.' Her shoulders drooped.

'Anyway, we were both there, and the rain was pounding on the roof, and I was shivering with cold. And he had some brandy. He'd been drinking it himself. I tasted it on his breath. And he was so strong. Far stronger than me. I couldn't do a thing to stop him.'

Jasper knelt in appalled silence, the only thing keeping him from crying out in anguish the memory that Dr. Fothergill had pronounced her a virgin. Whatever Lionel had done, whatever he was about to hear, he could at least be certain the cur had not fully raped her.

'He poured brandy down my throat till I thought I would drown in it. Then he pinned me to the floor, and described all the ways a man's body differs from a woman's, and all the ways a man can get pleasure from a woman's body although only one of them results in a woman having a baby. It seemed to go on for hours. And all the time he had his mouth to my ear, pouring his filthy words into my head, he was…' She shuddered. 'But at last, he got his pleasure, and he rolled off me. I staggered outside and was sick into the rhododendrons. He stood behind me, laughing while he did up his breeches. He said there was no point in telling anyone what had just happened, because there was no physical proof. It would be my word against his, just as it always was. Besides, it had been a week since he'd spent the night in my bed, and I hadn't complained then. And I reeked of brandy. He would say I was drunk, and egged him on, that he couldn't resist me. I ran back to the house with his taunts ringing in my ears. He was right. I couldn't tell anyone. I was as much to blame as he was. Besides, Aunt Susan was pregnant with Jenny at the time, and I didn't want to upset her.'

Jasper groaned. She would bear anything rather than distress anyone else. So she had needlessly borne the guilt of this horrific assault all these years.

'I was too scared to sleep in my room that night in case he came in and actually did any of the things he'd told me men like to do to women.' Her voice was strident now, as though she was forcing herself to come to yet another sticking point. How much more could there be? Jasper bowed his head, bracing himself for the worst.

'I took my quilt, and crept up to the attics to hide, and I burnt the dress he'd soiled in the grate. While it burnt, I prayed like I'd never prayed before that something would happen to stop him ever coming back to The Holme again. And it did. Gerard died.' She choked on a hysterical little sob. 'I…I killed him, Jasper. I prayed to the fire, and fire took Gerard. I…I am not the sort of woman any man should marry, especially not one like you. There is something evil in me…' she pressed her hands to her stomach '…something dark and destructive.'

He could not take any more. He gripped her shoulders and shook her. 'That's nonsense. Do you hear me? Nonsense. First of all, it was Lionel who assaulted you. And secondly, the fact Gerard died as he did was just a coincidence.'

He wasn't getting through to her. Her eyes were dark with horror in her pinched, white face. He reached inside himself.

'Listen to me. When my brother died, I felt that darkness that you have just described, inside me. Guilt that I was still alive, when he was dead.'

Her eyes turned towards his face at last, though they were still glazed with grief and guilt.

Ruthlessly he hauled her to her feet. 'And if you think for one minute that I am going to let you jilt me, because of something that happened six or seven years ago, you are very much mistaken. No Challinor has ever been jilted, and I am not about to be the first.'

'J…jilted?' Hester looked stricken. 'I'm not jilting you. Don't you see? I'm trying to spare you.'

'And how would making me look ridiculous spare me anything, you little fool?'

'At least you won't be married to a woman whose reputation is in tatters.'

'I won't be. Don't you think me capable of crushing a worm like Snelgrove? You should have just come and told me of this attempt at blackmail.'

She shook her head, closing her eyes. 'I couldn't. I never wanted to have to repeat any of this to anyone, least of all you. How you must despise me.'

'Despise you?'

Abruptly he let go of her shoulders. She thought he was angry with her. No wonder. He had been shouting, shaking her. 'I do not despise you.' He spoke through clenched teeth, keeping his tone as moderate as he could.

'But now you know,' she persisted, 'I've been living a lie for years. I am soiled, Jasper.'

He turned away and vented some of the fury at what Snelgrove had done to her by slashing at the bushes with his riding crop. Was there nothing he could do to root out the canker that the man had planted in her soul? She couldn't even bear to let him touch her any more.

Hearing the noise of skirts rustling, he turned to see Hester untying her bag from Nero's saddle.

'What do you think you are doing?'

'I'm going home. It's obvious you cannot marry me now you know it all.'

'Not to me it isn't.' He snatched the bag from her hand and tied it back to the pommel. 'Anyway, what good would it do to go back to your uncle? He won't be able to protect you. How long do you think it will be before Snelgrove makes another attempt on you? Do you want to fall into his hands like a ripe plum? For make no mistake, if you do not marry me, he will go after your inheritance again. Make your mind up, Hester. A lifetime running from Snelgrove, or a lifetime secure with me.'

'No, it wouldn't be like that.' She pressed her hand to her forehead. 'I can't think…'

'Then I will make the choice for you. You are not going to make a fool of me and make yourself miserable. You are marrying me and that's final.'

Mounting Nero, he yanked Hester up on to the saddle in front of him again.

'In fact, we are going to get married in the first church we come across today. I have been carrying a special licence about in my pocket since the day that damn fool doctor threatened to lock you away. Not he, nor Snelgrove, nor your own desire for martyrdom are going to stop this wedding going ahead.'

Hester quailed at his anger. He had only decided to marry her in the first place because Lionel had thrown them together, and now he felt obliged to carry it through rather than face the ridicule of being jilted. Or expose her to ridicule by crying off.

He was saving her from disgrace yet again. She wrapped her arms about his waist and buried her head in the crook of his shoulder. While he had to concentrate on picking a way through the dense undergrowth to get back to the road, he couldn't shake her off, no matter how disgusted with her he was.

Hester was amazed at how much money it took to push a clandestine wedding ceremony through. The vicar's scruples against runaway matches had to be overcome, witnesses had to be bought. She had never seen so much cash change hands on such a nefarious pretext.

It was well into the afternoon when she found herself being hauled out of the dank little church where Jasper had growled, and she had whispered, vows.

'That's it then.' He stopped in the lych gate and turned her roughly to face him. 'Legally you are my wife now. You can forget all your silly notions of running away and hiding from Snelgrove, and others like him, for the rest of your life, do you hear?' He grasped her chin in his hand and forced her face up.

'You don't have to fight your own battles any more. It is my duty to protect you.'

Tears filled Hester's eyes, though she tried to blink them away. He was furious that she had got him into this mess, but he would always do his duty by her. He would defend her. Supply every material need. But now he knew the worst of her, he would never respect her.

Jasper swore and let her go. No wonder she was crying. She had never wanted to marry anyone. And now he knew why. That devil had poisoned her mind, making her shiver with revulsion every time a man touched her.

He let go of her chin and drew back. 'We can't go back to London till morning,' he said, leading her back to the yew tree where Nero was tethered. 'We must spend the night at an out-of-way inn I happen to know of.' He boosted her into the saddle and mounted up behind.

'People are used to seeing us riding early in the park. Stephen will meet us there with Strawberry, and we will all simply ride up Brook Street as we have done so many times before.'

It was dark by the time they dismounted outside a ramshackle building. Hester was grateful when Jasper put his arm round her waist as they went in. This was so obviously the sort of low place men frequented in pursuit of illicit pleasure that Hester felt just as ashamed as if she was the sort of woman the smirking landlord assumed, rather than a legally married wife.

She felt slightly sick that this was the place Jasper had chosen to consummate their ill-fated union. But it was in keeping with all that had gone before. Everything about their relationship was second best. She was not at all the type of woman he had gone to The Holme seeking, and now he felt he had to go to extreme lengths to make sure she could not run away from him again.

Silent tears slid down her cheeks as the landlord led them up a rickety staircase to their rooms. It was not going to be pleasant to face the ordeal she had always dreaded while Jasper was so angry. She knew it would hurt. Lionel had told her that if he had taken her in the summer house, when she was still a girl and he a fully grown man, they would hear her screams in Beckforth square.

Hester blinked at the surprisingly clean little sitting room, at the table with supper laid out for two, and her stomach roiled. The landlord retreated and Jasper strode across to the door that led to the bedroom. Casually he tossed her bag on to the double bed, and stripped off his coat. Her mouth went dry.

'Have you eaten anything today?' he asked, strolling towards the supper table as if this was all perfectly common-place. It probably was to him. He'd probably had dozens of secret assignations.

'You should try to eat something.' He took a bread roll from the dish and tore it in two with his great, strong hands.

'I can't.' Hester shut her eyes, waves of nausea drenching her with sweat. She felt Jasper catch her as she swayed on her feet, pulling her into his chest and holding her tight. She could hear his heart thundering beneath his waistcoat. Or was it hers?

He untied the ribbon to her bonnet, reaching up to draw out the hat pin that secured it in place. 'I'll take this, I think,' he said, pocketing the hat pin and tossing the bonnet on to a chest of drawers.

She looked at the grim set of his face. 'I won't fight you, Jasper,' she vowed, as much to herself as to him. She had so little to offer him that she would not deny him the heirs that were the sole reason he had decided to marry at all.

'I'm not taking any chances.' He began to unbutton her coat. 'I've seen you in action, don't forget.'

'But I'm your wife now. It is your right.'

'You are shaking from head to toe, Hester. You don't know

whether to make a bid for freedom or a last-ditch attempt to protect your virtue.' His mouth twisted with scorn as he tugged her coat down her arms. 'I've cornered you, trapped you, and you want to lash out at me. You haven't understood yet that I'm nothing like Snelgrove. That I will never hurt or humiliate you.'

'Yes, I have,' she protested. 'Else I couldn't have fallen in love with you. I can't help being afraid. I don't want to be afraid with you. It's just that...'

Her eyes flashed with determination. Her hands went to the buttons at the neck of her gown. 'Never mind supper—I think we should just get on with it!'

As Jasper's eyes widened, her fingers managed to fumble about three buttons open.

'No.' He seized her wrists and halted her attempt to undress for him. 'It's not going to be like that. I'm your husband, not a rapist. Do you think I want to just take and give nothing in return?'

Hester was utterly bewildered by his reaction.

'Oh, God, Hester,' he breathed, pulling her into his arms. 'You think you know so much, but you know so little, and what you do know is warped.'

As he rocked her, stroking her hair, he felt her trembling gradually subside. When her arms slid tentatively round his waist, he sighed with relief. This was working. She needed plenty of reassurance. He would need a great deal of patience, but he was determined to teach her that a man need not defile a woman in order to get his own pleasure.

There was a knock on the door, and a couple of chambermaids came in with all the paraphernalia required for a bath.

'You have been shivering on and off ever since I got you off the coach,' he murmured into her hair. 'I ordered the bath for you. I thought it would help you get warm, and relaxed.'

'That was thoughtful of you, Jasper.' She looked up at him

sadly. 'But I don't think I will feel relaxed being undressed and knowing you are in the next room.'

'I won't be in the next room.' It had suddenly dawned on him that there could be no better way to teach her that a man's touch could be gentle, than to bathe her. He would handle every last square inch of her, and when he'd finished she would feel both cleansed, and cherished. 'I will be with you every step of the way.'

She stiffened. 'You can't mean to watch me?' Her eyes widened and a flush spread from her cheeks right down her neck. Jasper followed its progress with his fingers, opening the buttons that obstructed his view.

'Not just watch...' His mouth followed his fingers, planting gentle kisses in the cleft between her breasts as the dress fell open. He cradled her head to his shoulder as the dress fell to the floor. 'Don't be afraid of me.' His hand ran up and down her spine, stroking, soothing.

'I...I'm not afraid.' She wasn't lying. Her fears had dissipated the moment he'd pulled her into his arms. She couldn't be afraid of anything when he held her like that, not even his masculine desires. And at the first tentative brush of his knuckle against her breast, the blood had begun to run hot through her veins.

And when he'd kissed her—she had no words to describe what that felt like. On the two occasions he had kissed her mouth, she had found it pleasant. But to feel his mouth on her body...

Now Jasper was kneeling at her feet, unlacing her boots. When he raised her foot to tug the first one off, she almost overbalanced. He looked up, grinning when she hopped in a most ungainly fashion towards a chair, his hand still grasping her ankle.

'Give me your other foot,' he ordered, and she found herself bracing her bare foot against his shoulder while he tugged off the second boot. When she would have lowered her foot to the floor, he caught it, kissing the instep before sliding his hands up her raised leg to remove her stocking. It was just as well she was already sitting down.

'Now your petticoats,' he said eventually.

'No.' Somehow she found the willpower to force her boneless legs to take her weight. Tottering towards the bath, she said, 'I'll manage now, thank you.'

She couldn't just sit there and let him strip her naked. As soon as she was out of his sight, she tore off the rest of her underclothes. She had hardly sat down in the warm, rose-scented water, when Jasper approached, rolling up his shirt sleeves. He had already removed his waistcoat and cravat.

Feeling she would die of self-consciousness, she hugged her knees to her chest.

'If I had any compassion for your shyness, I would give you some privacy, is that what you are thinking?' He knelt down beside the tub.

She nodded, her eyes watching him warily as he picked up the cake of soap.

'Well, I don't.' He dipped his hands into the water behind her, and began to work up a lather. 'You need to learn…' His voice trailed away as their eyes met, and held. He couldn't remember what he had been about to say. He just needed to get his hands on her.

She couldn't believe how gentle his hands were on her back. He massaged the bunched muscles at her shoulders and neck first, sweeping the length of her spine with firm, sure strokes. Was this what a cat felt like when stroked? She certainly wanted to arch into his caress. And purr.

Shame engulfed her when his warm breath feathered down behind her knees, and her nipples contracted in a painfully pleasurable response. She wasn't supposed to feel like this. She was completely naked, completely at his mercy, and she ought to be afraid, repelled.

With a groan, she hid her face in her knees. He took her right hand, peeling her arm from round her knees, slowly running his freshly soaped hand the full length of it. When he got to her fingers, he soaped between them, interlacing his own fingers with hers, and drawing her hand to rest on the rim of the tub. Then he reached for her left arm.

She kept her knees tucked up to her chin while he methodically washed her, raising her face to watch him when he moved to the foot of the bath. He was kneeling facing her as he reached below the water line and gently grasped her foot. She gripped the edges of the bath tightly as he drew it out of the water, knowing her left breast would be exposed to his gaze as he extended her leg.

She couldn't take her eyes off his face, as he worked soapy fingers over and in between every single toe before rubbing the arch of her foot with his thumbs. He looked totally absorbed in what he was doing, concentrating his dark gaze on whichever part of her leg he was caressing, kneading, learning. She slid lower in the water as his hands worked their way inexorably higher, tensing as his knuckles brushed the place where she most feared a man's touch.

But then he ran his hands down the length of her leg, propping her ankle on the rim of the bath as he soaped his hands again. When he reached into the water for her right foot, she gasped as a shocking thrill of anticipation shot through her. He was going to repeat the whole delicious process all over again, and this time, because of the way he had positioned her foot, her legs were sprawled indecorously apart, making her throbbingly aware of his ultimate destination.

She made no move to resist him, or alter the way he had positioned her limbs. She was boneless, mindless, just a piece of clay for him to mould however he saw fit. Again he teased her with a touch that was not quite there, before releasing her leg. She stirred impatiently as he slowly soaped his hands yet again, her lips parting as he leaned over her to draw aside a ringlet that curled around her left nipple. When he kissed it, before gently draping it over her shoulder, she had to fight down a very strong urge to pull his head down to her breast, so she could feel his mouth there.

But when he slid his soap-slick hands down her flanks, she could keep still no longer. She found her waist flexed first one way, then the other as his hands swept round and over the clenched muscles of her stomach, and up her rib cage. She bit down hard on the urge to cry out when at last he cupped her breasts, but she could not stop herself wrapping her arms round his neck, and burying her face in his shoulder. She just clung to him, panting, as he kept on caressing, kneading, stoking the fires that were banked in her belly higher and higher.

'Jasper,' she breathed, turning her face up to his, her mouth blindly seeking his, opening to him as one hand slid beneath the waterline. She was on fire. Her blood pounded through her veins, making her restless for something, for more.

And then Jasper's knowing fingers were giving her what she hadn't known she craved. She clung to him, moaning as he rotated the heel of his hand against the juncture of her thighs, stoking the craving to a furnace of need. When he slid one soaped finger gently inside her, she instinctively clamped her thighs together against the intrusion, her eyes flying open in shock. But the action only intensified the pleasure, and he kept up the gentle, insistent pressure, until she found herself bucking up against his hand, and finally arching up almost out of the water as something like a lightning bolt of bliss streaked from the pit of her stomach to the tip of her toes. Then every muscle in her body went completely slack. She was as limp as a rag doll when Jasper lifted her out of the water, wrapped her in a huge bath sheet, and settled her on his lap, with a rather smug grin on his face.

Dreamily she gazed back as he patted her dry.

'I've ruined your shirt,' she observed. It was soap-stained and sopping wet from when she had clung to him in rapture. She wondered how he had known he could make her feel like this.

Some of her pleasure in the moment ebbed away as she worked out how he must have gained this sort of expertise.

Jasper saw the troubled expression return to her eyes and knew that he must not push her any more tonight. She truly did love him. He had thought she had just mouthed the words to soften the blow of rejection. But she could not have manufactured the trust that blazed from her eyes as she yielded to him, like a flower unfurling her petals to the sun.

She loved him. The truth of it was in her amazing, at first hesitant, then finally rapturous response. His own arousal was ferocious, but he dare not slake it. It would shatter her trust if he pinned her to that bed and degraded her beautiful moment of sexual awakening by ending it with a few minutes' savage rutting.

Especially, he did not want to consummate their union here. He did not want her waking up to nightmares in the future, in which his face, his actions, were muddled with Snelgrove's by association with low taverns. When they came together, it would be in more fitting surroundings. Snelgrove and all he stood for must be utterly expunged in an experience so wondrous it would be like a holy sacrament.

He got up, walked with her in his arms to the bedroom and deposited her on a chair. Deliberately turning his back on her, he pulled her nightgown from her bag.

'You'd better put this on,' he said sternly.

Wondering what she had done wrong, Hester covered herself up while Jasper pulled back the bedclothes.

'Get in,' he ordered, and she obeyed, sliding down against the linen, amazed at how good her freshly washed, newly awakened body felt.

And it was all thanks to him. In the space of a few minutes, he had shattered the bonds that Lionel had bound her with all those years ago.

With her heart full of love, she watched as he got ready for bed. His torso was quite the most beautiful sight she had ever seen. It was strange to consider a man beautiful, to regard muscular arms, a tapering waist, even the patterns of rough black hair swirling round his nipples and arrowing down into the waistband of his breeches as nature's work of art. Most strange of all was to want to feel all that masculine muscularity pressed against her soft and yielding feminine flesh.

She had always dreaded becoming intimate with a man. But now, oh, now she just wanted to hold him close while he found the same pleasure he had just gifted to her.

'I never want you to feel dirty or ashamed again, Hester.' His voice sounded strangely harsh.

'I know,' she said. And her heart began to beat wildly in anticipation.

Chapter Seventeen

Jasper got into bed on top of the sheet that covered her, rolled on to his side, and turned his back to her.

For a moment or two Hester just lay there, baffled. They were married. Why didn't he mount her? What had she done wrong?

Heat flooded her face at the memory of just how wild she had gone in the bath. She had clung to him, and writhed, and water had sloshed all over the floor and she had made... noises.

Had her ecstatic response caused Jasper to wonder about the veracity of her account of what Lionel had done to her? Did he wonder if she had enjoyed it as much as she enjoyed his caresses just now? Did he think that she might have encouraged Lionel, then twisted the story to make herself sound like an innocent victim?

A shaft of ice speared her through. Perhaps it had been her fault. Perhaps she did have a dark core to her nature that only needed a spark to make it flare into fully fledged depravity. Somehow Lionel had discerned it. And now Jasper had too.

He couldn't bring himself to touch her again. He had attempted to symbolically wash her, somehow understanding how dirty she felt, deep down inside. But it had not worked.

For a while she had forgotten everything but the feel of his hands on her body, but now doubts and fears assailed her from every side, and as she drifted off to sleep, the guilt broke free in a wave of jumbled memories more powerful and terrifying than the reality had been. She could hear the rain drumming on the roof. She could taste acrid smoke in her mouth, and feel Lionel's weight pinning her to the rough planks of the floor.

As she tried to fight free of him, she felt a hand stroking her hair, heard a voice that compelled her to listen.

'Hush, Hester,' the voice said. 'It's only a dream. Nothing can hurt you now. I'm here.'

And in her sleep she turned to the source of comfort, trusting the solid warmth of the body she clung to to shield her. She wept, in her dream, that although she had found a safe harbour at last, in finding it, she had lost something infinitely precious.

It was still dark when Jasper shook her awake.

'Get dressed,' he said, turning his back and reaching for his own shirt.

Humiliation slammed into her like a fist, and she pulled the sheet to her chin. With her hair rioting across the pillows, she knew she must look like one of Bacchus's wild maenads. No wonder he couldn't bear to look at her.

'Is there anything of value in your overnight case?' Jasper reached down and picked his breeches up from the floor.

'N…not really.' There was a comb. She would value time to ply it now, but she guessed that was not what he had meant. She saw that her chemise was draped across the foot of the bed. Keeping the blankets clutched to her chin, she shuffled down the mattress and made a grab for it.

'Then you must leave it behind.'

She tried not to gape at his bulky thighs as he stepped into his breeches.

'When we meet up with Miss Dean and Stephen in the park, we need to make it look as though we are just returning from our usual early morning ride. The presence of luggage may give rise to curiosity.'

Hester struggled out of her nightgown and into her chemise under the blankets. 'Whatever shall we say to your mother, though? She has been looking forward to our wedding, and now she's missed it.'

The chair across which her dress lay was beyond her reach. She was going to have to get out of bed wearing only her flimsy chemise, walk across the room, move Jasper's coat…

'We are not going to tell anyone we are married, Hester.'

'What?' She stopped in the middle of the room, her mouth gaping.

'Think about it.' He eyed her dispassionately as he stamped his feet into his boots. 'What possible reason could we give for running off, scarce two weeks before our wedding? If this information gets out, the very gossip that I am endeavouring to suppress on your behalf would run like wildfire through the *ton*.'

He reached round her, then calmly handed Hester her dress, bringing her cringingly back to awareness that she was practically naked. Turning her back, she stepped into the gown and frantically did up the buttons.

'We must go through with the public wedding as if nothing untoward has occurred.'

'B…but Lionel can still…'

'Leave him to me, Hester. Now that I am in full possession of the facts, I know exactly how to deal with him.'

He wanted to crush Snelgrove for his attempt to harry his own, dear, brave wife into adulthood, after having effectively robbed her of her childhood. He was certainly not going to permit the scoundrel to get anywhere near Hester ever again. It might mean enlisting help to flush him out of whatever hole he was hiding in, but he had friends on whose discretion he could rely. Farrar was already in this business up to his neck. Captain Fawley, too, would do whatever was necessary to protect the one woman in London who had treated him like a whole man, not a cripple.

His face looked so fierce as he tugged the door open that Hester's stomach clenched in fright. He kept his anger reined in, but, sat up on the saddle in front of him, she could feel the rigidity of his body, the way he tried to keep contact between them to the minimum. Discovering all there was to know of her had clearly filled him with revulsion.

It was Stephen who helped her down when they got to the rendezvous, while Jasper watched, in brooding silence; Stephen who boosted her into Strawberry's saddle once Em had helped her to tie the ribbons of her riding hat in place.

When they finally dismounted at the foot of the steps that led up to Lady Augusta's front door, Hester's courage almost failed her.

'I don't know how I'm going to face her,' she admitted, grabbing wildly for Em's hand.

'Then don't.'

She spun round at the first remark Jasper had made since leaving that wretched inn. 'Go to your room.' He glowered down at her. 'Have breakfast, get changed…' he made a vague gesture with his hand '…whatever you would normally do. I will speak to her for you.'

Another battle he was going to have to fight for her.

She couldn't bear it. The proud name of Challinor was on the brink of scandal, all because of her. And he was furious.

She waited until he had disappeared into the bowels of the house before she went in, dashing up the stairs two at a time and slamming her bedroom door behind her.

She stayed there for two full days.

On the third day she went to Lady Augusta's room during the breakfast hour.

'My uncle and aunt are arriving in town tomorrow,' she began, fixing her eyes on the snowy white hands that rested atop the satin quilt. 'It would be sensible, don't you think, if I were to remove to Vosbey House, to make sure their stay is as comfortable as I can make it?'

'Sensible?' Lady Augusta bit down on her lower lip. Jasper had told her she was not to badger Hester about the details of exactly what steps he had taken to ensure she would not bolt again. But she was no fool. He was so head over heels in love with this skinny little freckle-faced chit that he had dashed off into the wilds disguised as a highwayman and bedded her to make sure she could never escape. Since then, Hester had cowered in her room, unable to face anyone. She wouldn't even receive Jasper, not even when he called to take her out riding. And every rejection had sent her son sliding deeper into the sort of despondency that only thwarted passion could inflict.

She only wished she had someone to share the joke with. He was still strutting round the drawing rooms of London, looking down his proud nose at lesser mortals as if he was the epitome of sang-froid, maintaining the fiction that he was content with the convenient marriage his mother had arranged, when all the time he was in so deep he hardly knew what to do with himself.

'Jenny and Julia and Phoebe all need to procure dresses, since they are to be my bridesmaids,' Hester persisted. 'And since Uncle Thomas is going to give me away it would be more logical for me to stay at Vosbey House with them all.'

'Logical...' Her voice shook slightly. 'Of course it is.'

'Not that I'm not very grateful for all you've done for me.'

'But naturally you want to spend these last few days of your legal girlhood with your family.'

'Exactly.'

Lady Augusta coughed into her handkerchief before saying, 'Naturally Jasper will call upon you and your family, to pay his respects. And escort you all to whatever functions you wish to attend.'

'Oh.' Hester went white.

'You will naturally wish to introduce them about.'

'Yes, I will, won't I?'

Lady Augusta couldn't resist turning the screw one last twist. 'And of course you must bring my goddaughter to call here. And I, of course, will positively haunt your drawing room—it has been so long since I have talked, really talked with my dear friend, your aunt Susan. Jasper can escort me. I dare say we will all see so much of each other, it will hardly be as though you are living apart from us at all.'

Hester had shot herself in the foot. If only she had not come up with the stupid plan to escape Brook Street. She could have kept on using the excuse of ill health to stay in her rooms and avoid Jasper right up till the morning of their wedding. Now she had pledged herself to entertaining her family, she would be obliged to go out and about. She would have to face him. Speak to him.

How did women do it? How did anyone bear the pain of being hopelessly in love with a man who did not want emotion of any sort to feature in his marriage? Who was at this moment so angry that he could hardly bear to look at her?

She soon found it was impossible. All he had to do, the first time she saw him again, was bow over her hand and murmur 'good evening' for her to feel horridly conscious that he had seen her naked, in a most ungainly position, gasping and shuddering, while his skilful hands had roamed all over her eager body. It was beyond her power to stutter a conventional response, let alone look him in the face. All she could think to do was escape him, and by dint of becoming very busy entertaining their guests, and convincing her family that she was happy, when inside her heart felt like a lead weight, that was what shc did.

But wherever she went, she could feel his hard black eyes boring into her with disquiet.

Jasper could see she was quivering under the strain of keeping up a cheerful front, but since he believed that nothing but Snelgrove's utter destruction would ever bring her true peace of mind, he disdained the very notion of offering her empty platitudes.

To his great relief, two days before their public wedding, he received news that Captain Fawley had run the villain to ground. Dismissing the footman who had brought him the message informing him that his trap was in the very process of being sprung, he crossed the room to where Hester sat rigid between his mother and her aunt, pretending to listen to the soprano who had been hired for that evening's entertainment.

Leaning over the back of her chair, he murmured into her ear, 'A word, if you please, in private.'

When she would have denied him, he took the simple expedient of taking her by the arm, lifting her from her chair, and towing her from the room.

'This will end tonight,' he promised her. 'Tomorrow you will go riding with me, as we did when first you came to London.'

Conscious that somebody might overhear, he gruffly added, 'I have a matter to discuss with you, that must be for your ears alone. Before the wedding ceremony. Do you understand?'

Miserably she nodded her head, mentally preparing herself for a scolding. Or perhaps he was just going to lay out the terms for their marriage. He'd had time to consider how to deal with her, and her past. He would definitely want to ensure that she got into no more scrapes. He would probably have a list of exactly how she was to behave as his wife. He certainly had not approved of her behaviour in public since they had secretly married. Whenever she dared take a glance at him, he had been scowling at her, looking as though he wondered what on earth had possessed him to choose her above her lovely, placid, blameless cousins.

When he strode from the room, she lifted her chin, and returned to her seat, from where she gazed with unseeing eyes at the opera singer. She would accept whatever restrictions he imposed on her. He couldn't unmarry her now. So she had her whole lifetime to demonstrate that though her past had been chequered, she would do all in her power to be a conformable wife.

And in time, his desire for an heir must override his distaste for the woman he was legally shackled to.

Mustn't it?

Jasper's heart was pounding with anticipation as he strode through the streets to Captain Fawley's rooms, the prearranged venue for Snelgrove's demise. Stephen Farrar was already there, his face grim with purpose. They waited in silence, both rising to their feet when at last they heard the unmistakeable sound of Captain Fawley's uneven gait upon the stairs. Farrar went to the door. The moment Fawley stumbled into the room, supported by a red-faced, wheezing Snelgrove, he slammed the door shut behind them and leaned against it, his arms folded across his chest.

Snelgrove's eyes narrowed when he caught sight of Lord Lensborough, lounging at the green baize table beside the hearth, then widened when Captain Fawley abruptly straightened up and walked steadily across to the sideboard to pour himself a drink, all trace of the pathetic drunken cripple that he'd half-dragged back from the tavern in the East End where they'd met having vanished.

'I believe you have something you wish to ask me, Snelgrove.' Lord Lensborough's voice was cold. 'A matter of five thousand pounds, I believe.'

Snelgrove's eyes darted furtively about the room, noting that his only escape route was blocked by the athletic-looking Mr Farrar.

'I am sure you don't wish to discuss this matter before witnesses, my lord.' Snelgrove's voice was oily, like his smile.

'Oh?' Lensborough's left eyebrow rose the merest fraction. 'But I thought you particularly wished as many people as possible to hear your version of events.'

'What I wish, and what you wish, are not necessarily the same, though, are they, my lord? Hence the request for five thousand pounds to keep my mouth shut regarding what I know about your intended.'

'You know nothing I do not know myself. Lady Hester has no secrets from me.' He paused, as though considering the matter, though he had long since decided how he would handle this cur. 'Shall we regard these two gentlemen as... seconds?'

At the implication that this meeting had been arranged for the sole purpose of arranging a duel, some of Lionel's bluster ebbed away.

'Although, I shouldn't wonder if, by the time we have concluded this interview, you wouldn't like to pay me five thousand pounds to keep my mouth shut regarding what I know about you.'

'That's preposterous.'

'Is it, though? I wonder how many doors would remain open to you once the tale got out that you attempted the rape of a little girl, the sister of your closest friend, no less, under whose roof you were staying at the time? That tale, coupled with my own very public denunciation of you as a man without honour would be enough to finish you. My influence is considerable, as is that of those I consider friends.'

'You wouldn't do that.' Snelgrove's face flushed angrily. 'If you bring me down, I take your wife down with me.'

Lensborough appeared to consider this, then shook his head. 'Possibly, although what proof can you offer that anything actually occurred? It would be your word against hers.' He took delight in flinging the very taunt Snelgrove had employed against Hester back in his own face. 'And since I have documented proof that Hester is a virgin, all you would succeed in doing is make yourself look like the filthy, lying scoundrel that you are. You would destroy yourself from your own lips.'

'Proof? You can't have proof.'

'Oh, but I have. As soon as Hester arrived in London, I had a doctor check her…credentials for becoming my wife most meticulously. I can supply you with his name, if you like.'

'You cold-hearted bastard. What kind of a man does a thing like that to his fiancée?'

'As you have said.' Lensborough's smile at Snelgrove's obvious horror was positively cruel. 'Do you know nothing of the Challinor family's reputation? Do you think a man of my station would walk into marriage without knowing exactly what I was getting? I wouldn't even buy a horse for my stud without having it thoroughly checked over.'

Snelgrove was sweating now as he looked from one implacably hostile face to another. 'So, you do mean to force me to a duel?'

'Well, I should like to shoot you like the dog you are,' Lensborough drawled, 'but since technically that would be murder, and as a peer of the realm my duty is to uphold the law…' he tapped the deck of cards that lay on the table before him with his forefinger '…perhaps we should let the cards decide your fate.'

'The cards?'

'Yes, we'll cut, shall we? Whoever cuts highest, wins.'

'Agreed.' Snelgrove had sat at the table, had even reached

out his hand for the pack, before realisation dawned. He swallowed. 'Who wins what, exactly?'

'Exactly?' Lensborough's malicious smile sent a shiver of dread down Snelgrove's spine.

'How about, if you win, you have the right to say whatever you like about my wife, and I will not contest it?'

Snelgrove's brain reeled. 'Hang on! You have just said that if I do that, nobody will believe me, that I would be ruined.'

Lensborough shrugged indifferently. 'It was your idea in the first place. I would just be letting you do as you wish and taking the consequences.'

'I w...wouldn't have really gone through with it. I just needed the money—' Snelgrove bleated.

'Don't you want to know what happens if I draw the higher card?' Lensborough cut him off.

Thoroughly disconcerted, Snelgrove nodded his head.

'Well, the thing is, I don't want my wife troubled by your nasty insinuations. Ever again. What I really want is for you to leave the country altogether. So if I cut the higher card, I shall pay off your debts and buy you a commission in some regiment currently serving overseas. On the strict understanding that you never return. Should you ever set foot on English soil again, however...' His smile put Snelgrove in mind of a crouched tiger greedily eyeing a nervous gazelle.

With a hand that trembled, Snelgrove reached for the pack, and took a card. With his eyes still fixed on his enemy, Lensborough drew another.

Snelgrove glanced at his card, and licked his chalk-white lips. 'Ah, we never determined...are aces high or low?'

Lensborough looked at his card, a smile slowly spreading across his face.

'It is really not for me to decide. Fawley? What say you?'

Fawley let him sweat for a full five minutes, before glaring at him from his one good eye, and announcing, 'Low.'

Snelgrove ran his finger round the neck of his cravat and laid the eight of spades upon the table. At the sight of Lensborough's king of clubs, he slumped over the table, whimpering with relief. When Lensborough rose from his chair, Farrar took Snelgrove by one arm, and Fawley the other, lifted him to his feet, and marched him into the bedroom.

Lensborough knew they would not let the man out of their sight until his papers were duly signed. They had both sworn to do whatever was necessary to protect Lady Hester.

'You do not need me to tell you that I will never forget this,' he had vowed in his turn. 'If there is ever anything I can do to repay you, you have only to ask.'

Now he couldn't wait for the morning to come, so that he could release Hester from the foul shadow that had hung over her for so many years. This was the best wedding present he could give her.

There was an air of suppressed elation about him this morning, Hester decided as they cantered towards what she had come to regard as their stand of beech trees. Perhaps he was not quite so averse to the idea of marrying her as she had begun to fear.

'I have something for you,' he said, swinging her down from the saddle the moment she brought Strawberry to a halt behind the screen of foliage.

'It is only a token, but it will serve as an excuse for my insistence on this meeting. That, and the chance to snatch a few clandestine kisses, of course.'

Before she had a chance to register what he had said, Jasper drew her into his arms and brought his mouth down upon hers, in a kiss of such fierce possessiveness that it left her gasping.

'Here,' he said, reaching into his pocket while she made a feeble attempt to straighten her skewed riding hat. 'It is something I hope will remind you of me.'

Her heart, which had been beating wildly with hope, skipped a beat altogether. If he wished to give her a reminder of him, did this mean he was planning to leave her? But then why had he kissed her like that?

She opened the lid of the box he was holding out to her warily, wondering what sort of thing a man gave to his bride as a parting gift. Inside, nestling on a bed of black velvet, was a brooch. A cluster of yellow diamonds, surrounding…

'Your tiger's-eye pin,' she exclaimed, running her finger over its smooth surface. How often she had compared Jasper to that fierce, untameable creature, until just having him near made all other terrors pale in comparison.

'Well, you seemed so fond of it.'

She shot him a puzzled look.

'I thought at one time you were cured of the habit of addressing my neckcloth, but of late you have reverted to a fascination with that item of my apparel. So…' He shrugged eloquently.

'I have been abominably rude, haven't I?' Hester hung her head. 'It is just that after…that is, I feel so aware of you.'

'Aware,' he echoed with a sigh. The poor girl was still terrified of the full act of intimacy. Even after coming apart in his arms. She was trembling, red-faced, flustered, but at least she hadn't drawn back from the kiss he hadn't been able to resist giving her. She had her face averted from him now, though. He smiled fondly at the top of her head, a feature which she had presented to him with regularity.

'The gem was a gift from my brother Bertram,' he explained as she ran her finger over the jewel that had always reminded her of the colour of his knowing dark eyes. 'I cannot say it is the most expensive among my collection, but it has always been my favourite. He bought it out of his army pay, when he could scarce afford to.'

'Oh.' Hester's eyes misted. 'And you have given it to me.'

She looked up at him with a heart full of hope again. He must care about her to some degree if he could give her something of such value to him. 'I shall always treasure it.' He had worn that pin close to his heart. Was this his way of showing her that he knew how to value what was only semi-precious, when it was given with true affection? That he accepted she came to him with a heart full of love, even though she was not a diamond of the first water?

'This is not my real wedding present to you, though,' he said, throwing her into confusion again.

'Last night, we…that is, I,' he hastily amended, not wishing her to know that others had become privy to some of the distressing details of her past, 'dispatched Snelgrove. He will never bother you again.'

Her reaction was not what he had hoped for. Going ghostly pale, she swayed on her feet. 'You have killed him.'

'What? No.' He caught her about the waist and drew her to his chest when it appeared she would have recoiled. 'Not that I wasn't sorely tempted, believe me.' He tipped her chin up with one forefinger. 'Do you really believe me capable of cold-blooded murder?' He studied her anxious face with a feeling of foreboding. If she thought that of him, how was he ever going to get near enough to her to teach her that physical love could bring joy, rather than shame?

She then promptly flung her arms about his waist, burying her face in the folds of his riding coat, presenting the top of her head to his bemused gaze once again.

She believed he could commit murder, yet she clung to him like a limpet. Perhaps there was hope for him after all. With patience, by showing her the utmost consideration, in time he would break down the barriers she had erected in her mind to protect herself from Snelgrove's vile influence.

'If you didn't kill him,' she breathed into his waistcoat, 'then how can you be really sure?' He felt a shudder rack her body. 'He has this nasty habit of appearing to go away and then popping up again when you least expect him.'

'Hester, Hester.' He sighed, rocking her as he might a frightened child. 'I can assure you that I gave him no alternative. He will never dare so much as set foot in England again.'

She tipped her head back then, gazing up into his face with a frown pleating her forehead. 'It must have cost you a great deal to send him abroad. The least you can let me do is to reimburse you.'

Shock sent him reeling back from her. 'Reimburse me?' he roared. 'Why in Hades should I wish you to do that? You are my wife. It is my duty to protect you.'

'I know,' she moaned, turning from him. 'Don't think I am unaware of just how much trouble you are always having to go to for my sake. Especially when I am not the bride you would have chosen.'

'Not the bride…what do you mean? Of course I chose you, Hester.'

'Yes, but only because being in that inn together compromised you. I know that, and I don't mind so much now.' She turned her face to his, desperate to make him understand. 'I know you only came to The Holme to find a woman who would simply be a mother to your children, and not disrupt your present mode of life. And all I have done so far is cause you disruption. At least let me settle the debt myself, as a pledge that I will not—'

'For God's sake, woman,' Jasper groaned, closing his eyes on her anguished expression. Guilt flayed him when he went back over their association, and he saw how she had reached that erroneous conclusion about his feelings for her. He had shouted at her, barked orders at her, said and thought the most insulting things. In his desperate, overwhelming desire to possess her he'd acted like the worst sort of bully.

Clenching his fists, he roared, 'When will you get it through that stubborn head of yours that I *want* to take care of you?'

'But you can't possibly. I am nothing like the kind of wife you said you wanted.'

'No.' He shook his head. 'I was full of foolish notions when I came to The Holme, till you knocked them out of my thick skull with your forthright comments and your queenly disdain. Nobody has attempted to correct my manners since I was out of short coats, and even then, my pride was fostered as a very fitting attribute for my rank. You…you turned me upside down that very first time we ran into each other.'

'I'm sorry.'

'Don't be,' he grated, grasping her by the shoulders and pulling her back into his arms. 'Don't ever be sorry we met, Hester.'

And then, because she was looking at him with such hope, such longing, and she felt so warm and pliant in his arms, he kissed her again. And again.

'We will be married again tomorrow,' he reminded himself, trying to regain control. 'When the ceremony is over, you and I must have a long talk.' Resting his forehead against hers, he groaned, 'You have a busy day ahead of you. I promised to have you home in good time. Besides, if we linger here much longer…' He gave a rueful laugh as Hester ducked out of his arms, her face flaming.

He didn't want her to be sorry they had met, she reflected, mounting Strawberry in a daze. That must mean he wasn't sorry, mustn't it? And he had kissed her. Really kissed her. Remembering his unfeigned ardour sent her blushing all over each time she recalled it. She floated through all the last-minute preparations, the final fitting, in a kind of dream. A man could not fake that reaction to the woman he held in his arms. Jasper wanted her.

He really did.

* * *

And somehow her wedding day was upon her, and she was standing before the mirror checking her appearance one last time before going down to the hall where Uncle Thomas was waiting to escort her to church. Her aunt and cousins and Em had all told her how lovely she looked.

But all she cared about was what Jasper would think of her appearance. She knew she wasn't beautiful, but there was something about her today that was, oh, she didn't know, at least elegant. The pale gold silk of her gown seemed to flow like liquid sunshine over her slender figure, while the diamond tiara that Lady Augusta had insisted she wore atop the rich, glossy waves that flowed over her pale shoulders made her feel like a princess.

Her eyes sought him the minute she set foot in the church. She was oblivious to the faces of the great and good of the land craning to examine her dress, deaf to the comments being whispered behind gloved hands. She only had eyes for Jasper, the man she was so proud to call her husband. And when he turned to glance at her over his shoulder, it was all she could do to keep herself from flying down the aisle, flinging her arms round his neck, and thanking him for being there for her, in spite of everything. She wasn't sure how she managed to keep to the languid pace Madame Pichot had told her befitted a marchioness—and which, incidentally, displayed the fluid cut of the gown to best effect.

She wasn't quite sure how she managed to get through the very long, and very public, celebrations that her mother-in-law had deemed necessary, either. Being so close to Jasper was driving her insane. He had only to take her hand for her nipples to peak dramatically at the memory of how those callused palms had felt gliding over her soap-slicked breasts. Every time he brought a morsel of food to his lips, she recalled how delicious his kisses had been.

She was so very much in love with her husband that her entire body pulsed with a longing that she was ashamed to think must be transparent to everyone.

'You are being dreadfully unfashionable, you know,' Lady Augusta chided her when at last, at long last, the time came for her to leave with Jasper and gain the privacy of Challinor house. 'You too.' She turned towards her son.

From the moment he had turned and seen her walking down the aisle towards him, he had been unable to conceal the depth of his emotions a moment longer. It was plain for all to see the pair were besotted with each other.

'Didn't Hester make a radiant bride, Mama?' was his only response to her teasing. He took her arm then, and steered her through the crowd of well-wishers, his jaw determinedly set.

He tried not to read too much into her apparent eagerness to leave the scene of the wedding breakfast, and embark on their new life together. He couldn't forget the way she had begun to tear her own clothes off in determination to get the dreadful deed over with on their first wedding night.

However, he had gone to great lengths to ensure tonight would be nothing like anything she could have imagined.

His heart skipped a beat as he handed her into the coach for the short drive to Challinor House. This was such a new venture for him. He hoped he was not about to make a colossal fool of himself. He bit down on the selfish desire to preserve his own dignity with disgust. In the face of Hester's need, what did his own pride matter? He had already been rewarded for reining in his lust on their clandestine night together. She had walked down the aisle with her head held high. If she had not been a virgin, she would have felt such a fraud her guilt would have been plain for all to see. Knowing she was free of Snelgrove must have been a great source of comfort to her, too.

Hester darted a nervous glance at Jasper's brooding profile. He had withdrawn into his granite shell and she didn't know how to reach him. And she was so very aware of the size of his body in the close confines of the coach. The very air she breathed was redolent of his distinctive and intoxicatingly male scent. She was glad when the coach finally stopped, a grinning footman opened the door and she was able to get out. Jasper was in a very strange mood, veering between stony silence that spoke of a simmering anger, and a noble attempt to be conciliatory towards her. Did he know what he wanted from her at all? Because if he didn't, how could she ever learn to be the kind of wife he wanted?

She blinked up at the magnificent façade of Challinor House. Liveried servants, each holding a torch, flanked the steps. Every single one of them eyed her with frank curiosity, and many of them, as she passed, grinned at their master in what looked like a conspiratorial fashion.

What was going on? What kind of household did he run here? She entered a beautifully appointed hall with a sense of bewildered wariness, wishing that she had made the time to visit before entering this house as its mistress. She should have made a point of getting to know the staff she would be governing, more of whom had gathered about the foot of the stairs. They were all smiling, however, so her lapse had apparently not caused a breach before she had even come amongst them.

'Haven't any of you anything better to do than loiter in the hall?' Jasper suddenly bellowed, scattering them in a flurry of suppressed laughter. She recalled Em's assessment that his groom regarded him as a benevolent despot in the stables. His household staff clearly felt the same way.

Jasper opened a door on the left of the hall, asking her, 'Would you care for a nightcap before we retire?'

He looked…apprehensive.

It was the last straw.

'Can't we just go straight to bed?' she pleaded.

'Ah.' Jasper looked at his feet. 'Hester. I have to tell you...I'm not...' He looked at her beseechingly, as though for under-standing. 'I won't ever ride roughshod over your feelings.'

'I know that.' But she also knew that whatever he felt, or didn't feel for her, he had married because he wanted an heir. 'But it is my duty to give you children.'

'Very well.' Her hand still clasped in his, they slowly began to mount the stairs. 'I take my duty very seriously.'

Well, she knew that already. Duty was what had driven him to take her, rather than one of her prettier, more amenable cousins, after all.

'There is one duty that I am particularly keen to carry out.'

She clung harder to his hand as her foot almost missed one of the risers. She couldn't believe how much it hurt to hear that he regarded getting her pregnant in the light of carrying out a duty. Particularly since his words the morning before in the park had given her hope that he might really want her for herself.

'A husband's duty to cherish his wife.'

They had reached the first landing, and she paused reflect-ing on his last words. 'Cherish?' she finally managed to whisper.

'Cherish,' he affirmed, leading her to a second flight of stairs. 'And to that end, I have spent some considerable thought on the decor of your room here.' He led her along a carpeted landing, and pushed open the first door on the right.

The sight that met her eyes made Hester gasp in amaze-ment. She stepped, enchanted, into what looked like a moonlit forest glade. There was not a single stick of conventional fur-niture in the room. The walls were handpainted with the most realistic sylvan scene: trees and delicately perfumed flower-ing shrubs apparently surrounding a small glade. A moon glowed over its reflection in a crystal-clear pond.

'How did you...?' She craned her neck to examine the ceiling, which had been made to look like a starlit night by means of hundreds of tiny candles refracting through crystals, which were suspended somehow on a canopy of black velvet. The moon was similarly a lantern suspended behind a screen of gauze.

She couldn't resist kneeling beside the pond, trailing her fingers through the shallow water, then over the grass-effect cushions that surrounded it.

'It is not real grass, alas.' Jasper's voice sounded strangely hoarse. 'But the velvet is a close enough approximation.' He closed the door behind him. 'I wanted a waterfall as well, but the carpenter went on at great length about the necessity for reinforcing joists, and warned me that the noise that the pump needed to keep the water circulating would ruin the romantic atmosphere I wished to create.'

'Romantic?' Hester gazed wide eyed at the man who disdained any show of emotion, pacing about the room, twitching a frond of fern nervously between his fingers. 'This is supposed to be romantic?'

He went still. 'Isn't it?' He frowned. 'I have never attempted anything like this before, so I wasn't sure. I just wanted the bridal chamber to be perfect for you. There are no windows, see?' He gestured towards the screened and painted walls. 'I wanted you to feel safe, utterly safe with me, here tonight.'

Hester got to her feet. 'There is no bed, either,' she pointed out.

He cleared his throat, crushing the fern frond completely as she faced him, her head tilted to one side. 'Ever since our first meeting, I knew you were different from anyone I had ever known. You are not a predictable, domesticated product of civilization. You are…a creature of nature. When you came to London, and tried to conform to all the strictures my mother placed on you, it was like seeing a wood nymph bound in chains. Hester…' He took a step towards her. 'You don't belong in a drawing room, mouthing meaningless platitudes. You belong outside, my little dappled fawn.' He drew nearer still, reaching out to run one finger over her freckled nose. 'Far away from all other men, the men who would frighten you, and hurt you.'

He drew her to what looked like a grassy knoll, and pulled her down beside him.

'All this…' he waved his hand to indicate the room '…is the proper setting for you.'

The knoll was incredibly soft. 'Is this stuffed with feathers?' she asked as she sank into it.

He nodded, murmuring, 'You are too rare to dwell in the dreary, commonplace world of men.' He raised her hand to his mouth, and began to kiss her fingertips. 'This poor mortal would worship at your shrine, if you will permit.' He turned her hand and pressed a fervent kiss in her palm.

'W…worship?' The kiss had sent heat directly to her womb, leaving her melting between the velvet cushions and the hard strength of his body.

'With my body I thee worship,' he repeated, stunning her by dropping to his knees before her and raising the hem of her gown to his lips.

'I will never take, in the way Snelgrove threatened to take from you. I will only ever give.' Her heartbeat increased as he drew off her gold satin slippers.

'Don't be afraid of me.' He began to kiss her toes. 'I won't push you where you don't want to go.' One by one, he drew them into the heat of his mouth. Hester sank deeper into the cushions, as her whole body turned to liquid heat. 'I will wait as long as you need before consummating our union fully.' He reached up and removed the diamond tiara from her hair, tossing it carelessly aside so that he could plunge his fingers into her hair. It splashed, unheeded, into the artificial lake as Hester wound her arms about his neck and drew him down.

'I am not afraid of you,' she declared, bravely planting a kiss on his mouth.

He smiled sadly. 'My darling, ever since I forced you into

that secret marriage you have not been able to look me in the face. I made you confront your fears when I bathed you, and…'

'No. No.' She took his face between her hands, and looked him straight in the eye. 'I was not afraid of you. Only your rejection. Every time I looked at you I could feel your hands on my body, and then the awful coldness of your rejection.'

'What rejection? I didn't reject you.' He swore. 'Was that what you thought?' he groaned. 'It wasn't a rejection, my sweet innocent. I was trying to spare you. When you quivered under my hands I very nearly exploded with reciprocal lust. I dared not touch you. I would have taken you with such brutality it would have undone all the trust I had begun to build.'

Hester's face lit up. 'You wanted me then?'

'I ache with wanting you, but don't worry. I can control my lustful urges. I am not like Snelgrove.'

She thumped his shoulder. 'Jasper, you great idiot. I know you are not like Lionel. The very first time you kissed me I understood that it was not kissing that filled me with disgust, but him. He wanted to humiliate and degrade me, so his touch sent me straight to a hell of his own devising. But you…' she laid her open palm against his cheek '…you transported me to heaven on our secret wedding night. Because I love you. And,' she added shyly, 'I ache with wanting you too. Now that everyone knows we are married…'

'Are you sure?' He tensed, kneeling over her, gazing deep into her eyes for any sign she was only sacrificing herself to please him.

Hester smiled and began to undo the buttons of his waistcoat.

'You don't have to…' His words choked out as she determinedly pushed the garment off his shoulders and set to work on his neckcloth. With a groan, he scooped her into his arms and brought them both down next to one another on the mound of artificial grass.

'God, Hester, tonight?' He buried his face in the mass of

hair that was tumbling about her shoulders. 'This is so much more than I had hoped for.' With hands that trembled, he unbuckled the clasps that held her gown together, and pushed the fabric from her shoulder. 'I would have waited,' he panted between the kisses that he trailed along her collar bone, 'a humble penitent—' up her neck '—at your feet—' he found the sweet, moist haven of her mouth and ravaged it thoroughly '—for all eternity.'

A gurgle of the most seductive laughter he had ever heard issued from her throat. He bent to kiss it again as she said, 'Humble! You?'

'Loving you has brought me to my knees,' he confessed, pushing her dress to her waist and demonstrating his need by suckling her breasts.

She was not quite so lost to sensation that she missed that. 'You love me?'

Jasper tensed, rolled on to his back, and laid his arm across his face, hiding his eyes. 'I didn't mean to say that.'

Hester knelt up and tugged at his arm. Her heart was beating so fast now she felt as if it might burst through her rib cage. 'Then why did you say it? If you didn't mean it?' His arm didn't budge. She climbed astride him to get a better purchase. She had to see his face.

Suddenly, he seemed to accept defeat. His arm flopped to his side, and he lay gazing mournfully up at her. 'Oh, I mean it. That's just the trouble. I love you so much I have to resort to this sort of tomfoolery to demonstrate it.' He waved despairingly at the elaborately constructed bridal bower. 'I have spent a small fortune constructing what has to be the most ridiculously romantic bridal bower any groom has ever dreamt up to woo his bride. I had hoped to preserve some dignity by holding out until you presented me with our first son before confessing to feeling such a vulgar, unfashionable, lowering emotion.' His face grimaced in self-disgust. 'Since meeting you, my behaviour has become increasingly erratic. I brawl in taverns, kick down doors, hold up stagecoaches, kidnap innocent maidens…'

Hester cut through to what she saw as the heart of the matter. 'How were we ever going to get a son if you planned to wait patiently to the end of time before consummating this marriage?'

'Ah…the flaw in my logic. You see what you have done to me, Hester? My brain does not function correctly any more. The only part of me that seems to be working at all efficiently, in fact, is this part.'

It was a gamble to take hold of her hand and draw it to the front of his breeches, but with her sitting astride him, her breasts bared to his gaze, it was too great a temptation to resist.

Her eyes widened as she felt the full extent of his desire pulsing beneath her hand. For a fleeting second, the very size of him induced a thread of fear. Then she looked into his eyes and saw his longing, and hope, his very heart open to the risk that she might reject him.

'Idiot.' She sighed affectionately, leaning forward and kissing his forehead tenderly. A look of profound relief washed over his taut features, just a split second before he very naughtily gathered the breast that dangled so temptingly close to his lips deeply into his mouth. As he suckled, Hester gave way to curiosity, tentatively exploring the explicitly masculine contours that lay beneath her hand.

'I can't help noticing,' Jasper said after a while, 'that you are getting well acquainted with my one fully functioning part.'

Hester blushed and hid her face in his shoulder. 'Jasper, I have to admit I am still a little afraid. Before I met you I was terrified at the prospect of ever becoming completely a woman.' She raised her face to look at him, casting all caution to the winds. 'P…please, my husband. Won't you chase all my fears away? For good?' Deliberately, she tightened her fingers around the length of him.

With a rather wicked smile, he rolled her on to her back and gazed down lovingly into what for him was the most beautiful face in the world.

'It will be good. That I can promise. My whole life will be dedicated from this moment forth to chasing your fears away. On a regular basis.'

Just before his mouth claimed hers she whispered her thanks. Then he set about making good his promise.

Devilish Lord,
Mysterious Miss

For Peter and Ruth,
Steadfast Friends

Chapter One

Lord Matthison reached for the area railings to steady himself, blinking up at the façade of the house where Miss Winters lived.

With her ambitious mother.

And her ruthless father.

He had no idea how he'd fetched up on Curzon Street, at the house of the scheming jade who had stripped him of his last vestige of hope.

He was drunk, of course. He had been drinking steadily since just before midnight. Any man who'd had the week he'd just had would have done exactly the same—made for the nearest gin shop and called for a bottle. Though he had assiduously avoided taking the road that led to oblivion during the past seven years, when the cards had turned against him, and he'd gone down to the tune of five hundred guineas for the third night in a row, he'd had to accept it was over.

'Cora,' he moaned, as the pain of her loss struck him

with an intensity he had not felt since the first day she'd gone. Gin was so deceitful! It promised to relieve all woe, but all it had done was strip him of the ability to pretend he did not care. He'd assumed he would have found at least a measure of respite, before coming round in some gutter. Possibly even staggering back to his own lodgings. He'd never dreamed he would turn out to have such a hard head, he would still be on his feet by dawn. Or that those wayward feet would have brought him to the last place on earth he would willingly have gone.

'But I won't marry you!' he yelled, shaking his fist at the shuttered windows.

A milkmaid who was passing eyed him with suspicion, and gave him a wide berth. He scarcely noticed her as he straightened up with renewed resolve. What did he care if Miss Winters was ruined!

He had not lured her into her father's study, tousled her hair, and torn the bodice of her gown. No, she'd done all that herself. Then launched herself at him just as the door swung open, making it look as though they had been locked in a passionate embrace.

Not that she wanted to marry him so much now, he laughed mirthlessly. He'd soon wiped that triumphant smile from her face!

'So, you want to dance with the devil, do you?' he had mocked, seizing her by the upper arms when she would have broken free.

'You are hurting me,' she had protested, beginning to look a little uncertain.

'But that is the kind of man I am,' he had answered. 'Have you not heard the rumours? Damsels of a sensitive nature practically swoon with fright whenever I walk into a room. With good reason, wouldn't you say?'

The confusion in her eyes had made him wonder if she really did not know. It was just possible. Her family did not mix in the best circles. Her mother had no intimates privy to the type of gossip circulating about him. They might have managed to secure a house at a fashionable address, but Miss Winters was never going to receive vouchers for Almack's.

'Or were you fooled by the fact that I still get invited everywhere?' he had mused. 'That was naïve of you. But as you do not seem to understand the ways of the *ton*, I will explain. Some of them ignore my reputation, because of the vast amount of wealth I have accrued since I made my pact with the devil. They claim not to care how I came by it, because my birth is sufficiently exalted for them to turn a blind eye. But they would never let me near any of their daughters.

'And there are others who are fascinated by the aura of evil I carry with me. They get quite a thrill from telling people they've been daring enough to ask the man who murdered his fiancée to attend one of their insipid gatherings. Oh,' he'd said, when a look of horror had spread across her face. 'So you had not heard? That I had made a pact with the devil, or that I had been engaged, long ago? To the innocent and unsuspecting Miss Montague…'

Suddenly it had felt like a kind of blasphemy, to

speak *her* name aloud while he was holding another woman in his arms. He had flung the trembling Miss Winters from him, but kept between her and the door. He had not finished with her yet!

'They never found her body,' he relished informing her, 'so they could never bring me to trial. But, since it was my best friend, the man who had known me since childhood, who brought the accusation against me, I must have done it, must I not?'

Miss Winters had begun to rub at the spot on her arms where he'd been holding her, but he'd felt not one ounce of remorse. He deliberately discarded the ice-cold persona he had adopted to disguise his state of mind, expressing all the bitterness that he normally held in check, through his next words.

'Since the day she disappeared, I have had phenomenal luck at the tables. Is that not proof that I have stained my soul with the blood of a virgin? I often wonder,' he'd grated, 'why people still sit down to play cards with me, when they know I can't lose. Just as I wonder—' he had paced slowly towards her, his fury unchecked '—why you expected this little charade to have any effect upon me. You do not suppose a man whose soul is as black as mine, is going to send off a notice to the *Morning Post* just because someone saw me in a compromising position with a virgin, do you?'

He had thought that would have been an end to it. Last thing he'd seen of her, she'd fled from the room, sobbing, and flung herself into her mother's arms. His mouth twisted into a cynical sneer as he recalled what a short distance she'd had to go. Her mother had been hovering right outside the door.

Anyway, he shrugged, she had definitely changed her mind about wanting to marry him.

Her father, though, was made of sterner stuff.

'Now look here!' he'd blustered, storming into Lord Matthison's rooms late the next afternoon. 'You cannot go about compromising young girls, and then scaring them off with half-baked tales that sound as though they've come out of a Gothic novel!'

'Is that so?' he'd drawled, not even bothering to raise his eyes from the deck of cards he was shuffling from his left hand into his right.

'It most certainly is! As a gentleman, you owe it to my daughter to offer marriage!'

'Out of the question,' he'd replied, taking the pack in his right hand, splitting it in half, and dextrously folding it over on itself with supple, practised fingers. 'I am already betrothed.'

That assertion had not silenced Mr Winters for more than a couple of seconds. 'Ah. You are referring to the Montague girl!'

Lord Matthison had felt the shock of hearing the man speak her name in such an offhand way clear through to his bones. And when Mr Winters had gone on to say, 'She's dead, ain't she?' the cards had spluttered from his hand to land in a confused jumble on the table top.

He'd got up, stalked across the room and leaned his forearm against the window frame, staring sightlessly down into the bustling courtyard while he grappled with the urge to do his visitor some serious bodily harm.

'Yes,' he had finally managed to say, with lethal calm. For nobody knew better than he that Cora walked the spirit world. 'Technically, I suppose you could claim I am free to marry again. But since nobody has ever managed to discover her body, her family prefer to think of her as missing. And I, therefore, am still legally bound to her.' With bonds that went beyond the realm of mere legalities, far tighter than any mortal man could ever suspect.

A nasty smile had spread across Mr Winters's avaricious face. 'Then we will just have to, legally, unbind you, will we not? So you can have no more excuse to avoid making an honest woman of my daughter.'

Before he could express his opinion that nobody had the power to make his daughter honest, since duplicity was such an intrinsic part of her nature, Mr Winters had declared, 'I do not care what it costs, or how long it takes. I *will* have Miss Montague declared legally dead. And then, my lord, we shall have you!'

Three days ago, that had been. Three days since Mr. Winters had declared his intent to instigate the proceedings that would kill Cora Montague all over again.

But he did not know Robbie Montague. Good ol' Robbie, he grimaced, folding his arms across his chest and leaning back against the area railings.

Robbie would have no truck with Mr Winters's suggestion that it was time to let go of his sister by holding a memorial service and finally putting up a gravestone.

Robbie would never set him free to marry again, and fill Kingsmede with children that were not his sister's. If he could not see him hang, Robbie's only satisfaction would be to make sure he remained suspended in a legal limbo.

Mr Winters, he smirked, had quite a fight on his hands.

The amount of hawkers pushing their handcarts up to the big houses, and the shortening of the shadows on his side of the street told him that it was well past daybreak now. Of the fourth day. His smirk turned to a grimace of despair. For the three consecutive nights since Mr. Winters had declared war on Cora's memory, he'd lost heavily at the card tables.

Last night, he had finally accepted what that meant.

He had thrown down his losing hand, tossed what he owed onto the green baize tablecloth, and stumbled from the gaming hell into the street. To confront his own personal hell. He'd had to clutch at the door frame for a few seconds, his heart had been beating so fast, while he'd fought down a rising tide of horror.

Not that he cared one whit for the money he'd lost. It was no longer financial necessity that kept him going back to the tables, night after night, but need of an entirely different nature.

'Cora,' he'd moaned uselessly into the empty alley way. 'I couldn't help it!' But there had not even been an answering echo.

She was not there.

For the first time in seven years, he could not feel her presence, anywhere.

He'd damned Mrs Winters for conspiring with her daughter to compromise him. He'd damned Miss Winters for forcing her lips against his in that unholy parody of a kiss. And he'd damned Mr. Winters for daring to speak of Cora as though she was of no account. Between the three of them, they had managed to do what even death could not.

They had driven her away.

He had never told anybody that she haunted him. They would have thought he had gone crazy. Hell, he often wondered about his sanity himself!

But it had only been a few days after the last time he had touched her warm soft skin, that he had felt her spirit hovering close by.

At a race track, of all places.

He had gone there with Robbie's accusations and curses ringing in his ears. He had been stunned when Robbie had accused him of murdering his sister. 'If you can believe that of me, then you will want this back!' he had yelled, throwing what was left of the money Robbie had lent him to pay for the wedding at his chest. 'I thought you were my friend!'

The purse had fallen unheeded to the floor. 'You have enough friends in these parts, it seems,' Robbie had sneered. 'Nobody will say one word against ye. And without a body, that magistrate says he dare not put the only son of the local lord on trial.'

They had flung increasingly harsh words at each other, which had culminated in Robbie yelling, 'Curse you and your title! May you rot in hell with it!'

Hell, he'd mused. Yes, he had felt as though he was in hell. And like so many of the damned, he had set out on a path of deliberate self-destruction, staking all that was left of Cora's wedding fund on a horse that was certain to lose.

He'd eyed up the runners, and been drawn to one that was being soundly whipped by its infuriated jockey. It was frothing at the mouth, its eyes rolling as it went round and round in circles. The jockey had lashed at it some more. He still couldn't get it to the starting line.

That horse doesn't want to be here any more than you do, he could imagine his tender-hearted Cora saying. *Poor creature.*

And that was when he knew he had to lay her blood money on the horse she would have felt sorry for.

When had it romped home a length ahead of its nearest rival, he heard her delighted laughter. He would swear to it. And pictured her clapping her hands in glee.

In a daze, he'd gone back to the betting post, feeling like Judas at the thought of the cascade of silver that would soon be poured into his hands. In the next race, he'd backed the most broken-down nag he could see in a last-ditch attempt to purge away his overriding sense of guilt. He *had* to get rid of that money. Robbie had cursed it!

As the pack set off, he thought he felt Cora sigh as the sorry specimen he'd backed lumbered wearily along the track. Dammit if he hadn't wagered on the very horse she would have chosen again! This time, he had felt there was a certain inevitability about the outcome of the race. Two furlongs from the finish, a riderless horse ran across the field, causing the leaders to stumble, and creating a few moments of mayhem, during which Cora's favourite wheezed up on the outside, crossing the finishing line while the rest were still disentangling themselves from the pile-up.

Cora had cheered. He'd heard her. No question.

The noisy crowds of race-goers faded from his consciousness as his mind had gone back to the day he had finally managed to place his ring on her finger.

'Nothing will be able to part us now,' he had said with grim satisfaction. And then, anticipating their wedding vows, he'd added, *'Except death.'*

'Not even that,' she had breathed, gazing up at him with naked adoration in her eyes.

And that was the moment he'd realised that no matter what Robbie might think, Cora was still his. He had felt her lay her hand on his sleeve, and hold him back when he would have tossed even those winnings away on the favourite in the next race. *'Enough now,'* she had cautioned him. And tears had sprung to his eyes, because he had known, beyond the shadow of a doubt, that she loved him far too much to want to watch him blight his future with reckless gambling. And he had walked away.

From that day forward, he had done nothing without considering what she would have made of it. And the more he asked her opinion, the more often he had felt her hovering close by.

Robbie had stormed off back to Scotland, his parents

had washed their hands of him, neighbours regarded him with suspicion, and former acquaintances shunned him.

But Cora had stood by him.

There had been times when he had sunk into such despair that he considered following her into the after-life.

But he could see her shaking her head in reproof, and hear her declaring that suicide was a mortal sin. He did not care if it was a sin, if it could bring them together. But something told him that whatever part of the after-world she inhabited would exclude sinners of that sort.

And so, since he knew she did not want him to take that course, he'd just had to go on existing. He could not call it living. Cut off from his family and friends, he had begun to haunt the lowest gaming hells in London. They were the only places whose doors were still open to him.

But even there, she watched over him, giggling at the stunned faces of the men from whom he'd won cash, deeds to mines, and shares in canal companies.

And it was she who urged him, when he had just donned the first set of good quality, brand-new clothes he had ever owned, to walk into White's and face them all down. She had crowed with laughter when he had walked out, £20,000 the richer.

It had brought him a measure of satisfaction to pay off the mortgage on Kingsmede, when his father had died. And to pay off his inherited debts out of winnings he'd gleaned from the very men who had fleeced his shiftless parent. Since then, he had gradually been able to make all the improvements to his estate Cora had talked about when she had been there. His tenants might whisper about him, and the way he came by his money, but it did not stop them from being glad he was re-thatching their cottages, or draining low-lying fields to improve their harvests.

Not that he cared what they thought of him. He was not doing it for them, but to please her. Her opinion was the only one that mattered to him.

She was the only person he felt any connection with any more.

Even though she was dead.

If that made him crazy, then so be it.

If it was madness that drove him back to the card tables, so that he could hear her muttering about the drunkenness of his opponents as he ruthlessly stripped them of their money, or feel her breath fan his cheek as she blew on his dice for luck, then it beat the alternative! He had not cared that her unseen presence, walking at his side, acted like a barrier between him and the rest of the world.

She was still there.

Until Miss Winters had kissed him.

'Cora,' he moaned again, sagging against the railings in defeat.

A seller of kindling, pushing his cart before him, shot him a piercing look, before shaking his head and hurrying on.

He knew what he must look like. He was standing here, in the first light of day, crying out for a woman who had been dead for seven dark, hellishly lonely years. And he didn't care what anyone might think. If he only had the supernatural powers that people attributed to him, by Lucifer and all that was unholy, he would use them now! If he really knew of some incantation…

A line from somewhere sprang to mind. Something about three times three times three…

And even as he muttered what he could remember of what he dimly suspected was something from Shakespeare, a movement from the area steps of a house further down the street caught his eye. A short young woman, modishly yet soberly dressed, in a dark blue coat and poke bonnet, was climbing up on to the pavement. At first, he did not know why, out of all the people bustling about their business, this one insignificant female had attracted his attention. But then she turned to scan the traffic before venturing out into the road, and he caught a glimpse of her face.

And it felt as though something had sucked all the air from his lungs.

It was Cora.

'Bloody hell!' he swore, clutching the railings even harder as his knees threatened to give way beneath him. Somehow, with all that three-times-three business, and invoking unholy powers, he had managed to conjure up her shade! For the last seven years, he had heard her, caught her scent on the breeze, felt her presence, but never, ever had she allowed him so much as one brief glimpse of her…

'Bloody hell!' he swore again. While he had been standing there, completely stunned at having called up her spirit, or whatever the hell it was had just happened, she had disappeared round the corner. She had walked away from him as though he was of no account. As though she had somewhere far more important to be.

Uttering another curse, he set off in pursuit. It should have been easy to catch up with her. She did not have that much of a head start. But as he attempted to break into a run, the pavement undulated beneath his feet as though it had a life of its own, throwing him into the path of a furniture mender carrying a bunch of rushes. Lord Matthison had to grab on to the man's shoulders to steady himself before he could lurch off in the direction Cora had gone.

For a few terrible minutes, he thought he would never see her again. The streets were full of tradesmen making early deliveries to the houses of the wealthy now, and it was as if the crowds had swallowed her up. Panic brought him out in a cold sweat, until he caught a glimpse of that dark blue coat on the far side of Berkeley Square, and he plunged into the gardens after her.

She was half-way up Bruton Street before he sighted her again, gliding effortlessly through the throng. He bit back a curse as a rabbit, dangling from the pole of its vendor, struck him full in the face.

'Cora!' he yelled in desperation as the rabbit seller laid hands on him, angrily demanding something…recompense for the damage to his wares probably, but he paid no heed. 'Wait!' he cried, thrusting the man rudely aside. He could not let anything prevent him from discovering where Cora was going!

He saw her half-turn. Felt the moment she recognised him with the force of a punch to the gut. For there was no tenderness, no understanding in her eyes. On the contrary, she recoiled from him, and with a look of horror hitched up her skirts and began to run.

He tried to run too, but she just kept on getting further and further away from him. She could melt through the throng, because she was a wraith. But his own body was all too solid, so that he was obliged to swerve around, or shove people aside. But he kept his eyes fixed on her. Until the very moment she darted into one of the shops on Conduit Street, and slammed the door behind her.

He stumbled to a halt on the pavement opposite what turned out to be a modiste's. A very high-class modiste with the name 'Madame Pichot' picked out in gold leaf on a signboard above the door.

His heart was hammering in his chest, which was still heaving with shortened breath. What was he to do now? Barge into the shop, which probably wasn't even open to customers yet, and demand they let him speak to the ghost he'd just seen take refuge inside? They would call for the watch, and have him locked up. In an asylum for the insane, most like.

He bent over, his hands resting on his knees as he fought to get his breath back. And make some sense of what had just happened.

Why, for God's sake, had Cora fled from him, the

very moment she had finally deigned to let him see her? And what was the significance of bringing him here?

He straightened up, staring at the shop front as though it might provide him with some answer to this unholy muddle.

'Evening gowns a speciality', read a card prominently displayed in the window, underneath a sample of the fabulously intricate beadwork that had become all the rage amongst the fashionable this year.

And a cold thread of foreboding slithered down his spine.

The very night after Mr Winters had declared his intention to lay Cora's ghost to rest for good, the first night he'd had a run of such spectacularly bad hands even he could do nothing with them, he had partnered a woman wearing a dress that came from this modiste. He had laid the blame for their defeat at whist at the feet of the woman wearing the expensive gown, a French chit, who had as little grasp of the game as she had of the English language. But in his heart he had known she had nothing to do with his wins or losses.

All gamblers were superstitious, but he supposed he must be the most superstitious of the lot. Knowing Cora's influence to be the source of his success, he had taken great pains, from the first day he had sensed her presence, to avoid offending her. He never touched strong liquor, nor did he succumb to the lures cast out by women who were fascinated by his aura of dark menace. How could he have contemplated bedding anyone, even if any woman had ever stirred him on any level, knowing that Cora hovered not far away, watching his every move? Not that she would have watched for long. Her puritanical soul would have been so shocked, she would have fled, perhaps never to return.

He had been right to take care. Cora's love was so strong it had reached out to him from beyond the grave. But a love strong enough to cheat death was not a force to be trifled with.

Miss Winters had kissed him, her father had begun to search for lawyers cunning enough to lay her spirit in the grave for good, and Cora had turned her back on him. And getting blind drunk, and shouting curses up at Miss Winters's windows, had not done him any favours. That slamming door was a clear enough message that even he could read it.

She had put back the barrier that existed between the living and the dead. And she was on the other side.

He ran a shaky hand over his face, feeling sick to his stomach.

He had only survived the last seven years because she had been right there with him. More real to him than all the gibbering idiots who populated the hells he frequented.

Would she come back to him, he wondered frantically, if he proclaimed the truth about her? He would not care if they declared him insane, and locked him up. He could afford to pay for a nice, cosy cell. It would almost be a relief to stop pretending his life made any sense. To stop hiding the anguish that tortured him night and day. He could just lie in the dark, and rant and curse to his heart's content.

Mr Winters would surely abandon his ambition to have his daughter marry a peer, if that peer was a raving lunatic! And even Robbie would reap some benefit. It would appease his quest for justice, to see the man he believed had murdered his sister finally locked away.

If that was what it took to appease Cora, he decided, his jaw firming, then it would be a small price to pay!

'You wanter cross or not, mister?' a little voice piped up, jerking him out of his darkly disturbing thoughts.

'Cross?'

A ragged boy with a dirty broom was standing, palm outstretched, gazing up at him expectantly.

A crossing sweeper.

'No,' he replied. There was no point.

No point to anything, any more. He had offended Cora. Driven her away.

'Want me to see if I can get a message to her?' the lad persisted.

'Message?'

'To the red-haired piece you chased up the street.'

'You saw her?' Lord Matthison stared at the boy in shock. He had assumed he was the only one who had been able to see her. Especially after the way she had melted through the crowds as though she and they existed on different planes.

The boy leaned closer, and took an experimental sniff, his perplexed face creasing into a grin.

'Clearer than you, I reckon, by the smell of your breath. Had a heavy night, have yer?'

Lord Matthison grimaced as the lad's words sank in.

He had not taken a drink in seven years. Had been astounded by what a tolerance for gin he seemed to have, marvelling at the fact he was still on his feet. Well, he might be on his feet, but he was sure as hell not sober.

The woman was real. He had not called some spirit up out of the pit. Cora had not deliberately turned her back on him, run from him, and slammed the door in his face. He had just seen some servant girl climb up the area steps from the servants' entrance, and go about her legitimate business.

Which had nothing to do with him.

The fact that she had looked uncannily like Cora was mere coincidence. Or…had she even born that much of a resemblance to his late fiancée? He frowned. He had not been close enough to see her face clearly. It had been her build, and the way she walked, that had convinced him he was seeing a ghost.

His head began to ache.

Typical!

He was getting a hangover before he was even sober.

He pressed the heels of his hands over his eyes, digging his fingers into his scalp. There was no point in trying to make sense of any of this until he had sobered up.

'Is this your patch?' he asked the crossing sweeper, running his fingers through his hair.

'Yessir!' said the lad, rather too loudly for Lord Matthison's liking.

'Then find out whatever you can about the red-head,' he said, dipping into his pocket, and flipping the lad a coin, 'and I shall give you another of these.'

The boy's face lit up when he saw it was a crown piece. 'Right you are! When will you be coming back?'

'I shall not,' he replied with a grimace of distaste. He despised men who loitered on street corners, hoping to catch a glimpse of the hapless female that was currently the object of their prurient interest.

'You will report to my lodgings. What is your name?'

'Grit,' said the boy, causing Lord Matthison to look at him sharply. And then press his fingers to his throbbing temples. It was all of a piece. The boy he was employing to spy on Cora's ghost could not possibly have a sensible name like Tom, or Jack! Everything about this night bore all the hallmarks of a nightmare.

'I will tell my manservant, then, that if a short, dirty person answering to the name of Grit comes knocking, that he is to admit you. Or, if I am not there, to extract what information you have, and reward you with another coachwheel.'

'And who might you be?'

'Lord Matthison.'

He watched the light die from the boy's eyes. Saw him swallow. Saw him try to hide his consternation. But Grit was too young to quite manage to conceal the belief he had just agreed to serve the devil's minion. He kissed goodbye to the prospect of ever finding out anything about the red-head who had worked him up into such a state. The lad would never pluck up the courage to venture to his lodgings. Or if he did, his conscience was bound to hold him in check. Even a dirt-poor gutter-snipe would think twice about selling information about a defenceless female to a man of Lord Matthison's reputation.

'In the meantime, perhaps you could find me a cab,' he drawled, eyeing the shop across the street one last time. And then, because he got a perverse kind of pleasure from playing up to the worst of what people expected of him, he added, 'I dislike being abroad in daylight.'

Chapter Two

Mary dashed across the main shop, through the velvet curtains that divided it from the working areas, and pounded up the three flights of stairs that led to the workroom. The one place where she had learned to feel secure.

She had no idea why the way that man had emerged from the shadows on the other side of Curzon Street, with his black clothes, black hair and forbidding expression, had shaken her so badly. Or why, for an instant, she had got the peculiar impression that the shadows themselves had thickened, solidified and spawned the living embodiment of her nightmares.

It *was* terrifying, though, to feel as if your nightmares had invaded your waking life. Particularly since those nightmares were so vague.

All she could remember when she woke up from one of them was that there had been something hovering behind her. Something she dared not turn and face.

Because she was sure that if she did, it would rear up and swallow her whole. And so she would curl up, trying to make herself disappear, so the Thing would not notice her. But she could always feel it coming nearer and nearer, its shadow growing bigger and bigger, until eventually, in sheer terror, she would leap up and try to run away.

In her dreams, she never managed to move one step. But her legs would always start to thrash around the bed.

'Wake up, Mary,' one of the other girls would complain, prodding her with their sharp elbows. 'You're having one of your dreams again.'

They would tell her to lie still, and she would, clutching the sheets to her chin, staring up at the ceiling, terrified to close her eyes lest the dream stalked her again.

She sighed, rubbing the heels of her hands against her eyes. Deep down she knew that shadows did not turn into men, and chase girls down the street.

Though it had not stopped her running from him.

Just as she fled from whatever it was that stalked her dreams.

'Mary!' The angry voice of her employer made every girl in the workroom jump to attention. The fact that Madame Pichot had left her office at this hour of the morning did not bode well for any of them.

'What is the matter with you now? You are as white as a sheet! You are not going to be ill again, are you?'

Mary could not blame her for looking so exasperated. She was nowhere near as robust as the other girls who sewed for Madame. Never had been.

'That doctor promised me that if you took regular walks, your constitution would improve,' Madame complained. 'I cannot afford for you to take to your bed at this time of year!' Although the workload had slackened off slightly, now that the presentations in the Queen's drawing rooms had mostly taken place, there were still enough orders coming in for Madame to keep her girls working from dawn till they dropped into bed from sheer exhaustion.

Madame Pichot stalked across the bare floor and laid her hand on Mary's forehead.

'I am n-not ill,' Mary stammered, as much alarmed now by Madame's censure, as by what had happened in the street. 'B-but there w-was a m-man…'

Madame Pichot rolled her eyes, raising her hands to the ceiling in one of her Gallic expressions of exasperation. 'The streets are always full of men. I am sure none of them would be interested in a little dab of nothing like you!' she snapped, tugging off Mary's gloves, and untying her bonnet ribbons.

'N-no, he was shouting,' Mary exclaimed, recalling that fact for the first time herself.

'There are a lot of men hawking their wares at this time of the morning,' Madame scoffed. 'He wasn't shouting at you.'

'But I think he was,' she murmured, trying to examine what had happened without letting the panic that had gripped her on the street from clouding her perception. 'He chased me!' Though why some man she had never seen before should suddenly take it into his head to pursue her, shouting angrily, she could not imagine. But she had definitely seen him roughly pushing a tradesman out of his way. With his vengeful, dark eyes fixed on *her*. And for one awful moment, it had felt as though the curtain that separated what was real, from what existed only in her head, had been ripped in two. She had not known where she was. Or who she was.

That had been the most frightening moment of all.

'Mary, really,' Madame said, tugging her to her feet, and undoing her coat buttons, while the other girls in the workroom began to snigger, 'just because you saw a man running in the street, does not mean he was chasing you. Who on earth would want to chase a scrawny little creature like you, when there are willing, pretty girls for sale on every street corner?'

It should have been reassuring to hear Madame repeat the very fact that had her so bewildered. Except that she *knew* he had been chasing her. Her.

'Now, Mary,' said Madame firmly, shoving her back down on her work stool, and thrusting her spectacles into her hands, 'I forbid you to have one of your turns. There is no time for it today. Not when you have the bodice for the Countess of Walton's new gown to finish. Whatever happened outside, you must put it out of your head. Do you hear me?'

'Yes, Madame.' In truth, there was nothing she wanted more than to put it out of her mind. She was really glad she had such a complicated piece of work to do today. For concentrating on making something utterly beautiful had always had the power to keep her demons at bay. Even when she had been a little girl…

With a startled cry, Mary dropped her glasses. It always gave her a jolt, when one of these little glimpses of a past that was mostly a complete blank flared across her consciousness without warning.

Hearing Madame's huff of disapproval, Mary dropped to her knees to grope for them. They would not have slid far along the rough planks of the workroom. She would find them in mere seconds, pick them up, and be quickly able to get on with her work.

Why, she thought in anguish, could her mind not be as nimble as her fingers? Whenever she tried to catch hold of one of these little slivers of light that flashed into her mind, it was just like trying to take hold of a candle flame. There was nothing of any substance to latch on to. Except pain.

Well, only an idiot would keep on putting their hand into a flame, once they had learned that it burned, she thought, hooking her glasses over her ears. Instantly, everything beyond a few feet from her went out of focus, isolating her on her stool, like a shipwrecked mariner, clinging to a lone rock shrouded by fog.

When she had been a little girl, she sighed, unable to silence the echo of that memory straight away. Hastily she picked up a needle, but not fast enough to blot out the feeling that when she had been a little girl…with her head dutifully bent over her needle-work…

'*Pay no mind to anything but your sampler,*' she

heard a gentle voice telling her. And for a fleeting moment, it was not Madame standing over her, glowering, but a kindly, protective presence that she instinctively recognised as her mother.

'For the Lord's sake, keep your head down,' the voice…her mother…continued as she became aware there had been someone else with them. Looming over them. A man with a loud voice and hard fists…and fear rushed up to swamp her.

Past and present swirled and merged. The child in her bent over her sampler, to blot out the raised voices of the adults, the violence that hovered in the air. And the woman hitched her stool closer to her embroidery frame. She leant so close her nose was practically brushing the cream silk net so that every time she breathed in, her lungs were filled with the sweet, aromatic scent of brand new cloth. With fingers that shook, she threaded a string of tiny crystal droplets on to her bead needle. Then she took a second needle which she would use to couch down the tiny segments of beading. She bent all her powers of concentration on to the intricate work, deliberately pushing away the vague images of violence that had almost stepped fully formed, into the light, just as that dark man had done earlier.

She had become adept at pushing uncomfortable thoughts away since she had arrived in London, bruised, alone and scared. And soon, her world shrank until all she could feel was the texture of the luxurious fabric, all she could hear was the pluck of the needle piercing it, the hiss of the thread as she set each meticulously measured stitch.

Her breathing grew steadier. Her heart beat evenly again. All that was ugly and mean slithered back into the shadows, leaving Mary conscious only of the work that occupied her hands.

She sensed, rather than heard, Madame Pichot step away. They both knew that now Mary's mind had turned in a new direction, she would soon forget all about the alarming incident in Berkeley Square.

It had been a long time since Lord Matthison had played against the house. The owners of gambling hells, such as this one, had become reluctant to admit him, until he had restricted his play to private games, arranged for him with other gentlemen. Or men who called themselves gentlemen, he corrected himself as he glanced round the table at the flushed faces of Lord Sandiford, Mr Peters, and a young cub by the name of Carpenter who was looking distinctly green about the gills.

Peters fumbled with his cards, reached for a drink, then, seeing his glass was empty, called for a refill from a passing waiter.

Lord Matthison leaned back in his chair with a sneer. Taking yet another drink was not going to alter the fact that once Peters threw down his hand, he would have cleaned them all out.

His mockery turned inwards. Had he not discovered for himself how deceptive strong drink could be?

Thinking he had summoned up Cora's ghost, by muttering something about three times three indeed! As soon as he'd sobered up, he had realised that the vision he'd had of Cora had sprung like a genie from a bottle, formed from a heady mixture of gin fumes and wishful thinking.

He had not been able to bear the thought he might have lost her all over again, that was what it boiled down to. And so he had let the gin steer him down a path of self-delusion.

Just as brandy was steering Peters down the path of self-destruction, he reflected, as the man gulped down what the waiter had just poured.

The man would have done better to stick to coffee, as he had done, he mused, as Peters, with a defiant flourish, finally displayed his hand.

Then slumped back when he saw what Lord Matthison had been holding.

'One more hand,' he begged, as Lord Matthison reached for his winnings.

'You have nothing left to stake,' Lord Matthison replied coldly.

'I have a daughter,' the man interjected, his eyes fastened on the pile of coins, banknotes and hastily scrawled pledges Lord Matthison was sweeping into his capacious pockets.

Lord Matthison regarded him with contempt. 'Do you expect me to care?'

If Peters had a grain of worth in him, he would have been at home, managing his business, not wasting his substance in a gaming hell like this! He should have considered what it might mean to his daughter *before* he gambled it all away. It was no use appealing to him now.

His own father had been just the same. When gambling fever gripped him, he forgot all about his wife and son, the dependants who looked to him for their welfare. All that had mattered to him was the next turn of the card, the next roll of the dice.

'No, no!' the man gibbered. 'I am saying that I still have a daughter—' a nasty look spread across his face '—to stake. Just give me one last chance to win something back,' he begged.

'Out of the question,' he replied, despising the man who had just ruined himself.

'She's pretty. And still a virgin,' Peters gabbled, sweat breaking out on his florid face.

Lord Sandiford, who had gone down to the tune of four hundred guineas without batting an eyelid, sniggered. 'You are wasting your time there, old man. Better sell her outright to me. Lord Matthison has no use for women.'

'Not living ones,' he agreed, shooting a pointed look at the hell's newest hostess, who had been hovering by his shoulder all night. At one point, he had found her perfume so cloying that he had told her quite brusquely to move further off. She had pouted, and looked up at him from under half-closed lids, purring that she would await his pleasure later.

'What do you mean by that?' demanded Peters.

Everyone at the table fell silent. Very few people

had ever dared ask Lord Matthison whether there was any truth in the rumours circulating about him.

Mr Carpenter shot Lord Sandiford a look of disgust, which turned to loathing as his eyes swept past Lord Matthison, got up so quickly his chair overturned, and made hastily for the exit.

'The only woman I am interested in, Mr Peters,' Lord Matthison replied, choosing his words very carefully, 'is Miss Cora Montague.' He felt a ripple of shock go round the room as he finally spoke her name aloud in public. Several men at nearby tables twisted round in their seats, hoping to hear some new titbit about the scandal that had rocked society seven years earlier.

'In her case, I was willing to stake my very soul on just one throw of the dice,' he said enigmatically. 'And I lost it.' He got to his feet, wondering whether proclaiming his allegiance to her ghost in a hell-hole like this would be enough to entice her back to his side.

What had he got to lose?

'She has my soul, Mr Peters.' And then, considering the massive amount he had just won tonight, his breath quickened. Even though he had not felt her presence, his luck had definitely turned. 'Or perhaps,' he added, feeling as though a great weight had rolled from his shoulders, 'I have hers.'

The girl who had been trying to get his attention all night was standing by the door. The owner of the hell was holding her by the arm, and talking to her in an urgent undertone.

Lord Matthison pulled out a banknote and waved it under her nose.

'Still think you'd like to earn this?' he taunted her.

She shrank back, her face turning pale as the owner of the hell moved away, leaving her alone with him. Lord Matthison put the money back in his pocket.

'Clearly not,' he drawled. 'Very wise of you.'

It was a relief to get out into the street, and breathe air not tainted by cigar fumes and desperation. 'Did you see that, Cora?' he asked of the black-velvet shadows of the alleyway. 'Did you hear me tell them?'

But there was no reply. She did not come skipping to his side, to keep him company on the long walk home. Instead, he had a fleeting image of what that nameless daughter would feel like when Peters went home and told her he was going to sell her to Sandiford. Swiftly followed by the horrified look on the face of that woman he had mistaken for Cora two days before.

'It is not my fault Peters tried to sell his daughter to me,' he growled as he set off through the dark, damp streets. 'I only went to the tables to find you.'

But she had not been there. And so the money that was making his coat pockets bulge meant nothing to him. He had no use for it.

When he reached his rooms, he drew out all the banknotes that had formed part of the winning pot and thrust them into his manservant's hands.

'I ruined a man named Peters tonight,' he bit out. 'Take this money, and hand it over into the keeping of his daughter. Tell her she is not to let her father get hold of it. Or she will have me to answer to.'

'Sir.' Ephraims's eyebrows rose a fraction, but he went straight out, without asking any questions.

Until tonight, Lord Matthison had felt not one ounce of pity towards any of the men from whom he'd won money. To his knowledge, he had ruined three.

But tonight, he could not bear to keep one penny of that money. He had only gone to the tables to find Cora. Not to bring more misery to the child of a compulsive gambler.

He went to his room, and shrugged off his jacket, the coins spilling from his pockets and rattling across the boards.

'I did not want that money for myself, Cora,' he explained, sitting on a chair by the bed to tug off his boots. 'You know I don't need it. I've invested wisely these last few years.' Somehow that admission only made this evening's work seem worse.

'I have ensured the girl will be safe,' he protested, untying his neckcloth and letting it slither to the floor.

'Does that please you, Cora?' he addressed the shadowed corners of his room. But there was no answer.

With a groan of despair, he lay down on top of the bed, still fully clothed, and flung his arm over his eyes. If she was not going to come back, he did not know how he could bear to go on.

There was no satisfaction to be had in ruining one man, or bestowing largesse on another.

Not when she wasn't there to see it.

He needed *her*.

God, how he needed her!

He felt as though he had barely closed his eyes, when he was woken by the sound of somebody knocking on the door.

Persistently.

Ephraims must still be out, he thought, sitting up and running his fingers through his disordered hair. He would have to deal with whoever was visiting himself. Probably one of the men from whom he had taken promissory notes the night before, he decided as he padded barefoot to the outer door.

However, it was not a shamefaced gambler who stood on his doorstep, but the grubby street sweeper from the night of the vision on Curzon Street.

'Grit,' he observed, opening the door wider to admit the rather scared-looking boy. 'You had better come into my sitting room.'

'Her name is Mary,' the boy announced without preamble, the moment Lord Matthison sank wearily on to the sofa. He did not really want to hear anything the lad had to say. But he might as well let him earn his tip, since he had plucked up the courage to walk into the devil's lair.

'The red-head you was after. She come to Lunnon about six or so years ago as an apprentice, and has been working her way up. Well, not that she's indentured regular, like, on account of her being a charity case.'

Lord Matthison brushed aside the apparent coincidence of that female appearing on the scene about the time Cora had disappeared. Hundreds of working girls came up to London from the country every year.

'No one can match the stuff she turns out now,' Grit added, staring round Lord Matthison's study with apprehensive eyes, as though half-expecting to see a human skull perched on one of the shelves. 'The nobs fight to get a dress wot she's had a hand in.'

Cora had been exceptionally fond of sewing, he recalled. But then, so were lots of gently reared girls. It meant nothing. Nothing!

'If you want to meet her,' the boy said, after a slight pause, 'she'll be in the Flash of Lightning Friday night. Her friend, see, has an understanding with a jarvey wot drinks in there. And they mean to sneak out and meet him. 'Bout seven,' he finished, sticking out his hand hopefully.

'Go into my room,' said Lord Matthison, jerking his head in that direction, 'and you can pick up whatever you find on the floor.' There had been several crown pieces amongst the coinage he had won last night. Grit was welcome to them.

He sat forwards on the sofa, his head in his hands. Last night, he had thought he had got it all clear in his mind. The woman he had seen on Curzon Street could not have been Cora. He had just been drunk, and had imagined the likeness.

But now he was beginning to wonder all over again. Take the way Grit had described her as a red-head.

The woman he had chased had been wearing a poke bonnet that covered her hair completely. So how had he been so sure it was red?

As Cora's was red.

And what about the way the bleak chill that usually hung round him like a mantle had lifted the second he saw the early morning sun brush the curve of her cheek? The way his heart had raced. As though he was really alive, and not just a damned soul, trapped in a living body.

He was not going to find a moment's peace, he realised, until he had looked the seamstress in the face, and proved beyond a shadow of a doubt that she bore no more than a passing resemblance to Cora.

'Stop worrying, Mary,' Molly cajoled. 'Madame Pennypincher won't know nothing about it unless we tells her.'

'She'll know it shouldn't take us so long to make a delivery.'

Ever since Mary had come back from the Curzon Street errand with her nerves in shreds, Madame Pichot had sent Molly with her on her daily walks.

Molly had been cock-a-hoop at escaping their relentless drudgery, shamelessly making use of their daily excursions to arrange this clandestine meeting with Joe Higgis, who worked out of a hackney cab stand on the corner of Conduit Street.

Mary did not begrudge Molly her snatched moments of happiness, she just did not see how they would manage to get away with taking a detour to a gin shop in Covent Garden.

'All we have to do is think up a story and stick to it,' Molly persisted. 'We'll tell her the housekeeper asked us to take tea in the kitchen, or the lady had some query about the bill.'

'I don't...I can't...' Mary felt her face growing hot. The very thought of telling her employer a barefaced lie was making her insides churn.

Molly clicked her tongue and sighed. 'Just leave the talking to me, then, when we get back. You can keep yer mouth shut, can't yer?' She gripped Mary's arm quite hard. 'Ye understand it ain't right to snitch on yer friends, don't yer?'

'I would never snitch on you, Molly,' said Mary, meaning it.

When she had first come to work for Madame Pichot, she had existed in an almost constant state of sickening fear. London was so confusingly crowded, so nerve-jarringly noisy. She had found it hard to understand what Madame's other girls were saying at first, so peculiar did their accent sound, and so foreign the words they used. But Molly had always been patient with her, explaining her work slowly enough so she could understand, even putting a stop to the acts of petty spite some of the others had seemed to find hilarious.

'Anyhow, Madame ought to let us have an hour or two off, once in a while, and then we wouldn't have to sneak off on the sly!'

No, she would not say one word to Madame about where they had been.

She would not need to.

She looked round uneasily as Molly towed her into the overheated and evil-smelling den in which her Joe liked to take a heavy wet of an evening, with the other drivers who worked for the same firm as him. Madame would only have to breathe in as they walked past to know exactly where they had been.

Molly soon spotted her beau, who got his pals to make room for the two of them at the table where they were sitting. A slovenly-looking girl deposited two beakers on the sticky tabletop in front of them, and Joe flipped her a coin.

Molly dug Mary in the ribs.

'Say thank you to Joe for buying us both a draught of jacky, girl. Ever so generous of him, ain't it?' Molly beamed at him, and his eyes lit up. Sliding closer to her, he slid his arm round her waist, and gave her a squeeze. Molly giggled, turning pink with pleasure. Mary might as well not have existed for all the notice he took of her.

She reached for her beaker, and bent her eyes resolutely on the liquid it contained, feeling slightly nauseous. She could not understand what Mary saw in Joe Higgis. He had sloping shoulders and a thick neck. His fingernails were dirty, and, given the nature of his job, he probably smelt of horses. How could Molly let such a man paw at her like that, never mind encourage it?

Molly had explained that he made her laugh, and that in this miserable world, you didn't turn your nose up at a man who could make you laugh, no matter what.

For Molly's sake, and to avoid hurting Joe's feelings,

she supposed she ought to try to look as though she was grateful for the drink he had bought her. Besides, she thought, glancing about her nervously, if she appeared to be concentrating on her drink, she would not look so out of place as she felt.

Tentatively, she tasted it, and was surprised to find it had a lightly perfumed flavour. Gin was not unpleasant, she grudgingly admitted, taking another sip.

'Friend of Molly's, are yer?' asked the man beside her, who had been eyeing her speculatively ever since she had sat down.

Mary bit down a scathing retort. She had come in with Molly. She was sitting next to Molly. What else would she be, but a friend of Molly's?

'Now, none of your cheek, Fred!' Molly suddenly stirred herself to say. 'Nor none of you others, neither,' she addressed the other men who were sitting at their table. 'I won't have none of you taking advantage of Mary, just coz she's too simple to do it for herself. I'll darken the daylights of anyone who so much as lays a finger on her!' she declared belligerently.

Fred raised his hands in surrender. 'I was just being friendly,' he protested.

'Well, stop it!' snapped Molly. 'She don't like men. They make her…' She paused, considering her choice of words. Mary stared fixedly into the depths of her drink, torn between gratitude to Molly for defending her, and sickening dread at what she might be about to reveal.

'Jumpy! Yes,' Molly declared, 'that's what she is round men what don't mind their manners. So just watch it!'

Having settled the point to her satisfaction, Molly climbed on to Joe's lap, and took up where she had left off.

Mary felt like a coin that had been tossed in the air, unsure whether she was going to come down heads, humiliated at having her deficiencies broadcast, or tails, grateful for Molly's spirited defence. Though Molly had only spoken the truth. Men did make her jumpy. She had not wanted Fred to speak to her, and she certainly did not want to have to answer him. In fact, she wished she could just shrink down into her coat and disappear. To conceal her confusion, she took another, longer pull at her drink.

Once it had gone down, she found her initial surge of contrasting emotions had settled down into a sort of dull resentment.

Molly had just told all these people that she was simple, and she did not think she was, not really. It was true that when she first came to London she had been confused about a lot of things. But she had been ill. She had still been getting the headaches for months after Madame took her in.

But now she wondered if some of those headaches had been due to the fact she had slept so poorly back then. For one thing, the streets were so noisy, at all hours of the day and night, and for another, she was not used to sharing a bed…

Though how she was so sure of that, when so many other things that other people took for granted were complete mysteries to her… She sighed despondently.

Perhaps Madame and Molly and the others were right about her. Perhaps she was a simpleton.

In an effort to distract herself from the perplexing muddle of her thoughts, she applied herself to her gin. Gradually she felt the knot of anxiety that was normally lodged somewhere beneath her breastbone melt away. What did it matter, really, if there was something wrong with her mind? She had a good position, where the skills she did have were put to good use. And she had friends.

Joe's friends, too, she realised, raising her head to look about the table, were not such a bad bunch, for all that they were so repulsive looking. She felt a giggle rising up inside as it occurred to her that if she had to come into a dirty, smelly drinking den, she could not have better companions than a group of hackney-cab drivers. Experienced as they were with handling highly strung creatures for a living, they had taken Molly's words to heart, and acted on them. Oh, not overtly. But they were not speaking so loudly now as they had been doing before. They were not crowding her with their big, male bodies, and they seemed to be trying not to make any sudden movements, that might startle her.

It was…quite touching.

London, she mused, cradling her cup of gin to her chest, was turning out not to be such a dreadful place at all. It had taken her a long time, but she was slowly growing accustomed to it. The more she explored its alleys and byways, the more familiar it became, the fewer terrors it held.

She would be all right.

One day, she would…

'Why did you do it, Cora?' A man's harsh voice rudely interrupted her reverie.

She looked up to see a gentleman standing over her. *The* gentleman. The one who had chased her clear across Berkeley Square. Same dark clothes, same forbidding expression, same angry voice.

She sucked in a sharp breath, waiting to feel the onset of that fear that usually surged through her whenever she felt threatened by something unfamiliar.

It did not materialise.

She peered into her beaker, wondering if this was why so many women grew so fond of gin. It seemed to be making her uncharacteristically brave.

Or maybe, she pondered, it was knowing that this man was outnumbered by Joe's pals. That she was, in effect, surrounded by a burly, bewhiskered, badly dressed cohort of bodyguards.

And so she didn't tremble. She did not shrink away. She just sat there, calmly looking up at him.

His face grew darker.

'You have to make me understand it, Cora,' he grated. 'Why did you run away?'

Cora? Ah, so that was it! She must resemble…her. That was why he had chased her, shouting so angrily. He must have been waiting for…Cora…and been completely perplexed when she had taken fright and run away.

'You have mistaken me for someone else, I think, sir,' she said gently. For she could see that he was really upset, and had no wish to add to his distress.

Yet he looked at her as though she had slapped his face.

If he had been mistaken in her, it had been seven years ago, not seven days!

She had said she loved him so much she did not care if they had to live in a bothy, whatever that was. Yet one afternoon, when nobody was watching, she had sneaked out on him. Without warning. Without excuse. Without reason. And started a new life. Here in London. Not half a mile away from his own lodgings. He might have passed her in the street countless times and not known...

Sheer rage gripped him at the magnitude of her deception. His whole existence, for the past seven years, had been based on a tissue of lies. She had lied to him. Robbie had lied about him. He had been lying to himself.

'You are supposed to be dead,' he hissed between gritted teeth. That she wasn't made him feel like a complete fool. What kind of an idiot would harbour the maudlin, pathetic sentiment that a woman could ever be true, let alone from beyond the grave! Since the day she had...no, not died. Left him, was what she had done. Left him with an accusation of murder hanging over his head. But since that day, *he* might as well have been dead. For nothing had mattered any more.

But what irked him most was the fact that he had still wanted to carry on believing all that claptrap *after* he had seen her in Curzon Street. When he had sobered up, after a few fitful hours of sleep, he had been determined to deny the evidence of his own eyes, preferring to believe alcohol had fuddled his senses so much that he had imagined the resemblance, rather than let go of his insane delusion she was haunting him.

And if Grit had not been heartless enough to sell information to a man of his reputation, he would probably not be standing here now.

He had only come here to get confirmation that he had imagined the woman's resemblance to Cora.

He had never expected to find himself looking at Cora herself.

A slightly older, careworn version of Cora, but Cora none the less.

Her voice had changed. Her accent was now almost indistinguishable from that of the other girls who lived and worked in this area. But there was still an unmistakably soft Scottish burr underlying the sharper vowel sounds, and a cadence to her speech that proclaimed her origins. The rest of her had hardly altered at all. Same fair skin that would break out in freckles at the most fleeting exposure to sunlight, same delicate features that made her face look all eyes, same mannerisms. The way she held her cup, the way she tilted her head as she looked up at him, though those green eyes, that had once blazed at him with what he had believed was the sort of love poets wrote sonnets about, were cold now. Blank.

Empty.

The enormity of her betrayal, her sheer deceitfulness, struck him all over again. There was no consolation in knowing she was not dead after all! He slumped down on to the bench beside her, in the gap that had opened up when her co-worker had climbed into the hackney-cab driver's lap and sucked in a sharp pain. Why had he not seen how deceitful she was back then? Look at her now, calmly sipping her gin after colluding in a clandestine meeting between her co-worker and her fancy man. Abusing the comparative freedom of her trusted position without so much as a qualm! His upper lip curled into a sneer. This woman was not trustworthy! She had waltzed off with his heart and his ring...

His ring! How could he have forgotten that? That ring had been in his family for generations. It was the only item of jewellery his mother had managed to prevent his father from selling. It was extremely valuable. Far too valuable to waste on a deceitful, brazen... He grabbed her hand, determined to take it back.

Her ring finger was bare.

'You sold my ring!'

How had she managed that? He had put up a reward, which he had been ill able to afford at first, in the hope that if it turned up, it would lead back to her. The antique ring, a blood-red ruby surrounded by tiny pearls, was such an unusual piece that he had been sure he would have heard if it had come on to the market.

She had somehow outwitted him, even in that. She must have sold it and used the proceeds to fund her flight to London. He scoffed at his own naïvety in thinking the paltry reward he had put up would have tempted a fence to turn in his supplier!

'Why, Cora?' he asked her again. That was what he

simply could not comprehend. 'At least, tell me why you ran away.'

If she had changed her mind about wanting to marry him, why had she not just told him, broken off the engagement and gone home? There was no need to have gone to such lengths to disappear so completely.

Mary's heart went out to the poor gentleman who looked so bleakly baffled. For she knew exactly how he felt. At one point, her world had frequently seemed to make no sense at all. And that in turn left her feeling scared and lonely and confused.

And when she had felt like that, a few kind words, or a smile, had helped her get back on an even keel. Summoning up a smile that she hoped conveyed her sympathy for his state of mind, she gently explained, 'I really am not who you think I am, sir. My name is Mary.'

'How can you sit there and lie to me?' he snarled. 'To my face! You got on your horse and rode off without a backward glance...'

'A horse?' Mary's eyebrows rose in surprise. If this man thought she was capable of climbing right up on top of a horse, when she was far too timid to even bring herself to pat one—no matter how earnestly Joe promised it was quite safe—then that just proved how badly mistaken he was about her identity! The very prospect of touching one brought on waves of uncontrollable panic. Panic so strong she could smell it. The smell came flooding to her nostrils right now. She swallowed down hastily, but her heart was already pounding in her chest. And she could smell damp leaves, mixed

in with the scent of horse and leather, and taste that
horrid, metallic tang of blood…

'…leaving me to pick up the pieces! Now you will
not even do me the courtesy of explaining your outrageous behaviour! You said you loved me…'

His face dark with rage, he suddenly seized Mary's
shoulders, and kissed her hard on the mouth.

Mary was so surprised, she had no time to react. He
had not looked in the least like a man who was about
to kiss a woman.

But before she could do more than gasp, all hell
broke loose.

With an inarticulate bellow of rage, Fred rose up,
reached over her, seized the poor, deranged gentleman
by the lapels of his very expensive coat, and hauled him
to his feet.

His sudden action caused the bench on which they
were all sitting to topple over, sending Mary flying
backwards in a tangle of skirts. Joe, whose reactions
were lightning fast, had managed to leap to his feet as
the bench slid out from beneath him, but Molly had
tumbled to the floor alongside Mary.

'Quick, this way!' Molly shrieked, grabbing her by
the arm even as she herself started to scramble on all
fours out of the reach of the flailing boots of the three
men now struggling together where, just a moment
before, they had been sitting quietly drinking their porter.

By the time they reached the door, everyone in the
place seemed to have been sucked into the brawl.
Glancing over her shoulder as Molly hustled her out, she

saw one of the serving girls bringing her tray down on the head of a coal-heaver who had a bespectacled clerk in a bear hug, while one of Joe's pals accidentally elbowed Fred in the face as he drew back his fist to punch a man in naval uniform. But she could not make out the dark gentleman anywhere amidst the sea of struggling combatants.

'What a night!' Molly gasped as they made it to the safety of the street, her face alight with excitement.

'Are you not worried about Joe?'

From inside the gin shop Mary could hear the sounds of furniture breaking, and men cursing and yelling.

'Sounds like—' she broke off briefly at a tremendous crash of breaking glass '—he's having a smashing time.' Molly giggled as she straightened Mary's skewed bonnet. 'Did you see how fast he was?' she added, dancing on the spot, and throwing a few punches at imaginary opponents for good measure.

'I scarcely knew what was happening,' Mary admitted. 'It all happened so fast. One minute that man was kissing me, and then… Oh dear—' she paused, casting an anxious glance over her shoulder '—I hope they are not hurting him.'

'Well, strike me!' Molly looked at Mary as though she had never seen her before. 'Here was I thinking you'd be all of a quake, and all you can think of is whether Joe and the lads are hurting your beau!'

'He's not my beau! I just feel…sorry for him, that's all. He seemed to think I was someone he had known once, someone who said she loved him, but then left him. That must have been why he followed me the other day, I must look very like her.' Even sitting face to face with her, in the glaring light of the tavern's lanterns, he seemed convinced she was his lost love. It was so sad.

Molly tucked Mary's hand in the crook of her arm, and stepped out briskly, muttering, 'I done the right thing, then. I weren't sure,' she said a little louder, darting Mary a sidelong glance, 'but the thing is, Mary, girls like us don't have a lot of choice.'

'What do you mean? What have you done?'

'It's for your own good,' she replied, puzzling Mary still further. 'And it's not as if you're scared of him now, are you? Not like you was the other day?'

'No,' Mary confessed, shamefaced. 'I was just being silly that day. He startled me, that was all, leaping out of the shadows like that…'

'There, you see. It will be fine!'

'What will be fine? Molly,' Mary panted, 'do we have to walk this fast? Nobody is chasing us now.'

'Sorry,' said Molly, moderating her stride to accommodate Mary's. 'You know I've always watched out for you, haven't I?'

'Yes.'

'Well, that's what I'm doing now. When Grit came to ask me what he oughter do about the questions Lord Matthison was asking about you, I told him to tell the gentleman whatever he wanted to know. Coz I don't think he'll do you any harm, Mary. There's places what cater to gentlemen of that sort, and he don't go to them. Not that I've heard…'

'Molly, I don't understand what you are talking about!'

'No, I don't s'pose you do. Look,' she said earnestly, 'how long do you think Madame will keep you on, once your health goes completely? She puts up with you now, because the kind of beading you do is all the rage. But there'll be a new fashion next season. Or your eyesight might go. Or…or anything could happen! And then, out you'll go!'

Mary shook her head. 'Madame took a risk, taking me in and giving me a job. She's always been good to me.'

'I've worked for her a damn sight longer than you, girl, and I'm telling you, she's like an old spider, she is, sucking all the life out of us, and then throwing away the husks what ain't no good no more! Mary, she don't even pay you! You get your bed and board, while she's making her fortune out of what your clever fingers bring in. Do you know how much she charges the Earl of Walton for those gowns you embroider for his wife? And do you see a penny piece of it? No! Coz you're too simple to stand up for yourself. Well, I'm doing it for you! You've caught the eye of a real live lord, girl. One of the wealthiest in town.'

'Well, yes, but only because I look like someone he used to know.'

'Makes no difference why he wants you. It only matters that he *does* want you. Gents like him can be very generous, if you give them what they want. And when he tires of you, he won't just chuck you out on the street. Point of pride with men like him, to leave their ladybirds comfortably off.'

'L…ladybird?' Mary echoed in appalled disbelief.

'Oh, yes! I reckon he'll be making you an offer quite soon. And when he does, you take it! You hear? Play your cards right, and this could be the making of you.'

'The making of me?' Mary gasped. 'The ruining of me, you mean!'

'Lord, Mary, don't be any dafter than you have to be. You don't dislike him, do you?'

'It's not that. I do feel sorry for him, but…'

'Well, there you are. No harm in offering the poor man a spot of comfort, is there?'

No harm? She did not know where to begin to explain the sheer magnitude of the harm that would come to her if she sold her body to a man! She could never regard becoming a man's mistress as a step up in the world. It was all very well for Molly to describe it as a chance to gain the kind of financial security she could never hope for, not if she sewed for Madame for a hundred years, but as far as she was concerned, it would be the ultimate degradation!

But there was no point even trying to explain all that to Molly. She would just see her scruples as further proof of her stupidity.

She hunched her shoulders against her friend's well-meaning meddling, and walked back to the shop in Conduit Street feeling like the loneliest, most misunderstood girl in London.

Chapter Three

*M*ary was standing on the edge of a cliff. She could hear waves pounding the shore far below, but it was too dark to see them. It was too dark to see anything. One false move, and she might go tumbling down to her doom.

Her heart started to race. Her legs shook. And, just as she had somehow known it would, the ground beneath her feet crumbled away and she was falling, falling, her mouth open wide in a soundless scream...

She landed with a bump, in the bottom of a small boat, winded, but unharmed. The dark gentleman had been there, waiting to catch her. His arms broke her fall.

It was not dark down here in the boat with him. The sun was shining. She felt warm and secure lying in the dark gentleman's arms, being gently rocked as the waves lapped against the boat. She could hear gulls keening. She looked up into a vast, cloudless sky, the kind of sky you never saw in London, fettered as it was by rooftops rank with smoking chimneys.

He smiled down at her as she relaxed into his hold with a sigh.

'I know you want me to kiss you,' he said, and lowered his head...

With a jolt, Mary woke with the blankets twisted round her legs. The feeling of tranquillity dissipated under a sharp blast of shame. How could she be dreaming about kissing a man? *That* man! She could not seriously be considering Molly's suggestion she become his mistress!

Could she?

Sick with self-disgust, Mary pulled her nightgown out from under Molly's leg, and wriggled out of the bed she shared with her and Kitty, one of the other seamstresses who lived with them over the shop.

She pulled her wrapper round her shoulders, and padded barefoot up to the workroom. The sun was not yet up, so she lit one of the lamps Madame Pichot kept available when her girls had to work beyond the hours of natural daylight, and settled onto her stool by her embroidery frame.

She had intended to distract herself from the disturbing feelings the dream had unleashed, by getting on with some work. But her mind stayed stubbornly focussed on the dark gentleman, like a stray dog gnawing at a stolen bone.

She had woken just before his mouth had touched hers, but she already knew what it would feel like. Though in the dream he would not have kissed her as he had done in the gin shop, with frustrated anger. No, he would have kissed her tenderly, lovingly, exactly as she would want him to…

No! She did not want him to kiss her! She was not that sort of girl! She did not want to snuggle up to him, and put her arms round him, and…and…comfort him with her own kisses…why that would make her no better than a harlot!

She could not understand the person she had become in the Flash of Lightning. Before last night, she would have sworn that she feared and reviled men. All men. She had never wanted to receive the sort of lewd advances that other girls found flattering.

So why had she not felt the slightest inclination to jerk her hand out of his when he had grasped it? Why had she not wanted to struggle away from him when he had crushed her to his chest and kissed her?

She supposed she could argue that she would have been glad of anything that distracted her from sliding down into one of her panics. And she had certainly not been able to think about horses once he had swept her into his arms.

He had overwhelmed every one of her senses. His breath had been warm against her face, his hands strong and determined, yet they had not bruised her shoulders when he had pulled her against the hard wall of his chest, where her nostrils had filled with the scents of him. Expensive linen and fine milled soap and warm, clean man…

She sucked in a sharp, shocked breath. There she went again, savouring an experience that should by rights have scared her. Why had the feel of his arms closing round her felt likc…she forced herself to admit it…like coming home? She rubbed at a dull, nagging ache that was thrumming at the base of her skull. It was ridiculous! He was a complete stranger to her.

A stranger who had managed to breach all her defences with one kiss!

One kiss, she sighed, and she could not stop thinking about him.

Oh, she pressed her palms against her flushed cheeks, she hoped she never saw him again!

If Molly was right, and he was about to make her a dishonourable offer, she did not rightly know how she would answer. She knew what she *ought* to answer. Of course she did. But would she be strong enough to say no? If he spoke to her again, kissed her again, this time gently, persuasively, as he had been about to kiss her in her dream, would she have the courage to stand firm in her beliefs?

Because, for one blissfully sinful moment, until Fred had come to her rescue, she had felt as though there was nowhere else she would rather be.

She, who had felt alone amongst strangers for as long as she could remember, had felt a connection with him that defied explanation.

Surely she had the moral strength to resist the temptation to go away with the first person who had ever made her feel as though she belonged somewhere?

No wonder, she sighed, so many women abandoned honest, hard toil, and took to a life of vice. If she could feel this torn after one fleeting encounter with a man she knew practically nothing about… She shivered. Perhaps her first instinctive reaction to his advent in her life had been the right one. To run far, far away to a place where he could never find her. Because he was dangerous. Dangerous to her.

'Heavens, girl, what's to do with you now?'

Mary started, discovering Madame Pichot hovering over her, her lips pursed with disapproval. She had not heard her come into the workroom. Not that that was so unusual in itself. She was often so immersed in her work that hours passed without her being conscious of anything else that went on in the room around her.

What was unusual was that Madame had caught her staring into space, her hands idle.

No wonder Madame looked displeased. Mary had not been herself since the day she had come running home in a panic from her errand to Curzon Street. Her nights were full of disturbing dreams of the dark man. And all day long her thoughts kept straying in his direction. She had to keep yanking them back to her work by force of will. She hung her head, embarrassed to have to acknowledge that for the first time ever, she was behind with her work.

Madame reached down, took hold of Mary's chin in her strong, capable fingers, and jerked her face up.

'Stars in your eyes,' she muttered angrily. 'You've come back from wherever Molly took you last night with stars in your eyes.' Her fingers squeezed more tightly as Mary squirmed guiltily. She had known Madame would see through Molly's excuses for taking so long over what should have been a straightforward errand. She had sent the girls straight up to their room without comment, and Molly seemed to think they had got away with it. But Madame's next words chilled Mary to the bone.

'Once the gentry start going back to their summer homes, I'm turning that girl off for last night's work.' She looked right through Mary as she voiced her thoughts aloud, treating her, as she had done from the first, as though she was a half-wit. Mary could understand how that attitude had originated. She had been in a terrible state on the day she had arrived. Almost beside herself after the rigours of the journey, and what had happened to her before setting out. For weeks, the slightest thing had triggered debilitating episodes of blind panic, which had meant she hardly got any work done.

The other workers had soon learned it was not safe to ask her questions about where she came from. Whenever she had tried to provide explanations, groping back into the unrelenting blackness where the knowledge should have been, she was overwhelmed by such a devastating sense of loss that it brought her actual, physical pain. So severe she could scarcely breathe through it. It was like…drowning.

Pretty soon, the girls stopped asking her. And Mary stopped trying to probe into that maelstrom of darkness and pain. It was a bit like coming to an uneasy truce with herself. She did not deliberately try to provoke her memory, and for the most part, it left her alone.

And Madame, discovering that when Mary was calm

she could do far more than merely sew a seam, that she was in fact far more highly skilled with her needle than any of her other workers, had begun to treat her like a pet dog. A dog that could perform amazing tricks, and was therefore worth cosseting, but not quite on a par with a real person.

'I can get another such as her for the crooking of my finger,' Madame continued relentlessly. 'Girls who can sew fall over themselves to work in an establishment such as mine, Mary, where they can get fair wages for an honest day's work.'

Most girls, yes, but not her. Madame had only agreed to take her on as a favour to the friend who had sent her to London. Mary had her board and food. She got nice clothes, which she made for herself during the winter months, when custom was slack. She had sturdy boots, and attractive bonnets and warm gloves, for Madame insisted her girls looked well turned out when they went to church.

But hard coin never came into her hands.

'I trusted you to go out and take your prescribed exercise, because I thought you were different from the other girls. That you were so scared of men that you would never idle away my time flirting with footmen in the houses I send you to, or loitering on the streets to see if you can catch the eye of some Bond Street buck. And then you come back here, reeking of the tavern, with stars in your eyes!'

She let go of Mary's chin then, as though she was disgusted by the prolonged physical contact.

'I thought all you needed to keep you happy was a piece of satin, and a dish of beads! The longer you worked for me, the calmer you seemed to become. Are you not happy working for me?'

Mary heard the threat implicit in Madame's question and went cold inside. What would become of her if Madame turned her off? She had no family, no friends outside this workroom. Nor did she possess the survival skills of Molly and her ilk.

Mary stared at her, aghast. She no longer looked like the patient benefactress who tolerated her deficiencies because she had a charitable nature, but like a hard-headed businesswoman who had risen to the top of her profession by sheer determination. With her slightly protuberant eyes, her dark, wispy hair coiled round her head in a plait, and the way she had held Mary's chin with fingers that felt like steel pincers, she could see exactly how Molly could liken her to a spider, grasping hold of a fly she had caught in her web. Molly and the other girls had always seen this side of her. Because they had their wits about them.

Now she, too, saw how precarious her position was. How totally dependant she was on this woman's good will.

'Please don't turn me off when the Season is over,' Mary pleaded. 'I promise I won't go into a tavern ever again! Indeed, I did not like it!'

Madame glared at her for a few seconds, before apparently coming to a decision.

'I cannot go on pampering you as I have done, if

this is how you repay me,' she said coldly. 'A daily walk, indeed! None of the other girls are granted such indulgence.'

None of the other girls worked quite so hard as she did, though, Mary surprised herself by thinking mutinously. They did not get so caught up in their task that they forgot to eat. They chattered, and got up to stretch and peer out of the window, or peek at the titled customers that came into the downstairs showrooms, while Mary kept her head down, and worked relentlessly, exhausting herself so that when she was finally permitted to leave her station, she hoped she would fall into bed and sleep dreamlessly.

'Well, I shall certainly not permit you to leave these premises again until I can be certain I can trust you not to go making assignations. And no more sitting about, mooning over whoever it was you dallied with last night either. No man ever brought a woman anything but trouble. You must forget him! Do I make myself plain?'

'Yes, Madame,' said Mary with heartfelt relief. She was not, apparently, going to lose her job, and her home along with it, for the foreseeable future. Nor was she going to be going outside where she might risk running into the disturbingly seductive dark gentleman, either. And by the time Madame's temper had cooled down, so would his ardour. People of his class, from her experience of the spoilt débutantes and titled ladies who came into the shop downstairs, did not possess a scrap of patience. They all wanted their whims satisfied quickly, or they grew petulant. And he was a lord, she recalled. Molly had mentioned his title. It was something like Harrison. Something with a lot of 's' s in it, anyway. And a lord would not hanker after one particular seamstress for very long, if she knew anything about it. By the time she next ventured out of doors, he would have tracked down someone else who reminded him of his lost lady, and forgotten all about her.

'Well, then, go and get some clothes on,' Madame snapped. 'And do not even think about getting any breakfast. You have wasted enough of my time today as it is!'

It was a fitting penance. Every time her stomach rumbled, Mary would remember how tempted she had been by the deceptive kisses of a stranger.

'Thank you, Madame,' Mary breathed, thankful the entire episode was over. She only hoped she would soon stop feeling guilty. It was not as if she had invited the man to accost her. No, he had rudely invaded, and taken up residence in her thoughts without the slightest bit of encouragement from her.

She would just have to turn her back on thoughts of him, just as she shut out the other shadows that tried to creep up and menace her hard-won sense of tranquillity.

That was all she really wanted.

To be at peace.

Lord Matthison winced as Ephraims applied a fresh piece of raw steak to his rapidly blackening eye. His knuckles were grazed, and it hurt to breathe too deeply, but by God, it had felt good to hit someone. Several someones. Seven years of holding back his grief, his anger and despair, had erupted last night in the Flash of Lightning, he realised.

But the satisfaction in inflicting as much pain upon everyone around him as he bore within himself had only brought temporary relief. By the time he had limped home, his mind had been in complete turmoil over the red-head.

One minute he was convinced she was Cora. Then his whole being would revolt at the very notion.

Because if that woman was Cora, then what the hell had been going on for the last seven years? He certainly had not imagined the extraordinary success her shade had brought him at the tables.

Unless…he sat forwards, clutching the steak to his eye as Ephraims gathered his bloodied shirt up from the floor. Supposing winning on those horses had just been a fluke. One of those lucky streaks that happen to gamblers from time to time. He had been barely twenty years old, half out of his mind with grief, spurned by his family and friends at a time when he needed them most. Had he just clung to the idea there was still one person who would not turn her back on him?

And his subsequent successes—could they have more to do with the fact that he never played but when he was stone-cold sober? And that he knew when to stop?

He shot to his feet, flinging the steak on to the dish on the table, dismissing it and Ephraims with a peremptory wave of his hand.

'Don't be angry with me, Cora,' he pleaded, terrified

lest she be offended by this lack of faith in her. 'I still believe in you. I do!'

He refused to believe that red-headed woman could possibly be Cora! Why, she'd had no idea who he was or what he was talking about. He paced across the room, running his fingers through his hair. Cora would never have forgotten him! They had been everything to each other! Besides, the woman he had mistaken for Cora had looked completely at home amongst the denizens of that gin shop. Whereas Cora had been shy. And opposed to strong drink. It was unthinkable that she could have changed so much!

And Cora had no reason to flee to London. Not one that made any sense.

He paced the room for several minutes, torturing himself with an imaginary lover, with whom she had eloped. Of an illicit pregnancy, which she dared not confess to her brother.

He went cold inside. Robbie's temper was formidable. She might have been afraid of what Robbie might do. But surely, he groaned, she could have confided in him?

He went to the washstand, where he bowed over the basin, and dashed a jug of cold water over his head. And was flooded with relief at the recollection that there had been no mention of a child of any sort in Grit's report.

Of course not.

Cora had not taken a lover. Or been pregnant. She had loved him!

The woman was not Cora, that was all there was to it!

But what if she was? a persistent little voice nagged at him.

'Dammit all to hell!' he growled, reaching for a towel and burying his face in it. If the woman he had seen in the gin shop was Cora, then she owed him an explanation for the suffering he had endured on her account! And if not…he tossed the soiled towel to the floor.

Well, he was not going to break faith with Cora. He might have kissed the woman, but that was only because he had been so sure, in that instant…

He was just going to have to establish, beyond a shadow of a doubt, that she was *not* Cora, that was all.

And the quickest way to do that, he suspected, would be to walk back into that gin shop, and start to make enquiries amongst the people she associated with.

But not straight away.

He deliberately waited the few days it took him to regain his sense of equilibrium before returning to the gin shop where he had caught her carousing with…no, not scum. The men she had been with were at least honest and hard working. He paused on the threshold of the Flash of Lightning, scanning the room until he spied the men she had been with the night he had seen her, held her, kissed her…

Muttering a curse, he stalked across the room to the very same table where he had committed that act of gross folly. And stood there, calmly letting the conversation dry up as the men, one by one, became aware of his presence.

The one who had been sitting next to Cora, the one who had been so eager to rush to her defence, rose slowly to his feet.

'Thought we'd seen you off for good on Friday,' he growled. 'You got no right coming back here.'

The other men around the table growled their agreement.

Rather than argue that he had a perfect right to enter any drinking den in London, or anywhere else he chose, Lord Matthison kept his expression neutral as he replied, 'I have returned to compensate the landlord for any breakages that occurred. And to offer my apologies for poaching on your territory,' he addressed Cora's defender directly. 'She bears such a remarkable resemblance to my late fiancée, that for a moment or two...' He tailed off, with a slight shrug of his shoulders. 'I hope you will believe me when I tell you I intended no insult to your...wife.'

He had no idea what connection the red-head had to these men. But he had seen them all leap to her defence from what they interpreted as his assault, as if she was one of their own. If he wanted to find out more about her, this was the place to start.

'Mary's not my wife!' Fred protested, turning red as a couple of the other men at the table sniggered. 'But nor could I just sit there and let someone grab her like that. No, not if he was a royal Duke I couldn't!'

'Scurvy thing to do,' said another of the group. 'Taking advantage of a simpleton in that way.'

'It was as well it was Fred as saw you trying to steal

a kiss,' said another, 'after what Molly threatened not five minutes before you walked in.' There was a moment's thoughtful silence, then the entire group burst out laughing.

'She'd have torn you limb from limb!' declared the one who had been cuddling Cora's female companion, wiping tears of laughter from his eyes. 'You couldn't have employed that right hook against her!'

Taking advantage of the relaxation in the atmosphere, Lord Matthison took a place at the table, and clicked his fingers for service. After he had ordered a round of drinks, Fred clapped him on the shoulder, admitting,

'If it hadn't been you, it'd uv bin someone else. There's nearly always a fight in here of a Friday night.'

'Usually a woman what starts it, too, one way or another,' bitterly asserted a man on the other side of the table whose fists, Lord Matthison recalled ruefully, had made such an indelible impression on his ribs.

When he told him as much, the man's scowl turned to a grin of pride. 'For a gent, you pack quite a punch yourself. Spar with Gentleman Jackson, I suppose?'

He allowed the conversation to dwell for some time on the merits of the science that could be learned at such establishments, compared to the tricks learned in less salubrious surroundings.

There was a slight lull when the serving girl brought their tray of drinks, and once they had all toasted his punishing right, he turned to the topic he had really come in to investigate.

'What did you mean when you referred to…Mary,' he forced himself to call her, though he was by no means certain it was her real name, 'as a simpleton?'

They had spoken of her that way several times, and attributed their defence of her largely to that cause.

'Just that,' replied the one who had reminded him his name was Joe. His jaw, Lord Matthison noted with grim pride, was still rather swollen. 'She ain't all there. My Molly looks out for her at work, but…' He raised his tankard, and took a long pull.

'And she don't like men,' pointed out Fred, sympathetically. 'No disrespect to you, sir, but she's jumpier than an unbroke filly round men she don't know well. Couldn't let you go a scaring of a poor maid like that.'

'Molly reckons,' said Joe, setting down his tankard and aligning the handle with great precision, 'she's been took advantage of, before she come to London.' There was a murmur of assent from the other men. 'Not that she's ever spoke of it. Says she don't remember much of anything before she fetched up in town. Molly said she was a lot worse back then even than she is now. Headaches, and sort of fits, and that.'

Lord Matthison went cold. The girl had no memory of the time before she came to London? Six years ago? Could that account for the blank look in her eyes?

'Always having the doctor out to her…'

'Ought to have the doctor out to some of them others, rather than turning them off when she's wore 'em out,' put in the bitter jarvey with the rib-crunching fists.

He took a long pull on his tankard, listening to their

diatribe on the lot of girls who worked for grim-faced old gorgons like Madame Pinchpenny, as they called her. The long hours spent hunched over their work that ruined their eyes, rotted their lungs and generally sapped their stamina by inches.

'And all so the gentry can dance the night away in their silken gowns,' muttered Fred with disgust. 'They don't care the girls what make their finery ain't treated no better than slaves.'

'It's that old besom she works for I blame,' Joe argued. 'She don't need to drive them quite so hard.'

If this woman was Cora, Lord Matthison reflected, even if she had done the very worst he had suspected of her, she had more than atoned for it. He felt his anger towards her dissipate. She might have put him through hell, but she had been enduring her own form of purgatory. He recalled her pinched face, pallid in the lantern light. She had always been dainty, but on Friday night she had looked as frail as thistledown. As though one more blast of misfortune could shatter her, scattering what was left to the four winds. And the emptiness in her eyes…

'You got no call to worry about her,' Fred put in, misinterpreting the troubled expression on Lord Matthison's face. 'She didn't seem too bothered by you kissing her.'

'Well, the gin probably helped,' Joe pointed out.

Was this what Cora had sunk to? Drowning her sorrows in gin, like so many other working class women?

No. He slammed his tankard down on the table. Her eyes had been blank. Not glazed. And she most definitely had not been drunk the morning he had chased her down Curzon Street. He should know. It was impossible to run that fast, or display such agility in dodging the crowds, with the senses dulled by alcohol.

No. Something else had put that blank look in her eyes. These men all firmly believed she had something wrong with her mind. Something that had its origins in an assault she had sustained before she came to London. An assault that had left her afraid of men.

He felt as though an iron hand had reached into his chest and squeezed his heart until it almost lost the ability to beat.

There were only a few facts regarding Cora's disappearance he knew for certain. She had gone out riding one afternoon, alone, and had never come back. The horse had returned to the stables in a state of terror, mud and leaves all over its foaming flanks. At first everyone had assumed she had met with an accident. It was only when they could find no trace of her after days of increasingly desperate searching that Robbie had turned on him. After that, instead of pooling their resources to widen the search, each had shut the other out.

He had often wondered if she had been attacked and robbed. But robbers would have left her lying in the forest where the crime took place, surely? That theory did not account for her turning up in London.

He began to feel a bit sick. If this woman was Cora, then she had vanished from his estate, only to turn up several weeks later in London, so shattered by whatever had happened to her that she had never recovered her memory of it.

He felt ashamed of himself for experiencing a glimmer of relief at the thought that somebody might have taken her, used her cruelly, then disposed of her. Because if that was the case, terrible though it was, it meant that she had not willingly left him.

She had been taken. But she had not *wanted* to go.

All he had been left with, after Cora had vanished, was the conviction she would not leave him. And now, if it turned out this woman was her...

He breathed in deeply, closing his eyes on a surge of emotion he was completely at a loss to name.

It had been so long since he'd permitted himself to feel anything much at all. For the last seven years only his rigid self-control had kept him functioning with any semblance of normality. But getting drunk, and raging at his fate, had been like setting the spade to ground frozen by winter's hard frost. Now, one emotion after another was beginning to break through the fractures.

Maybe he should have got drunk years ago. Mourned her. Let her go.

But he had not been ready to let her go.

His jaw hardened with determination. He was still not ready to let her go.

If there was any possibility, no matter how slight, that this poor, abused woman could be his Cora, then he would do his utmost to rescue her from this life of drudgery, and restore her to full health.

He would need to find a really good doctor. One

who had experience in treating ailments of the mind, as well as of the body.

He had half-risen from the table before he saw the flaw in his plan. How was he to get her to see such a man? He had no influence over her any more. As far as she knew, he was a stranger.

He could not see any responsible employer letting one of her staff go off with a strange man. Especially not when the girl in question was afraid of men.

There was little chance he might be able to earn her trust, either. He had already chased her, run her to earth in this drinking den, railed at her and kissed her. Any approach he made now was likely to terrify her. She might even do something as drastic as running away if he made his intentions known. He slumped down on the bench, a dark frown marring his features. It had taken him seven years to find her. He did not wish to scare her so badly he ended up spending another seven hunting her down.

There was only one person who might be able to help him to persuade her employer to give her over into his keeping.

Robbie.

Robbie would only have to take one look at her, to know who she was! If his own judgement was clouded by wishful thinking, he could trust Robbie, at least, to look at the situation more dispassionately. He would never permit an impostor to take Cora's place in his life.

He would write to him, and tell him that he had found her. That he needed to come to London as soon as he could. Madame Pichot would not be able to argue with both her brother, and her fiancé!

In the meantime, she was safe enough where she was, he supposed. Madame Pichot guarded all her girls, he gathered from Joe's acid comments about the difficulties involved in seeing his sweetheart.

A malicious smile came to his lips as he realised that at least he could instruct his lawyers to block any moves Mr Winters might make with regards to his quest to declare her dead.

Cora would never be dead to him. And whoever this red-head turned out to be, he was not going to allow anybody to say she was!

Chapter Four

Kitty pounded up the stairs, poked her head round the workshop door, and panted, 'Such a to-do, you'd best come quick!'

Kitty worked mainly in the showroom because not only was she attractive, but she was also quite well spoken. But she never forgot the needlewomen hidden up in the attics. She would always try to alert them when someone really famous came in. Or, if she could not find an opportunity to do that, she would study the celebrity carefully, and give them her usually highly disrespectful impersonation of them later, in their bedroom.

All but Mary immediately set their work aside, thrilled at having something to break up the monotony of their day.

'You too, Mary, this time,' Kitty darted back to insist. 'And hurry up, do, else we'll miss all the fireworks!'

After only the briefest hesitation, Mary toed off her

shoes, as all the other girls had already done, and tiptoed across the bare floor. For once, she admitted, she was glad of an excuse to get up and walk away from work that no longer had the power to completely absorb her.

The other girls were already crowded together on the top four treads by the time Mary reached the back stairs, those who had been swiftest pressing their faces up to the knotholes in the partition wall. Which meant the fireworks Kitty had promised them were going off in Madame's private office. The knotholes that allowed them to peep into the showroom were all much further down the staircase.

'Unless you take steps to put a halt to this outrageous affair,' Mary could hear a strident female voice complaining, 'I shall see your business ruined!'

'Please calm yourself,' Madame Pichot replied, in an even, soothing tone. 'I choose all my girls with great care, and watch them assiduously.'

Mary had no problem hearing Madame almost as clearly as she could hear the complaining woman. The partition wall was flimsy, its only function to prevent Madame's wealthy clients from the terrible misfortune of catching a glimpse of the conditions that prevailed beyond all the opulence of Madame's plush showroom.

'I can assure you,' Madame said haughtily, 'that neither Mary, nor any of my other girls, is having an affair with Lord Matthison.'

The girls all turned to stare at Mary in mingled shock and excitement. She shrugged her shoulders, palms spread wide to indicate she had no idea what was going on.

'Not yet, perhaps, but he certainly has plans for her! He is intent on making my daughter an object of ridicule!' the first voice wailed. 'First he wilfully compromised her, and now he is trying to wriggle out of marrying her by claiming to have discovered his long-lost fiancée.'

Ah! The woman must be complaining about the handsome dark gentleman who had kissed her in the Flash of Lightning. His name was not Harrison at all. But Matthison. Lord Matthison.

'…working of all things as a seamstress! When everyone knows she is dead!'

'You are supposed to be dead,' he had muttered, looking at her as though he had seen a ghost. Oh, the poor man! He must be so convinced she was that Cora person that he had gone to the complaining woman's house, and told her… No, but wait a minute, Mary frowned. Something about all this did not add up. The woman said he had compromised her daughter. She shook her head, baffled. They could not be talking about the same man. The man she had met was so besotted with the woman who had died, she was sure he would never…unless this woman's daughter looked like Cora too. That was why he had kissed *her*, after all.

'There is no question of Mary agreeing to any such thing.' Madame's tone was still quietly contemptuous, in stark contrast to the almost hysterical tirade of the other woman in her office.

'Girls of that sort will do anything for the kind of money Lord Matthison could give her!' the other woman protested. 'And even if she did not wish to go along with it, he is ruthless enough to compel her! He might kidnap her, and terrorise her into doing his bidding. He is evil, I tell you, evil!'

It crossed Mary's mind that it was mighty peculiar of the woman to insist Lord Matthison had to marry her daughter, if she really believed he was evil.

'And if that happens,' the unbalanced female almost shrieked, 'we will not be the only ones to suffer! I shall make sure you are ruined! What do you think will happen to your business once word leaks out that you supply girls for gentlemen with unusual appetites? For that is what I shall tell the world. Do you think you will still get earls and dukes bringing their wives here if they think it is just a front for a bawdyhouse? Do you think any half-decent sort of man will allow his daughters to be dressed in gowns made by…by harlots?'

'My girls are all completely respectable.' Madame sounded a little shaken. 'There has never been any whisper—'

'There will be more than whispers if Lord Matthison gets his hands on that Mary! There will be such scandal that your reputation will never recover!'

There was a slight pause, then Madame said, in a voice that had regained its composure, 'He will not. I shall make sure of it. You have my word. Now, if that will be all…?'

She heard the determined rustle of expensive clothing, footsteps, and a door latch being lifted.

So did the others, who scrambled swiftly on their

stockinged feet back up to the workroom. Only when they were back at their respective stations, with the door to the back stairs safely shut behind them, and their feet decently shod, did the whispering and nudging begin.

'Mary,' said Molly, through a mouthful of pins as she deftly tacked a length of silk chenille round the sleeves of a bronze-gold evening gown, 'you won't go doing anything daft, will you?'

'Daft?' echoed Mary, trailing her fingers distract-edly through a dish of iridescent turquoise sequins.

'Yes, like running off with that Lord they was going on about,' Molly muttered.

'But,' objected Mary, 'on Friday night you were saying that if he made me an offer I ought to accept.'

'That was then, this is now!' she snapped. 'I thought then that if you could come to some arrangement, you could ask him for a big fat parting present, and you would be set up for life. I was going to suggest you ask him to set you up in a little shop so's I could come and help you run it…what?' She rounded on the others, who had begun to mutter behind her back. 'Don't say you wouldn't jump at the chance to get out of here if you could do it!' She turned back to her garment, jabbing a pin into its bodice with unnecessary force. 'Now it looks as though I shall have to marry Joe and raise a pack of tow-haired snot-nosed brats.'

'I thought you liked Joe,' protested Mary faintly.

'Liking has nothing to do with it. It is one thing coming to an understanding with a man, where you both get something out of it. Quite another being completely under his thumb…'

'That's right, Mary,' put in Josephine, a plump girl with a gap between her front teeth. 'Accepting *carte blanche* from a gentleman, and letting him set you up in style, is a far cry from being stolen out of your place and being held against your will by some depraved monster.'

'Like you would know anything about being kept in style,' sneered Lotty, a sallow-complexioned, slender girl with stooped shoulders. Lotty and Josephine were currently at odds. Any conversation that took place up here lately seemed to fuel their simmering resentment of one another.

Before the conversation could descend into yet another slanging match, Mary hastily interrupted. 'Lord Matthison will not kidnap me.'

'How would you know?' breathed Josephine in a thrilled tone. 'You heard what that woman downstairs said.'

'Well, for one thing, Madame will not let me outside any more, so I don't see how he could possibly do it. And for another, he, well, he just would not.'

When Lotty made a noise that exactly expressed the depth of her contempt for such a naïve comment, Mary exclaimed, 'He is not evil! Even that woman did not really think so, or she would not be so set on having him marry her daughter.' That did give the other girls pause, she could see. Emboldened, she went on, 'I think he is just confused. I mean—' she frowned, trying to find words to explain how she was certain he felt towards her '—I am quite sure that he really, truly believes I am his long-lost fiancée. He asked me why I had run away.'

'Ooh,' breathed Josephine, 'do you think you are really a runaway heiress?'

'Don't be daft!' snorted Molly. 'Why would an heiress want to run away? Especially if she was betrothed to someone as rich and good looking as that Lord Matthison. No one in their right mind would give up that kind of life, to work in a place like this!' She gestured round the spartan room with contempt. It had skylights, as well as floor-to-ceiling windows on the south-facing wall, to maximise the hours of daylight, during which Madame Pichot could keep the girls working without the expense of having to light the oil lamps. It meant the room was like a hothouse in summer, yet impossible to keep warm in winter.

It took Lotty only a few seconds to come up with the scathing rejoinder, 'But then, we all know our Mary ain't exactly *in* her right mind.'

Everyone, except Mary, began to snigger quietly. She went to her stool and sat down, her cheeks burning with humiliation. It was not as if she was that bad! Not nowadays! Yes, she still got confused and scared sometimes. But she could read and write. And once, when she had caught a glimpse of Madame's account books, she had been able to grasp the significance of all the neat little columns. And had she not learned to find her way about the labyrinthine courts and alleys of London?

Madame never worried that she might get lost when she sent her out on errands!

What she could not do, though, she accepted with mounting chagrin, was to come back with some really cutting remark that would put a stop to their mockery as effectively as scissors snipping off a loose thread. She was still desperately trying to come up with one, when she heard Madame's heavy footsteps on the stair. They all bent to their work with renewed concentration.

When Madame Pichot marched into the room a few seconds later, she went straight to Mary. Raking a look over her embroidery frame, she said, 'How long will it take you to finish this up?'

Mary looked down at the intricate tracery of roses in their varying stages of bloom, which were to decorate a pair of evening gloves. She had already worked the same design on to a spectacularly opulent evening gown, and the satin slippers that went with it.

'There are several hours work left still.'

'Then get to it!' Madame snapped. 'Molly, when it is time for the noon break, make sure Mary comes down to my office.' With that, she turned and swept out of the workroom.

'Phew!' Lotty whistled. 'You're for it, Mary. Marching orders.' She drew one finger across her neck in a gesture denoting her fate was sealed.

Mary made no reply. Her mind was in turmoil. She could not decide whether it would be better to eke out her work, in the hope that Madame would keep her on until it was finished, or whether shirking would make her more likely to lose her job altogether. A shaft of pure terror shivered through her, at the sudden realisation that any of the other girls in this room could have accomplished as much as she had done, this week, even on a design as complex as this one.

Worry had reduced her to such a state that by the time Molly pushed her from her stool, and nudged her towards the stairs, she had set scarcely one stitch that would not have to be unpicked and reworked.

'Take a seat, Mary,' said Madame, when Mary timidly entered her office. Madame pointed to a low stool beside a table that was set for a light lunch. Mary decided it was a good omen when she noted two thick slices of plum cake as well as an array of sandwiches. Surely, if Madame was about to turn her off, she would not be doing it over a beautifully prepared repast, served up on the second-best china? She took her place at table, feeling somewhat relieved.

'Now, Mary, I do not want you getting upset by what I have to say. I do not believe a word of it myself, but I have a business to run, and the welfare of the other girls under my employ to consider.' She cocked her head, examining Mary with pursed lips, muttering, 'Not that I suppose you will understand the half of it, but there…nobody will be able to say I did not do my best.'

With a resigned sigh, she poured tea into Mary's cup, adding a splash of milk, and, after an infinitesimal hesitation, half a teaspoon of sugar.

'Sadly, because of a complaint I received today, I am

going to have to send you away from London for a while.'

Leave London! Just when it had finally started to feel like home. And go somewhere else, where she would have to start all over again! Her heart began to pound hard. 'No, Madame, please—'

'It is for your own good,' Madame Pichot broke in. 'London is not safe for you any longer. I told you,' she repeated with exaggerated patience, as though to an imbecile, 'a woman came here this morning and lodged a complaint against you.'

Mary was finding it hard to breathe now. She clutched at the arms of the chair, as though clinging to something tangible could somehow prevent Madame from forcing her to leave.

'I have not done anything—' she began.

'I am sure you have not!' Madame Pichot interposed, with an imperious gesture of her hand. 'Nevertheless, I have to demonstrate that I have taken steps to clear my name. You do understand, don't you?'

Madame squeezed her eyes shut as though recoiling from the impossibility of what she had just said. 'Well, even if you do not, the fact is, just having you under my roof is enough to jeopardise everything I have worked so hard to build up here. So you cannot remain under my roof.'

Mary wondered whether it was worth reminding Madame that she would not even be under this particular roof, if it wasn't for her. When she had first come to work for Madame Pichot, her shop had been only mod-

erately successful. Mary's malady had completely trans-
formed the whole nature of her business. She needed to
work like other people needed air to breathe. She accomplished whatever task Madame gave her with a
fervour wholly alien to girls who were only there to earn
their pay. It was not long before Mary began to turn out
gowns that were works of art. Soon, anyone who was
anyone simply had to have at least one gown from the
previously obscure French dressmaker. Madame had
begun to be more discriminating about the clients she
took on, and moved into larger premises in the more
fashionable Conduit Street.

Mary must have made some inarticulate sound,
because Madame's eyes flew open, and she looked at her
sharply. 'You need not be alarmed, girl. I am quite sure
the whole ghastly business will blow itself out before the
end of the Season, and then, well...' She shrugged in that
expansive way that indicated anything might be possible.

'You mean, I can come back?'

'You have always been a good worker,' Madame
replied, with a wry smile. 'Better than I expected when
I took you on. Drink some tea, girl,' she said in a bracing
tone, 'and stop looking as though you were facing the
end of the world. I am only sending you to Bath.'

'Bath?'

'Yes, on the six o' clock mail. I have already purchased your ticket. Have you finished that piece of work
yet? Because if you have not, I shall have to get one of
the others to pack your overnight bag. And put the rest of
your things into a trunk, which I shall send on by carrier.'

'Bath,' Mary repeated, in a daze.

'Yes, Bath. Not so fashionable as it once was, but still full of shops that cater to the wealthy patrons of the city. And plenty of work available for a girl with your skills with a needle. I still have contacts with several dressmakers in the town. While Molly is packing up your things, I shall be writing a letter for you to take with you.'

Bath. She was not simply being turned out on to the streets to fend for herself. She would have work, and presumably somewhere to live. But before she could gather her thoughts and form them into questions, Madame put an end to the interview.

The afternoon rushed past in a flurry of activity, during which she had no leisure to speak to anyone except in snatched, furtive asides. Madame seemed to be everywhere at once, getting a trunk and a small valise hauled out of storage, and thoroughly dusted down, sending Molly to separate her things into two piles, one to tide her over the first few days, and the rest for sending on later.

Joe winked at her solemnly as they got into the cab that was to take them to Cheapside, reminding her again of the threat Madame had made regarding Molly's position.

'You will need Molly more now, won't you?' she managed to pluck up the courage to say once they set out for the coaching inn. 'Since I am leaving. You will not turn her off now, will you?'

'Impudence!' Madame muttered, turning her head away sharply.

Mary knew there would be no point in arguing any more. From the grim set of Madame's mouth, she had already made up her mind. The further they got from Madame's shop, the more upset Mary became.

Her one, meagre consolation was that she had managed to scribble a note on a slip of tracing paper, and hide it in Molly's scissor sheath, warning her that Madame did not mean to keep her on once the Season ended. It might give her the chance to make plans, at least. Perhaps she would finally marry Joe.

It was not easy to clamber out of the cab with her overnight case in one hand, and the basket of provisions Kitty had made up for her, in the other. But Madame did not stop to offer her any assistance. She strode off down the passage that led to the Swan with Two Necks, forcing Mary to trot to catch up with her.

She paused for a moment when they entered the yard, stunned by the sheer volume of noise that reverberated round the enclosed space. Horses whinnied and snorted as grooms led them towards the line of coaches drawn up beneath an overhanging balcony. There was the regular thumping of bags being tossed into the boots of coaches, the occasional crash of another being dumped onto the cobbles. The owners of the goods thus casually handled protested, and were answered with a volley of derision from insolent ostlers. The whole place appeared to her like a scene of utter confusion. Scores of people seemed to be scurrying about, ducking into doorways, or emerging from them with bewildering rapidity.

Mary instinctively clutched her belongings tightly, as though they were her only safe anchor in this whirlpool of transient humanity.

'There is your coach,' Madame suddenly announced, plunging through the maelstrom towards one of the smaller vehicles, a black, rather dusty-looking coach with the royal coat of arms emblazoned on the doors. The lower half of its body, she saw when she got a bit closer, was not covered in dried mud as she had supposed, but painted a dull brown. Mailbags were already piled high on its roof, while various other items of luggage were still being lifted from the ground, and tossed into the forward boot.

A large man, swathed in a wide-skirted green coat with large brass buttons swaggered up to the coach, clambered on to the driving seat, settled himself with a regal air, and pulled out his pocket watch. The bustling around his particular vehicle increased in frenzy.

Mary's own heart picked up speed.

'Make haste,' said Madame Pichot, pushing her in the small of her back. 'I know you do not wish to leave, any more than I wish to part with you, but at least in Bath you will be safe from That Man.'

'Yes,' Mary replied, her eyes skittering over the flaking paint, which made the coat of arms look like a crumbly cheese, to the rather gloomy interior of the coach. She could just, barely, make out a double stripe of crimson through the mud that coated the worn carpet. 'Yes,' she repeated, bolstering herself with the thought that it was far better to have honest work, than to fall into the clutches of a man about whom she knew virtually nothing. Leaving London would at least deliver her from the temptation he had been posing. And she would get used to Bath. Same as she had got used to London. 'I want to be safe,' she declared, ducking her head as she got inside, and took the one remaining seat.

She placed her valise on the floor between her feet, and set the basket on her lap.

'Here,' said Madame, leaning in and holding out a coin. 'You will need this to tip the guard.'

Mary took the proffered half-crown from Madame's outstretched hand with a rush of heartfelt gratitude. Madame had not *had* to pay the extra for an inside seat. She need not have arranged for her to get work in Bath at all, come to that. She knew Madame was motivated more by practicality than true charity, and yet, over the years she had grown quite fond of the gruff, no-nonsense woman who had taken such a risk in employing her at all.

'I will miss you, Madame,' she admitted shyly. 'I hope I may come back soon.'

Madame reared back, two spots of colour staining her cheeks. But she did not have the chance to make any reply. Somebody slammed the door, the guard blew the horn, and the coach lurched forwards. Mary pressed her face to the window to wave farewell, and saw Madame standing with her fists clenched, her brows drawn down into a fierce scowl as she watched the coach depart.

The scowl put some heart back into Mary. Madame seemed really angry at having to do without her, even temporarily. She might have known Madame would not want to lose the worker who had achieved so much for her, at so little cost.

She patted her pocket, feeling the letter that Madame had given her rustle reassuringly. She still felt somewhat nervous to be leaving the only home she could remember, but it was not as if it would be for ever. Madame valued her enough to want her to return.

She couldn't help contrasting the way she felt now at leaving the noisy, bustling metropolis, from the day she had first come here. She kept her face glued to the window as the coach rattled through familiar streets, bidding them a silent farewell. She had been almost beside herself with fear, back then, the letter of introduction she'd had in her pocket then bringing her no reassurance whatsoever. It had been even worse when she had alighted. The citizens of London were all so busy. Far too busy to stop and give directions to a bedraggled little waif fresh from the country.

But she had made it to Madame's shop, she reminded herself, lifting her chin. Madame had taken her in, and encouraged her to focus on what she could achieve, rather than getting all worked up about things she had no control over. That was what she must do now.

She had no idea what her new employer would be like, or if she would find another friend like Molly to help her settle into her new surroundings. But she had survived a far bigger upheaval in her life once. And she was stronger, calmer and more confident now than she had been when she'd arrived.

The choked city streets gave way to suburbs that were completely alien to her far sooner than she would have believed possible. Jostling buildings petered out into hamlets interspersed with fields. She craned her neck to keep her eyes fixed on the pall of smoke that hung over the horizon where the town's chimneys still breathed, but eventually even that last link with the only home she had ever known was severed.

Only then did she sit back in her seat and glance timidly at the other occupants of the coach. When she had boarded, she had only taken note of three bundles of assorted clothing occupying three corners of the dingy interior. Now they resolved themselves into human form.

All three, she noted on a swallow of dismay, were men.

Quickly, before any of them noticed her furtive glances, she looked down at the basket on her lap, her heart thudding alarmingly. It would be hours and hours until they reached Bath. The coach travelled non-stop right through the night. Already the shadows of the trees and hedges they were rattling past were growing longer. Soon it would be completely dark, and she would be shut up in here with three strange men... She sniffed, suddenly recognising the sweet fruity smell of spirits that hung in the air. Three strange men who were very far from sober.

Her stomach lurched. And not only because of the pothole the coach had bounced over.

She gripped the handle of her basket tightly, keeping her attention focused on its contents. The men would take no notice of her, if she took no notice of them. Why should they? As Madame was always telling her, she was naught but a scrap of skin and bone, of no interest to any red-blooded male…

Except Lord Matthison, a defiant spark of pride contradicted Madame's scathing tones.

Ah, well, but he was only drawn to her because she looked a bit like someone he had once cared about, pointed out Madame's voice with crushing accuracy.

Mary sighed wistfully. She did not suppose she would ever look into those dark, haunted eyes again. Or feel that hard mouth seeking a response from her startled, untried lips.

And that was for the best, she decided, unpicking the knot of the muslin square in which her supper was tied. Far better to sigh over what might have been, than plunge headlong into a course of action that could only be ruinous.

The cloth parted, and she discovered it contained a chicken leg, a wedge of cheese, an apple and a couple of slices of the plum cake she'd had at lunch.

At least eating gave her something to take her mind off the fact that she was shut up in cramped quarters with three complete strangers.

By the time she had finished her supper, two of the other passengers were snoring loudly. With their bodies slumped into their respective corners, hats over their eyes, they had gone right back to resembling nothing so much as untidy heaps of laundry.

That would be the way to cope with them. To think

of them as sacks of laundry, rather than men. In fact, if she shut her eyes, not only would it blot them from her sight, but she might even be able to doze a little, too. After all, they all seemed to be managing it.

Men, though, she soon found out, were far less inhibited creatures than women, even when asleep. She had to retreat deeper and deeper into her corner as their lax limbs sprawled all over the place. They produced a lot more unpleasant smells, too, at far greater volume than she had believed the human body capable of emitting. And even if it had not been for the sprawling, and the snoring, and the belching—not to mention the other noxious effusions they all began to produce at regular intervals—Mary would not have been able to sleep for more than a few snatched moments at a time, because the guard blew his horn at every turnpike, loudly enough to rouse even the slender young gentleman next to her, who was the most obviously inebriated of them all.

Mary was the only passenger who got out every time the coach stopped for a change of horses. She welcomed the chance to breathe fresh air for a few minutes, and walked up and down to stretch out her cramped limbs.

By the time they pulled up in the yard of the White Hart, just before ten the next morning, she felt as though she had been through a wringer. She eyed the others with resentment as they unfolded themselves from their respective corners. Though they looked a little crumpled, every one of them managed to collect their luggage, and then disperse, flapping across the yard like washing torn from the line by a gusting wind.

She flopped down the steps, limp and shaky, and would have slithered onto the cobbles if the guard had not grabbed her by the arm, and held her upright until she steadied.

'Someone comin' to meet yer?' he asked gruffly.

Mary hoped he did not notice how badly she wanted him to remove his great meaty paw from her arm. He was only trying to be helpful.

Mustering up a wan smile, she shook her head, explaining, 'I only have to get as far as Orange Grove, though. I believe it is not far?'

He shrugged. 'You best ask the landlord.'

To her relief, he let go of her arm then, to point to one of the doors leading off the yard. 'Get something warm inside you while you're at it.'

'Thank you,' she said, nodding as though she planned to follow his sage advice to the letter. Then she reached into her pocket and handed over the half-crown Madame had provided for her to tip him.

It worked like a charm. With a grin and a nod, he pocketed the money and stumped off towards the posting offices.

Mary lingered on the premises only long enough to get directions from one of the many porters employed there. She did not have any money to buy refreshments, and was besides so weary that all she wanted was to reach her destination, find a horizontal surface that was not bouncing about, and sleep the clock round.

She took the road the porter had pointed out, and the right-hand junction that he said led down to Orange Grove. It came out in the middle of a thoroughfare, which ran as far as she could see in either direction. To begin with, Mary turned the wrong way. She had to retrace her steps before finding Number Eight.

Which was a wig-maker's.

Puzzled, Mary pulled the letter from her pocket and looked at the address again, in case she had remembered it wrong. But, no. In Madame's neat round hand, it clearly stated *Cleopatra's, 8 Orange Grove, Bath.*

Perhaps, in all the hurry, Madame had put down the wrong number. Perhaps Cleopatra's was at number eighteen, or eight and twenty. Mary walked all the way up one side of the street, then all the way down the other, but none of the shops bore the name she sought.

Completely perplexed, she made her way back to the wig-maker's. Perhaps this had been the correct address, but the modiste had moved on. If so, she only hoped the new shopkeeper knew where the former tenant had gone.

To her dismay, the rather forbidding gentleman who came to the counter informed her in extremely frosty accents, when she asked if he had recently taken over the business from a modiste, that his shop had belonged to his father before him, and to his father's father before that. She left hastily, feeling embarrassed at having offended him, and unsure what to do next.

There had been, she recalled, a milliner on the corner, towards the High Street. She might have heard of Cleopatra's.

The milliner had not, but when, in a burst of inspiration, Mary further enquired if there was anyone in Bath who might have a connection with Madame Pichot, her eyes lit up.

'The French *émigrée* who makes such exquisite gowns for the *ton*?' she breathed. 'I did not know she had ever set foot in Bath!'

Mary frowned. Mentioning feet had reminded her how badly her own were hurting. Her boots seemed to have shrunk during the night, and felt as though they were sawing through the knuckles of her toes. Her head was beginning to ache, too, as she grew more confused and tired.

Had Madame actually said she had worked in Bath? She shook her head, bewildered. That conversation had grown hazy. She could not remember *exactly* what she had said. Only that she had mentioned having connections here. She looked down at the letter, which was beginning to look rather the worse for wear, wondering exactly what the connection with this Cleopatra was.

'If it is a high-class modiste you are seeking,' put in the milliner kindly, on seeing Mary's strained face, 'you might do better looking on Milsom Street.'

'Thank you,' said Mary, grateful for any suggestion that might lead her to the elusive salon. And, though her legs felt as though they belonged to a newborn foal, she set out in the direction the kindly woman had pointed with renewed determination.

Milsom Street was full of shops, the pavements thronging with their smartly dressed customers. But none of them, she ascertained by walking all the way up one side, and right back down the other, bore the name of Cleopatra above the door. The only thing she could think of was to go into every one that had anything even remotely to do with fashion, or might conceivably employ workers with a talent for stitchery. None of them could help her. And, as it came on to rain, and her appearance grew increasingly bedraggled, they became less than polite in the way they expressed their inability to be of help.

Cleopatra's must be somewhere! Why could nobody tell her where it was? Or had she somehow muddled up the directions? 'Stop and think,' she muttered under her breath. She had to get out of the rain, and try to work out what to do!

Ducking into a doorway out of the worst of the rain, Mary pulled the rather dog-eared letter out of her pocket yet again, and looked at the direction, half expecting it to be completely different from what she remembered seeing the last time she had looked.

But it still said Number Eight, Orange Grove.

It went against all her principles, but she knew the only way to get any more information about the mysteriously elusive Cleopatra was to open the letter and read it herself. Setting her bags down on the step, out of the puddles, she tugged off her gloves, turned the letter over, and broke the wafer sealing the single sheet of paper closed.

And her eyes widened in sheer disbelief.

There was nothing written on it at all.

She was holding a blank piece of paper in her hand.

She went cold inside as she realised what this meant.

There was no job. Probably no such person as Cleopatra. She was all alone, in a strange town, without a penny to her name.

For some reason, what hurt her the most was the way Madame had smiled when she had given her money to tip the guard. He was probably tucked up in snug lodgings right now, his belly full of tavern fare paid for with her half-crown, while she...her stomach clenched, feeling completely hollow, yet full of ice at the same time.

And that was when she began to shake.

She had trusted Madame. Molly had warned her what the woman was like, and she had still trusted her. She had got into the coach and actually *thanked* her for sending her away.

A gust of wind blew rain into the doorway, sprinkling the sheet of paper at which she was still staring in blank horror. And a wave of desolation swamped her, black and sickeningly familiar. She knew she had been alone, and cold and wet and miserable before. Feeling betrayed and deceived...

At that very moment, a shadow fell across the doorway. Even before she lifted her head, she knew who would be standing there. For some reason, she just knew that Lord Matthison would materialise out of the driving rain and deepening shadows to embody her feelings of misery and betrayal. She lifted her head with a sense of inevitability, and held out the blank sheet of paper, where her future security should have been written.

'It is all your fault,' she said.

He took it from her, frowning when he turned it over, and saw what Madame Pichot had done to her.

Then he looked straight at her, his expression as blank as the piece of paper he held.

'Not all of it, Cora. But even so, I shall put it all to rights.'

She did not ask him what he meant. She knew why he had come. Had known the second he called her Cora.

He picked up her valise, and held out his arm.

There was nowhere to run, no other choice she could make.

Head bowed, she laid her hand on his sleeve, and set out into the rain beside him.

Chapter Five

Mary was lost too deep in the maze of her own
thoughts to notice where he was taking her. Why had
Madame done this to her? Why? How could she have
deliberately stranded her in a strange place, with no
money, when she knew how badly it would scare her!

She stumbled, as something inside her seemed to
curl up, twisting painfully at the thought of how stupid
she must have looked, thanking Madame for sending
her to Bath, and saying how she would miss her! She
clung a little tighter to Lord Matthison's arm as she
imagined Madame chuckling all the way back to the
shop. For the price of a ticket on the mail, and half a
crown to tip the guard, she had persuaded Mary to leave
London quietly, thus averting the scandal the complaining woman had threatened to unleash. By making it
look as though she *had* provided generously for Mary,
she had dealt with the prospect of having to preside over
workers simmering with resentment, too. Not that there

would be much any of them could do, but she knew that if they learned of her current plight, they would all be angry on her behalf. For she had become one of them. Against all her expectations, considering the way they had once intimidated her with their cocksure ways and coarse language, she had forged a place for herself in that workroom.

She pictured them, clustered on the stairs, listening to that final interview she'd had in Madame's office, with their eyes to the knotholes, taking in the significance of the plum cake and the second-best china. And a cold hand seemed to reach into her chest and squeeze. Could Madame have known they were watching? Was that why she had been so determined to spell out exactly why she was sending her away, even though she was convinced Mary would not understand the half of it?

It all made a horrible kind of sense. If Madame *had* known her workers were in the habit of spying on her, she had used that knowledge to her own advantage, rather than reprimanding them.

'As I expected,' she heard Lord Matthison saying, 'the journey down has exhausted my wife. I trust you have our room ready?'

Mary blinked in bewilderment at finding herself standing in the foyer of what she had to assume was a respectable hotel, judging from the elegance of its décor.

'Indeed,' a neatly dressed man she supposed must be the landlord replied. 'If you would come this way?'

Wife? She frowned. 'But…'

'Not now,' Lord Matthison bent to murmur in her ear.

'You may berate me as soundly as you please once we are in private, but not just yet, hmm?'

He slipped his arm round her waist, and with all the appearance of a solicitous husband supported her up the stairs and along the maze of corridors that led to their room.

Their room. As she crossed the threshold, she took note of the single large tester bed standing at one end of the rectangular room, along with a washstand and clothes press. At the other, set before a cheerfully blazing fire, stood a small table and two inviting wing-backed chairs. A far cry from the kind of opulence she guessed a man of Lord Matthison's means would be used to. But then, as he led her towards the seating area, she caught the landlord eyeing her dishevelled appearance, then flicking an assessing glance at the plain overcoat that completely concealed Lord Matthison's exquisite tailoring. To him, they probably looked like any moderately well-to-do couple, who could not afford a suite.

As the landlord made to leave, Lord Matthison turned towards him, and began issuing a series of requests. Mary scarcely took them in. The sight of the fire had reminded her how very cold and wet she was. She left his side, and kept on going till she stood right in front of it. Crouching down by the fender, she held out her hands to the flames. She was not wearing her gloves. That was right, she had taken them off to open the letter. The letter that was no letter at all, but a symbol of the most horrible cruelty, perpetrated by a mean-spirited woman on a stupid, gullible fool...

Shaking with the force of her indignation, Mary reached into her pocket where she had shoved the letter after Lord Matthison had handed it back to her.

Molly had been right all along! She ripped the page in half. All Madame cared about was profit! She ripped the pieces in half again. She'd had Kitty packing up a meal, and Molly packing her trunk. Rip. Which, she suddenly realised on a fresh wave of anger, the old miser had no intention of sending on. Rip. Indeed she could not, because she knew very well Mary had nowhere to go. The pieces were now so small that Mary was having a struggle to tear them again. Furious at her inability to even tear the letter to bits small enough to satisfy her, she flung them into the flames with a cry of utter vexation.

'That's better,' said a dark voice from behind her, making her jump. She had almost forgotten Lord Matthison was there, for a moment, so completely consumed was she by the dreadful sense of betrayal she had felt, as she had stumbled through the devious workings of Madame's mind.

Lord Matthison thanked God he had employed Grit to keep an eye on the comings and goings at Madame Pichot's emporium. The lad had been bright enough to recognise the significance of the French woman taking Mary off in a cab, laden with luggage rather than carrying the neatly wrapped parcels that one might expect to see coming out of a dressmaker's shop.

He had known he had no chance of catching up with the night mail, but the amount of money he'd disbursed at the White Hart had soon bought him the information he needed. After securing a room at the Pelican he had made for Orange Grove, all fired up to enquire at every shop until he had located Cora. In the event, he had not needed to. She had been wandering up and down, in a bewildered state, alternately looking at the letter she held in her hand, and examining the numbers over shop doors. He had not intended to approach her today. The things he had learned from the jarveys had made him wary of frightening her. He just needed to find out where she was going to live before returning to his own hotel where he could work out what to do next.

As the day had worn on, he had witnessed her descent into exhaustion and despair. And eventually realised he could not leave her alone to deal with whatever it was that had so shocked her about the letter she had been clutching like a talisman.

He had crossed the street, all thoughts of remaining concealed from her erased by the conviction he had to help her. He had experienced a flare of triumph when he had perceived that she had no option but to accept his immediate protection.

But that triumph had been short-lived. The moment she had laid her hand on his sleeve in a gesture of weary defeat had been like suffering a blow to his heart. He had thought she looked fragile when he had discovered her in the Flash of Lightning. But it was only a foretaste of how she looked now. He'd had to half-carry her up the stairs, and the dazed look in her eyes had made him wonder if she was on the verge of a complete collapse.

So it was a relief to see a resurgence of some spirit, to see her rip up that damnable sheet of paper, and utter that cry of protest against all that life had flung at her. To know that this latest ordeal had not been the breaking of her after all.

'You will feel better still, once you have got out of your wet clothing, and had something to eat,' he said.

'You have no idea what will make me feel better!'

How could he stand there, so calmly, talking about eating, when her life lay in ruins?

Because he did not care. He had brought her to this. He had betrayed her! Held her in his arms, and kissed her, when all the time...

She lurched to her feet on a wave of anguish and fury. Her fists were already raised before she knew how badly she wanted to hit him. But she did not manage to land a single blow. He caught hold of her wrists, his reactions lightning swift.

She flailed out at his imprisoning hands, kicking ineffectually at his booted legs. His eyes widened in horror, then narrowed with grim purpose as he lifted her bodily off her feet and began to drag her across the room.

Her anger flipped to wild, ungovernable panic at the realisation that she could do nothing to prevent him forcing her on to the bed. She began to twist in his hold, clawing at him like a cat.

It took her a full five minutes before she realised that, far from flinging her on to the bed and ravishing her, he was merely restraining her in one of the armchairs.

She stopped trying to escape him, and looked up into his face. She was wrecked from the exertions of struggling against a being so much stronger than herself, but he was not even breathing hard. He looked completely in control of himself. While she had just behaved like some kind of…a wild woman!

Oh, it was all true, what they said about her! She was not right in the head! How could she have attacked the poor man like that! *He* was not the one who had betrayed her, and robbed her of the future she had worked so hard for so many years to secure. It was Madame Pichot who had done all that.

With a whimper of shame, she let her head fall forwards, on to his breast. And as her breathing slowed, and her heart quieted, the odour of singed wool permeated her senses.

And she felt even worse. When she had leapt to her feet, she had been careless of her proximity to the fire. Lord Matthison had only been pulling her away from the flames.

'I…I'm s-sorry,' she gulped.

His hands eased the pressure they had been exerting on her shoulders.

'Can I let you go now? Will you stay in that chair, and do nothing that might put yourself in danger?'

She nodded, too ashamed of her loss of control to muster up an adequate apology for having so badly misjudged his intentions.

It was only when he pulled away, and went to sit on the chair on the other side of the hearth that she could tell how shaken he was, too. His face was white, and his hands, as they curled round the arms of the chair, were trembling. It must be frightening, she expected, to have a crazy woman leap on you!

'You *do* need to get out of your wet clothes, though, Cora,' he repeated.

'My name is Mary,' she reminded him defiantly as she began to fumble at the buttons of her coat. That episode had stripped her of what little remained of her dignity. She had to claw it back somehow! And reminding herself that *he* was just as capable of leaping to the wrong conclusions about a person was a start.

'Whatever you call yourself,' he said so patiently it roused a strong desire to throw her sodden, singed coat at him, 'you need to accept the fact that I have no wish to see you hurt yourself. Nor,' he went on more firmly, 'will I let anyone else hurt you. I just want to look after you now. Protect you.'

Her fingers stilled on the strings of her bonnet. Protect her! Offering a woman protection was just another way of saying he wanted to make her his mistress, she knew that much, however simple everybody thought her.

But surely, if he really believed she was his lost love, he would not be offering her that kind of relationship? She eyed him with renewed suspicion. Had he known all along she was not the dead woman who had taken his heart to the grave? Was he not the tortured soul she had thought him at all?

She heaved a sigh as she lifted the bonnet from her

head. She was clearly no judge of character. Look at how wrong she had been about Madame Pichot.

The complaining woman from the showroom had accused him of trying to evade doing his duty to her daughter. Claiming Mary was his long-lost fiancée would get him off the hook all right...but not, she frowned as she leaned down to place her bonnet in the hearth to dry, if he only planned to make her his mistress! Many married men still kept mistresses.

And she had said he was evil. Kitty had said there were whispers he was in league with the devil. That all his luck at the gaming tables stemmed from a horrible murder he had committed of a young woman who he'd lured to his estate. Learning about that was what had made Molly change her mind about the advisability of Mary embarking on a relationship with him. It did seem odd, she thought, darting him a sideways glance, the way he had materialised out of the rain just when she was at her most vulnerable. How had he known she was in Bath? Let alone arriving the very minute she had discovered she was completely and utterly destitute?

A shiver racked her whole body, and instinctively she wrapped her arms about her waist.

'I don't care how much you pay me,' she said as firmly as she dared, 'I won't pretend to be somebody I am not, just so that you can get out of marrying someone you should never have asked in the first place if you do not love her.'

'What?' Lord Matthison sat bolt upright, staring at her as though she had just sprouted two heads.

But before either of them could say another word, a hotel waiter had knocked and entered, bearing a tray of coffee and sandwiches. While he was setting it down on the table, they sat eyeing each other, like two prizefighters getting their breath back between rounds.

'Will that be all, sir?'

'Not quite,' Lord Matthison bit out. 'Would you be so good as to take my wife's coat and bonnet, and dry them? And her boots, too, if you would not mind waiting for a moment.'

And then he was on his knees at her feet, deftly unlacing her boots, sliding them off, and handing them over to the wooden-faced waiter.

'Madam's things will be dried, brushed and returned first thing in the morning,' the man assured them, almost managing to conceal his disgust at the state of Mary's clothing. It wasn't until he had left the room with her coat draped over his arm, her boots dangling from his fingers, that it hit her that she was now trapped in this room overnight, with a man who was so determined to make her his mistress, he had pursued her all the way to Bath. She had just been so glad to see the back of those wretchedly uncomfortable boots she had not paused to think what the consequences of handing them over would be.

It would be useless to apply to any of the hotel staff for aid, now. She had walked into this establishment leaning on her would-be seducer's arm. They would not believe her excuse that she had been too dazed by the enormity of Madame's cruelty to know what she had been doing.

Besides, if she did attempt to escape him, where would she go? What could she do? She knew of nobody who might help her find work. Not just here in Bath. Not anywhere.

While she sat in gloomy contemplation of her utter stupidity in playing right into his hands, Lord Matthison calmly began pouring the coffee and making a selection from the plate of sandwiches, which he then handed to her.

The fragrant aroma of coffee made her nostrils twitch, and the daintily cut sandwiches set her mouth watering. She promptly decided that whatever was going to happen next, there was no point in trying to deal with it on an empty stomach.

And so it was that the chambermaid who came in not five minutes later with a can of hot water, found them sitting by the fire, facing each other, sipping coffee and tucking into their sandwiches like any unremarkable, staid married couple.

She felt her last chance of explaining to a member of the hotel staff that she was being kidnapped, or seduced, or at the very least, being forced into a situation that was completely repugnant to her, slip away while Lord Matthison ordered the disposing of the hot water, basin and towels.

And then he was kneeling at her feet again, a towel slung over his shoulder.

'Do not make a fuss about this,' he said sternly. 'Just remove your stockings so I can tend to your feet.'

The idea of a lord washing the feet of a seamstress was so shocking that Mary just sat there gaping at him.

'If you do not remove them,' he warned her, 'I shall be obliged to do it for you.'

'W-why?' she said stupidly. Why would he want to wash her feet?

'They are bleeding. Did you not know?'

She looked down, and saw that he was right. Her toes were numb with cold, but there was no mistaking the bloodstains on her stockings from where the boots had rubbed her feet raw. It would be silly to fight him over an issue like this, she decided, putting her half-eaten sandwich down. Besides, they had already established that when it came to a contest of brute strength, he must always be the victor.

As she reached up under her skirts to untie her garters, Lord Matthison turned away, bringing the basin of warm water closer to her chair, so that she could put her bared feet straight into it.

It seemed a remarkably considerate thing for an evil seducer and murderer of women to do. It would have been more in character for him to leer lasciviously as she peeled off her stockings. She studied the top of his bent head as he lathered his hands.

'I beg your pardon,' he murmured when she winced as he gently began to soap the raw skin.

His strong hands were incredibly gentle as he lifted her feet on to the towel he had spread over his thigh, and patted them dry. She felt tears spring to her eyes at the tenderness of his ministrations. It was all a far cry from how she might have expected him to treat her.

Could a man in league with the devil be capable of acting with such kindness?

'How, then?' she murmured as she wondered how he had managed to appear like a genie from a lamp at the most opportune moment. 'I mean,' she explained at his puzzled frown, 'how did you find me?'

'I followed you, as soon as I heard your employer had put you on the night mail, of course.'

'How did you hear I had got on the night mail?'

'I had been having you watched.'

She shuddered at the thought that someone had been watching her movements without her suspecting a thing. It was almost as horrible as thinking he had been able to locate her by supernatural means. Her revulsion must have shown on her face, because he said,

'I have had you watched from the day I found you. You didn't think I would let you slip through my fingers again, did you? After all I have been through these last seven years?'

'People don't behave like this,' she said, wondering what on earth possessed him to act in such a way. And then she closed her eyes, on a wave of giddiness. Everything she had believed about everyone she knew had been turned upside down so many times this day! 'This is like…a nightmare…'

'The nightmare is over, now,' he insisted. 'I have told you, I will look after you now. You have nothing to fear. I won't let you fall into the hands of unscrupulous people like that seamstress who treated you little better than a slave.'

She opened her eyes, saw the determined set of his jaw, and realised it was pointless getting upset with him.

It was not his fault she looked like the woman he had loved and lost. Not his fault Madame had vented her spite by pitching her into the worst possible scenario she could have invented. In fact, if anything, she felt sorry for him. For a moment, she had a crazy urge to reach out and put her arms round him. To tell him that she understood he believed he was doing the right thing, and did not hold it against him.

Instead, she ran her hand shakily round to the nape of her neck, closing her eyes against the need burning from his. He might say she had nothing to fear from him, but wealthy men did not pursue poor girls for any other reason than to amuse themselves for a while in bed. She might feel sorry for him, she might accept he sincerely believed he was coming to her rescue, but that did not mean she was going to abandon all her principles!

Even as she wondered how on earth she could find the words to explain all that was going on in her mind, when she was not sure she fully understood herself, he rose to his knees, placing one hand on each of the arms of her chair.

'Cora,' he grated, in a voice so full of pain and longing it touched her at the deepest level, 'wake up and love me again.'

She knew the second before he did it that he was going to kiss her. Or at least, kiss the image of Cora that she represented.

She had not the heart to repulse him, after that heart-felt plea. So she made no move to stop him.

Just before his mouth brushed against hers, she tensed, expecting to feel the dismay and revulsion that normally overcame her when a man got too close. But it did not materialise. Instead she felt a very strong wish that she could somehow take away his pain. A single tear slipped from behind her tightly closed eyelids as she put her arms round him, and began, very inexpertly, to kiss him back.

Her heart speeded up. She had dreamed of him kissing her like this, night after night.

Oh, how she wished she *was* the woman he had loved so much he was incapable of letting her go.

But she was not.

Her eyes flew open in dismay.

'No,' she said, her hands sliding from behind his neck, to push against his shoulders. 'This is all wrong. I am not *her*.'

'You are!' he insisted, the anguish in his eyes bringing fresh tears to her own. 'I did not believe it myself at first,' he said. 'I thought you were a ghost. And then, when I had sobered up, that you were just a woman who resembled Cora somewhat. That was why I came to find you. To prove to myself that it was a trick of the light, or…' He ran his fingers through his hair, leaving the damp locks ridged and furrowed. 'But then you spoke. And I touched you. Cora…' He seized her hands and began squeezing them repeatedly, as though assuring himself she was still there. 'No woman has ever been able to stir my blood the way you do. It is as though I've come back to life, after seven long years of wishing I was dead!'

She blinked at him, a shock running right through her. For she knew exactly what he meant. When he held her in his arms, and kissed her, it was as though she had come to life, too. She knew no other man could have this effect on her.

It *was* as though they belonged together.

But it could not be…

Seeing her tiny shake of the head, he groaned, and buried his face in her neck, clutching her to him so tightly it was a wonder she could still breathe.

'I'm sorry,' she murmured, stroking his hair. 'So sorry.'

She wished she did not have to hurt him. If only she was the kind of girl, like Molly perhaps, who would not mind pretending to be who he wanted her to be.

It seemed to take a long time before he stopped shaking. But even then, she could not bring herself to let him go. Holding him was a harmless enough way of comforting him. If only there was some other way she could help ease his suffering, without sacrificing her principles.

And perhaps there was.

'If,' she began hesitantly, 'I really was Cora, would you be treating me like this?'

'What?' he reared back, looking thunderstruck.

'She was a proper lady, was she not?' She must have been if she had been betrothed to this lord. 'You would not have taken her into a hotel, and kissed her and held her like this. You would have cared about protecting her reputation.'

She could see him take her argument on board, struggle with it briefly, then toss it ruthlessly aside.

'I am not letting you out of my sight again. Who knows where you might vanish off to if I once let down my guard!' He leapt to his feet, paced away, then rounded on her, fists clenched at his sides. 'And it is not as if you have any reputation left for me, or any other man to ruin is it? Not any more!'

Mary wondered why she did not feel in the least bit scared by this blatant display of masculine outrage.

But then it hit her that it was because it was not aimed at her, but at Cora.

And that it was Cora who had to answer his objections, if Mary was to stay safe.

'Are you saying you no longer care about my reputation?' she challenged him.

'No, I am not, damn you!' he snarled. 'It is your physical safety, your well-being that matter to me, not some damn stupid convention that would have us lying apart in separate beds all night. Cora, I need to hold you, to know I have you back! Do you think I would sleep a wink if you were in another room, when I have already spent the last seven years wondering where you are? Don't ask me to leave you.'

No, she sighed, she could not ask that of him. Not

when it would be such a cruel thing to do. She had already experienced far too much of cruelty for one day.

'Very well,' she sighed, though she knew she was going to regret it. 'I will not ask you to leave. But,' she said, lifting her chin in a gesture of defiance that was probably futile, 'I will not share your bed.'

'Not until we are married,' he agreed, a look of profound relief on his face.

'Married? I cannot marry you!'

'But of course we are going to be married. What do you think I meant when I said I would not let you out of my sight?' He looked wounded. 'Cora, you cannot think that because I said you had no reputation now that I could possibly be offering you anything less than marriage?' He looked as though she had struck him. 'I see that you did. What have I done to make you think that of me?'

Nothing, she realised. She had been troubled by the rumours others whispered about him, but she had never quite been able to believe them completely. Somehow she had always known that Lord Matthison was not evil. He was hurt, and angry and confused. That was what made him act in a way that seemed reprehensible to others. But she ought to have known better.

'It is nothing you have done,' she said in a contrite voice. 'It is who you are. Men of your class *never* offer marriage to girls of mine.'

He spun back to her, his face clearing.

'Of course. You still don't believe you are my Cora, do you?'

He returned to the chair opposite hers, and sat forwards, his hands clasped between his knees, looking intently at her.

'Very well, if you are not Cora, then who are you?'

Her heart leapt. 'Are you ready to hear the truth at last?'

And then it plunged. If she made him believe it, what then? The only thing that gave her any hold over him was his belief she was a lady. Once he accepted she was just a poor seamstress, she would have no means to prevent him doing exactly what she feared the most.

'Yes. Tell me…' He paused, then said with deliberation, 'Mary, where do you come from? Who were your parents?'

It was the first time he had addressed her by her real name. The truth was going to come out, now, no matter what the outcome.

She looked into the black depths of his eyes, and felt the shadows creeping closer. 'The truth,' she managed on a strangled whisper. She wished now she had not challenged him to seek the truth. Whenever she had tried to examine what lurked buried in the depths of her mind, all she had ever discovered was that it was dark and horrible and painful.

Uttering a little whimper, she began to massage the back of her neck, where the muscles had gone rigid with stress.

'I don't know!' she finally managed to admit. 'I don't know who my parents were. Though, sometimes, I think I remember my mother.'

Because he had asked it of her, she delved inwards, towards the vague image of the kindly, calming presence that had urged her to keep her mind on her sampler. 'She taught me to sew.'

'That is good,' Lord Matthison murmured. 'Is there any more?'

He reached across the space between them and laid his hand over the one with which she was clutching at the arm of the chair. 'What of your father?'

There was that menacing figure beyond her mother. The one she had never quite dared to try to examine. The one her mother had been so determined to shield her from. The one with the loud voice and the hard fists.

'He used to hit me!' Now she knew why it was second nature for her to sit quietly at her needlework, striving to become invisible to anyone else that might be in the room. 'He was always angry. Nothing I did was ever good enough.'

And then, before she could prevent it, a horrible image flashed into her mind. Of a woman lying on the floor, curled up on her side, with a man crouching over her, pounding her with his fists.

'Cora, Cora, what is it, where have you gone?'

She blinked, coming back to the present to find Lord Matthison holding both her hands between his, his dark eyes full of concern.

'He used to beat her, too...' She shivered. The image was so stark, so terrifying, the sense of loss and horror so deeply imbedded in her psyche that she suddenly knew why she flinched from the prospect of reclaiming any of her memories. 'I think he might have killed her.'

She had to block out this shattering revelation from her past! She had to turn her mind away from the horror. But she had no work to occupy her hands. No soothing, repetitive activity to calm her troubled mind. She got to her feet, in agitation, her breath coming in thin, reedy gasps.

In an instant, Lord Matthison was on his feet beside her. He hauled her into his arms, and began to rock her, crooning soft, soothing nonsense into her ears. And because there was nothing else she could use to block out those images, she concentrated completely on him. On the feel of his hands, running up and down her back. The sound of his voice, telling her over and over again that she was safe. The scent of his skin where her nose butted up against his neck. And the violent images gradually faded away, her breathing slowed, and the panic receded. She was not *there* any more. She was standing in a hotel room in Bath, with the fire crackling cheerfully in the grate, and the coffee cooling in the cups on the table. In Lord Matthison's arms.

'Your father could not have killed your mother,' he said, when at last she stopped spasmodically clutching at his jacket sleeves. 'He was a man of the cloth.'

The man who had been crouching over her mother had been wearing the clothes of a cleric.

She shook her head, vehemently pushing the disturbing image back into the shadows.

'Cora's father may have been a man of the cloth,' she

argued, pulling out of his arms and turning away. '*My* father was a drunken bully.'

It was one of those truths that slipped from her mouth without her knowing where it had come from. Yes, she sighed. She knew that was true. That was how she had been able to identify the sweet, fruity odour in the coach as spirits lingering on a man's breath. The other passengers must have spent some time in the taproom whilst waiting for the journey to start. It was the reason they had all slept so soundly, no matter how loud the guard blew the horn, or how deep the potholes that they bounced over.

Lord Matthison gently set her back on her chair, and went to his own, his face creased in perplexity.

'If you are not Cora Montague,' he said, shaken, 'then who the hell are you? Why do you look so much like her? And why did you only appear in London six years ago? Less than two months after she disappeared. With no clear memories of your past!'

'N-not clear memories, no,' she admitted. 'Just snatches, mostly.'

He sat forwards, his eyes narrowing. 'What do you mean, mostly? What have you not told me?'

'Well,' she admitted, feeling horribly guilty for not mentioning it before. 'I do remember the place where I lived before they sent me to work for Madame Pichot. A great house it was, in the country.'

'Where was it?' he demanded sharply. 'Tell me everything!'

'I...I can't!' she gasped, getting to her feet and pacing the floor in an agitated manner.

'Can't or won't?'

'Why are you torturing me like this?' she whirled on him. 'What do you hope to gain?'

He got to his feet too, and pulled her into his arms again, cradling her against his chest. In spite of her accusation that he was torturing her, she subsided into his embrace as though he was her only rock in a sea of uncertainty.

'You know what I want,' he groaned. 'I want you to be Cora! I want to find out what happened to you that day you went out riding and never came back. And how you ended up in London. But if—' he took her face in his hands and raised it so she had to gaze directly into his eyes '—if you turn out to be someone else…a girl perhaps who ran away from home after witnessing the brutal murder of her mother by her father…then I promise you, I will still take care of you. I swear, you have nothing to fear from me, whatever we find out.

'But don't you want to know the truth about yourself? I think,' he said, looking at her challengingly, 'we both need to unravel the mystery of your past, before either of us can begin to live freely again.'

'Y-you will take care of me?'

'Yes. It is not your fault you look like Cora. You have done nothing to merit losing your post and ending up in a town where you know nobody. If you are not Cora, then I swear, I will make amends for all of this.'

She knew he spoke the truth. Whoever she turned out to be, he would be responsible for her.

Just as Molly had said he would.

She pulled out of his arms, rubbing her hands up and down the sleeves of her dress. Now was the moment any sensible woman would negotiate terms. Tell him she wanted him to set her up in a shop when he was finished with her.

But, she realised on a shocked, indrawn breath, that was not what she wanted at all!

Somewhere during this long, confusing day, she had begun to wish she really could be his Cora. That she was fit to marry him, and could stay with him for ever! That was why she had allowed her memories to begin to tally with what he kept on telling her.

She sank down on to her chair.

'W-will you do something for me?' she asked in a tortured whisper.

'If I can.'

'W-will you treat me, as though I was…Cora, until we find out the truth?'

She did not think she could bear it if he treated her like a disposable commodity, not now she had caught a glimpse of how deeply this man could love.

'Nothing would please me more,' he said, his face relaxing into something approaching a smile.

It almost broke her heart. She was encouraging him to live out his fantasy, when she knew it would only be a matter of time before the truth blew it all to smithereens.

She was not the woman he loved.

It was one of those things she just knew.

Chapter Six

It was not as pleasant, having an enormous bed all to herself, as Mary had thought it would be.

She rolled over on to her side, tugging the blankets up round her ears as she went, wondering how it could be so hard to get to sleep when she was so exhausted. To think, when Lord Matthison had told her she could take this bed, while he made himself comfortable on a chair by the fire, she had felt nothing but relief! She had even mustered up a timid smile when he had pulled the velvet bed-hangings closed round her, assuring her that he would not intrude on her privacy. She had briefly imagined stretching out her aching limbs on the invitingly soft mattress and falling instantly into a blissfully deep and dreamless sleep.

As yet, she had not even managed to keep her eyes closed for more than a few seconds at a time.

It was too dark.

Almost as soon as Lord Matthison had drawn the

dusty brown curtains round her, she'd had to fumble her way to the edge of the bed and open them a chink. She had brought her overnight bag into her private cocoon, but dreaded groping for it in that thick darkness, and trying to locate her nightdress in its depths by sense of touch alone. It had been extremely awkward, wriggling out of her clothes, and into her nightdress whilst kneeling up on a surface that had the consistency of sponge cake. And when she'd finally succeeded, instead of relaxing back into the bank of pillows, she had kept on kneeling there, chewing on her lower lip, while she wondered what to do about her dress. She had felt how stiff the hem was as she'd tugged it over her head. What she really wanted to do was to rinse the mud out before settling for the night. She was sure, if she could hang it over one of the chair backs, before the fire, it would be almost dry by morning.

But that would mean venturing out into Lord Matthison's territory.

In her nightgown.

Swallowing down hard, Mary had draped her soiled dress over the footboard, telling herself that there were worse things than having to put on travel-stained clothing.

Far worse. She had experienced some of them today. When she remembered how desolate she had felt, standing in that doorway with that blank piece of paper in her hand, her insides clenched up and she had to wrap her arms about her stomach.

And it was not only what had really happened today that had left her feeling so raw. It was the glimpse of the past that Lord Matthison had goaded her into looking at. She could still see her father pounding his fists into her mother's curled-up body, every time she shut her eyes.

She sat bolt upright, her own fists clenched. She had always known that there was something so ugly in her past that her mind recoiled from remembering it! But worse, far worse, was the horrible, sickening certainty that there was more to come. She could sense it, lurking just out of sight, like a beast crouching in the shadows, lashing its tail as it prepared to pounce the moment she let her guard down...

Mary grabbed one of the pillows, and buried her face in it as she hugged it to her knees. If only she were back in London, with Molly on one side of her, and Kitty on the other. They would not have let her so much as roll over, never mind sit up and toss pillows about. But then, with the girls on either side of her, she would not be feeling so vulnerable. Even if they did not fully wake up, one of them would always reach out, and pat her sleepily, and tell her to pay no mind to her dreams. Without them to guard her, she gasped, blinking blindly into the inky blackness that surrounded her, she would never dare to go to sleep. With nobody to wake her, she might fall deeper and deeper into her nightmares until they swallowed her whole!

Her heart was beating so fast, her whole body shook with its force. She felt so utterly, completely defence-less, here in this town where nothing was familiar to her. In London, there was always noise, no matter what time of night it was. The rattle of carriage wheels passing in the street, the cries of the night watchmen, drunken revellers singing as they staggered home. Signs of life.

This place was as silent as the grave. She felt as though the very quietness of the hotel room was conspiring with its darkness to suffocate her in this velvet tomb.

And then she heard the creak of a chair as Lord Matthison shifted position. Some of the tension drained from her shoulders and she lay down, staring straight up where she knew there was a canopy over her head. If she fell asleep, and if she had a nightmare, he would hear her cry out. And he would wake her, wouldn't he? Before she went in too deep?

When the chair creaked again, Mary ruefully compared their positions. It didn't sound as if he could get comfortable. She should have taken the chair, and let him have the bed. She could have curled her smaller body up in a blanket, and watched the flames dancing in the grate. He could have stretched out here, in the kind of luxury he was used to. And at least one of them would have been able to get some sleep.

Instead, she lay rigid, listening to the sounds of his wakefulness, yearning for daybreak to put an end to their mutual discomfort.

She found it almost impossible to look him in the face the next morning. She was painfully aware that he had chased halfway across the country to rescue her, and rescue it had been—she shuddered to think what might have become of her if he had not been there. And far from expressing so much as a hint of gratitude, she had reacted with hostility and suspicion, and finally demanded he accord her the kind of respect he would show a woman of his own class.

'I will hire a post-chaise to convey us back to London,' he said, once they were seated at the table where a fresh-faced young waiter had set out a substantial breakfast.

'London?' she echoed, her curiosity roused enough to dart a timid glance at him. Immediately, she felt quite wretched to see the dark shadows that spending a sleepless night in a chair had put under his eyes.

'Yes, London,' he replied, cutting a slice from the succulent slab of sirloin that lay on his plate. 'That is the logical place to begin to hunt for clues to your true identity.'

Mary dejectedly bit into a roll she had mechanically slathered with butter and honey. He was not going to give this up. He was not going to rest until he had ferreted out the very deepest of her secrets.

'You say you worked in a big house before you went to Madame Pichot?'

She nodded, her mouth suddenly too dry to swallow, let alone form words.

'She must know something about your former employer. They must have given you a reference?'

Mary reached for her cup of chocolate and took a large gulp. Once Madame related the circumstances that had led to her being sent to London…

'She…Madame…might not be willing to tell us anything,' she said hopefully.

Lord Matthison looked at her sharply, and she hung her head. It was all he could do not to curse out loud. The dressmaker would *not* want to help them, that was what she meant.

He stabbed into his steak, savagely hacking off another slice and impaling it on his fork. Madame Pichot was a spiteful woman, to have served a girl she believed to be a simpleton such a cruel trick.

But it was his fault that she had turned on Cora at all.

He flung his fork, complete with the untasted morsel of rare steak, back on to the plate with a clatter. He had spent a large part of the night re-examining the events of the past few days, trying to come to terms with Cora's reactions to him. In particular, wondering why she assumed he had proposed marriage to another woman, when nothing was further from the truth. She could only have heard that there was any thought of an engagement from some member of the Winters family. Nobody else knew anything about it.

One of them must have gone to Madame Pichot and fed her a pack of lies. Probably breathing threats of scandal that could jeopardise the business.

He could curse them all for their cruelty towards a defenceless woman till the cows came home, but in the end, he had to accept that it was his own actions that had resulted in Cora losing her job and ending up on the streets, so lonely and scared she had accepted the protection of a man who was a virtual stranger to her.

No wonder she could not bear to look at him.

'She may not want to help us, but she will,' he said in a tone so implacable, his face going so hard that, for the very briefest moment, Mary felt a twinge of pity for her former employer. She could almost see why people believed this man was in league with the devil, when his eyes could burn with such malevolence.

Travelling in a post-chaise, Mary soon discovered, was an entirely different prospect from taking the mail coach. For one thing, the interior was too small to take more than two passengers. For another, they were not tied to anybody's schedule but their own. When they stopped to change horses and postilions, they could take a meal, or even a stroll if they felt so inclined.

The leisurely pace was less taxing, it was true, but it had the disadvantage that they would not reach London in one stage. And though Mary was in no hurry to face Madame Pichot, she still felt awkward about sharing a room with Lord Matthison. And she knew he would insist that they did.

Though, she mused, as they sat down to a light supper, set out in the private parlour he had obtained, she no longer worried he might not treat her with respect. He had been so attentive to her needs, getting ostlers to jump to attention, and landlords to scramble to serve them, with just one lancing look from his night-dark eyes. How she wished she was a real lady, and could always expect such consideration!

He was such a perfect gentleman, she sighed, wiping

her lips with a napkin, and laying it on the table beside her plate. He deserved to be with someone so much better than her.

'You can take the bed tonight,' she declared, the moment Lord Matthison closed the door to their bedchamber behind them. Marching across to the bed, she whisked off the quilt, helped herself to one of the pillows, and arranged them on the chesterfield that sagged on bowed legs under the window.

'And please, do not argue about this, my mind is made up,' she said when she saw a whole raft of objections flit across his face. 'I am so tired I could sleep anywhere. I can be quite comfortable on the couch, being so much smaller than you,' she pointed out.

With a weary shrug of his shoulder, Lord Matthison sat on the edge of the bed, tugged off his boots, then disappeared into the damasked folds of its hangings. To fall instantly asleep, she expected, curling up in the nest she had made for herself.

She did not think it would take her long to fall asleep tonight either. The shocks of the previous day had receded from the forefront of her mind. She had felt herself relaxing in Lord Matthison's company more and more as the day had progressed. He had been a perfect travelling companion, kind and attentive, and always treating her with the utmost propriety. She was really glad he would be staying in the room with her, though naturally, she would never admit as much to him!

Even so, when she closed her eyes, for a while she

had the peculiar impression that she was still bouncing along in the post-chaise. Her muscles had got so used to clenching and straining to compensate for the vehicle's lurching motion that it seemed to take them a while to accept they could all just let go.

But gradually, as exhaustion claimed her, her mind translated the bouncing movement of the coach that her body was still experiencing, into a dream of rocking, on a gentle swell, in a rowing boat, out on the open loch. She could hear seagulls keening as they wheeled overhead. And, of course, Lord Matthison was there. She felt his strong arms wrap her in a blanket of pure contentment. She nestled closer to him, laying her head on his chest, so that she could listen to the steady, reassuring thud of his heart as the waves lapped against the hull of their boat.

And woke with a jolt, to find herself curled up on the bed, cradled against Lord Matthison's chest.

He must have waited until she fell asleep, then carried her to the bed, intending to… She gulped. He had intended to swap places with her, of course! He must have succumbed to the temptation of holding her for a while, and fallen asleep again.

Well, it would not do.

Slowly, stealthily, so as not to disturb him, Mary tried to disentangle herself from the quilt in which she was wrapped like a swaddled baby.

'No…' he moaned, clutching her more tightly, and rolling over so that his leg now pinned hers down.

Without even opening his eyes.

Mary's heart melted. The poor man needed to keep her close. She knew just how he felt. Had she not missed the company of her bedmates the night before?

Did she really want to escape his hold badly enough to wake him? Where was the harm in staying exactly where she was? He was not going to do anything but hold her while he slept.

They would both get more rest, if she just closed her eyes again and shifted into a more comfortable position.

And she did feel warm and comfortable. And happier than she could ever remember feeling. The girls she slept with might have provided company, and warmth on a winter night, but they did not cling to her as though she was a rare treasure.

As though she mattered.

When she awoke in the morning, she was alone in the bed, with the curtains drawn closed. But she did not feel in the least lonely or scared, because she could hear Lord Matthison moving about the room. He splashed about at the washstand, and then she heard him huffing slightly as he dried himself, and then the rustle of fabric that told her he was putting on his clothes.

It felt peculiarly intimate, to hear him going about such everyday tasks, after spending the night held in his arms. When he approached the bed, and cleared his throat, before drawing back the hangings on one side, her whole body blushed with awareness. Every single one of her pores felt sensitive to his intense, dark gaze as he stood over her, for what felt like an eternity, while she drank in every detail of his appearance.

The look in her eyes reached right down into him, stirring feelings that he had thought were beyond recall.

She must be Cora! Surely, no other woman could affect him this way?

And yet, would the Cora he knew have been able to share a room with a man she barely knew? And wake up looking so calm?

This woman appeared to have a core of inner strength that Cora had lacked. Oh, there were times when she was unsure of herself. But then, she had no memory. Of course she experienced anxiety.

But despite that handicap, she had bravely forged a new life for herself in unfamiliar surroundings.

And look how she had stood up to him!

It must have been frightening to fall into the clutches of a devil like him. And the way he had behaved in Bath, falling to his knees and begging her to love him, must have convinced her he was as mad as a March hare.

Yet all she had done was hold him. Though she was clearly afraid, she had generously offered what comfort she could, when he had been at his lowest ebb. Without compromising her beliefs. She had stood firm on that point, insisting he treat her as though she was a lady.

She *was* a lady! Every inch of her. From the crown of those tangled curls, to the tips of her blistered toes. With as big a heart as Cora had ever had. Last night, seeing how weary he was, she had put his needs before her own, insisting he took the bed.

Until last night, Cora had been the only person who had ever seen what he needed, without having to be told. He did not want to lose that again.

He did not want to lose her.

If she was not Cora…

He recoiled from the alarming prospect.

'I shall wait for you in the parlour while you get dressed,' he said gruffly, breaking whatever spell it was that had rendered her powerless to do anything but gaze back at him with utter fascination. 'Will you be ready to breakfast in half an hour?'

Mary nodded, dimly aware of a vague sense of disquiet. It was not until she had finished her wash, and was stepping into her increasingly disreputable-looking gown, that she realised what had disturbed her. Lord Matthison might have phrased it as a request, but in effect, he had ordered her to bestir herself, and be downstairs within half an hour.

He had decided they were going back to London.

He had decided that they needed to unearth the secrets of her past that she would just as soon leave buried.

He had given her no say.

He had taken over her life.

And there was not a thing she could do about it.

By the time the post-chaise lurched to a halt before some buildings she recognised as being bachelor chambers in Albany, Mary was feeling more than a little resentful. He had promised to treat her exactly as he would have treated Cora, but she was certain he would never have brought *her* here.

He would have escorted her to a hotel…

The mere thought of being stuck in one of those rooms, all on her own, to lie all night in a great expanse of empty bed, with all those suffocating swathes of fabric round her, brought her out in a cold sweat. Thank heavens he *was* only paying lip service to the notion of treating her like a lady! She reached out and clung on to his arm as he steadily mounted the steps.

He looked down at her sharply.

'Don't be afraid,' he said gently. 'I will never hurt you. I just mean to see you settled in comfortably, before I go to deal with Madame Pichot—'

'No!' The prospect of being abandoned, the minute they had set foot in London, was almost as dreadful as the thought of being banished to a hotel.

'D-don't leave me on my own!'

She gazed up imploringly into his eyes, feeling profoundly relieved when she could not detect any hint of annoyance creeping into them. A man with a less even temper would be exceedingly put out by her contrariness. One minute she was complaining she did not wish to see Madame Pichot, the next she was refusing to let him go without her!

But he just laid his hand over her fingers where they curled into the material of his jacket like claws.

'I won't leave you alone,' he vowed. 'Never.'

For a moment or two, they stood there, gazes locked.

At what precise moment had Lord Matthison become indispensable to her peace of mind? During the journey, when he had demonstrated how kind he could be? Or during the night spent blissfully wrapped in his arms? However it had happened, she only knew that he had become a bulwark against life's alarms. She felt as though she would fall to pieces if she let him out of her sight for a minute.

And he just stood there, letting her search his eyes for as long as it took her to realise he understood, and even welcomed her dawning need of him.

'Come,' he said gently, 'let us go inside, and wash away the dust of travel. Would you care for something to eat before we go to beard the Gorgon in her den?'

She darted him an uncertain look as he led her inexorably up the stairs.

'Together,' he reassured her. 'Ephraims,' he said when a short stocky man with curly brown hair opened the door on which he had just knocked. 'We have a guest. She will be staying with us for the foreseeable future.'

While Lord Matthison issued a string of instructions, Mary surreptitiously took stock of the servant's reactions. She was pleased to note his swiftly concealed look of surprise when he had seen her clinging to his master's arm. And positively heartened by the way his eyes grew round when Lord Matthison instructed him to prepare the guest room for her use. It meant that he was not in the habit of bringing women up to these rooms. Whatever was happening between them was as extraordinary for him as it was for her.

'My name is Mary,' she told the servant over her shoulder, as Lord Matthison ushered her into a sitting room. She was glad he had not introduced her as Cora. It would feel like living a lie if he went round telling other people that was who she was, when she knew full well she was not.

She subsided into the chair he indicated he wished her to sit in, chewing on her lower lip. The truth was, she was only here at all because of his erroneous belief. But once they had visited Madame Pichot, and he found out who she was, and what she had done, all this concern would be snuffed out like a guttering candle.

She gazed up at him, her heart plunging at the thought that he would soon cease treating her as though she was a person that mattered.

'You have noted,' he said in a rather defensive manner, as soon as the servant had left the room, 'that I have ordered Ephraims to prepare the guest room for your use while we are staying here.' He paced across to the fireplace and turned to face her, running his fingers through his hair. 'I know I promised to treat you as though we had already established you really are Cora…and it is true that as you were, when I last saw you…seventeen, and untouched…' A look of anguish flitted across his face. He turned, staring into the empty grate for a while, and when he turned back to her it was like looking at a stranger. There was no trace of compassion in those world-weary eyes. She was, she realised, looking at the hardened gambler who had made his fortune ruining anyone who showed the slightest trace of weakness in his presence.

'Back then,' he drawled, 'yes, I admit it would have been outrageous for you to spend a night in a single gentleman's rooms. Or to travel with me, unchaperoned, as we have done. But things are different now. For the past seven years you have been out of society, living in a way that is bound to raise eyebrows…and I do not see that sticking to a set of restrictive regulations at this point will do anything to quell the gossip that will erupt once we marry.'

Mary plucked at the folds of her skirts. 'I dare say Cora would have objected to being brought here.' She scanned the room with inquisitive eyes, taking in the heavy, masculine furniture, gentlemen's magazines piled neatly on a side table, several decks of cards stacked on a felt-topped table under the window. 'But I do not.' She hung her head briefly, remembering her feeling of resentment that although he was paying lip service to the idea of treating her like a lady, he was not quite managing it.

'You—' she tried a tentative smile '—you are *trying* to treat me with respect. Far more respect than most gentlemen would accord a simple dressmaker.'

'But I am not quite treating you as though you were a lady born, though am I?' He grimaced. 'Dammit, this is so complicated. The sooner we have established who and what you are, the better!'

Though Mary could not agree with his statement, she kept that thought to herself. They barely spoke again while they shared the collection of cold cuts and bread and butter that Ephraims brought in. But his comment kept going round and round her mind while she freshened up in the room to which Ephraims later escorted her.

A room that Lord Matthison had promised was for her use alone. Now that he had her in his own territory, he did not seem to think it was necessary to keep such a close watch on her. And it was a nice room, she noted. It had carpeting on the floor beside the bed and by the washstand, lovely, leafy-green damasked hangings around the bed and at the window, and all the furniture was made of the same dark, heavy wood, with matching patterns inlaid in a lighter colour.

She wished she could stay here indefinitely. With Lord Matthison always close at hand to keep her feeling safe, and a servant to do all the cooking and cleaning, fetching and carrying. It would be lovely not to have to work until she dropped from exhaustion every night.

But once he discovered she was not Cora... She splashed her face with water, trying to wash away the creeping worries that kept on besetting her. He had promised he would look after her, no matter who she was, she reminded herself, patting her face dry on the softest towel she had ever held against her skin. She could trust him to keep his word. He was a gentleman.

She picked up a silver-backed hairbrush, and began to work it through her tangles, meditatively. Two weeks ago, she would have sworn she would never, ever, have considered becoming a man's mistress. But if that was the only way she could stay in his life...

And she did want to stay near him. She had never met anyone who made her feel like he did. So safe, and cherished. He even understood her confusion. He did not mock her, or pity her, or make her feel she lacked anything at all.

It was strange to think that a man others whispered was in league with the devil should rouse such feelings of trust in her, when she was apt to be scared of her own shadow. She tilted her head to one side, to work through the curls over her left ear.

Well, the rumours about him were quite ridiculous, that was why they did not bother her! For a start, he would not be so sure she was Cora, if he had done away with that woman all those years ago. And since his pact with the devil was supposed to have been sealed in that girl's blood, it was blatantly a piece of malicious gossip, made up by someone who... Angrily she set the brush down on the highly polished dressing table top. One of those people he had beaten at cards, she expected. And, no, she had no idea how he managed to be so amazingly successful at the gaming tables, when it was impossible to imagine him cheating. A man who was honourable enough to feel guilty for not keeping strictly to his promise to treat a dressmaker like a real lady, no, that was not a man who could cheat at cards! Or murder anyone. Or have any truck with anything unholy at all!

Most of the class who called themselves gentlemen would not have turned a hair at taking advantage of her in either of the inns they had stayed in. They would not have taken a chair, or just held her in their arms. Nor left her bed early, so that she should not even be troubled by the knowledge he had held her!

She was not sorry, she decided, lifting her chin defiantly, that he had taken over her life. The only thing she was sorry for was the hurt he would feel when he found out who she really was.

He would be so disappointed she was not the woman he had sought for so long. How would he feel about her then? What if he found it too painful to have her near, a constant reminder of all he had lost? She had no doubt he would set her up in a shop, if she asked him, but...

The prospect that he might send her away made her feel quite ill. She leapt to her feet, the brush dropping unheeded to the floor as she dashed back to the sitting room, suddenly fearful that he might have gone out without her.

He was leaning against the mantelpiece, his arms folded across his chest, his eyes fixed on the door.

Waiting for her.

She paused in the doorway, her heart beating wildly as she castigated herself for her lack of faith.

He had told her, over and over again, that he couldn't bear to let her out of his sight. And suddenly, for the first time, she knew he really meant it. That spike of panic that had just pierced her was the exact same feeling that had put that haunted look in his eyes, the one that had dissipated the moment she walked into the room.

For a moment or two she felt such an inexpressible sense of joy she scarcely knew how to contain it. But then he said, 'We should leave now. The sooner we get this visit to Madame Pichot over with, the better.'

And Mary's bubble burst. *She* was not really the

person that mattered to him. It was Cora who had this effect on him. She had to turn away, lest he detect the jealousy that ripped through her. If she ever came face to face with the woman who had reduced such an honourable man to this state of chronic need, she would be hard pressed not to slap her face.

He unfolded his arms, and came across to where she stood in the doorway, a frown still creasing his brows.

'We shall have to get you some new clothes,' he said, eyeing the sadly soiled garments she'd had to put back on.

He was looking magnificent, in a fresh suit of exquisitely tailored clothing. He might have dressed completely in black, but the cloth was of the finest quality, and cut by an expert hand, to set off his leanly muscular figure. The splendour of his tailoring made her more aware than ever of the discrepancy in their stations. With her mud-encrusted, crumpled dress, singed coat, and boots stiffened from their soaking, she knew she looked exactly like the penniless nobody she really was.

'I have my own things,' she heard herself say defiantly. 'I want to wear my own things.' She had slid far enough down the slippery slope of temptation where he was concerned. It was bad enough that he was demolishing her principles one by one. Once she started letting him buy her clothing, he would own her completely.

He raised one eyebrow.

'Molly packed them all up for me the day Madame sent me to Bath. She was going to send them...' She paused, shaking her head. 'The trunk must still be in one of the store rooms…unless she has already taken it to a dealer in second-hand clothes.' She bit down on her lower lip to stop the incipient tremor. She felt as though part of her identity had been packed away in that trunk. If she did not get her own things back, she would have to let Lord Matthison clothe her. And she would become entirely his creation.

'Then I shall make sure you get them,' he vowed, making her contrarily even more jealous of Cora. He would let Cora have her way about anything!

It felt strange to walk through the front door of Madame's shop on Lord Matthison's arm, as though she was a customer. It must have looked strange, too, because when Kitty saw them, her mouth gaped open in surprise. She backed through the blue velvet curtain to fetch Madame, as though she could not bear to tear her eyes away. And then she heard her pounding up the back stairs as Madame emerged from her office.

Her expression was decidedly frosty.

'I do not make gowns for anything but ladies,' she sneered, pointedly looking at the way Mary was clinging to Lord Matthison's arm.

'Then it is just as well we have no intention of purchasing anything from you,' replied Lord Matthison in equally chilling tones. 'Our business with you is of a personal nature, and I would be obliged if we could conduct it in private. I am quite sure you do not wish to run the risk of one of your clients coming in and hearing what a swindling, corrupt and downright cruel woman you are?'

Madame's eyes bulged, her cheeks turning red, but it was not long before she turned on her heel and stalked down the corridor that led to her office, at the back of the building.

As they walked along behind her, Mary's ears strained to hear the sound of her former workmates congregating on the stairs. The second they reached Madame's office, her eyes darted to the wall, where she knew the knotholes gave a view over everything that was about to happen. Then they swivelled back to Madame, who was taking her seat behind the desk. As Lord Matthison held one of the ladder-backed chairs for Mary, making sure she was seated, before taking a chair for himself, she could picture Lotty's eyes growing round. She knew how the girls would interpret this sign of chivalry towards her. They would assume she was his mistress already!

It was all she could do not to turn round, and mouth an explanation that it was not what it looked like.

'We have only come here for some information,' Lord Matthison began, when Madame sat glaring at him in brimming silence.

'And my trunk,' put in Mary, her hand reaching out to touch his sleeve anxiously.

This time, she did dart one look upwards, towards the spot where she knew the girls clustered.

'Ah, yes, the trunk,' Lord Matthison drawled, leaning back in his chair and crossing his legs. 'Which you had one of your other girls pack, under the delusion you would be sending it on to the carrier's.'

'I have not had time to do so,' Madame blustered. 'But of course, now that I know Mary is back in London, under your protection—' her voice took on a derisory tone '—I will arrange to have it sent to your address.'

'Will you?' he replied in a tone that indicated he did not believe her. Mary could almost feel the girls suck in shocked breaths at his thinly veiled accusation. 'I rather think Mary would prefer me to send my man to collect it in person.'

'Yes, I would,' she said. She no longer cared why Lord Matthison was humouring her over this matter, when she was sure he would rather dress her to suit his own tastes. Every pair of gloves, each change of stockings packed up in that trunk, represented hours of painstakingly earning her place in the world. She was proud of what she had achieved since coming to London. Whatever else anybody said about her, they all acknowledged her superior talent with a needle. And those skills had not just been the means by which she survived. No, they had launched Madame Pichot, and all her workers, into a new sphere. Mary had only to take one look at a client, to know what would suit them. While Madame did the cutting, it had often been Mary who made the initial sketches, though her greatest talent had been the intricate beadwork that required such intense concentration. Few girls could do that.

She felt as though her whole life, for the past seven years, was packed away in that trunk. She was not going to leave it behind! Nor could she bear to think of

Madame selling those gowns, when she had already profited so much from Mary's skills.

'And now,' Lord Matthison said, 'you will give me some information, if you please.'

'I do not know what you think I can tell you...'

'To begin with, you will tell me where Mary worked before she came to you.'

'I see no reason why I should do any such thing.'

'Be careful, Madame,' he said, his eyes narrowing in the way that had already sent shivers of apprehension down Mary's spine, 'that you do nothing to make me your enemy.'

'What more do you think you can do to me?' Madame replied, laying her hands flat on the desk, and rising to her feet. 'Stalking one of my girls, and leading her astray, and leaving me open to charges of keeping some sort of...of brothel? When I have worked my fingers to the bone since coming to this benighted country, raising myself out of the gutter with sheer hard work, to become one of the top modistes of the town?'

Her large, protuberant eyes were watering now, her whole body quivering.

Mary struggled with conflicting emotions. She could not help feeling some sympathy for her. Even though the woman had treated her so cruelly at the end, she thought she could understand what had driven her to do it. She must have been furious to lose Mary's particular skills. The fickle fashionables would turn to someone else once they knew they could no longer get the fabulously embroidered gowns that had recently become

Madame's trademark. Her clientele would dwindle. To keep up with her expenses, she would be obliged to accept commissions from people outside the *haut ton*. And then, once she lost her exclusivity, when it became clear that one could meet *anyone* in Madame's fitting rooms, the downward slide would accelerate.

'I do not think it is your fingers that have been worked to any extent,' Lord Matthison drawled. 'I rather think it is your unfortunate employees whose health has suffered in order to line your pockets. But, that point aside, let me remind you to choose your enemies carefully. There is bound to be gossip about this…' He waved his hand to encompass the three of them, sitting in the office. 'There will be no escaping it. The effect it has on your business, however, will largely depend on whose side you decide to take. And I should warn you that the Winters family are not highly thought of by people that matter. They have no background, no breeding. What money they have derives from trade,' he said with a curl to his lip that denoted exactly what members of the *ton* thought of vulgar mushrooms who pushed themselves in where they did not belong. 'Once Mary is my wife, nothing the Winters say about her, or her *friends*, will be considered anything more than spite.'

Madame's lips worked soundlessly as she weighed up her alternatives. Eventually, she said, 'You really intend to marry her?'

'I do.'

A nasty smile twitched at her lips. 'Then I shall be

only too delighted to tell you where she came from. It was a place called Oakham Hall, in the county of Surrey. She worked as a seamstress for Lady Sandiford. But they had to turn her off, because of her violent outbursts.'

The smile broadened, as her gloating eyes turned to Mary. 'Attacked and maimed a man, she did. The son of the house. Ah…' she sighed, as Lord Matthison leapt to his feet, his face twisted with rage. 'She didn't tell you about that unsavoury little episode, did she?'

Chapter Seven

Lord Matthison held out his arm for Mary to take. He opened the door for her, held back the curtain so they could pass through it into the showroom, and handed her into the waiting carriage with punctilious correctness.

But his face was white, and his eyes had taken on a murderous look.

Mary's heart was racing. Her stomach had been churning even before Madame had blurted out the truth she had hoped Lord Matthison would never hear. She could see he was barely containing his fury. She was not afraid he might do her any physical harm. But she dreaded what he would say once he got her alone. Now that he knew what she had done, he was bound to throw her out.

The bitter taste of betrayal rose in her throat. She choked back a sob.

His promises had meant nothing! Men never stuck to their word. They said whatever they thought would achieve the desired result, but there was no loyalty in them.

* * *

By the time they reached his chambers, her hurt had curdled into anger. It was his own fault if he was disappointed in her. She had repeatedly told him she was not what he thought she was.

'Don't you at least want to hear my side of it?' she said, as Ephraims took his master's hat, coat and gloves.

A spasm of something like disgust flitted across his set white features. He took her by the arm, and roughly dragged her into the sitting room, kicking the door shut behind them.

'Only,' he breathed, 'if you *want* to tell me about it. But you don't, do you? My God, I'm so sorry,' he groaned, taking her completely by surprise by hauling her into his arms and enveloping her in a hold so strong she could scarcely breathe. 'I should have left it all in the dark, not forced it into the light. That bastard Sandiford!' He let her go, but only to cup her face in his hands so that he could look into her eyes.

She blinked back at him in confusion.

'Y-you are not angry with me?'

'With you?' He looked stunned. 'For fighting off a brute like that? Of course not!'

She shook her head. 'Did you not hear what Madame said? How that I attacked him? Were you not listening?'

'I was listening to a spiteful woman trying to drive a wedge between us,' he bit back. 'But I know you, Cora. And I know Sandiford. So it is quite obvious what happened.'

'You do *not* know me!' she protested. If he had not

called her Cora, she might have taken comfort in his blind faith. But it was not faith in *her*. He was just so besotted with the memory of his fiancée that he could not see her getting involved in a scene so sordid, it had the power to make her feel ill to this very day.

She tore herself away from him, and faced him down, her fists clenched at her sides. How could he go on clinging to his delusion even when faced with the truth? She could stand it no longer.

'I did stab him!' she sobbed. 'Again and again and again! There was blood everywhere!'

The room seemed to go misty around the edges. Her lips went numb. Shakily, she reached for the nearest article of furniture, which happened to be a sofa, and dropped down on to it, covering her face with her hands.

She heard Lord Matthison cross to the sideboard, remove the stopper from a decanter, and pour something into a glass.

Then he was beside her, kneeling on the floor, pressing a glass into her hands. When he saw how badly she was shaking, he raised the glass to her lips, and poured the golden liquid between her chattering teeth. She spluttered a little as it burned its way down her throat. But once it hit her stomach, and she felt its warm tendrils snaking through her blood, she grasped the glass for herself, and took another gulp.

'You were only trying to defend yourself,' he said. 'You have no need to feel guilty about hurting him.'

'How do you know that?' she spat, raising her head to challenge him. The concern she saw in his eyes pierced her like a dagger. He only assumed she must have been the innocent victim rather than the instigator of the violence, because he thought she was that gentle, pure, nobly born Cora who could do no wrong!

Mutinously, she pried the brandy glass from him completely, and took another fortifying swig. 'Well, I *was* defending myself, as it happens,' she said sullenly, averting her face so she would not have to see the respect for Cora that blazed from his eyes.

'I know,' he said. 'Sandiford abducted you, did he not, and carried you off to Oakham Hall?'

'What? No!' cried Mary. 'I was working there as a seamstress!' It was not as satisfying to see him reel back, a look of confusion on his face, as she had thought it would be. 'He was not even there when I got taken on.'

'How did you come to be there, then?' he asked, looking completely perplexed.

'I…I don't recall, precisely,' she had to admit. 'There just is not anything much—' she tapped her temple with her forefinger '—before the big house…that is, Oakham Hall.' She drained what was left of the brandy, and set the empty glass on the floor at her feet. 'I can remember standing in the housekeeper's office, the day I got the job. And the lady who had taken me there saying they could only give me light work, because I had been ill. The housekeeper said they happened to be in need of a seamstress, and the other lady said I was a good needlewoman, and I can remember feeling very surprised. But I found all the tasks they set me very easy, so then I knew it was true. I *was* a good needlewoman.'

'You had been ill?' Lord Matthison levered himself off the floor, and sat on the sofa next to her, his hands clasped between his knees.

'I kept having these terrible headaches…' She ran her hand across the back of her neck, in a gesture that was becoming familiar to Lord Matthison. 'But I had been there for a *long* time before Lady Sandiford's son came home. He'd been away. I don't know where. And he…' She paled perceptibly. 'He kept coming up to the sewing room, to see the new girl, he said. That was me. And he would stand over me, and ask me how I was settling in. Did I like my work…?'

Her stomach contracted into a knot as she remembered his low voice, the foul stench of his breath as it gusted into her face. 'I could always smell liquor on his breath, no matter what time of day it was. And he would always stand just a bit too close. But I could not say anything. He was the son of my employer. Then he began to stroke my hair, and the kind of questions he asked frightened me. Even though I did not properly understand them, not back then.'

She paused for a moment, her pale lips pressed together tightly. Then she took a deep breath and plunged on, in a small voice. 'But I never asked him to stop. So I suppose it was my fault that he thought he could touch me.' She gestured towards her breasts, her cheeks colouring. Lord Matthison took Mary's hand as a single tear slid down her cheek.

'He squeezed very hard. It hurt me, and shocked me out of the state of servile acceptance that had made me cower before him. I jumped off my stool and backed away. He laughed, and made a grab for me. And I just acted without thinking. I still had the embroidery scissors in my hand, and when he reached for me, I…stabbed at his hands. And then everything happened so fast…' She hung her head, her shoulders hunching. 'He was howling, and there was blood every-where…and people came running, and he grabbed me by the neck, and somehow we were on the floor and I was on top of him, and I kept on stabbing at his hands with the scissors to try to make him let go…and then two footmen were there, pulling me away, and he was screaming that I had gone mad and ought to be locked up…and they dragged me down to the wine cellar, which had the stoutest door in the house, but it was so dark in there—' she shivered '—when they shut the door, and so cold.' Tears were streaming down Mary's face now, as she recounted the horror of that time.

'I was so scared they would send me to prison. He was yelling about sending for the magistrate. I was sure nobody would believe a word I said in my defence. Why should they, when I did not know the first thing about myself? That was the most frightening thing of all. The awful space in my mind where there should have been…something! Anything! I did not even know my own name. When the lady who brought me there told the housekeeper my name was Mary, I felt dreadful. How could my own name come as a surprise to me?'

'Because it was not your name. It *is* not your name. You are Cora.'

'No, no! Have you not heard a word I have said?'

'Yes,' he said with infuriating calm. 'You have already told me more than you know,' he said, laying one arm gently about her shoulders while he pressed a handkerchief into her hands. 'But I still need to hear how you escaped from the wine cellar.'

'She let me out. The housekeeper,' said Mary, blowing her nose. 'I could barely see. It seemed so bright after being shut down there for so long. I felt as though the darkness had become a part of me,' she admitted, scrunching the handkerchief into a ball. 'It had seeped right inside me, and was eating away at me from the inside, until I had begun to fear there would be nothing left of me. I…I still have nightmares about it.'

And then, even though some traces of anger and resentment towards him remained, Mary found herself burying her face against Lord Matthison's shoulder.

'You are safe now,' he murmured against the crown of her head. 'I will never let anyone hurt you again.'

It was not his words that had her releasing her breath in a great juddering sigh. It was the solid warmth of his body, the strength of his arms as he held her tight. The scent of clean linen and the citrus tang that lingered on his skin from the soap he used. They were what drove the feelings of being cold and alone, locked up in the dark, from her mind.

'She…' She sat up jerkily. 'She did not believe his story either.' She reached up and laid her palm against his lean cheek. 'Just like you. She did not need to ask me anything. She said he had preyed on the young female servants for long enough and had only got what he deserved.'

Lord Matthison's stern face relaxed into something resembling a smile. 'She sounds like a sensible woman.'

'She wrapped me in a warm cloak and got one of the outdoor workers to put me on the stage for London, with a letter of introduction to Madame Pichot. Madame read the letter,' said Mary, completely skipping over the terrors she had suffered on that coach journey, 'and said she was willing to hide me if I promised to work hard and behave myself. She said she would feed and house me as a favour to her friend, and that if I was any good at my work, she would see about some wages, as well. She was very kind to me, back then,' put in Mary hastily, when Lord Matthison scowled at the mention of wages he knew very well had never materialised. 'She could see I was scared, and she sat me down with a cup of tea while Molly went and got me a clean dress. She said I wasn't to worry about that kind of thing happening as long as I worked for her, because she didn't allow no gentlemen to enter her premises and bother her girls.'

Mary looked up at him with an entreaty in her eyes. How she wanted him to understand!

Eventually, his face softened, and he nodded. 'You looked on that place as your sanctuary, did you not? And Madame Pichot as your saviour. You never really cared about the wages, did you?'

She shook her head, absurdly pleased that he had understood.

'My poor darling,' he said, when she had finished. 'You have endured so much.' He took a deep breath, and said resolutely, 'Though you may not like to hear me say so, I think it was a great pity that the housekeeper did not hand you over to the magistrate.'

When Mary reared back, anguished incomprehension on her face, he grasped hold of her hands tightly, saying, 'We would have had you home. You need never have gone to London and spent all these years wondering who you are!'

'I know who I am!' she insisted. 'I am Mary. A dressmaker!'

Lord Matthison's face set in obdurate lines. 'I can see that we will need to establish how you got from Kingsmede to Oakham Hall before you will believe it. The lady you mentioned, the one who spoke to the housekeeper for you, she must hold the key. What can you tell me about her?'

Mary snatched her hands back, and wrapped her arms round her waist.

'I can tell you nothing!'

'Then let me tell you a few things,' he replied sternly. 'It is less than thirty miles between Kingsmede and Oakham Hall. You were staying at Kingsmede with me. We were going to be married in the chapel on the estate. We were all busy with the arrangements. We were so happy.'

His eyes took on a faraway look that made Mary feel as though she had just disappeared.

'One afternoon,' he went on, oblivious to her growing

disquiet, 'you went out riding alone. Your horse came back to the stables riderless, with mud and leaves all over the saddle. At first we thought you must have taken a tumble in the woods. There had been a terrific thunderstorm. A bolt of lightning, or a loud thunderclap, could have spooked your horse. We were all in a panic. We did not even know in which direction you had ridden out. We searched until it got dark, and then went back for lanterns, and kept on looking. And when there was no trace of you anywhere…' His face suddenly closed up.

He got to his feet, and began to pace the room. 'Perhaps you *were* stunned in a fall, woke up wet, and confused, and made for shelter, somewhere. Probably with the lady who eventually took you to Oakham Hall. Though I must say—' he frowned '—it seems mighty peculiar of her not to have contacted us. After that first night, we organised search parties. There was not a house for miles around we did not visit. Everyone knew a young lady had vanished from my estate. Especially,' he added bitterly, 'once I was accused of your murder. After that, I admit, the area of inquiry narrowed considerably.' His face took on what she thought of as his devilish look. 'My coveys, ponds, haystacks, even the ice-house—they looked everywhere I might conceivably have concealed your body.'

'I'm sorry,' she said, feeling unaccountably guilty.

He shrugged one shoulder, turning to her with a grim smile. 'You have no need to be. It was clearly not your fault. But dammit,' he snarled, striding across the room to glare down at her, 'every time I get an answer to one piece of the puzzle, that answer only throws up another set of questions in its place. Who was that woman? Why were you under her care? And why did she take you to Oakham Hall, for God's sake, a place where nobody with an ounce of compassion would send a defenceless girl to work? Try to think, Cora.' He sat down and took her by the shoulders. 'Can you remember anything about the time you spent with that woman? Anything that might help us fill in the missing pieces?' He spread his arms wide in a gesture of desperation. 'Anything at all!'

Mary screwed her eyes tight shut, wrapping her arms even tighter round herself. It was useless to keep on protesting that she was not his Cora. The things he had just told her about what had happened back then, the staggering coincidences that had placed her so close to the scene of his tragedy, had helped her to see why he was more convinced than ever that she was that girl.

But she knew she could never have ridden a horse, like he said.

'I wish I could help you sir, I really do,' she forced herself to say. 'But whenever I try to reach back to those days, what comes to me, more strongly than the little snatches of things that happened, are feelings.' They were rising up now. 'Pain,' she moaned, rocking herself. 'And loss, and…' A great wave of utter desolation came crashing over her. 'I can't, oh, I can't go there,' she moaned.

'Hell,' he swore, immediately contrite. 'I should not

have pushed you this far.' He swept her into his arms, and rocked her as though she were a frightened child. 'Let it go, darling. Let it all go, and I will find the answers myself.' He smoothed her damp hair back from her tearstained face, saying, 'I can soon find Sandiford, and wring some answers out of him.'

'No! You must not! Please do not tell him where I am!' She clutched at the lapels of his coat. 'He will have me thrown in jail, or worse…'

His face hardened. 'Credit me with a little more sense than that! I have ways of getting information out of the man that will not involve revealing anything about your whereabouts.'

He got to his feet.

'You are going now?' Mary was aghast. 'Right this minute? But you said you would not leave me. You promised!'

A flicker of impatience crossed his face. 'You will not be alone. Ephraims will be here, to see to your every need. You have only to ring for him.' He indicated the bell-pull by the fireplace.

Mary felt herself shrivel inside. He said she meant a great deal to him, but the truth was that he was more interested in solving the riddle of his fiancée's disappearance than looking after her.

'And do not even think about coming with me,' he added sternly. 'You know the kind of man Sandiford is. I may need to trawl through quite a few places that cater to men of his tastes in order to find him.'

She promptly forgot her own grievances at the

thought he might be going into danger. 'You will be careful, won't you?' she said, rising to her feet and twisting the crumpled handkerchief between her fingers.

He reached out and stroked her cheek with one forefinger. 'I would descend to the lower reaches of hell to set you free,' he grated. And then, as abruptly as it had come, the look of tenderness in his eyes gave way to one of determination. 'You need not worry about my safety. The people who inhabit the kind of dens Sandiford frequents know all about me, and my so-called pact with the devil.' His face twisted in self-mockery. 'They would not dare cross me. But in the event somebody should be reckless enough to try anything, I am amply prepared. I fence regularly at an exclusive academy, and box at Gentleman Jackson's. In my trade—' he smiled cynically '—it pays to be able to take care of myself.'

'Please,' she said, plucking up every ounce of courage she possessed, 'do not go after Sandiford.'

His face shuttered. 'You must be tired after the rigours of the last few days. You must wish to retire to your room. Take a book.' He waved his hand towards an alcove whose shelves were crammed with an assortment of books and periodicals.

In spite of herself, she could not resist darting one covetous look at his impressive collection of reading materials. It felt like an age since she'd had the leisure to just sit and read.

He was perceptive enough to notice the longing that gripped her.

'You always did love to read,' he said.

'Cora loved reading, you mean,' she protested, tearing her eyes away from the treasure trove on his shelves.

'You know,' he said a touch irritably, 'if you really are just a humble dressmaker, from a lowly background, do you not wonder how come you can sense that you love reading novels? I doubt many working girls have the leisure to indulge in such a pursuit.'

Her shoulders hunched defensively. She had *never* had the leisure to read a book while she had been employed by Madame Pichot. So she did not know how she knew she loved reading. Just the same as she did not know from where her strict moral code came, the code which had put such a distance between her and the other girls she worked with.

'Perhaps my parents were well educated,' she said defiantly. 'Genteel but poor...'

'That is nearer the truth than you want to admit,' he said sardonically. Then, with obvious impatience, 'Why are you fighting me every step of the way? Can you not just be grateful to have the chance to indulge in an evening of leisure? Whoever you think you are?'

Then he turned and stalked from the room, leaving her stunned by his uncharacteristic outburst.

She went cold inside.

He was growing tired of her determination to maintain the identity she had fought so hard to establish. Was this only a foretaste of what she might expect if she did not begin to play along with his fantasy?

Could she really abandon her principles, though, and

play-act at being Cora, if that was the only way to avoid his displeasure?

She did not know how long she sat there, wrestling with the moral dilemma she faced. But eventually, she realised she was only working herself into a state of near panic by imagining increasingly unpleasant scenarios she might have to face. She would have to distract herself, or go mad.

Until now, she had relied on work to set her mind on a more productive path. But she was not going to find any materials for sewing in this bachelor residence! So she got to her feet, went to the bookshelves, and grabbed the first book that came to hand.

As soon as she flipped it open, the scent of good quality, printed paper reached out to her. After taking a couple of deep breaths, with her eyes half-closed, her nose a scant inch from the page, she ran her fingers over the slightly raised lettering on the title page. Feeling calmer already, she took the tale of *Rackrent Castle* to a chair by the fire, hoping that Maria Edgeworth would be able to take her mind off its own troubles, and send it to a happier place.

But the story was not powerful enough to completely absorb her. She found herself reading the same lines over and over again, or getting to the end of a page and having no idea how the story had progressed.

She could not help wondering where Lord Matthison was. Whether he had found Lord Sandiford, and if he had, what they were saying about her. And every time she heard footsteps on the stairwell, she tensed, wondering if it was him, returning.

But the only person to intrude on her lonely vigil was Ephraims, come to bank up the fire, he said, and to tidy up for the night. After snuffing most of the candles, and straightening everything in the room that was an inch out of place, he cleared his throat, and asked, 'Will you be wanting anything else tonight, miss? Only his lordship did intimate that you would be wishful of retiring early.' He glanced at the clock on the mantel. It showed close on midnight. 'Perhaps some hot chocolate?'

Feeling rather like a child being sent to bed, Mary trailed to the door which Ephraims leapt to open for her. She could as well read her book in her room as here.

She checked on the threshold. She had thought it lovely before, but since the last time she had been there, somebody had wrought a transformation in it. A vase of cream and gold roses now stood on the dressing table, which had been polished to a high gloss. She could smell the beeswax mingling with the sweet scent of the roses. Various other little touches told her that Ephraims had gone to some trouble to provide her with a feminine sanctuary in the midst of this distinctly masculine apartment. She would have to make sure she thanked him properly, in the morning.

Her trunk now stood at the foot of the bed, which had been made up with fresh linen. And a nightdress lay on top of a luxurious satin quilt.

She was glad to see the trunk, but less pleased to think Ephraims had been going through her things. She flung open the lid, bracing herself at the thought he might have unpacked for her. But all her things lay undisturbed, just as Molly had packed them.

She took a second look at the nightdress. It was not hers. She had never owned anything made of such fine silk. And a wrapper that matched it hung across the arm of the bedside chair. Lord Matthison must have bought them for her, just in case she did not have a spare in her trunk!

Nobody had ever bought her such a beautiful gift before. She sat back on her heels, her brow furrowing. To her knowledge, nobody had ever bought her *any* kind of gift before. She reached out, and ran her fingers reverently over the beautiful garment.

Then, trembling with anticipation, she undid her gown and pulled it off, went to the washstand and poured warm water from the pitcher into the basin. The quality of that nightgown demanded she wash before trying it on!

The soap, she discovered on working it into a lather, was not the same as the one she had used before. It was more finely milled, and smelled of roses.

Her favourite.

She froze, water dripping from her eyelashes and nose. It was uncanny, the way Lord Matthison seemed to know what she liked, without her having to tell him.

She reached for a towel and blotted her face dry, her pleasure in the room completely destroyed.

He was a clever man, Lord Matthison. He was employing every strategy he could come up with to convince her she might be his missing fiancée. And she was almost foolish enough to fall for them. Almost.

But she was not the only woman who loved the scent of roses. Nor the only one who craved the feel of silk against her skin. It did not mean Lord Matthison knew anything about her in particular!

She scowled down at the nightgown for several seconds before angrily sweeping it off the quilt, and thrusting it into one of the dressing-table drawers. In her trunk she had a perfectly adequate, clean nightgown of her own. She had made it herself from several roll ends of fine lawn. She had no need of his extravagant gifts.

She tugged it over her head, tied the ribbons into tight bows, right up to her neck, and clambered into bed, her breathing laboured.

Mary opened the book, at the page she thought she had been at before Ephraims had put an end to her vigil. The candle burned low, and began to gutter, but still she sat bolt upright in bed, clutching the book she could barely make out through the gloom, while her mind darted this way and that, like a wild bird trapped in a cage.

It was growing light when she heard the hall door slam shut. The book landed on the floor as she scrambled out of bed. It did not matter that she was still angry with him for trying to coerce her into going along with his fantasy; she had to know if he had found Lord Sandiford. And what the man had said. If he had been able to name the woman who had brought her to Oakham Hall, and whether she had any connection to Kings…wood? Kings Combe? She shook her head impatiently. It did not matter what the name of the place was where *Cora* had last been seen. It was *her* future that hung in the balance.

She went straight across the corridor, and knocked on the door that led into his bedroom. It never occurred to her that it was most improper to be running about barefoot, clad only in a flimsy nightgown, in the early hours of the morning. She was too worked up to think of anything but what Lord Matthison had discovered.

He was sitting on the bedside chair in a room that was the mirror image of hers, though somehow indefinably masculine. Ephraims was kneeling at his feet, removing his boots. Both men stared at her in equal surprise.

'What is it?' Lord Matthison snapped.

She faltered on hearing the less-than-welcoming tone of his voice.

Ephraims set the boots aside, while Lord Matthison got to his feet. The servant calmly helped his master off with his jacket.

Mary swallowed, her fingers clenching on the doorknob. Her eyes skittered away from the sight of Lord Matthison removing his clothes, only to come to rest on his shaving equipment, set out on the washstand.

'That will be all for tonight,' he said brusquely, drawing her mortified gaze back to where he stood, in his stockinged feet, by the dressing table. Only to realise, with relief, that it was Ephraims he had dismissed, not her.

She sidled into the room as Ephraims left it, her back pressed against the wall.

'Why are you here?' Lord Matthison said wearily as he unwound his neck cloth and dropped it to the floor. 'What do you want of me now?'

Mary fetched up with a bump against the edge of the wardrobe.

'I—I'm sorry,' she stammered, her eyes transfixed by the triangle of flesh that had just appeared where he had unfastened his shirt. There was a smattering of dark hair growing there. 'I...will l-leave you in peace,' she stuttered, edging her way back along the wall towards the door.

'The hell you will,' he snarled, crossing the room in two strides and seizing her by the wrist.

'I have had no peace for the last seven years! And you are not going to provide it by walking away from me after coming in here, practically naked, and making me think—' he swallowed '—making me hope—' He squeezed his eyes shut, muttered a low curse, then flung her from him abruptly. Turning away, he ran his fingers through his hair, and, keeping his back to her, he growled, 'Go, then! Just get out and leave me to burn in my own particular version of hell.'

'I—I d-don't want to,' she heard herself whisper. It was strange, but the minute she saw how hurt and angry he was, she remembered how very kind he had been to her whenever she had been similarly upset. He had not abandoned her to her fears. He had held her. Comforted her.

She closed the distance between them, and timidly laid one hand on his shoulder. He was standing with his back to her, his hands gripping the edge of the dressing table, his head bowed. He tensed when he felt her touch, but she sensed it was not with revulsion.

He wanted her to stay. Even though he had ordered her to leave.

He was being torn in two.

Just as she was being torn apart by her own conflicting emotions.

'It is not just your hell,' she said, stepping closer, sliding her arms about his waist, and laying her cheek against his rigid back. 'It is mine too. I am in it with you.'

He spun round then, and took hold of her wrists, holding her at arms' length.

'You don't burn for me, though, do you? Like I burn for you?'

She did not think he did burn for her, not really. It was the dead woman who held him in thrall.

'That was not what I meant,' she protested. 'You and I—' she frowned, trying to find the right words '—we are both out of step with the rest of the world. It is as though everyone else is indoors, in a ballroom lit by a million candles, and they are all dancing a complicated minuet. And we are outside, on the terrace, in the cold moonlight, waltzing to a tune only we can hear.'

Some of the anguish faded from his face. He took her into his arms, and held her tightly.

'I failed you tonight,' he admitted. 'The man could tell me nothing of any use. Oh, he talked.' A shudder ran through him, and Mary responded by wrapping her arms round his waist, and hugging him for all she was worth.

'He said a great many things I shall never repeat. Things that turned my stomach. God, that man is vile!'

'It does not matter,' she said, running her hands up and down his back, in an attempt to soothe him.

He buried his face in her hair, breathing her in as though his life depended on it. They stood like that, entwined in each other's arms, for several minutes.

When he eventually whispered, 'Let me kiss you,' she had no thought of denying him. She simply raised her face to his in mute surrender.

He groaned in heartfelt relief when she parted her lips to let him in.

Mary was only startled for a second or two by the ridge of hardening flesh that she could feel pressing into her stomach. She had learned a lot from the girls she had worked with in that stuffy little workroom. They had sometimes giggled about that part of a man's anatomy that ebbed and flowed with the tide of his lust. So she knew that it was the evidence of Lord Matthison's rising desire. Just as she knew that the molten sensation she was experiencing between her legs was her body making itself ready to accommodate him.

'I want you,' he moaned into her neck, before pressing such a heated kiss to her throat that it felt as if he was melting her bones. He nuzzled the neckline of her gown aside, his fingers working frantically at the ties so that he could bare her breasts.

She gasped at the thrill that shot through her when

his lips fastened round one pouting nipple, and began to suck. Now was the time to stop him, if she was determined she was not going to become his mistress.

'Stop me now,' he panted, echoing her thoughts, 'if you don't want me too. Or I shall not be able to stop.' He ground his hips against hers, his hands cupping her bottom to hold her in place.

'I don't,' she gasped, clinging to his shoulders, 'I don't want you to stop!' she cried, suddenly convinced that this was one thing the saintly Cora would never have granted him. She would never have deigned to come to a man's room, in her nightgown, and let him kiss her. Let him push her nightgown out of the way so he could feast on her breasts.

Before she had time to think better of it, Mary reached down and dextrously undid the buttons that held the fall of his breeches closed and delved inside. Molly had sometimes described the lengths she went to with Joe, in order to 'keep him on a leash'. Mary had never imagined she might be glad to have learned exactly what she needed to do to pleasure a man. But now all she felt was exultation as he gasped, and groaned, and strained against her hand. A fine sheen of sweat broke out on his brow as he grew harder still. She knew he was really, really close to release.

And she had brought him there!

She, Mary the simple-minded dressmaker, was able to give him something his idol never could. Because she was alive, and real, and…in love with him!

That was why the thought of him being angry with

her, of sending her away, had tormented her. Why she felt as though she would fall apart without him. She loved him.

She rained kisses over every part of him she could reach as he backed her towards the bed, feeling a sense of euphoria that she had roused him to such frantic urgency.

'I need you,' she cried as he swept her off her feet, and up on to the bed. It was as simple as that. He meant more to her than her pride, than her honour, than anything. 'I am yours!'

He reared back, tore off the remainder of his clothes, and came down on top of her.

Chapter Eight

There was a moment of searing pain.

'Cora,' he gasped.

Turning her pain to agony.

She had thought she could make him forget Cora. But even though it was *her* body spread-eagled, naked, beneath him, it was her rival he was making love to. He could not have wounded her more deeply if he had plunged a knife into her heart.

'My darling,' he murmured, stroking a tendril of hair from her damp brow. 'My love, I never meant to hurt you. I would rather die than hurt you. I just never imagined...' He shut his eyes briefly. 'Sandiford led me to believe that he...'

Her reticence to speak of what she could recall of her past had lent weight to Lord Sandiford's graphic description of the rape he had boasted of.

But it had all been a pack of lies!

God, how had she managed to remain pure, given the

circumstances to which she had been reduced? When he had seen her sitting in that gin shop, surrounded by jarveys, her eyes blank and weary, he had been ready to believe the worst. And ever since, he had been treating her accordingly. As a fallen woman.

Even though he had not held her to blame, at least, not for long, it had coloured all his actions. A man naturally thought of a woman with sexual experience, however gained, completely differently to the way he regarded a virgin.

But she had been a virgin. And rather than respecting her, he had just been so damned glad she was finally responding to him as he would wish, all he could think of was getting her to the bed before she could change her mind.

And now she was lying with her face averted, her eyes closed, her teeth clenched.

'I have heard that the first time can be painful,' he murmured, gently kissing her cheek. 'I should have prepared you better. I was impatient,' he admitted. 'But now that I am inside you, the pain will ease, I promise.'

It was the genuine remorse she could hear in his voice that got to her. With one final whimper of self-pity, Mary turned her face so that she could return his kiss.

'Yes, that's my brave girl,' he said, when she wound her arms around his neck. Though he instinctively wanted to bury himself deep inside her, he withdrew a little, and began to rotate his hips gently against hers. He wanted to give her pleasure, not just take his own.

It was not long before he could feel her tense inner muscles softening, her rigid body relaxing. He bent to suckle at her breasts, recalling how much she had enjoyed it when he'd done that before.

'I love you,' she whispered, sweeping her feet up and down the backs of his calves.

'I love you too,' he answered, initiating a series of gentle, rhythmic thrusts. Far from tensing up against his intrusion, she undulated beneath him, sinuous as a cat, even to making little mewing noises. He matched his thrusts to her gyrations, resisting the urge to plunge deeply until her own movements became demanding.

When he felt her come to a rippling climax, his sense of elation surpassed anything he had ever experienced before. His restraint shattered, he only had to thrust deep a few more times to bring about his own heady rush of pleasure.

'Cora,' he groaned, slamming into her one last time before collapsing on top of her, utterly spent.

Mary ran her arms up and down his back when she felt his hot tears scalding their way across her cheeks and neck.

It should have been her crying.

She knew she was not the first foolish, simple girl to let a handsome, wealthy man turn her head. But she guessed very few women would ever let a man use their body knowing full well he was in love with someone else.

She had nobody to blame but herself when he called out another woman's name at his moment of crisis. He had never tried to deceive her. On the contrary, he had done all he could to make her believe she was Cora, so that she could more easily cope with the role he wanted her to fill.

'What is it?' he said, once he had got his breath back. 'What is wrong?'

'Nothing.' She sighed despondently. 'What could possibly be wrong?'

He shifted so that he could look down into her face.

'I should not have done this,' he said ruefully. 'You trusted me, and I repaid you by taking your virginity.'

'I wanted you to take it,' she said, acknowledging to herself that this much, at least, was true. 'I wanted you to take me to bed,' she confessed, remembering how she had naïvely thought that, by doing so, she could defeat Cora. 'I want—' she blushed at the admission '—to be your mistress.'

One day he would come to his senses and realise she was not Cora. She would say something, or do something that would snap him back to reality where she was concerned. And then he would send her packing.

But until that day came, she would give herself to him completely. With her whole heart. No more qualms about the immorality of lying with a man to whom she was not married. She loved him. That was all there was to it.

'You will not be my mistress!' he protested. 'We will get married. Just as we should have done seven years ago.'

'I cannot be your wife.' She struggled out of his arms and sat up, pulling the sheets up to cover her breasts. 'I am just an ordinary girl, and you are a lord. If you won't have me as your mistress…' The thought of parting from him was so appalling she promptly burst into tears.

'I won't let you go,' he said, putting his arms round her and drawing her close. 'You are mine now you have given yourself to me. Are you not?'

She nodded into his chest, clinging to him as tightly as he held onto her.

'Then no more talk of parting. If I cannot convince you, once and for all, that you are Cora, then we will live together any way you please.'

They subsided back on to the pillows, wrapped in each other's arms. It was pointless to worry about how long their relationship might last. So far as she was concerned, he was the husband of her heart. Making love with him had been her way of showing him she would belong to him until the day she died. Only him. She would never love another man the way she loved him.

Lord Matthison stroked her hair soothingly until she fell asleep. Then lay there just watching her, his mind racing.

She needed him, this woman, in a way nobody had ever needed him before. She had nobody else, not even herself. What must it be like, to have no memories? To not know who you were, and where you came from?

He frowned. He had not understood what she meant earlier, about dancing to a different tune to the rest of the world, but he thought he could grasp it now. She was utterly alone. And he was an outsider because of what people believed about him. If only his parents had stood by him, everything might have been different. But their attitude had only served to give credence to Robbie's accusations. *'He must have done it,'* people had said, *'or his family would not have shown him the door.'*

Only *she* had demonstrated any faith in him. Though he could tell it went against all her principles, she had yielded her virginity to him. Even though she still thought she was Mary, and it would be impossible to marry him. A less scrupulous woman would have turned what she saw as his delusions to her own advantage. But not her. She just gave, and gave, and gave.

He wrapped his arms round her, and buried his face in her hair, a wave of possessiveness sweeping through him. He was not going to let her go, he vowed, no matter who she was!

When Mary woke, it was to find Lord Matthison, clad in a black velvet dressing gown, sitting on the bedside chair, studying her with brooding intensity.

Hastily, she reached for the covers, and drew them up to her neck, embarrassed to discover she had kicked them aside in her sleep.

He shook his head. 'I was enjoying watching you lying there, naked and flushed from our lovemaking. But you know—' he leant forward to tuck an errant curl behind her ear '—your instinctive modesty pleases me almost as much.'

He bent over and kissed her slowly, languorously on the lips. 'You are completely delightful.'

He got up abruptly, saying, 'But you must be

hungry.' He straightened up and went to the bell-pull by the fireplace. 'I shall have Ephraims bring our breakfast.'

When he saw her horrified gaze flick to the door, he said, 'Just draw the bed-hangings round you.'

She was grateful for his suggestion, but she still did not like to think of being naked, even behind the concealing curtains, with Ephraims in the room.

'My nightdress,' she said, pointing to where it lay on the floor. An understanding smile on his face, Lord Matthison picked it up, and had just handed it to her when Ephraims knocked on the door. With a squeak of alarm, Mary knelt up, desperately trying to pull the bed-hangings closed, whilst still clutching the blankets to her breasts with the other.

With a low chuckle, Lord Matthison shut them for her, before allowing Ephraims to enter. Gratefully, Mary scrambled into her crumpled nightgown, to emerge shyly only after the servant had deposited a breakfast tray on the console table by the door, and left again.

Lord Matthison was pouring her a cup of chocolate. 'How long will it take you to be ready to leave?' he enquired, handing her the brimming cup.

'L-leave?' Mary's heart came to a juddering halt in her chest. She had thought, after all he had said the night before, that he meant them to stay together. How had she got it so wrong?

'Don't look so appalled.' He frowned. 'You must surely realise I want to get you safe out of London as soon as I can. You have too many enemies here.' He broke open a roll, slathered it with butter and honey, as he explained, 'Madame Pichot has already demonstrated how spiteful she can be. Lord Sandiford, should he ever get wind of news that the girl who fought back, leaving his hands permanently scarred, is within his grasp...' He grimaced. 'And let us not forget the thwarted ambitions of Miss Winters. She has already attempted to destroy you once. I will be better able to protect you at Kingsmede.' He darted her an assessing glance, before adding, 'And of course, once we are there, we might be able to trace that woman. The one who took you to Oakham Hall.'

Mary laid her cup and saucer down on the bedside table and slumped down into the chair.

'We need to find her. Find some conclusive proof that you are Cora,' he persisted.

'Last night,' she remonstrated, 'you said we could live however I chose...'

'Once we have established your identity, yes! But dammit, I want to marry you!' he snapped. 'You should be able to take your rightful place at my side, not stay hidden away as though you have something to be ashamed of! And you told me that the only way you will agree to marry me is if I can prove to you that you are Cora,' he pointed out.

Mary shook her head from side to side, tears pricking her eyes.

'What are you so frightened of?' he asked when she began to tremble.

'That—' she gulped '—that once we find out who I

really am, you will send me away,' she finally managed to confess.

'No!' he bit out grimly. 'I shall never do that.' He came across to the chair, and knelt at her feet. With a visible effort, he softened the tone of his voice. 'I have already told you I will always take care of you. If, by some remote chance, we find out that you are not Cora, but some girl who is all alone in the world without family, or friends, it would be unthinkable to abandon you. You will need me all the more.'

He put his arms around her, and she leant forwards, resting her head on his shoulder with a sigh of relief.

'So, now you have nothing to fear, perhaps you can find it in yourself to tell me what you remember about that woman.'

Lord Matthison would never rest until he had solved the mystery of her identity. No matter how hard she wished he would. For in spite of his promises, she had a horrible, sick certainty that the minute they had established who she was, and where she had come from, it would all be over between them.

But all the fight had drained out of her. His will was far stronger than hers. He would keep on and on asking questions until she gave in and told him all she knew. She might as well get it over with.

'The first thing I remember,' she sighed, 'is waking up in a room that I have always believed was an attic. It smelled of dust and decay, and there was all sorts of old broken furniture stacked up in jumbled heaps. And no proper window. Just a skylight, at the far end, by the door.'

She felt his shoulder tense under her forehead. She knew he was thrilled that she was giving him more information, but she could not share his excitement. A pall of misery had descended over her.

'She only came in once or twice a day, with a jug of water, and a plate of what looked like the leftovers from someone else's meal. She thought me a great nuisance for being there. She never said, but I could tell. She would stand there, staring down at me as though she hated me.'

'What did she look like?' Lord Matthison broke in to ask. 'It sounds as if you were in a biggish house. Perhaps I know her.'

'She looked exactly how you would expect a female prison warder to look. Hard-faced, and hefty. Plain, serviceable clothing. Hard eyes. Hard hands…'

'You are doing well,' he said, running his hands up and down her back, and dropping a kiss onto her temple. 'Can you recall anything else?'

With his arms round her, the feelings that usually swamped her along with her memories had far less power.

And it struck her that when she had been bold enough to face him, in the Flash of Lightning, she had learned that he was just a man after all, and not some horrible phantom. She had realised that she had been silly to run from him that day in Curzon Street. She wondered if any of the things she shied from remembering were really as bad as she feared. Maybe, if she turned and faced those shadowy images that lurked in the hidden corners of her mind, they would all turn out to be equally harmless?

Had she not learned that things were hardly ever as bad as she feared? The girls who had so scared her, that first time she had walked into Madame's workrooms, for instance, with their rough, aggressive manners. They had become her friends.

Tentatively, she went back to the way she had felt that day, when she had woken in that attic. She had not known who she was, or where she was, and that had frightened her. But most of all, she had felt unbearably unhappy. So unhappy that she would lie there wishing she was dead, without understanding why. She could remember that it hardly seemed worth the trouble of eating, and keeping herself alive. She had only picked at what her warder brought because she had been afraid of what the woman would do if she came back and found the tray untouched.

'She used to come up to the attics at night, when she thought I was asleep. She would go to an old bureau that was half-buried under a mound of mouldering linen, open one of the drawers, reach her hand inside and press a hidden catch. I would hear the loud click, and then the sound of a panel dropping to the floor. And she would stoop, and pick up a ring.'

'A ring?' He disentangled himself from her, and held her by the shoulders, so that he could look straight into her eyes. 'What sort of a ring?'

'It was a big, heavy-looking thing. It looked very old, somehow. The setting…' She frowned, trying to picture it clearly. 'She would hold it up to the light, so that the flame flickered through the stone. It always gave me the shivers, because it would look as though it was bleeding.'

'A ruby,' he breathed. His hands had clenched so hard on her shoulders that it was almost painful. 'I think, I really believe, that it could have been your betrothal ring. It has been in the family for generations. It was the only item of her jewellery that my mother managed to keep hidden from my father. Our one and only family heirloom. He had sold or wagered everything else he could lay his hands on. When I told her we were to be married, she fetched it from wherever she had been hiding it, for me to give to you. Don't you see what this means?'

He got to his feet, running his fingers through his hair as he paced back and forth. 'You could have been set upon by robbers. She was probably the fence. In those circumstances, she would naturally have kept you concealed when we began searching the area. She would not want to give away her criminal connections...' He whirled to face her. 'Did you see anyone else while you were held in that house?'

A cold sensation slid down her spine. She had always had the conviction that the woman had no right to the ring. But she had been so weak, and that woman so strong and always angry, that she had never dared question her about it. Instead, she had told herself over and over again that it was nothing to do with her.

Something shimmied in the air, hovering just out of reach...

She shook her head. She had to stop this! She was

letting Lord Matthison influence the few things she did remember, now, because she wanted so desperately to be the woman he loved.

She focused on him as he kept on talking, and pacing the room. And as she watched the jerky movements that punctuated each sentence, the troubling sensation evened out, like ripples vanishing after a stone has dropped into a pond.

'Even if my surmise is correct about the motive for hiding you to begin with, it does not explain why she took you to Oakham Hall. Nor why the housekeeper was willing to take you on, just on this hefty woman's recommendation, when you were clearly hardly fit for any sort of work. And we cannot ask her. The one thing I did find out from Sandiford is that his former house-keeper died. He complained about how difficult he is finding it getting a replacement.' He paused, hands on his hips while he stared at her as though she was an in-triguing puzzle. 'It almost sounds as if your gaoler was a person of some standing, locally. But your descrip-tion does not fit anyone I know. Well, no matter,' he said, coming back to her, and sitting on the edge of the bed. 'We can circulate her description when we get down there.'

'Do we,' Mary said hesitantly, something inside her shrivelling at the prospect of searching for a woman she never wished to set eyes on again, 'do we really have to leave London? I know you say you are concerned for my safety here, but I would not want to take you away from your work.'

'My work?' He looked puzzled for a moment, then his face shuttered. 'You mean fleecing drunkards with more money than sense. I think you can safely say I shall not be sorry to leave all that behind.'

He looked at her, then at the wall behind her, then at his feet, then squared his shoulders.

'I have no need to earn a living that way. I have not needed to for some time. The only reason I kept going back to the tables...' His cheeks flushed a dull red. 'You are going to think I was quite mad.' He got up, stalked across to the table, and tore open a second bread roll.

'I had convinced myself that your ghost haunted me.' He jabbed his knife into the crock of butter. 'I attributed all my success at the tables to your benign influence. I went back, time and time again, just to feel you near me. How crazy is that?' He kept his back to her, as though spreading butter on to a roll required all his concentration. 'When I hate gambling.' He flung his knife onto the tray with a clatter.

His shoulders hunched as he braced his hands on the table top.

'I had a run of luck at the outset. The kind of winning streak real gamblers dream of. And then I began to tell myself you were guiding me, whenever I won. And if I did not win, I decided you were not in that particular hell, and went off to another one, searching till I found you.

'I despised the men who sat there, too drunk to know when they were throwing good money after bad, but all along I was far sicker than any of them.

'I was sleepwalking through some sort of...labyrinth of self-deception, making more money than I knew how to spend, when all the time…'

He straightened up slowly and turned to look at her, his face racked with guilt. 'You were within my reach all the time. Working yourself to the point of exhaustion for your food and lodging. If only I had kept on searching for you. If only I had…'

She got up and flung her arms round him, tugging his head down to the crook of her neck.

'Hush, don't,' she said. 'It is over now. Done with. I…' She steeled herself to be what he wanted, to say what he needed to hear in this moment. 'I am here now. And,' she continued, utterly sure that no woman could remain obdurate in the face of such sincere remorse, 'I do not blame you for any of it.' Whatever had happened to Cora, surely she would forgive him for carrying on living, the only way he knew how?

'I will make it up to you, Cora, I swear!' he vowed, tilting her face so he could kiss her. 'I want nothing so much as to leave London and its haunts of vice behind us, and make a fresh start. At Kingsmede.'

She returned his kiss with fervour, not really caring where he took her, so long as they stayed together.

'I suppose,' she said, reaching up to smooth the frown line from his brow, 'I would not like to run into Lord Sandiford on the street. And as for poor Miss Winters…I do not think it would be very kind of us to flaunt our affair in her face.'

'After what she would have done to you?' He looked incredulous.

'Well, she must have been heartbroken when she learned her engagement to you must come to an end…'

'Heartbroken? Not her! A more heartless creature it would be hard to find!'

'So why did you propose to her, then?'

'I did no such thing,' he growled. Then, seeing the sheer puzzlement on her face, he swept her into his arms and set her down on the bed. 'I can see,' he sighed, 'that I shall have to confess my stupidity in regard to Miss Winters, too.'

He went back to the console table, picked up the plate of buttered rolls, and pressed them into her hand. He took one, bit into it, then paced to the window, chewing.

'Mr Winters was a business acquaintance of mine. I have invested a good deal of the money I won at play in various enterprises. Usually, I carried out any business I had with Mr Winters in his offices, but occasionally he would invite me to his home. Along with other investors that might wish to have mutual dealings. His wife and daughter were sometimes present at certain parts of such gatherings. And—' he leaned his forearm against the window frame '—she impressed me, I have to admit. She was so different from the empty-headed society females who have been fluttering and cooing about me since it became known how successfully I had reversed my family's fortunes. She never attempted to flirt with me, but spoke to me in the same polite manner she addressed all her father's other guests.'

As he took another meditative bite out of his breakfast roll, Mary's heart sank.

'Did you find her pretty?' she found herself saying, though the thought of him admiring yet another female tore at her heart.

'Pretty?' He whirled round, an expression of complete bafflement on his face. 'What do her looks have to do with any of it? I have told you, she lulled me into a false sense of security, by behaving as though she had no interest in me whatsoever!'

The pain eased somewhat. Mary nibbled at her own breakfast roll as Lord Matthison resumed pacing.

'One night, I arrived at her home, to find her looking somewhat distressed. When I asked, as any gentleman would, if there was anything amiss, she…' He halted by the window, gazing down into the street as though whatever he could see out there had his full attention.

'She lured me into a room apart, on the pretext of saying she was in desperate need of advice she thought only I could give her. Of course, it was not advice she wanted from me at all. As soon as the door was shut, she flung herself at me…'

The disgust she could hear in his voice, the rigid set of his shoulders, paradoxically made Mary's own tension diminish.

'Naturally, our…clinch was witnessed. She had arranged it all down to the last detail.'

Mary's eyes strayed down the tense line of his spine, to where his legs protruded from the hem of his dressing gown. Bare legs. It had felt wonderful when she had stroked the soles of her feet over them.

'I wonder why she went to such lengths,' Mary

mused, her eyes riveted to his bare feet. It seemed strange to think of feet as objects of beauty, but Lord Matthison's were. 'She must have been quite desperate, don't you think? Or her family were. Do you think they compelled her to it?'

He whirled round to face her, an incredulous expression on his face.

'Oh, come now!' she said, licking honey from her fingers. 'You have a reputation for being dangerous. Fiendish even. I could never understand why Mrs Winters was so insistent that you marry her daughter, when she kept on emphasising how evil you were. They must be in some sort of financial difficulty.'

'Is it so impossible to believe she might have been in love with me?' he retorted.

'Do you think she was?'

He ran his fingers through his hair. 'Hell, no! If I have the measure of her father correctly, it was all about money and position. He wanted a title for his daughter, I suppose. But in the end, she was terrified of me. I made sure of it!'

'Really?' She drew her knees up to her chest, hugging them as she looked at him with her head cocked to one side. 'I cannot imagine being afraid of you.'

'You always saw the good in me when nobody else did,' he said. 'Even when…' A shadow flickered across his face. 'No, forget I said that. The circumstances at Kingsmede are completely different now, anyway, and…what are you laughing at?'

'You…you asked me to for…forget…' She giggled. 'When all you have wanted me to do up till now is to remember. I do wish you would make up your mind…'

It felt as though the sun had come out. This was his Cora, just as she used to be. Laughing at his absurdities. Making him feel life was not the serious business he believed, but a game they could play together. Chasing away his shadows with her sunny nature, her natural inclination to see the good in everyone, not just him.

The night before, when he had held her in his arms, and he smelled the scent of roses on her skin, it had been as though he was transported back in time. The years had rolled away and he was a boy full of optimism, honoured to be the first one to kiss her. The first to make love to her.

But this…this was a moment he would treasure till the day he died. She was sitting in his bed, her glorious hair tumbling round her pale shoulders, laughing again. A woman with less spirit would have forgotten how to laugh after all she had been through.

'You are happy,' he said, with satisfaction.

'Yes,' she said, smiling as she held out her hand to him. 'Because I am here with you.'

'Nothing else matters, does it?' he said. This moment was precious, yet he sensed the fragility of it. Like a newly blown soap bubble, anything that touched it might burst it.

He walked to the bed, untying the belt of his dressing gown.

'Have you finished with your breakfast?' he asked,

taking the plate from her and setting it on the bedside chair.

She said nothing, but the hunger in her eyes was all the answer he needed.

'Kingsmede will still be there tomorrow,' he growled, tumbling her down among the rumpled sheets.

'And the day after,' she agreed, twining her arms round his neck.

Chapter Nine

She had no idea how long they spent in that room. They kept the shutters closed, sleeping when they were sated with lovemaking, sending out for food when they were hungry.

But she knew their magical time out of time had come to an end when she awoke to the sound of Lord Matthison drawing the curtains. The pale grey light heralding the dawn of a new day had replaced the romantic glow of candles. One or two of them still smoked as though he had only just snuffed them. Her heart sank when she saw that he was fully dressed, with a determined look on his face.

'I have made the travel arrangements,' he said brusquely. 'Since you have not yet unpacked your trunk, we should be able to set out as soon as you have taken breakfast, and put some clothes on.'

When she made no attempt to stir from the bed, he frowned. 'I have spent long enough stumbling around in the dark. We need to return to Kingsmede.'

There was no point in arguing with him. When his mind was made up, she knew that nothing could sway him.

'I hope,' he said later, once he had handed her into the hired carriage, 'that you will not find life in the country too dull.'

He shot her an assessing glance. She had been so quiet this morning. And clearly unhappy about leaving London behind. Though she had not uttered one word of protest, she kept on looking out of the windows as they passed various landmarks, as though she was silently bidding them farewell.

'Many people find it somewhat flat, without all the amusements available in town.'

'Well, I did not see that side of life in London, did I? I spent sixteen hours out of every day shut up in an attic, sewing.'

He felt a rush of relief to have got a response from her, even if it was a rather negative one.

'So, it is not the prospect of boredom that has made you so waspish this morning.'

She turned to him in amazement. Surely he knew why she was upset? She would have been more than happy to have stayed in his room indefinitely. *He was the one who had grown bored. The one who needed more stimulation than she could provide.* The one who had opened the curtains, and let reality flood back into their lives.

'My mother,' he said when she made no contribution to the conversation, 'referred to Kingsmede as her prison. Though it was undoubtedly my father's prof-ligacy that made it so. She never ceased complaining that she could not even afford to escape up to London for a change of scenery, while my father hardly ever set foot in the place. Not enough diversions for a man of his temperament in a rural backwater,' he finished drily, his tone suggesting he was quoting what the man himself had said. 'It will not be the same for us. Should you ever feel like a jaunt up to town, I shall take you. It is about time I purchased a carriage for my own use, rather than hiring one…'

'There is no need to purchase a carriage on my account,' she protested. 'I have no wish to return to London, and risk running into Lord Sandiford. No, no, I am sure I shall find plenty to occupy me at Kingsmede. After all, it will all be quite new to me. I expect it will take some time before the novelty of it all begins to wear thin.'

'The countryside is really very pleasant, in a quiet sort of way,' he said. 'Though not, of course, possessed of the rugged beauty of Scotland.'

'Scotland? Why do you mention Scotland?'

'It is where you grew up.'

Where Cora had grown up, she silently corrected him.

'However did you meet her, then?' she plucked up the courage to say after a few minutes. Her antipathy towards the woman who'd had such a devastating impact on this man's life was no match for the force of her curiosity. 'C-Cora, that is.'

'I was at school with your brother,' he replied tersely, his face closing up.

When, after some minutes, it became apparent he was not going to divulge any more, Mary turned to stare out of the window despondently. It was all very well for him to probe into her past, searching and interrogating until she was almost hysterical. But let her ask him one question about his background, and he wrapped his privacy round him like a cloak.

They must have travelled almost a full mile before she felt him reach for her hand.

'It is not always easy to talk about the past, is it?' he said with contrition. 'Not when it is painful.'

When she returned the pressure of his hand, signifying her understanding, he said, 'Now that we are together again, though, everything will come right.'

His misplaced optimism plunged Mary even deeper into the gloom that had dogged her from the moment she had first opened her eyes that morning.

'We were very close friends, your brother and I. We even spent our school holidays visiting each other's homes. I had always thought Kingsmede a completely joyless place to live before he burst into it like a whirlwind. My parents, you see,' he said, raising her hand to his lips and kissing it, 'had never been interested in anything I did. They were never proud of any of my achievements. But he interpreted their indifference as the most marvellous freedom.' He tucked her hand into the crook of his arm.

'That summer, we roamed the fields and woods from dawn 'til dusk, catching fish from our lakes and streams and cooking them over open fires, and generally living off the bounty of my neglected estate like a pair of poachers. Or gypsies, or bandits, or whatever else we decided to be on any given day. During the next long vacation, your mother insisted on returning the invitation, in spite of your brother's protests that he would rather come back to Kingsmede.

'That was when,' he said, turning in his seat, 'I met you for the first time. You were a shy little thing, with long braids, bony wrists and a freckled face.' He reached out and teased a few coppery tendrils from the braid she had pinned up beneath her hat, and wound them round his fingers.

Then, with a crooked smile, he went on, 'You stared in awe at your big brother's friend, then ducked out of sight, and kept well away from us for the duration of my visit. I could not even get you to speak to me at mealtimes. Not that conversation was encouraged at table.' He grimaced.

'I soon understood why your brother loved the ramshackle housekeeping that prevailed at Kingsmede. Your father was the very antithesis of mine. He ruled over you all with a rod of iron. And as for the sermons he preached...' He shut his eyes and shook his head. 'They did not have quite the effect—' he opened his eyes, and grinned at her ruefully '—on growing boys that he intended. We came out of the kirk on Sundays so utterly sure we were doomed to spend eternity burning in hell-fire that we just had to go out and find some consolation en route.'

He paused, as though choosing his next words carefully. 'There was more opportunity, of course, for sinning at Kingsmede.

'Things only really changed after your parents died,' he went on. 'Your brother could not leave you on your own, so I had no choice but to travel to Scotland when I wanted to visit. He warned me I would have to take things as I found them. But I did not care for that, nor the length of the journey. I knew I would be far happier in Auchentay, with my friend, and his sister, than on my own at Kingsmede.

'But during that last visit, he really was too preoccupied with winding up your late father's rather tangled affairs to spend much time with me. And so it was left to you to entertain me.'

He smiled at her, running his finger along the line of her jaw. 'Finally, there was nothing to prevent us spending as much time with each other as we wanted. We took full advantage of our freedom.' His heart turned over in his chest as he recalled that idyllic summer. The sun seemed to have shone every day. And she had never stopped smiling.

There was little left of that laughing, lovely young girl in the gaunt, troubled woman who sat beside him now. Irritably he pushed the unflattering comparison aside. There was not much of the young man he had been either. After she had disappeared, he had abandoned his own aspirations to attend university. Pretty soon, the only books he studied were books of form. The only human contact he had was with drunks and sharps and bookmakers. He had only slowly clawed his way back to some semblance of normality. But it remained a thin veneer, concealing his ravaged, embittered core.

The years, he sighed, had twisted and warped them both almost beyond recognition.

Robbie, too. He had taken to drink to blot out the horror of what he believed his young friend had done to his only sister.

He would be a fool to think that any of them would ever be quite the same again.

Though last night, she had been all he had dreamed of, with her hair tumbling round her shoulders like living flame, and her eyes alight with love. He had felt triumphant at winning this woman's heart.

Just as he had thought he had won Cora's once before. He had risked everything, back then, to hold onto her for ever. Yet she had still slipped through his fingers.

If he should lose her again…

When they reached Kingsmede, this fragile, tenuous relationship they were beginning to form would be put to the test. She would feel self-conscious, he knew, about continuing their love affair under the watchful eyes of his household staff.

'It will not be long until we stop for a change of horses,' he said gruffly. 'We may as well put up there for the night.'

She looked out of the window, baffled. 'It is scarce past noon,' she pointed out.

He returned her puzzled look with a scowl. He had woken this morning yearning to discover the truth about this woman's past, so that he could bind her to him for ever.

But now, all that seemed important was clinging to what they had right this minute. The truth could wait for a little while longer. He would be a fool to jeopardise what he had found with this woman who called herself Mary!

'It will be dark when we close the curtains,' he replied.

Her eyes widened. She blushed. But she did not voice any objections.

With a growl of satisfaction, Lord Matthison pulled her into his arms, and began his intended ravishment at her lips.

To Mary's disappointment, they spent only one night on the road. And Lord Matthison was particularly terse with his instructions to pack up and set off again. But only mid-way through the next afternoon, he grasped her hand, saying 'Not far now.' He leaned forward to point through the window. 'We are just entering Bamford, our nearest market town.'

It did not take them long to pass through the bustling, prosperous-looking town. Then the carriage slowed as the road out of it became quite steep. Just before they reached the top of the long incline, the coachman nudged the straining horses into a left turn on to a road that hugged the brow of the hill. Through Mary's window she could see acres of lush farmland rippling down into the valley below.

But then the carriage veered sharply to the right, and the vista of what promised to be a bountiful harvest disappeared as they entered a belt of woodland.

Soon they were passing through a pair of stone

pillars, on to a carriage drive completely overhung by a tangle of trees. They crowded the drive so thickly that once or twice branches scraped the sides of the carriage, sounding like the talons of unseen phantoms, trying in vain to impede their progress.

Mary shivered, telling herself that it was only because they had gone from bright sunlight into the greenish, mouldering gloom that she had conjured up such a macabre image. But she could not shake off the feeling of foreboding. It grew stronger with each yard they penetrated deeper into the woodland.

'Cold, love?'

She jumped as Lord Matthison patted her hand. She had almost forgotten he was there, so focused was she on watching as the shadows, like long, hostile fingers, insinuated their way into the carriage, inching their way ever nearer, as though they wanted to close round her throat, and choke the life from her.

'N-not cold,' she stuttered through chattering teeth. 'Sc-scared.'

Because the shadows were not only creeping into the carriage from the outside. They were seething up inside her, gathering such strength she was not sure how much longer she could hold them at bay. Perhaps she should not try to. Had she not worked out that things were never as bad as you imagined they could be? She had been afraid of Lord Matthison, that first time he had stepped out of the shadows. And yet, once she had faced him, she had learned there was nothing about him to frighten her at all.

'We will be out of it soon,' he said, slipping his arm round her shoulder when she turned a tense white face towards him. 'When we round the next bend we will be into the park, and you will be able to see the house.'

Her eyes grew wider, and though they were fixed on him, he felt as though it was not him she was seeing at all.

Nor was she. An image had taken possession of her mind. The image of an ivy-clad Elizabethan manor house, with barley-twist chimneys and dozens upon dozens of windows, the thousands of tiny diamond-shaped panes glittering in the low sunlight making the walls look as though they were studded with jewels.

'I sent word to have your old room prepared for you. The one you had when you were here before. I thought it would help you settle more quickly, and I also thought establishing you straight away as my fiancée would spare you at least some gossip…'

A panicky feeling swirled in Mary's stomach.

'You are going to make me sleep in *her* room?' She could see it. Vividly. There would be an ancient, canopied bed, giving a view over the park down to a lake. An intricately carved wardrobe, full of dresses, and shoes ranged up on the floor below…would he expect her to wear the dead woman's clothes, as well as sleep in her bed?

Her breath caught in her chest.

'I can't,' she gasped, tearing at the bonnet ribbons that felt as though they were choking her. 'Can't breathe…'

She clawed frantically at the top buttons of her coat, which had grown so tight it was like a vice squeezing her chest. The world began to spin. Through the haze that clouded the interior of the coach, she felt Lord Matthison reach past her, to pull the window down. She felt the cold air slap her cheek, and his voice saying, 'There, is that better?'

But as she leaned forwards, to gulp in the sunlight that had suddenly come streaming in, she saw something that stopped her breathing altogether.

It was a house. An old, ivy-covered house, with barley-twist chimneys, and diamond-paned windows...

'Cora, darling, breathe...' she could hear him saying, from far, far away. But she could no longer see him. He was not in the coach with her. It was another man. A younger man. And he was saying, 'Just look at what a grand place ye're to be mistress of. Did you ever see the like?'

And her heart was sinking. She did not want to be mistress of the place. That was not why she had come.

'Don't call me Cora,' she choked. 'I don't belong there.' She pointed at the Elizabethan manor. 'I never have, and I never will...'

And then she could no longer hold back the great wave of certainty that she had travelled this road before, feeling exactly as she did now. It surged up from deep, deep within, breaking over her and washing aside everything she had achieved in the last seven years, until she was reduced to a quivering, pathetic, young girl, whose heart was irretrievably broken.

'No!' she cried in desperation. 'I am not her. I am Mary!'

She could hear the wheels crunching over gravel. She

felt his hands on her, lifting her, pulling her somewhere she did not want to go. She could not fight the shadows, but she could fight him. And she did. With hands curved like claws.

'I won't, I won't be Cora!' She did not want to go back there. It hurt too much. 'I don't want to be her!' she screamed. 'I'm Mary!'

But it was too late. Mary was drowning in Cora's pain. And Lord Matthison captured her flailing hands between his own, and used them to pull her out of the comparative safety of the coach, and on to the shadowed portico of Kingsmede.

A door behind him swung open, and out from it barrelled a great giant of a man with an unruly thatch of red hair and eyes like shards of bloodshot ice.

'Put ma' sister down, you lying, cheatin' swine, so I can gi' ye the thrashing ye deserve!'

And everything she had kept submerged for seven long years broke free, drenching her in total awareness, and choking the very last gasp of air from her lungs.

She gave one strangled, agonised cry, and fell headlong into darkness.

Lord Matthison caught her as she fainted, and swept her up into his arms. He barged his way into the house, yelling 'Get some smelling salts!' to his housekeeper, who had trailed on to the portico in the Scotsman's wake, and 'Get out of my way, you damn fool,' to the giant who tried to block his path.

'What have ye done to her?' yelled Robbie as Lord Matthison carried her through to the morning room.

He could see the way Robbie's mind was working and it made his blood boil. He had dragged his terrified sister from the carriage, her clothing dishevelled, and then she had fainted dead away.

'For God's sake!' he snapped as he lowered her gently on to the *chaise longue*. 'If I meant to rape her, do you suppose I'd have invited you here to witness the crime?'

'Who can ever tell what is going on in that infernally twisted mind of yours?' He thrust his face aggressively close to Lord Matthison's.

The alcoholic fumes made his eyes water.

'Where have you been hiding the poor wee lassie all these years?'

'I have not been hiding her anywhere, you drunken fool,' he replied, pushing him aside, so that he could attend to Cora. She was so deathly pale. She lay so still he could not even be sure she was breathing. He leaned closer, meaning to see if he could find a pulse, when, with a roar of outrage, Robbie grabbed him by his collar and yanked him backwards.

'Keep your filthy, lecherous hands off her!'

'Don't be more of an ass than you can help,' Lord Matthison grated, desperately striving to keep a leash on his own temper. 'She needs—'

But Robbie was in no mood for talking. In the old days, the swing he took at Lord Matthison would undoubtedly have floored him. Had it connected with his jaw. But Lord Matthison managed to dodge it with ease. As he did the next wild swing, and the next, and the one after that. Seven years of drunkenness had taken their toll on his former friend. Robbie's size and aggression were now no match for the science he had spent seven years learning from Gentleman Jackson, and the cunning he had picked up on the streets.

But his inability to land more than the occasional glancing blow on his opponent was stoking Robbie's anger to the point of madness. With a roar he lunged forwards, arms outstretched as though meaning to trap Lord Matthison in a crushing bear hug. Had he succeeded, they would both have landed on the *chaise longue*, on top of Cora.

So Lord Matthison jabbed Robbie hard in the stomach, halting his headlong rush, then got his own shoulder into the larger man's chest, pitching him sideways, away from the vulnerable woman lying unconscious.

Robbie wrapped his arms round Lord Matthison as he toppled sideways. They both landed on the rug by the side of the sofa, kicking and gouging when neither could land a solid blow on the other's body, locked in a fight that had been seven years coming.

As Cora slowly surfaced from the depths of her faint, the first thing she heard was the all-too-familiar sound of her brother, grunting and cursing as he beat the living daylights out of somebody.

She felt extreme reluctance to take a look at his victim, yet somehow, her eyelids drifted open anyhow.

And there he was, rolling around on the floor with Kit Brereton, his best friend. She felt a moment's confusion. Not because they were fighting. There was nothing new in that. But surely Father would never allow them to scrap in the house…

But Father was dead. And Robbie was the head of the household now, so he…no, wait a minute. The ceiling above her head was ornately plastered. There was no ceiling anything like this anywhere in their house. It looked far more like Kit's house…

Kingsmede.

That was right…she had come to Kingsmede, to marry Kit, because…

For a few seconds, past and present swirled and shimmied around her, the eddies almost dragging her back under. But then the two men rolled against the sofa leg with such violence that, had she still been insensible, she would have been tipped on to the floor.

Not that either of them would have noticed. They were too engrossed in beating the tar out of each other. They seemed to have forgotten she was there.

Or, if it did cross either of their minds, they would just assume she would run away from this uninhibited display of masculine brutality. And wait for one of them to come to her, and inform her of the outcome.

Like they had last time.

Gripped by a cold fury, she sat up.

She was not a child any more, too timid to stand up and speak for herself! She would determine her own future! She was not any man's possession, to dispose of as though she had no opinion of her own!

When the fight rolled sufficiently far from the sofa

for her to leave it safely, she got shakily to her feet, and made for the vase of roses she had seen on a table under the window. She stood with it in her hands for a second or two, wondering which one of them deserved she smash it over his head the more.

In the end, since there was not a second vase with which she could dispense equal justice, she had to settle for merely dashing its contents over the pair of them.

'For heaven's sake!' she snapped when they both ceased hostilities long enough to stare up at her in incredulity. 'You are not schoolboys any longer!'

Lord Matthison disentangled himself first, shoving her brother roughly to one side as he rose to one knee. 'Cora,' he spluttered through the water that was dripping from his hair into his eyes. 'Are you all right?'

'Much you care!' she stormed. 'You…you hypocrite! And as for you…' She glared down at her brother. 'My God, Robbie, you've turned out just like Father. Using your fists first, and asking questions later.'

'That's no' fair!' he protested, brushing dank flower petals from his chest. 'You were out cold when the fight started. You cannot possibly know who threw the first punch!'

She reeled back from the smell that wafted to her on his breath. 'Exactly like Father,' she said. 'After all you said when he died, all the promises you made me, you've taken to drink…'

Robbie sat up, glowering at her. 'You don't know what I've been through these past seven years. No man could have stood it without a wee dram now and again.'

'You see?' She laughed. 'You are even making the same excuses he did. Nothing was ever his fault, was it? Someone else always drove him to it. Either Mother drove him to the edge of his patience with her constant ailments, or I was too much of a disappointment for any man to contend with, or you provoked him with your wildness…and the answer was always to punish us. And that's what you're doing, is it not? Punishing Christopher…for something that was not his fault!'

She sat down abruptly on the sofa as a whole new set of memories came flooding to the surface, set free, apparently, by simply alluding to them.

'You've remembered…' Lord Matthison grated, moving towards her, on his knees. Blood was streaming from a split lip, water dripped from his hair, yet his eyes were alight with what, only this morning, she would have said was love. 'Cora…'

'Yes, I've remembered,' she said in a voice so cold it halted him in its tracks.

She steeled herself against his look of baffled hurt. For no matter how convincing it looked, she knew it was all an act. She meant nothing to him. She never had.

Wrapping her arms round herself as the only barrier left against the pain, she groaned, 'I remember everything.'

Chapter Ten

'I apprehend you no longer require the smelling salts?' Mrs Paulding stood in the doorway, surveying the wreckage of the drawing room with distaste.

Lord Matthison scrambled to his feet, his brows drawn into a frown.

'As you see, Miss Montague has recovered from her faint—'

'And would now like to retire to her room,' Cora said firmly. Her heart was pounding, her whole body shaking with the effort of behaving correctly when what she really wanted to do was rage and scream and howl.

'I will come to your room once I have changed,' Lord Matthison said in an urgent undertone. 'We must speak…'

'It would be most improper to admit you to my room,' she replied frostily. 'In future, anything you have to say to me, you will have the goodness to say in public.'

His eyes widened. His face turned white, making

the streak of blood trickling from his lip look an even darker red.

As she turned to leave the room, he made to seize her arm.

'Oh, no, you don't,' growled Robbie, lurching to his feet, scattering water droplets and broken rose stems in all directions.

'Dammit all to hell!' cried Lord Matthison. 'You cannot think I mean her any harm?'

'I saw the way she looked at you. That's enough for me,' said Robbie, interposing his large body between Lord Matthison and his sister.

'Robbie,' Cora sighed, 'I do wish you would stay out of this.' He was itching for an excuse to take up the fight where she had obliged him to leave it off. Stepping to one side so that she could see Lord Matthison beyond her brother's belligerent bulk, she said, 'Please just do as I ask, Christopher, and leave me alone! I need time to…' She squeezed her eyes shut against another surge of self-awareness left her feeling dizzy. 'I need to think.'

A muscle twitched in his jaw. Without taking his eyes from her, he rapped out, 'Mrs Paulding, make sure Miss Montague reaches her room safely. And see she has everything she needs. She has journeyed far, and suffered a severe shock.'

The housekeeper obediently placed her arm around Cora's waist, and supported her from the room. Too grateful to be spared any further browbeating from either of the men in that room, Cora made no protest until the door was shut behind them. Only then did she halt, and turn to the grey-haired woman. More grey than she remembered, and more lines on her face, but then hadn't the years taken their toll on them all?

'You can drop the show of concern now there is nobody to see us. I know you have never liked me.'

'It is not my place,' Mrs Paulding replied, 'to express any sort of opinion regarding the young ladies his lordship chooses to bring into his home.'

Cora reeled away from her at the implication Lord Matthison was always bringing women here. And Mrs Paulding just kept walking, rigid-backed, towards the dark oak staircase. Cora made it to the foot of the stair and grasped hold of the newel post for support, her pain redoubled by a fresh wave of memories. She was almost as breathless as she had been in the coach, but now, she was having to deal with them completely on her own.

It had been seeing Mrs Paulding's back, turned to her after delivering a cruel aside, that had done it this time. She sucked in a deep breath, as she mounted the first step, deliberately avoiding looking back at the morning room, where Christopher and Robbie were still closeted together. Last time she had been in there, the woman lying on that sofa had not been her, but Christopher's mother. Christopher had kept a tight hold of her hand as he had made the introductions with his chin up, and more than a hint of defiance in his voice.

'Oh, Christopher,' Lady Matthison had wailed, pressing one hand to her bosom, which had heaved dramatically. 'Surely you cannot mean to make me so unhappy because of—' and she had waved her other hand in Cora's direction, lowering her voice to a tragic moan '—that Creature? I could have understood it if she was in the least bit pretty,' she had added, reaching for a scrap of lace with which to dab at her eyes. 'But when you know how desperately Kingsmede stands in need of an heiress…'

Cora opened her eyes, which she had inadvertently shut against the sting of the reception she had endured all those years ago. Mrs Paulding had reached the landing, and was staring down at her, bristling with impatience.

For a moment or two, past and present merged, and she was just a nervous girl on her first visit to her fiancé's family home. She had just been mortally wounded by her future mother-in-law's reaction to her, and there stood Mrs Paulding, bidden to take her to her room, staring at her with open derision on her face.

She had scarcely seen Kit's mother after that. Lady Matthison had made no attempt at extending any hospitality to the girl she saw as her son's great mistake, taking all her meals in her room. Kit and Robbie had shrugged off her attitude, telling Cora that mealtimes would be more congenial without her drooping over the table. But Cora had taken it to heart. Neither of his parents had approved of her. His mother had showed it by refusing to welcome her properly to Kingsmede, and his father by not even bothering to come home to meet his son's intended bride at all. And she could quite understand their attitude. Because she was not a worthy bride for a man of Kit's standing. He *should* have been marrying somebody pretty, or wealthy, or both. A woman who came from his world, who would know how to deal with servants who despised them.

No wonder, she gasped, she had felt so aware of the discrepancy between her station in life and Lord Matthison's this time round. It echoed exactly what she had felt before. When she had been his fiancée.

Slowly, her eyes came back into focus, drawn to the stony-faced housekeeper who still waited for her at the head of the stairs.

Last time Cora had been here, the woman had gone out of her way to make her as uncomfortable as she could. And Cora had never had the confidence to complain. Instead, she had begun to wonder, along with Mrs Paulding, why such a handsome young lord should have taken up with a plain, ill-educated minister's daughter? Long before the housekeeper had enlightened her as to what was really going on, she had begun to feel as though she had only dreamed he had asked her to marry him, and that one day she would wake up, and find herself back in Auchentay. Every day she had spent at Kingsmede had increased her fear that one wrong move on her part could bring everything crashing down around her ears.

Pressing her lips tightly together, Cora climbed the remaining stairs, her eyes fixed on Mrs Paulding's face.

'You still do not want me to marry Lord Matthison, do you?' she said, once she was on a level with the dour woman.

'You are not,' the woman replied with venom, 'and never have been, any good for his lordship. While you stayed away, Lord Matthison has prospered. He has looked after his tenants, improved his lands, and refurbished this house. You have not been back in his life for five minutes, and already there's brawling in the drawing room. That is my opinion, madam, and I shall stick by it.'

Certain things had not changed, then. Cora remembered the gleeful way Mrs Paulding had finally managed to convince her how little Kit really cared for her. Her eyes had flashed with malicious triumph as she had informed Cora that everyone knew the young master had only proposed to her because her bully of a brother had forced him to it. And went on to say that if she had any integrity, she would not hold him to an engagement that had already caused a breach between him and his parents.

She had lain awake all that night, weeping as she recalled the events that had led up to Kit's proposing to her.

He had taken her out on to the loch in the rowing boat. And he had finally kissed her. She had been yearning for him to kiss her for days and days.

No, longer. She had always admired Robbie's solemn-eyed friend, right from the first moment he had stepped into their home. He had fascinated her. He was so different from the men who lived in the village, and even from her irascible father, and brother. He had good manners. What her mother termed breeding.

But it was not that alone that drew the young Cora to him. It was the fact that he was always so calm, and controlled. He never spoke without considering for a moment or two, unlike Robbie and her father, who invariably said whatever was at the forefront of their mind. And occasionally lashed out with their fists without bothering to explain their thinking at all.

She lived for the times he came to visit, though she rarely plucked up the courage to speak to him.

Until that last summer. Robbie had been so busy, he had not been able to prevent her from spending every waking hour with the object of her adoration. It caused her almost as much pain as pleasure, finally being able to spend whole days with him, whilst wondering if he was only tolerating her company out of deference to his friend's difficult situation. Not that he ever made her aware of how he must have felt. His manners were far too polished.

'Come on,' he had said, with that smile she had always found completely irresistible for being so rare, 'I will teach you to row.' And they had climbed into the boat.

In order to show her how to handle the oars, he'd had to take hold of her hands as they sat side by side on the narrow bench. She had been able to feel his hip through the material of her skirts, pressing up against her own as they had each plied their own oar. She had felt as though she was in heaven. The laughter, the sunshine, their close proximity—it had all gone to her head. She blushed even now to think of how shameless she had been. A large wave had jostled the oar from her hands, and instead of lunging for it, she had clung to Kit for safety as the boat rocked alarmingly. He had put his arms round her, to steady her, and she had gazed up into his face with naked adoration in her eyes. She must have done, for he had said, 'You want me to kiss you.' She had nodded. He had obliged.

It had been, she swallowed, a moment of pure magic. Her first kiss.

But not his.

Even back then, she had sensed that a boy did not get that level of mastery without having practised on dozens of other female lips. Not that the knowledge had prevented her enthusiastic response. Pretty soon, they had tumbled to the bottom of the boat, meshed together from shoulder to hip, her skirts tangling round his legs as she twined herself round him.

And the sun had beat down on their writhing bodies while the waves lapped gently against the hull, rocking them. The gulls wheeled in the clear blue sky overhead, keening, but she had shut her ears to their warning cries. Her heart had been so full of exultation, she had vowed to treasure this moment for the rest of her life.

And when he had come to her, later that same day, and asked her to marry him, it had seemed too good to be true.

'You cannot mean that!' she had cried. 'You hardly know me!'

'I have visited your home many times,' he had replied seriously. 'I know you well.'

She had shaken her head, still too dazed by her good fortune to believe he could be in earnest.

'We are too young,' she had persisted. She had heard

him talking about going to university. Could he afford to do that, if he married her? Besides, his family would surely want him to marry a woman of his own class, a woman who had been brought up knowing how to run the kind of estate he would one day govern. 'I am not the kind of girl you should marry,' she had concluded sadly.

'But you want to marry me, though, don't you?' he had frowned. 'You would not have kissed me so enthusiastically this afternoon unless you were already thinking along those lines. You are not that sort of girl.'

She had opened her mouth to protest that she had not been capable of thinking of anything that afternoon. She had just been swept away by the yearnings of her heart, the insistent clamour of her body. But he had stopped her mouth with a kiss before she could explain anything. And had kept on kissing her until all power of rational thought deserted her. 'Say yes,' he kept murmuring between kisses. Until she was so hazed with passion she could scarcely remember what her objections had been.

She blinked away the mist that obscured her eyes, and the malevolent form of Mrs Paulding swam back into focus.

Mrs Paulding, who had shattered her dreams with her ruthless delivery of a piece of information that both Robbie and Kit had kept from her.

'Your brother was walking home along the headland overlooking the bay, and saw you frolicking in the boat with the young master,' she had hissed, barely a week after Cora's arrival at Kingsmede. 'He caught up with him in the boat-house, and set upon him. He did not stop hitting him until he had forced the poor lad to agree to propose to you!'

It had felt like the missing piece of the jigsaw, finally falling into place. She had wondered what they had been fighting about, down on the shore, when they should have been indoors, getting changed for dinner. But she had seen them wrestling dozens of times over the years, and had not thought there was any particular significance to that fight. Especially since they had eventually come in with their arms round each other's shoulders, grinning.

She had thought it peculiar, though, when Robbie had made himself scarce after supper, leaving her alone with Kit when his habit before had been to send her away, so that he and his friend could indulge in 'man talk'.

No wonder Kit had brushed aside her feeble objections to his proposal. He was, first and foremost, Robbie's friend. And wished to remain so. So much that he was even prepared to marry his gauche, unattractive little sister after being caught kissing her.

She had been completely wretched at Kingsmede after that, seeing everything from the moment of that fateful boating trip in a new light.

Kit had not wanted to make her his wife because he had fallen headlong in love with her! She had cringed to recall the numerous times she had poured out all that had been in her heart, and he had just smiled, and kissed her. She could no longer excuse his silence by telling herself he was not the kind of man who spoke about his feelings. The truth was that he simply did not have any deep feelings for her. But he was far too much the gentleman to tell her to her face that she had trapped him into a marriage he did not want. He had even managed to maintain a cheerful demeanour for the remainder of his stay at Auchentay.

When all the time, he must have wished he had never met her.

She had wanted to die.

Instead...

With a start, she came to herself, finding she was standing on the upper landing, gazing sightlessly at Mrs Paulding.

'You did all you could to make me leave,' she breathed.

Mrs Paulding gave her a considering look. 'You did the right thing.' She frowned. 'I thought you understood how unsuitable you were—and still are—to become mistress of Kingsmede. I cannot comprehend why you have changed your mind and returned.'

Cora felt a flash of surprise. Just now, in the hall, when that part of her memory had returned, it had seemed obvious that Mrs Paulding had been behind all that had happened that last day. Yet her words now showed she had no knowledge of it.

She turned and stalked along the corridor that led to Cora's room. Cora drifted behind her in a daze. How wrong she had been about everything. Everyone. Even Mrs Paulding. Though the woman had never made any secret of her animosity towards her, she was no criminal. Just a woman with strong convictions, and utter loyalty to the family she served.

Cora paused on the threshold of her room, assailed by yet more images from her past. The last time she had been here, the bed-hangings had been dusty, the curtains frayed and faded, and the bed linen so fragile that she had put her foot straight through the top sheet the first time she'd got in. She had been so scared of informing Mrs Paulding of the damage she had done, she had sat up half the night sewing it sides to middle. Only to have the housekeeper inform her scathingly the next morning, with the offending article draped over her forearm, that in the residence of persons of quality there were maids to attend to the linen.

Everything was fresh and new now. There was even a pretty rug beside the bed, thick and soft and luxurious for bare feet to step on to first thing in the morning. Not like the ragged old thing she had always been catching her heels in. And, as she stepped into the room in which she had suffered such agonies of self-doubt, she could not help noticing that everywhere smelled different too. The Kingsmede of old had smelled of dust and mildew. Now, the scent of beeswax and lavender hung in the air.

Mrs Paulding stood in the middle of the room, her hands clasped at her waist, her expression wavering between defiance and…apprehension.

It struck Cora that, this time around, she had far more power over events than she'd had before. If she really were to marry Lord Matthison, she could fire Mrs Paulding from her post.

Given the way she had treated her in the past, this

was clearly what the housekeeper expected. Cora frowned. Though she could not like the woman, she did not know if she had the heart to fire her. It would be hard for her to seek another post at her age. And utterly humiliating to ask for references from a woman she despised.

Suddenly the tension in the room became too much. She went to the armchair by the empty fireplace and sank into it wearily.

'Would you please get me some tea?'

'Tea?' the woman echoed. 'Or something stronger?' And then after an infinitesimal pause, 'His lordship did say you had suffered a shock.'

Cora might have been imagining the taunt, but she did not think so. Mrs Paulding was bracketing her with her brother, who no doubt had a decanter of something 'stronger' in his own room, to which he applied all too frequently, judging by the pungency of his breath.

Last time she had been here, she had put up with Mrs Paulding's attitude, because she felt the woman had only been following the line taken by Kit's parents, and because she did not have the experience to know what to do. But she was not a timid seventeen-year-old, with everything to lose should she put a foot wrong, any more.

'If you do not wish to continue working here, I shall quite understand,' she said coldly.

Mrs Paulding's mouth snapped shut. With one last defiant toss of her head she stalked to the door, leaving Cora to wonder whether she would be getting a tray of tea and cakes, as befitted a female guest, or a pint of gin, in keeping with the low opinion the woman held of her.

Uttering a groan, Cora lowered her head to her hands, almost wishing she could choose Robbie's road to oblivion. It had to be easier than wrestling with the maelstrom of thoughts and impressions that were whirling through her head. She felt dizzy with them. Sick.

How she wished Kit had never brought her here! She could have gone on being Mary, his mistress, and they could both have known some measure of happiness. Instead of which everything was coming unravelled.

From the moment they had driven into that dark, brooding forest that surrounded Kingsmede, she had been pitched back in time seven years. To the very day life as she had known it had come to an end.

She rubbed at the dull ache that was building from the nape of her neck. She had slowly been learning to let go of her fear of the unknown, that was the trouble. The very first time she had glimpsed Lord Matthison in the street, and she had sensed her shadowy past reaching out to grab her, she had acted out of instinct, and run from him. But she had not quite managed to outrun the persistent feelings he aroused. She had begun to daydream about him. The daydreams she had smothered by focusing on her work. And the dreams, that were now, she realised, based on things that had actually happened, she dealt with by waking herself up from them.

That was a trick she had developed, to save herself from the recurring nightmares about being locked in the cellar. And before that…in the attic room, where she had sensed danger hovering close by, she had wrapped herself round with a cloak of ignorance. It had been her only refuge against her gaoler. She had kept on hiding behind it, even when she no longer had any need to. Pushing away any stray thought that might threaten her hard-earned tranquillity. Because she had enough to contend with, just recovering from Lord Sandiford's attack, and learning to survive in the harsh conditions of Madame Pichot's sweatshop, without the added burden of the pain she would have brought with her from her former life.

Time and circumstances had given her material to shore up her defences against the truth, too. For she had fallen in love with a polite, shabbily dressed boy called Christopher Brereton. Kit, to her. He bore only a faint resemblance to the hard-eyed, wealthy gentleman who had accosted her so angrily. And she could truthfully tell herself she had never met anyone by the name of Lord Matthison before. Because she had not. The man who had borne that name seven years previously had been Kit's father. And from what he and Robbie had told her, she had always pictured him as an elderly, portly, carelessly dressed man with a complexion coarsened from drink and dissipation.

Without even knowing she was doing it, she had stubbornly resisted recognising him, cunningly shielding herself from risk of further pain.

She slapped the arm of her chair in vexation. It did not matter if she worked out how her mind had managed to protect itself from the prospect of unbearable hurt, her respite was well and truly over now.

A knock on the door, heralding the arrival of a maid with the tea things, could not have come at a more timely moment for Cora. Heartily relieved to have a diversion from the tortuous workings of her mind, she got up, and opened the door herself.

The young girl, standing on the other side, looked rather startled, but hastily recovered and bobbed a curtsy. The maid, who bore a tray stacked with pots, cups, cream and sugar bowls, was followed by a footman with a cake stand laden with cakes, sandwiches, slices of bread and butter, and pots of jewel-bright preserves. Behind him came a second maid with two cans of hot water, and a third with arms full of fluffy towels.

Cora could not help contrasting all this attention with the neglect she had suffered in this room before. Hot water! An unheard-of luxury in the Kingsmede she had known, but Cora could definitely see steam wisping from the can as the girl took it into the dressing room. She had never been able to wash in anything even approaching tepid before, and when she had been hungry, she, Robbie and Kit had occasionally raided the larder for ingredients that she had thrown together into something resembling a meal on the kitchen table.

Either Mrs Paulding had decided she wanted to keep her job after all, or Cora had allies amongst the lower staff, none of whom, she now noticed, had served under the previous Lord and Lady Matthison. By the way the maids and footman were all bowing and scraping, she guessed the latter. They all seemed extremely keen to ingratiate themselves with the woman they believed was about to become the new mistress of Kingsmede.

She frowned. Last time she had been here, everyone had believed she was about to become the new mistress of Kingsmede, too, but that had not prevented them from uniting against her behind Mrs Paulding's formidable antagonism.

The only person who had even *pretended* to be friendly had been Frances Farrell. The vicar's daughter.

She did not want to think about her. She really didn't, but she had rashly opened the floodgate in her mind, by the tiniest crack, and the force of what had built up behind it was too powerful to let her slam it back shut.

Tottering to the tea table by the window, she sank to the chair, and accepted a large slice of fruit-cake from the obsequious footman.

'Yes, that will be all,' she managed to say, once the footman had poured her tea exactly as she liked it. Part of her wanted to beg the servants to stay. With them to distract her, she could almost manage to ignore the latest pack of memories that had come baying round her like hounds scenting a fresh kill.

She had felt so lonely and friendless and insecure back then that she had welcomed the slightly older girl's overtures of friendship. Because Frances was Mrs Paulding's niece by marriage, she had been a frequent visitor to Kingsmede. In spite of her family connection, Cora had soon begun to look forward to her visits. Robbie had spoken about Frances before she had arrived, telling her she was a grand lass. And Frances had been such a good listener that Cora had opened her heart to her. She had confided her intention of impressing Mrs Paulding with her grasp of household economy. She had admitted she would not care if Christopher could not afford to dress her fashionably, or show her the entertainments London had to offer. She would be content to stay on his rundown estate all year round, if need be, so long as they were together. She had waxed lyrical about how she would be as good as any heiress for him, with her plans for economy and good house-keeping. And her boundless love.

She set her cup down in her saucer with a snap.

Stupid, stupid, stupid!

She could not believe how stupid she had been. How blind to what had been going on around her.

The moist fruit-cake turned to ashes in her mouth, which almost choked her as she forced herself to swallow the knowledge of her monumental idiocy.

Frances, just like her aunt, had eventually been only too pleased to enlighten the starry-eyed Cora about Christopher Brereton's nature.

'I am so sorry to have to be the one to tell you this,' Frances had said, laying her hand on Cora's forearm, 'but Christopher is playing you false. He has gone to meet the young lady in question this very morning.'

'He has gone out with Robbie!' she had protested.

'They have ridden over to Bamford to see the tailor about wedding clothes!'

Frances had shaken her head pityingly. 'I have no idea where your brother may be, but Christopher has gone to a certain woodman's hut in the western beech wood, where he always meets her. If you do not believe me, why don't you go there and see for yourself?'

She had flounced down to the stables in a blaze of outrage, determined to prove Frances wrong. The first blow had been to find Kit's horse in its stall. If he had gone to Bamford, he would have ridden there. She had gone cold inside. Why had he lied about going to Bamford? More by luck than judgement, she had managed to get the massive creature saddled, and scrambled on to its back with scant regard for the propriety of hitching her morning dress up round her hips.

And soon she'd had proof he had lied about everything. Through the grimy window of the tumbledown hut she had seen him holding a practically naked woman in his arms. She had stood there long enough to see him kiss the woman whose bared breasts were crushed against his waistcoat and then, at the thought she had let those lying lips loose against her own mouth, she had fallen to her knees and lost her breakfast.

Everything after that had taken on the quality of a nightmare. She had managed to remount the horse, just as the heavens had opened, and the creature had taken off on a course she had not cared to correct. She had no idea where she wanted to go anyway. Where *could* she go to escape from Kit's betrayal? Against a backdrop of flashing lightning, and the thunder of horse's hooves, she had felt her heart tearing apart in her breast.

Cora drew in a great, shuddering breath, and wrapped her arms about herself.

She was not a seventeen-year-old virgin any longer, with no experience of the base nature of men. She could appreciate now that, technically, Kit had never lied to her. For he had never once told her he loved her, or promised to be faithful. She had believed what she wanted to believe, without being offered one scrap of evidence.

She got to her feet, too sickened by her own culpability to stomach so much as the smell of food, and found herself wandering over to the wardrobe.

It was the one item of furniture in the room that looked exactly as she remembered it. It appeared frozen in time, with one of the hinges still slightly askew, and the carved oak-leaf panels peppered with woodworm.

Had he preserved it, she wondered on a swell of something like hope, for some sentimental reason? When they had talked about this room in the coach earlier, she had gained the impression he regarded it as a shrine to her memory. She had dreaded the thought he might want her to put on a dead woman's clothes…

But now, the thought that he might have kept all her things, preserving them, treasuring them…

With wildly beating heart, she tugged the door open.

It was empty.

Something inside her crystallized and froze solid.

Of course the wardrobe was empty.

Just as his black heart was empty!

The only reason, it came to her in a flash, that he had made such a show of clinging to her memory, was to get rid of poor Miss Winters!

But if he thought she was going to let him use her to break another poor young woman's heart, as he had broken hers…

'No!' she cried, slamming the door on the empty wardrobe and marching over to her trunk, which sat at the foot of the bed.

It was time to change her gown, and go downstairs, and set a few things straight.

Kneeling down, she flung open the lid, and plunged her hands into the jumble of goods she had amassed in her life as Mary. The mingled smells of hard work, cheap soap, and Molly's scent that wafted up as she rummaged for the gown she sought were vastly comforting.

Ah, there it was! Her Sunday best. A long-sleeved gown of bronze silk with a square neckline. Probably not the sort of thing ladies wore to dinner in the country, but she did not care. She was not a lady. And she had no intention of becoming one.

There was more of Mary in her now, than Cora. Not that Cora had been a lady either. In fact, Cora had not been very much of anything, she huffed as she pulled off her stained travelling gown. No wonder she had never regained the strength to resurface after having all her hopes so comprehensively trampled in the mud.

She had been, she frowned, tugging her fresh gown over her head, a timid child to start with who had been prevented by an overbearing father from developing any opinions of her own. Never mind expressing them! And then her mother had taught her how to become more or less invisible. There had only been a brief period where she had tried to unfurl her wings. That summer, after her parents had died, while Robbie was too busy to keep her caged. She had flown free with Kit, like a butterfly newly emerged from its chrysalis…until the day he had ripped her wings from her heart and she had spiralled downward into despair.

But Mary was made of sterner stuff. She lifted her chin and regarded her reflection squarely in the mirror. Mary had fought off the lecherous Lord Sandiford, preserving her virtue whilst leaving her mark on his vile, grasping hands. She had gone to London, got a job, excelled at it and then, when she had felt so inclined, had been bold enough to take a lover.

Cora would never have been capable of doing any of that!

Giving Cora's prim reflection one last derisive glance, Mary squared her shoulders and went downstairs.

Lord Matthison and Robbie were waiting for her in the antechamber that led to the dining room. Both got to their feet as she entered.

'I hope you will be in a fit state to travel in the morning, Robbie,' she said tartly, eyeing the almost empty glass dangling from his fingers. 'So that you can take me home to Auchentay.'

It was only as she took a comfortably upholstered chair, and accepted a glass of wine from the same footman who had brought her tea, that it occurred to her that Robbie might not live there any longer. That he might even have a wife, who would have something to say about a stray sister turning up uninvited on her doorstep.

But it was Lord Matthison who answered her, once he had dismissed the footman from the room.

'Your home is here with me now, in case you have forgotten.'

'There is no need to mock me, my lord,' she snapped back. 'I may have been suffering from some kind of...' She shook her head as she failed to find words to adequately describe what had been like a dam, holding back all those overwhelmingly painful memories. 'Some kind of blockade in my mind,' she eventually continued. 'But now that it has collapsed, I remember all too clearly the reasons why I should never have agreed to marry you in the first place!'

Lord Matthison got to his feet, his face ominously grim.

'Do you mean to tell me you ran out on me seven years ago?'

She had just taken a breath, to explain what had happened to her shortly after she had galloped away from the woodcutter's hut, when Lord Matthison flung his glass into the fireplace with such force that it exploded into a cloudburst of splinters.

'You faithless bitch!' He swore, turning away and striding to the far side of the room. When he turned round his face was contorted with rage. 'After all the protestations of love you made, you did not even have

the decency to come to me and break off the engagement to my face!'

'No…' Of course she hadn't! She had not had the
chance. 'You see…'

But he did not let her finish. Striding over to where
Robbie sat slumped in his chair, following the argument
through narrowed eyes, he said, 'For seven years you've
let your brother mourn you. And as for me…hah!' He
looked her brother straight in the eye as he said, 'For
seven years I have had to bear the burden of having the
man who was once my best friend believing I had killed
you! Do you know he accused me to the magistrate,
Cora, after you ran off? I could have hanged! Only that
they could not find a body…'

'Of course not,' she began. Because she had not died.
Only lost her memory.

And how she wished it had never come back!
Bearing his indifference back then had all but destroyed
her. Facing his contempt was tearing her apart all over
again.

'No, because you were never dead. In spite of letting
us all believe it! How little you care for anyone but
yourself! Well, let me tell you something.' He strode
back to her, leaning his hands on the arms of the chair,
making her cringe back in her seat. 'I have no intention
of letting you run out on me a second time. You are not
going to crawl back to Scotland and evade your respon-
sibilities towards me this time!'

'You…you cannot stop me,' she gasped, almost afraid
of this man's unleashed anger. 'R-Robbie…' she pleaded.

'Don't think your brother will take you back into his home now. Not now I have bedded you!'

She heard Robbie gasp. She wanted to turn her head to see what he was thinking, but somehow she could not tear her eyes away from Kit's.

'You could be carrying my child,' he growled, his eyes raking down the front of her gown, coming to rest on the small mound of her belly.

Why, oh, why had he gone and told Robbie that? If only he had kept that quiet, she could have gone home to Scotland and lived a quiet, spinster existence, keeping house for her brother. But now Robbie would never rest until they were married. Look how adamant he had been that Kit should marry her, when all he had done was kiss her!

But how could he imagine she might contemplate any kind of relationship with him when he could accuse her of such dreadful things, with such implacable hatred for her burning from his eyes?

And then he dealt the death blow to any last, lingering hope they might be able to salvage anything from the current situation.

'You owe me seven years, Cora,' he snarled. 'Seven dark, blighted, hellish years…'

'I don't owe you anything!' she cried, finally finding the strength to close her eyes and turn her head aside. She owed him nothing if he could believe she had lied about how she felt about him back then. Or was capable of just walking away without one word of explanation.

And then she heard Robbie growl, 'You have to marry him, Cora. Nothing else for it now you've slept with him. A man's heir, you know…'

And she saw another door slamming in her face.

She might have known Robbie would side with Kit against her. Men did not care how miserable women were made by their decisions.

Beasts, the lot of them!

With a wild cry, she raised her arms, and pushed Lord Matthison hard in the chest, forcing him far enough back for her to get to her feet.

'I hate you both,' she panted, looking wildly from one to the other. For years, growing up, their friendship had excluded her, the little girl who did not have the freedom to escape the stultifying atmosphere at home. How she had envied them their education, their freedom to stay out of doors all day long, their freedom to choose each other for a companion! For a brief time, when she travelled with them for the first time to Kingsmede, she had thought they would include her. But they had not. They had both lied to her, and evaded her, and now they were siding together, to thwart her, and contain her, and control her.

She cried out again, an inarticulate sound that expressed all her rage and pain and betrayal. She did not need either of them! For the last seven years she had earned her own living, and she could jolly well do it all over again if necessary!

The door opened. 'Dinner is—'

The butler got no further than that, as Cora pushed

past him in her desperate need to get out of the room, and away from the two men who had so spectacularly betrayed her. Again.

Chapter Eleven

She was too distraught to hear the sound of footsteps pounding up the stairs after her. Not 'til she reached her room, and yanked open the door, did she become aware that Lord Matthison had chased after her.

But she was too quick for him. By the time he caught up with her, she had slammed the door, and locked it.

'Cora, let me in, damn you!' he yelled, pounding on the door.

'No!' she yelled back in defiance. 'Go back to London and marry Miss Winters! She can have your blasted money and your rotten title. I don't want any of it. I don't want you!'

And then her legs folded under her.

She had been desperately trying to hold herself together ever since her memory had returned. Now she had completely run out of will-power. She bowed her head, and yielded to the grief she had held in check for seven years, her only concession to dignity being to muffle the sound of her sobs by burying her face in the carpet.

When she eventually ran out of tears, she could not say she felt any better for having given way to her emotions. Her eyes were swollen, her head throbbed and every muscle in her body was shaking. Her hair had come down and hanks of it were plastered to her face and neck.

When she tried, she could not get to her feet. So she crawled to the dressing room where she dipped a wash-cloth in cold water, and wiped it over her face.

And then she sat down on the pile of towels on the stool, wondering what on earth she had been crying for.

This emotional storm had been sparked off by Kit's angry insistence that she marry him. Should that not have made her heart leap with joy? She had loved him for as long as she could remember. Even when her mind had not allowed her to recognise him, her heart had somehow known it belonged to him.

She eyed her reflection with some hostility. She rather suspected it had been Cora doing all the weeping. Mary had always been too determined to hang on to her self-control to let her emotions get the better of her. Yes, she turned more fully towards the mirror. But then Cora had just discovered the man she adored did not love her back.

That was what all the weeping had been about. She was having to deal with the pain her seventeen-year-old self had never had the chance to purge from her system. She had just remembered exactly how she had felt when she had seen that woman opening her bodice and offering Kit her bared breasts. When he had walked towards her with a smile, taken her in his arms and kissed her, she had felt as though he had plunged a dagger into her heart. For a few minutes, she had been out of her mind with grief…

And then she had gone down to dinner, the intervening years gone in the blink of an eye. She was still reeling with the sense of his betrayal, and instead of him giving her any sort of explanation, or even an apology, he had accused her of all sorts of crass behaviour. How dared he?

She straightened up with a sniff, anger restoring her backbone. Unable to find a handkerchief about her person, she inelegantly wiped her nose on her sleeve. Her gown needed laundering anyway, after rolling about on the floor in it.

Seven years, she reminded her reflection crossly. It had all happened seven years ago, not yesterday! Even though that was what it felt like.

She twisted the washcloth between her fingers, studying it, rather than the woebegone reflection that inhabited the mirror. It was all very confusing. One minute she felt like Cora, the heartbroken girl who had just discovered her idol had feet of clay. Then next, she was Mary, older, wiser…but no less in love with the same man.

She sighed, cupping her chin in her hands and regarding herself in the mirror with resignation. It made little difference which version of herself she felt like; both of them were hopelessly in love with a man who did not love her back. As the starry-eyed Cora, she had shut her eyes to reality, grasping at a fairy-tale ending where the prince married the peasant and they all lived happily ever after in his castle. She had not even noticed the wicked witch hovering in the background, casting her spells over the gullible young princess-to-be.

She shook off the fancy, returning to the knotty problem of why she recoiled from the prospect of marrying a man she had been in love with, one way or another, her whole life.

She could not entirely blame her reluctance on the idealistic, youthful, Cora part of her. Even Mary, who knew the value of financial security, respectability and freedom from drudgery had baulked at the prospect of marrying him. Mary, who had loved him so much she had tossed her scruples aside, had declared she would rather be his mistress.

Well, it would have been impossible for a seamstress to marry a wealthy Viscount. But now she knew she was Cora…why should she not marry him? Her father had been a gentleman, after all. And her mother from a perfectly respectable family. There was not such a vast gap between their ranks that a match was ineligible.

And she belonged to him. Even when her mind had refused to let her remember what had passed between them before, her heart had leapt at the very sight of him. For he held it in the palm of his hand, to cherish or crush as the whim took him.

She gasped.

That was it! She was afraid he would inflict untold misery upon her. She did not want to be enslaved by the love she bore for a man who could not return even a tenth of her feelings.

What, then, should she do?

As if in answer, her stomach growled. It was hardly surprising. She had eaten virtually nothing all day. She crossed to the bell-pull, and yanked on it to summon a maid. Dealing with her hunger was at least something practical she could see about. A self-deprecating smile came to her lips. Putting off thinking about unpleasant topics was something that Mary had always been extremely good at.

It was not long before she heard a tentative knocking on her bedroom door.

Her head spun a little as she rose to answer it, confirming that her decision to send for food had been a wise one. There was no sense in making herself ill, on top of everything else.

'Cora, are you all right? You look so pale.'

It was not a maid, standing in the doorway, but Lord Matthison.

'Don't lock the door again,' he pleaded, his hand shooting out to push the door wider. 'I will not come in, if that is what you want, but...' He thrust his fingers through already disordered hair. 'If anything should happen to you...'

To look at his haggard expression, anyone would think he really cared about her. But a little voice that she could not quite manage to silence pointed out that he had already been accused of murdering her once. He had spent seven years under that cloud. It would get even worse if any harm befell her now, whilst she was under his roof.

'I rang for a maid,' she said resentfully. 'I need something to eat.'

An expression of incredulity flashed across his face. Then he straightened up, his eyes hardening.

'Of course.' For the first time she noticed the girl who had brought her tea earlier, hovering further down the corridor. At a brusque gesture from Lord Matthison, the girl scuttled off on her errand.

'You cannot remain in your room indefinitely,' he said coldly. 'We have matters to discuss. Arrangements to make.'

'Yes.' She leaned against the doorframe, her arms folded round her waist. 'But not now. Not tonight. Please…' She could not bring herself to look him in the eye any longer. The coldness emanating from him in waves was already making her shiver. 'Please, just let me have tonight to myself,' she begged him. Just standing here talking to him was more than she felt able to cope with.

'We can discuss—' her broken heart, her unrequited love, the other women in his life '—matters tomorrow, if you are determined to proceed with the betrothal we entered into seven years ago.' She still could not quite understand his determination to marry her, when he could look at her so coldly. 'I suppose, technically, it still stands.'

Could it be as simple as that? He had made a pledge? And a man of honour did not withdraw, once he had given his word. She did look up at him then, but his eyes had narrowed, and he was looking at her as though she was a complete stranger.

She supposed she was in a way. She was certainly a stranger to herself. Part Cora, part Mary, and completely muddled.

'You came to my bed,' he grated, as though he now found it hard to believe.

How cruel of him to remind her how weak she had been! And yet, she realised miserably, if he were to put his arms round her this minute, and murmur a few soft words, she would cling to him, and beg him to come into her room, and stay with her all night. How she wanted him to hold her, as he had held her last night! Tenderly, as though she was precious!

'You could be carrying my child,' he said, growing noticeably angrier.

She flinched. Cora had only trapped him with a kiss. Mary had done it with a potential pregnancy. He had been gentleman enough to spare Cora any expression of resentment. Mary, the wanton, could expect no such consideration. She felt tears stinging her eyes again. She had survived waking in the shattered, blasted ruins of the life she had dreamed of as a girl. But she did not think she could bear hearing him systematically destroying the illusion that taking her to his bed had meant as much to him as it had to her.

'Please, Christopher, don't say another word! I cannot bear any more! If I am carrying your child...' Oh, how she wished he wanted her to be the mother of his children! 'But even if I am not...' She faltered. If she was not pregnant, she might be able to persuade him to let her go. A vision of a future without him in it stretched out like a wasteland before her. It would be unbearable! She shuddered. She could see herself going to her grave loving him, and him alone. It was hopeless. 'I could never marry anyone else.'

Unable to bear standing so close to him, yet feeling so far apart, she retreated into her room.

Lord Matthison stared balefully at the door she had shut in his face. Cora did not want him in her room. She did not want to marry him. The thought that she might be carrying his child had been so distressing it had brought her to the verge of tears.

But she could not marry anyone else now. By taking her to his bed, he had effectively ruined her!

God, how he wished he had not insisted on waking Cora! Mary had loved him unreservedly, giving him her whole heart along with her virginity. She had trusted him with her future, even though she believed she could only ever be his mistress.

But he, damn fool that he was, had wanted to be able to marry her. As Cora.

And now, without knowing quite how or why, he had lost them both.

The maid returned, and nervously cleared her throat. She could not get to the door while he was standing with his nose to it, glaring at it as though he could blast it to smithereens by force of will alone.

Muttering a curse, he stepped away. The girl darted him a wary glance, tapped timidly on the door, and scuttled inside with Cora's supper. She looked as though she thought her employer had lost his mind. She was probably right. It had been a long time since he had known anything remotely resembling sanity. Every time he had thought he'd begun to make sense out of the chaos Cora had left behind, a new twist in his path had made him re-assess where he really was. And always, always, she had been dancing just out of reach, like some elusive sprite.

From the very first, it had been that elusive quality about her that had tantalised him. The slender girl who had darted shy glances at him across the table when she thought her father was not looking. The prim, untouchable maiden who had taken on the burden of housekeeping for her exacting father after her mother's death. That ethereal, otherworldly quality she possessed had been what had made it so easy to think of her as a spirit, wandering the earth. Last night as he'd held her in his arms, he had thought he'd captured her at last, but today...

He stepped back from the door that separated them, a shaft of pain lancing through him.

She still eluded him. Even as Mary, there had been a part of her he could not reach. She could have been his mistress, but never his wife. He had thought he would get what he wanted once she knew she was Cora. Instead, she had gone and slammed the door in his face. And turned his world upside down all over again.

Had she ever really loved him?

If she had, surely seeing him again would have restored her memory? But no, it had been coming back to Kingsmede, and hearing her brother's voice, that had freed her mind from the chains that bound it.

He found himself halfway down the stairs, his hand clenching the banister, breathing hard. Why had she told him she loved him if she had not meant it? Why, he thumped the banister with his clenched fist, had she felt the need to make such a colossal fool of him?

She had made him believe she welcomed his kisses. That day he had taken her rowing and she had wound up in his arms, and he had finally thrown caution to the winds...she had responded with an eagerness he thought matched his own! He had really believed they could overcome all the barriers he had feared might keep them apart. Her youth, his rank, their complete lack of funds.

That, he decided grimly, that was the moment he had lost his mind. He had been crazy to have thought they could make it work.

Crazy.

'Christopher!'

He lifted his head at the sound of Robbie calling his name, to find he was standing in the middle of the hall, so completely lost in thought he had forgotten why he had gone down the stairs at all, never mind which room he had been heading for.

Robbie was standing in the open doorway to the library.

'What you said to Cora,' he growled. 'Before dinner. It did na' make sense to me.' He shook his shaggy head. 'I've been thinking about it all evening. You accused her of leaving you.' He scowled, shaking his finger at him.

'But when you wrote me, ye said she had lost her memory and did nae know who she was when you found her. Which is it? For I canna see how both can hold true.'

He stood back, inviting Lord Matthison to join him in the library. 'I think it is high time we had a long talk, and worked out just what the hell has been going on.'

Cora groaned and rolled over in bed.

She would have sworn she had not slept a wink all night, but sunlight was streaming through a chink in the curtains, and last time she had opened her eyes the room had been completely dark.

Her throat was raw, her tongue felt too big for her mouth, and her head ached all the way down to her knees. In fact, she felt so dreadful, she might just as well have drunk the contents of the decanter that had come up on her supper tray the night before.

Oh, no, no! She shook her head, flinging back the covers and setting her feet on the luxuriously soft rug. One thing she had decided during the long hours of the night was that she would never succumb to the false comfort alcohol offered.

There were those who let the circumstances of life crush them. The streets and alleys of London were littered with them. Both men and women who gave up hope, and turned to drink, or worse. She had heard of women who would let their babies starve while they spent their last pennies on gin. But there were others, afflicted with like circumstances, who just gritted their teeth, and got on with it. Mary had been on the verge of collapse when she had found herself in London, with no memory of her past, terrified by her colleagues within doors, and the bustling, noisy, threatening crowds without. But she had gritted her teeth, performed every task that was set before her, and doggedly refused to let her mind dwell on those nameless fears that seemed to lurk round every corner.

Or had that been Cora?

Both of them, all of her, she no longer knew how to describe herself, but one thing she had learned about herself through all this, she nodded, tugging hard on the bell-pull: she was a survivor.

The person she was now was stronger than the naïve, dreamy Cora, or the self-effacing Mary. Nothing had managed to destroy her so far, and she was not going to succumb to the kind of self-pity that might do so now!

She was no longer a silly child who had never set foot outside her village. She was not going to throw away her entire future happiness because the man she loved had committed an indiscretion.

Two, if you counted the passionate affair he had begun with her, when he was still not quite sure who she was.

And at least she could be sure she ranked higher in his esteem than poor Miss Winters.

He was quite determined not to marry Miss Winters, no matter what stratagems she might employ to snare him.

And equally determined he *would* marry her. For whatever reason.

And she was going to accept him.

Cora had been devastated by witnessing her fiancé kissing a half-naked woman. But Mary had learned a lot about the nature of men from listening to her work mates talking about their lives. A man could see nothing wrong with marrying one woman, and keeping another as a mistress. They did not seem to think fidelity was an essential ingredient of being a husband.

And that one glimpse she'd had, of what her life without him would be like, had been too bleak to contemplate.

As she waited for the maid to answer her summons, she went to the little ormolu clock that sat on the mantel. It showed almost eleven o'clock. Not too late for a woman who was about to become Lady Matthison to be ringing for some breakfast! That was what fine ladies did. Lounged in bed half the day, taking their meals on a tray.

She had a sudden vision of the former Lady Matthison doing exactly that. Wallowing in self-pity! She pressed her lips together, disgusted with herself for even contemplating going down that road. She would be nothing like her predecessor!

She marched herself to the dressing room and poured the last of the water from the jug into the basin. The night before, she had, out of long years of habit, emptied the wash water into the enamel bucket under the stand, for the maid to remove this morning.

She expected Mrs Paulding would frown on her saving her staff so much work. The thought rather cheered her as she finished her brisk wash, and pulled her wrap back round her just as she heard a knock on the outer door to her chamber.

His lordship and her brother, the girl informed her when she asked, had breakfasted earlier, and then gone out riding together.

'Of course they have,' Cora replied with a tight smile. Healing the breach that had grown between them would be extremely important to him. Kit had never had many friends, and none so close as Robbie. When she had disappeared, he had lost what he held most dear. Oh, she did not flatter herself that it was her, so much! But his best friend, and his reputation. All gone, at a stroke. He would regain it all by marrying her.

She had it within her power, to grant him his heart's desire. Of course she would not deny him that!

She trailed over to the window, gazing out over the park where they had gone riding, just as they had done each day when she had last been here. How left out she had felt.

How much more would she hurt from now on, knowing she would have his name, but not his heart? But she would get used to it. It would not be anywhere near as painful as leaving Kingsmede, perhaps never to see him again.

She ate her scrambled eggs, and drank her tea slowly, wondering how she would fill her days as Lady Matthison. If the place had been as dilapidated as it had been seven years ago, she would have enjoyed setting it all to rights.

But Lord Matthison had done it all on his own.

Feeling restless and disgruntled, she decided to take a tour of the house, and see what other improvements he had made, apart from the ones she had already noticed. She did not ring for the housekeeper, whose task it should have been to escort her new mistress over her domain. She had enough on her mind already, without having to deal with her open hostility.

It was not long before she found herself in the portrait gallery, gazing up at the canvas that Kit's grandparents had commissioned on the occasion of his parents' betrothal.

The former Lady Matthison had been pretty as a girl. She was shown sitting on an armchair out on the front lawn, with the façade of Kingsmede angled behind her to reveal a stylised version of the surrounding lands spread out beyond. She looked very young, and very happy as she smiled down at the enormous ruby ring that adorned her finger. Kit's father lounged languidly against the bole of a tree looking down at her. Cora had never met the man, but she could just see that bored young fop turning into the rackety gamester Kit had described.

Twenty years of being married to him had reduced the happy, smiling girl in the portrait into the fretful woman who had been desperate for her only son to marry an heiress.

But she would not end up like her! Kit had promised, in the coach on the way here, that they would never suffer from the financial constrictions that had driven a wedge between his own parents. And that he would not neglect her, or make her unhappy.

And whatever happened, she would never, ever treat

any child of hers the way those two had treated poor Kit. They had been so wrapped up in their own problems, they had completely neglected him. And turned their backs on him when he had most needed their support.

Her breath hitched in her throat. Last night, all she had been able to think about had been seeing Kit with that half-naked woman. She had not spared one thought for what he had been through, in the seven years since she had lost her memory.

He had suffered a great deal. Whatever that incident in the hut had been about, it did not alter the fact that he had never stopped wanting Cora. Missing her so much that he had even invented a ghost to haunt him. He had been half out of his mind when she had met up with him again. She could not forget the look of anguish in his eyes when he had grabbed her in the Flash of Lightning, and asked why she had run away from him.

She felt quite indignant on his behalf. Surely somebody could have stood by him, no matter what he'd done? But nobody had. Not Robbie. Not his parents…

She pressed her hands to her mouth to stifle a sob. Not her, either. She had been as self-absorbed as his parents. She had been so focused on her own problems last night, she had turned her back on him. Left him all night to wonder if she was going to leave him all over again, which was his greatest fear.

'Oh, Kit!' she moaned.

Being unfaithful was not such a heinous crime that he deserved to suffer complete ostracism for seven years. Especially not when she took into consideration the fact that he had been coerced into proposing to her.

She felt thoroughly ashamed of herself for joining the ranks of people who had let him down.

She went to the window, and looked over towards the woods where her love for him had undergone its greatest trial. If she had not met with that accident, would she have had the courage to have fought for his love? To have marched up to him, and demanded an explanation? To insist he give up that woman if he wanted to marry her...oh, dear, she feared not! She had been so sure by that time that she was unworthy of his hand, that...

She remembered the way he had held her hand, all the while he had been introducing her to his mother. And the defiance in his voice. And his insistence that Lady Matthison hand over the betrothal ring that had been in his family for generations.

Her heart began to beat very fast. She had been quite wrong to let others persuade her he did not love her at all. She only had to consider the wreck he had been when she met him again, and the way he had subsequently treated her, to know he cared for her to some degree. More than his father seemed to have cared for his mother.

If she really loved him, would she not prove it by standing by him, no matter what he did or how he felt? And she did love him. As Cora, she had fallen in love with the sombre, cultured boy who had offered to make her a lady. As Mary, her heart had gone out to the hardened, bitter gambler who had sworn he would always take care of her.

And now…she loved him still. Through all the changes that suffering had wrought on him, he was still her Kit. The only man for her, no matter what he had done or who she was.

She had to find him, and tell him! She whirled round to make her way downstairs, only to almost jump out of her skin to find the butler standing right behind her.

'Excuse me, Miss Montague,' he said. 'You have a visitor. Miss Farrell,' the butler continued, 'walked over as usual this morning to visit Mrs Paulding, and when she heard of your return, asked if she might have the privilege of being the first of your neighbours to welcome you back.'

'Did she, indeed?' Cora supposed she had to admire the woman's sheer nerve. She had temporarily pushed the Frances Farrell issue to the back of her mind, while she had wrestled with the more important question of how she was going to cope with marrying Kit.

'I did say you had been unwell last night, and that his lordship had said you were not to be disturbed this morning.'

Had he? Oh, see! He did care for her! It might not be the all-consuming love she felt for him, but…

'But Mrs Paulding told her you were up and had breakfasted, and Miss Farrell was most insistent that I enquire as to whether you are receiving.'

She had the perfect excuse to avoid dealing with Frances.

But had she not decided to grit her teeth and get on with her new life? No hiding from reality by blotting

out painful memories, or fuzzing her perception with
alcohol, nor, she stood a little straighter, hiding in her
room like the last Lady Matthison. Or using butlers to
avoid unpleasant scenes.

'Thank you. That was thoughtful of you, but I shall
see her.'

Frances had all but destroyed Cora, by making her
believe she was not a fit bride for Kit Brereton.

But since then, she had spent seven years working
for a living. She had learned to stand on her own two
feet. She had established a position for herself, in that
workroom above Madame Pichot's shop.

It struck her that once separated from her domineering male relatives, and with no preconceptions about
how she ought to behave, she had been set free to
become herself.

She had finally learned who she really was.

And now, armed with the knowledge of Cora's
social position, bolstered by Mary's hard-won sense of
self-worth, she was more than ready to go downstairs
and tell Frances Farrell that she no longer had the
power to scare her!

'Miss Farrell is in the morning room,' said the butler.
'Do you wish me to escort you down?'

'No, thank you. I know the way. Tell her I shall be
down presently.'

The butler glided away, while Cora turned back to
the painting and regarded Kit's mother one last time.

The ring she was wearing in the portrait was unmistakably the one Kit had slipped on to her finger in spite

of his mother's protests. The same one she had seen Frances trying on, during the nights she had lain, drenched with fever, imprisoned in the attics at the vicarage.

Suddenly she was glad Kit and Robbie had gone out. This was something she had to deal with for herself. She had not had the courage or the self-confidence to fight for Kit's love last time she had been here. She had ended up cowering under the blankets while Frances flaunted her victory.

But the ring belonged to Lord Matthison's betrothed! She whirled round and marched down the corridor, fists clenched at her sides.

And it was up to her to insist that the thieving witch gave it back!

Chapter Twelve

Frances Farrell was sitting on what Cora had once, long ago, thought of as Lady Matthison's sofa. Lady Matthison *had* sometimes come downstairs, when Frances had come to call, and received her there in state. 'Such an obliging girl,' she would say to Mrs Paulding, in Cora's hearing. And then it would be, 'Frances dear, I know you won't mind me asking…so fatiguing for me…' and they would put their heads together and discuss people and places she had never heard of. And then Frances would go off on whatever errand Lady Matthison had given her. Once or twice, on her way out, seeing Cora's crestfallen expression, Frances had paused and patted her hand and promised that one day, perhaps once she had settled in a little better, she could go with her and meet the tenants she was visiting on behalf of the lady of the manor. And Lady Matthison would sniff, and turn on her heel, and float back up the stairs trailing shawls and scarves behind her.

Cora blinked away the slights heaped upon her in the past, and advanced on Frances Farrell with her shoulders squared.

Frances looked up at her and smiled. The open, friendly smile she had once upon a time employed to such devastating effect.

'Would you care for some tea?' she asked pleasantly.

In front of Lady Matthison's sofa was a low table that held cups, saucers, a sugar bowl and a plate of freshly baked biscuits. All the paraphernalia associated with the ritual of receiving morning callers.

Cora halted in her tracks as Frances lifted the teapot.

It all looked so civilised, so normal.

Except that *she* was presiding over the teapot as though *she* were the hostess and Cora was the one who was visiting!

'How dare you stroll in here, and sit on that sofa—' Cora jabbed her forefinger at the floral-patterned upholstery of the bow-legged, claw-footed *chaise longue* on which Lady Matthison had loved to recline '—and offer me tea, as though…as though butter wouldn't melt in your mouth!'

'Oh, dear,' said Frances, putting down the teapot and eyeing Cora with disdain. 'I see your manners have not improved since last we met. A lady who aspires to become mistress of Kingsmede,' she went on witheringly, 'really should know how to receive morning callers.'

At one time Cora had stood in awe of Miss Farrell's vast store of knowledge about the running of Kingsmede, gleaned not only from her kinship with Mrs

Paulding, but also her relationship with Lady Matthison. Frances had always been dropping 'hints' about how the future mistress of Kingsmede ought to behave. And Cora had drunk it all in, assuming Frances was trying to help her. But now she knew that all those hints had been dripped into her ears like so much poison, causing what little self-esteem she'd had to shrivel until she felt she was not even worthy to visit the place, never mind marry the man who would one day inherit it!

'That tone won't work on me any more,' said Cora defiantly. 'Because I know what you are now. I have remembered what you did. You should be in prison, not wandering about freely—' she sucked in a deep breath, her sense of outrage growing by the second '—offering people tea!'

Frances rose gracefully to her feet, her greater height making it all the easier to look down her nose at Cora. 'Perhaps we should take a stroll in the gardens,' she said, going over to the French windows that led out on to the terrace. 'So that the stridency of your voice may not reach the ears of the servants. We would not want them thinking his lordship has brought home a fishwife, now would we?'

With a supercilious smile, Frances unbolted the doors, and went outside. For a moment, Cora stood stock still in the middle of the floor, stunned by the way Frances was treating the place as if it were her own. And, most annoyingly of all, forcing Cora to trot along behind her, like some kind of supplicant if she wished to continue with the conversation.

Which of course she did.

'You mean you don't want to risk anyone overhearing what I have to say to you,' she retorted, plunging through the French doors in pursuit.

Frances had gone down the terrace steps, and was crossing the velvet-smooth lawn towards one of the rose borders.

'I trusted you!' Cora panted, catching up with Frances, who was examining the bushes with a critical eye.

'You made me believe you were my friend. But all the time, you were looking for ways to hurt me!'

'Not at all,' Frances replied mildly. 'I only wanted you to go back where you had come from. I had hoped,' she said with a doleful shake of her head, 'that seeing him with his paramour would have made you realise there was nothing for you here. My purpose was not to hurt you, but to open your eyes. You do remember,' she said with apparent concern, 'seeing him with that woman? You did just say your memory has returned.'

'Of course I remember seeing him with her, but...'

Frances frowned quizzically. 'Then why have you come back? Have you not learned what he is like yet? Or are you still claiming to be infatuated with him, so that you can pretend to be blind to his faults?'

The dart struck home. Was that not exactly what she had just been doing? Deciding to turn a blind eye to his infidelities, because she could not bear to contemplate living without him?

'You...you are twisting everything!' she cried.

'Besides, it is not his faults I came out here to discuss with you…'

'Good. Then we may discuss yours.'

'Mine?' gasped Cora, as Frances frowned, then stooped to snap a withered bloom from its stalk.

'You have no education, no fortune—' she tossed the spent bloom into the hedge at the back of the border with a grimace '—and no connections. You have never been a suitable partner for his lordship. And now—' she shook her head reprovingly '—I cannot think what has made you believe you can push your way back into his life.'

'It is not like that! It was his decision to bring me here. Besides, what right have you to say I am not suitable?'

'I only say what everyone thinks.' Frances turned away abruptly, her skirts releasing a cloud of fragrance into the air as they brushed against one of the low-growing lavender bushes.

'Nobody approved of his choice. Especially not his parents! None of his tenants would ever have accepted you, either. For we all knew how you and that brother of yours trapped him into making a proposal of marriage. Robbie,' she said, smiling maliciously over her shoulder, 'told me all about it.'

So that was where Mrs Paulding had got the story of the fight by the boat-house from. She felt slightly sick. Robbie had confided in Frances about how he had made Kit propose to her. How could he?

She watched Frances progress along the border,

stopping to sniff at a full-blown rose here, snapping off a spent one there... Frances, who had tricked her into believing she was friendly, when all the time she had been looking for ways to get rid of her. She had duped Robbie too. He had thought the world of her. He had spent a great deal of time going over to the vicarage. At one point, she had wondered if the two of them would make a match of it. She shuddered at the thought.

'You used that knowledge to try to get rid of me,' she said, and then, because Frances had nearly reached the end of the rose border, hitched up her skirts and trotted after her. 'What right had you to interfere?'

'Well, somebody had to do something about it. Poor Lady Matthison was prostrate with distress. And Christopher was far too much of a gentleman to tell you to your face that he could not stand the sight of you.'

The shaft went wide. For she knew now that Kit did indeed want her. He could not keep his hands off her! Oh, he might not feel the romantic love she had dreamed about inspiring when she had been a girl. But he certainly desired her, in a very basic way. Why, he enjoyed taking her to bed so much that he had stopped the carriage on the way here, and spent an entire afternoon naked in her arms, when he could just as easily have pressed on and arrived at Kingsmede in time for supper.

'Frances...' Cora stepped up to her and looked her straight in the eye. 'You and I both know that is a lie. Christopher wants to marry me.' For whatever reason. 'He told me he organised search parties—'

'Only to satisfy your brother!'

'No, Frances, that is not true. You have to stop this right now! He wanted to find me. You know he did.' It seemed so obvious now, she did not know why she had not seen it before. 'That was why you deliberately kept me hidden away up in the vicarage attic!'

'I was tending your injuries,' Frances argued, her eyes darting away. 'You were too ill to move.'

'You moved me from your hallway when I collapsed on your doorstep!' Cora scoffed. 'It would have been far less trouble to carry me into your parlour, and send word to Kingsmede that you had found me, than it was to heave me up all those stairs! And if you were really concerned about how ill I was, why did you never send for a doctor? No, you cannot use that excuse on me. Even back then, though I had a high fever, and had no idea who I was, or how I came to be there, I was fully aware that you hated me. You hated me so much, you sent me to Oakham Hall. You knew you were handing me over to a…a rapist, didn't you!'

Frances looked a little contrite. 'Yes, I did regret the necessity of taking that step. But by that time, it had become clear to me that little, short of death, would halt your ambitions. When the horse threw you, and I saw you lying there all covered with leaves, your head and limbs at such peculiar angles—' she tilted her head to one side, a reminiscent smile playing about her lips '—like a little broken doll.' Her eyes snapped back to Cora. 'I thought, for a few, blissful hours, that it had all been taken out of my hands. That death had provided the ultimate answer to the problems you posed. Even if the fall had not quite killed you, I was sure that lying on the ground in all that rain would have finished you off. Instead, you crawled to my door. It was quite a shock to see you standing there wringing wet, and with blood running down your face, asking me for help. You are like—' her face spasmed with disgust '—a pernicious weed, that will keep springing back up. You had to be rooted out for good!'

'You saw me fall? And did nothing to help?' No, it was worse than that. She screwed up her face as she tried to remember the actual words Frances had used when telling her about Kit's tryst in the woodcutter's hut. It was all terribly hazy...but unless Frances had put the idea in her head, she could not see why she would have gone to the stables and saddled a horse that was far too spirited for a novice to ride, when she could as easily have walked to the hut, as Kit had done.

'Frances!' she gasped. 'You tried to kill me!'

'Don't be silly,' Frances retorted. 'I merely concealed your whereabouts while considering what to do with you.'

Cora blinked in temporary confusion, until she realised that Frances was thinking about her stay in the vicarage, rather than the 'accident' in the forest.

'Your head injury had left you confused, which gave me a little time to come up with a solution to the problem you posed. For a few days, you became so ill that I began to hope you might just die and put us all out of our misery. But no...' She sighed. 'You began to recover. I feared it might only be a matter of time before you remembered who you were, and would start demanding you return to Kingsmede. So I went to visit the housekeeper at Oakham Hall. She was always in need of staff. The turnover there was very high.'

'And you told her I was an orphan, dependant on the parish…'

'In need of light work because you had been ill,' Frances nodded. 'A brilliant plan, I thought.'

'You deliberately put me in the way of Lord Sandiford, expecting him to…?'

Frances nodded sombrely. 'I dare say it must have been terribly unpleasant for you. But you had to learn your lesson. Your sin was overweening ambition. You wanted a lord. Well,' she tittered, 'I gave you to a lord who would humble you! So the punishment fit the crime. It was a very neat solution. A man of Christopher's standing would never marry a woman who had been sullied. Particularly not by a man of Lord Sandiford's reputation. So that even when your memory returned, and you found your way back to Kingsmede, I knew you would no longer pose a threat.'

'I cannot believe you are admitting to all this so calmly.' Cora felt as though she was in a waking nightmare. 'To talk of wishing me dead, of conniving at my utter ruin…are you not ashamed? Your father is a vicar, for heaven's sake!'

'Why should I be ashamed? I only did what was best for everyone concerned.'

'You are unbelievable! No decent person would have acted as you did…'

'You are such a simpleton,' Frances sneered as she unlatched the gate that led through to the orchard. 'History is full of good Christian folk girding up their loins, and acting decisively to save those around them from a greater evil. Just think of all those men of the cloth who condemned heretics to burn at the stake,' she said triumphantly, striding into the trees, her skirts flattening a trail through the long grass. 'It cannot have been easy to send a woman to die such a horrible death. And yet they did it. Because they knew it was the right thing to do, to purge the church from a greater evil.'

'I am not evil!' Cora gasped as she followed in Frances's wake. 'And nobody thinks it right to burn people at the stake any more. Frances, you have taken leave of your senses!'

Frances stopped so suddenly Cora almost ran into the back of her.

'No! I am the only one who sees things clearly. You are not fit to be Lord Matthison's wife! Not then, and especially not now! Not after spending seven years hiding away in shame, earning your living as a dressmaker and no doubt keeping low company.' She bent down, and hissed into Cora's face, 'Did you bear Lord Sandiford a child, Miss Montague? I have often wondered if he managed to make you pregnant before you escaped, like so many of the other girls who took employment at Oakham Hall. I could get no news of you once you had left. But then, of course, they are well used to covering up Lord Sandiford's peccadilloes.'

Cora reeled back. 'No! He did not manage to rape me.' She lifted her chin proudly. 'I fought him off.'

Frances raised a disbelieving eyebrow.

'Ah, so *that* is the tale you have told Christopher. That is how you persuaded him to take you back.' She shook her head and clucked her tongue in reproof. 'You really are shameless in your determination to ensnare him, are you not? And he, being the gentleman he is, will not question the word of his dearest friend's sister.' Her pale eyes turned flint hard. 'But I am warning you now, nobody else will believe you, once they hear you worked at Oakham Hall. Nobody will receive you. You will be a social pariah!'

'And you will make sure they know, won't you, Frances?' Cora retorted, the past becoming clearer as Frances spelled out what her future would be like. When she had first arrived at Kingsmede, as a shy young girl, the staff had been somewhat surprised that master Christopher had brought back a fiancée. Surprised, and warily watchful, but not hostile. That attitude had only developed gradually. As Frances, she now saw, had worked behind the scenes to paint a picture of her as a greedy, scheming seductress.

'Well,' said Frances with a calculating look. 'It all depends on you. I take no delight in spreading gossip, you know,' she said piously. 'I would much rather not have to speak about such a sordid incident. If you were to just break off this ridiculous engagement, and go back to where you came from, there would be no need for any more unpleasantness. And, my dear—' she placed her hand on Cora's forearm, and looked intently into her eyes '—if you have any real affection for him, you must surely see that the best thing you can do for him is to release him from the intolerable burden of this unequal alliance. Sometimes it is necessary to sacrifice our personal happiness, for the good of those we love.'

Cora swayed. If Frances had come to her last time she had been here, and delivered that little speech, with such sincerity that she had managed to bring tears to her eyes, Cora might have done exactly as she suggested. Frances might have won!

But she had not. No, Frances had sent her out on a horse she could scarcely ride, hoping to break her heart, if not her bones. And then locked her away, denying her the medical treatment she had so badly needed. She had lain in that attic, shaking with fear and fever while Frances sat at the foot of her bed, turning her hand this way and that so that the ruby ring she wore on her finger gleamed and pulsed in the candlelight. With a gloating expression on her face.

Angrily, Cora flung Frances's hand from her arm.

'You want him for yourself, don't you!' She did not know why she had not seen it before. But every time Frances mentioned Christopher's name, her eyes shone. Her whole face softened. 'That is why you have worked so hard to get rid of me. All that talk about working for the greater good is so much sanctimonious claptrap!'

Frances's mouth thinned with disapproval. She took a breath to refute Cora's accusations, but this time Cora was not prepared to listen.

'Don't bother to come up with any more of your clever little stories to try to hoax me! You took his ring from my finger, and you wore it. I saw the expression on your face as you sat there, night after night, hoping I would die.'

Cora's legs were shaking. She had never had the courage to stand up to anyone before, and she was not sure where she was getting the strength to do it now. It was just unthinkable to leave without saying what she had specifically come here to say.

'Frances, you must return the ring you stole. If you do not, I will have to tell Lord Matthison that you have it.'

'I did not steal it!' Frances looked outraged. 'I was keeping it safe. I have kept it safe for years. Lady Matthison asked me to hide it when her husband would have sold it off to pay his gaming debts.'

'And then she asked you to bring it back, so that Kit could give it to me,' Cora deduced.

'She did not want you to have it!' Frances spat. 'She wept when she told me how Christopher was throwing it away on an unworthy woman.'

'But it is Christopher's right to throw it away, if that is what he wants to do. It is not for you to decide who should wear it.'

'It will not be you!' Frances hissed, total hatred blazing from her eyes.

'Nor you!' Cora retorted without thinking.

'Why should it not be me?' Frances seized her upper arms and shook her. 'You hooked him, and you are only a parson's daughter!' She flung Cora from her with such force she stumbled, and would have fallen if the lower branch of a pear tree had not struck her in the small of her back. She clutched wildly at the trunk of the tree, steadying herself while Frances continued to rant.

'He has known me all his life. I was his friend before he even met Robbie! Lady Matthison looked on me as a daughter. I know his land, his people, in a way you never could, and never will. You have no idea what it means to be mistress of Kingsmede!'

The wild desperation in her eyes tugged a strand of sympathy from Cora. For some time she had known there was something not quite right about Frances. Now she saw that the woman had been so hopelessly entangled in the coils of unrequited love for such a long time that it had affected her ability to reason.

'Have I not been waiting patiently for him all this time? Helping him refurbish Kingsmede?' Frances gesticulated towards the house. 'Showing him what a comfort I could be,' she finished, tears welling in her pale eyes, 'when he was sad?'

What was sad, was that Frances had convinced herself that what she was saying was true. But it wasn't. Oh, she might have had a hand in redecorating the house. But Lord Matthison had never once mentioned Frances, not in any context, let alone as a friend who brought him comfort. When he described the years she had been missing, he had spoken of loneliness, pointlessness and hellish darkness.

Frances half-turned away, fumbling with the strings

of her reticule. After the amount of tears Cora had shed over the past few days, she had provided herself with several clean handkerchiefs when she had dressed that morning. Feeling heartily sorry for Frances's heartache, she pulled one from her sleeve, and went to offer it to her.

But Frances had already found what she had been searching for in her reticule. And it was not a handkerchief.

It was a little knife.

For a few seconds Cora stood there, holding out her handkerchief, while the dappled sunlight glinted on the lethal-looking little blade as the wind ruffled the over-hanging branches.

And then Frances came at her.

Cora instinctively flung up her arm to protect her face as Frances slashed out viciously. She felt a sharp sting, and then a spreading warmth as blood streamed from a wound that had been intended to disfigure her.

'Frances!' Cora gasped in appalled disbelief. There remained no trace of the genteel, pious façade that Frances employed to deceive people as to her true nature. She was no longer bothering to conceal the murderous hatred that had simmered inside her for years. Her eyes burned with a kind of devilish excitement as she swung the lethal little blade in a wide arc, almost as though she was taunting Cora.

Cora took a hasty step back, her heart pounding so hard it felt as though it was trying to punch its way out of her chest.

Frances took a step forwards, keeping the distance

between them equal. 'If I can get rid of you,' she said, with a chilling smile, 'he will turn to me!'

Cora's heart sank. They were too far from the house for anyone to hear if she cried out for help. And she would not get far if she tried to make a run for it. She had barely been able to keep up with Frances when she broke into a brisk walk!

But she had, once, seen the landlord of a tavern disarm a customer who had come at him with a knife. He had done it by seizing his attacker's arm as he lunged, deflecting the knife's trajectory. He'd then slammed his fist into the other man's face, and the pair had gone down in a welter of mud and blood and beer. She didn't know how effective punching Frances might be. In any case, she rather thought, given the woman's superior height and strength, she would need to use both hands to simply block any blow Frances might strike.

But she had to at least try to disarm her.

No sooner had the vague plan for self-defence begun to form in Cora's mind, than Frances stopped toying with her, and came at her with a wild cry.

The first part of Cora's plan went surprisingly well. She managed to grab her knife hand and deflect the blade away from her face. The impetus of Frances's attack carried Cora backwards, and they both fell to the ground, with Frances on top, the weight of her body slamming the breath from Cora's lungs. And the knife went flying.

But Cora only experienced a fleeting moment of

relief, because Frances promptly fastened both her hands about Cora's neck, and began to squeeze.

Cora scrabbled at Frances's fingers, trying to prise them from her neck. She was already winded from the fall, and she feared that if she couldn't take a breath soon, it would be all up with her. But she could not break her stranglehold.

Desperately, she tried to pitch her attacker off, but Frances was bigger than her, stronger than her, and was pressing all her weight down on Cora's windpipe. Cora's strength was fading swiftly. In one last effort to save herself, she reached up, trying to claw at her attacker's face. Frances reared back, laughing in open mockery. Her arms were longer than Cora's. She was having no difficulty in squeezing the life from her victim, while Cora could not even mark her face.

Blackness was creeping in round the periphery of her vision. Stars began exploding in front of her eyes. Dimly, from beyond the sound of a murderess's demonic laughter, she thought she could perceive Kit's voice, calling her name.

And then suddenly, just when it seemed all hope was lost, someone loomed up behind Frances, and another pair of hands was trying to break her grip. Frances fought to keep up the pressure on her throat to the last, her nails clawing at Cora's neck even as she was dragged bodily away.

And then Kit's face swam into view.

And she could definitely hear him calling her name, above the noise Frances was making as she was dragged away, kicking and screaming the kind of curses no vicar's daughter should have known.

She felt Kit haul her into his arms, urging her to breathe. But it still felt as though Frances had her by the throat. No matter how desperately she tried, she could not seem to draw any air past the constriction she could still feel there.

The darkness was creeping between them now. But as his voice began to fade, she felt a wave of immense gratitude that she had lasted long enough to die in his arms. The last sound she would hear on this earth would not be the demonic laughter of a woman who hated her, but his voice, so beloved, begging her not to leave him.

Chapter Thirteen

'Cora, don't be dead. Oh, dear God, please don't let her die!'

It was too dark, down in the void where she drifted, to see anything, but she could hear his voice, calling to her.

'Come back to me, Cora. I swear I won't force you to marry me if you can't bear the thought of it, only don't die. I couldn't stand it!'

'Kit…' He sounded so upset, she wanted to comfort him, but nothing emerged from her throat but an agonised croak. Oh, it hurt to try to speak. In fact, it hurt to breathe. She wished she did not have to bother. It would be so much easier to sink back down into the velvety soft darkness…

'Oh, thank God! Thank God!' she heard him say. 'She tried to speak. She's waking up! Come back to me, Cora, and I will give you anything you ask. Only don't leave me alone!'

No, she did not want to leave him alone. And so she breathed. And reached out for him.

And a room materialised around her.

The morning room. And she...she bit back a groan...in spite of determining she would never do so again, she had wound up lying on Lady Matthison's sofa!

'You will give me anything?' she rasped. 'Truly?'

He was kneeling on the floor beside her, his eyes glistening with what she suspected were unshed tears.

'You heard that?' His face went white. But then a look of resolution came over him. 'Whatever you ask of me, I will give it. Just tell me what you want!'

'I want you to burn this sofa,' she whispered, discovering that whispering caused her less pain that proper speech.

His eyes widened in surprise, but making a swift recovery, he said, 'If that is what you want...'

'And a drink...' Her hand fluttered to her throat, which felt bruised inside and out. Though there was not an inch of her that did not hurt to some extent. Her back, her legs, and especially her arms. Her right arm also felt strangely stiff and awkward. Raising it slightly, she saw that someone had torn the sleeve off her dress, and applied a bandage to her forearm where Frances had cut her.

'Do not try to talk any more,' he said, darting away and coming back with a tumbler of what looked and smelled like brandy. He slipped one arm under her shoulders, and raised her head while he held the glass to her lips.

'I know you don't like spirits,' he said, as she opened

her mouth to voice a protest, 'but this is one of those times when nothing else will do.'

Ruthlessly he tipped the liquid into her mouth. She spluttered a little as it burnt its way down, but presently she welcomed the reviving warmth it sent flowing through her veins.

She welcomed the feel of his arm round her shoulders, too. And the depth of concern she read in his eyes, and the persistent way he had kept on calling to her. He had not let her go.

She breathed in deeply through her nose, savouring the spicy scent of his soap, and his clean linen, and his warm skin. She tilted her head so that she could rest it on his shoulder, and sighed out her gratitude. She was alive. And for quite some time it was enough just to lie there, feeling him close as she breathed in and out.

But eventually she knew she would have to find out what had happened.

'Where is Frances?'

Lord Matthison's shoulder tensed under her cheek. 'Locked up,' he said grimly. 'She has gone completely mad! Even after Robbie dragged her off you, she kept trying to break free and get at you. In the end, I had to pick you up and run with you to the house, or I don't know what she might have done.' His arm tightened protectively round her shoulder. 'It took both footmen and the butler to subdue her. She did not calm down completely until the doctor who came to tend your injuries, gave her a sleeping draught. And even asleep...'

'Not in the dark!' she gasped. It was horrible to hear

of another woman suffering the same indignities that had been heaped on her. But then she recalled Frances's pious tone as she had declared that the punishment should fit the crime...

No! No, she did not want *anyone* to go through what she had done.

'Don't lock her up in the dark, alone. Frances is sick,' she whispered. 'She needs care, not punishment.'

Lord Matthison nodded gravely. 'Her aunt is with her for now. They are up in one of the guest rooms, which has a good stout lock on the door. But I will find a place where she can get the help she needs. Where they will treat her kindly.'

She relaxed immediately. But then she felt him shake his head. 'I am so sorry I left you unprotected. I brought you back to Kingsmede, promising to protect you from your enemies. Instead I exposed you to the most dangerous of them all.'

'You did not know what she was like,' Cora murmured.

'Not when I brought you here,' he said earnestly. 'But after last night...' He shifted his position, looking so guilty that she reached out and took his hand. He grasped it, as though she had flung him a lifeline.

'Robbie and I sat up for hours last night, going over it all, and gradually piecing together what happened to you. It was Robbie who worked out that the woman who kept you up in her attic was Miss Farrell. I did not recognise her from the description you gave, in fact I argued that it could not have been her. But he was adamant we at least check out his theory. Because he had seen that other side of Miss Farrell, during that last summer when he had begun courting her in earnest. He discovered she had eyes for nobody but me.' He cleared his throat self-consciously. 'He never told me about her infatuation. He did not have the time. It was shortly before you disappeared, and then everything fell apart between us...' He pressed a kiss to the hand he had been crushing between his fingers.

'Last night he told me that your description of a hard-faced, hard-eyed woman tallied exactly with the opinion he had formed of Miss Farrell just before he returned to Scotland. Her behaviour towards him was...unforgivable,' he grated. 'She offered him no sympathy, no condolences on his loss. Just told him it was all for the best. The best!'

Lord Matthison ground his teeth. She felt his jaw working against her forehead. She looped her injured arm about his waist, and hugged him.

He snatched in a ragged breath. Then another. Then, with a strangled moan, he flung both arms round her, and hung on to her tightly.

It seemed to take him an effort to continue talking, but eventually he went on, 'This morning, we went over to the vicarage, and once we saw her leaving, we... This will sound reprehensible, Cora, but we broke in. Well, not exactly broke in. The back door was open. Sneaked in, is what we did. And ransacked the attics. And we found it.'

He drew the arm that had been round her waist away, and dipped into his pocket. When he withdrew it, he was holding the ring.

The ruby ring.

'It was concealed in a secret drawer of an old bureau, under a mound of moth-eaten curtains, just as you described it.' He turned it slightly, so that it caught the light, making it gleam and throb as though it had a pulse of its own.

Cora stared at it in sick fascination as he continued, 'When we got back to the house, and heard that Frances had come to visit you, we came straight in here to confront her with what we had found. But by then, you were entering the orchard. I could not understand why you had gone so far from the house, but Robbie, bless him, knew at once she was up to no good. He ran out after you. And caught up with you just in time. I was only a second or two behind him. But it was as well he got to you first.' He tilted up her chin, and ran the backs of his fingers gently over the scratches she could feel scoring the skin of her throat. 'That woman has the strength of ten men. I never want to have to see a sight like that, ever again.' And he lowered his head, and touched his lips gently to the livid wounds.

The sensation sent a shiver of longing through her. She felt his lips curve briefly into a smile against her neck.

'Does that response mean what I hope it means?' he said, reaching down for her hand, and positioned the blood-red ring over her third finger.

'No!' Cora snatched her hand away.

'Don't...don't you want to marry me?' His voice was as hoarse as her own when he went on, 'Can you at least explain why? I deserve to know that much, don't I?' He withdrew his arms and sat back on his heels so that he could see her face. His own eyes were bleak, his mouth a taut line bracketed by two deep grooves.

'I have always wanted to marry you,' she whispered, determined he should not suffer even one more second of pain on her account. If only Robbie had not seen them kissing!

'And even though I learned that it was not your choice to begin with, if you really, truly want to marry me now...'

'Not my choice?' He reared back. 'What are you talking about?'

'I know that Robbie forced you to propose to me. After he saw us kissing in the boat...'

'He did no such thing!'

'You don't need to try to cover it up, Kit,' she said wearily. 'I don't care about that any more.'

'Just you listen to me, dammit!' he growled. 'It is true Robbie confronted me about us kissing out on the loch. He accused me of toying with you, the minute his back was turned. Said I had betrayed his trust, and I would never be welcome in any home of his again. How he could have thought...' He laughed bitterly. 'Well, his opinion of me was so poor that not long after he accused me of murdering you!'

His face took on what she thought of as his devilish mask.

'He would have thrown me out of his house right then, only I refused to go. Not until I had the chance to at least find out if you were willing to have me. That was when he went berserk. And said he would never consent to a penniless degenerate like me marrying his little sister. I had to fight him for the right to let you make up your own mind, Cora.'

'You fought him for the right…' Her mind was in a whirl. 'Does that mean…?' but she lacked the courage to ask what she really wanted to know. She turned her head away, shutting her eyes against the foolish hope she could not bear to have snatched from her.

'What else could it have meant? I was in love with you. Desperately in love.'

Her eyes flew open. She stared at him in wonder, still hardly daring to believe she had heard him correctly.

'I think I had been in love with you for years. It was not only Robbie I came to Auchentay to see. I looked forward to seeing the changes in you, as you grew from an enchanting girl, into a lovely young woman.'

'But you never said…'

'Your father guarded you too closely for me to get anywhere near you. And you were so shy.' He stroked the curve of her cheek with the back of his forefinger. 'I feared that if I went blundering in, telling you…' He thrust his fingers through his hair, his cheeks flushing a dull red. 'Well, what would I have spoken to you of, at that age? A boy's thoughts are of touching, and kissing, not love and marriage! And you were so prim and proper…

'Only the way you looked at me sometimes kept my hopes alive. And the little things you did for me.' He knelt up, and took her hands between his own. 'I will never forget opening my trunk when I got back to school, and finding you had tucked a couple of new shirts in amongst my ragged collection of clothing. And recalling how many nights, during my visit, you had sat sewing, with a little smile playing about your lips.' He bowed his head and kissed her fingers one by one.

'I put my heart into every stitch,' she admitted, raising her free hand to stroke his hair.

'When your parents died,' he went on, 'and Robbie was making all those plans for your future…there was some aunt or other he said he was going to send you to…well—' he looked up at her as though pleading for understanding '—I knew very well that you were far too young to be thinking of marriage, but I could not bear the thought I might never see you again. I felt as though it was my last chance. I know it was wrong, the way I went about binding you to me, but I did at least ask your permission before I kissed you,' he pointed out. 'I know things got out of control pretty quickly…hell, I'm not surprised Robbie was furious with me. I threw you down in the bottom of that boat and practically ravished you!'

Cora blinked at him, wondering how two people could have such divergent memories of the same event.

'And then, when you kept raising objections to my proposal… I…kissed you into submission. That afternoon, in the boat…you came alive in my arms. You had been repressed for so long, that when I began to rouse you, it was like letting the genie out of the bottle. We both discovered what a sensual person you are. And I shamelessly used that discovery against you. Because you are highly moral, too. I did not believe you could accept feeling that degree of passion, without linking it to a deep emotional commitment. So I stoked up the passion until you fancied yourself in love with me. Don't deny it,' he said, when she would have interrupted. 'Subsequent events have shown me that it was never more than lust that I could rouse in you. But, oh, how I longed to believe you meant all those things you said to me…'

'I did mean them,' she husked. 'I do! I love you so much.'

His answering smile was sardonic. 'But you won't marry me.' He glanced at the ruby ring he still held in his hand, and the determined way she was keeping her left hand well out of its reach.

'Do you love me, Kit?' she asked him earnestly. 'Do you really want to marry me?'

'I do not know how you can even ask me that,' he replied bleakly.

'Because I saw you with that other woman!'

He looked completely baffled.

'Other woman?'

'In the hut. In the forest. That last day!'

He shook his head slowly. 'There was no other woman. There has never been another woman for me, Cora.'

She felt his denial like a blow. 'Why bother to lie about it now?' she hissed angrily. 'I saw you with my own eyes. She had hardly any clothes on. And you kissed her!'

'In a hut…' he echoed, mystified. And then his expression cleared. 'Maggie.' He shut his eyes, and bowed his head. When he opened them, they were flat, and dead looking. 'I had forgotten all about that, in the light of everything else that happened that day…' He leaped to his feet. 'You seem determined not to believe a word I say!' He stalked across to the window, where he stood with his back to her.

Cora struggled to sit up, every muscle in her body protesting. 'Kit,' she croaked. Then, forcing as much volume from her battered vocal cords as she could, 'Kit, please! I need to know why you lied to me. You told me you were going to Bamford, when really you were going to meet that woman. What was I supposed to think?'

'Oh, obviously—' he spun round and looked at her bitterly '—that I was being unfaithful.'

She sank back, exhausted. But with her eyes fixed on his silhouette, outlined against the bright sunshine that poured into the room, she grated, 'Kit, you had never once told me you loved me. I thought Robbie had forced you to propose to me. And then Frances told me you loved that other woman. It was…awful…' She covered her face in her hands as the tears began to flow.

But then she felt the cushions dip as he sat next to her.

'Frances again, damn her!' he grated, and pulled her into his arms. 'She was lying, Cora. About everything.

She knew I was never in love with Maggie. Maggie was just…one of the reasons Robbie thought I was not fit to go near you. And you saw her, for goodness' sake. You must have seen she was a good bit older than me.'

'I was not looking at her face,' she mumbled into his neckcloth.

'Ah, yes, the enthusiasm of her greeting took me by surprise, I must confess. But did you not see that a kiss was all that passed between us?'

Cora shook her head. 'The kiss was all it took to make me lose my breakfast.'

His arms tightened convulsively about her. 'And then you galloped off in that storm, and Bobby threw you. My God, I can see it all now. You were too upset to think straight.'

'It felt as though my heart was breaking,' she admitted.

'You did not mean to run away for ever,' he said, a tremor of hope in his voice. 'You galloped away from that hut, all upset because you thought I had played you false,' he mused, as though to himself. 'You were never all that good a rider. Because of the storm, and your state, you lost control of Bobby, and fell. When you came to, you did not know who you were, did you? It had all been wiped away. What did you do, make your way to the nearest house?'

'I saw a light,' she whispered.

'The vicarage. Frances opened the door…the vicar was here most of that night, trying to bring us consolation…but I have never felt any, until now. Cora, you don't know what it means to finally know you did not mean to leave me.' He hugged her tight. 'You didn't, did you?'

She shook her head. 'I think I would have come back here eventually, when I had calmed down, and told you I could not bear to share you with another woman, and begged you to give her up.'

'I *was* giving her up,' he broke in. 'That was why I sent for her! Maggie could not read or write. So I had to meet her, one last time, to tell her I was getting married. I did not want her to hear it from anyone else, and think I did not care about her feelings. She did not deserve that. Besides, I needed to make sure there were no…obligations I needed to meet.'

'She was—' Cora sniffed '—just your mistress?'

'Not even that. She was a very generous woman, willing to share her favours with a growing lad. I am sorry you had to find out about my baser instincts the way you did. Would it do any good to explain that it meant nothing? That all young men experiment to some degree…'

'You met her to end it,' she sighed. And then she re-examined the scene that had all but destroyed her, because Frances had primed her to see Kit meeting the woman he loved. All she had actually seen was Kit, entering a tumbledown hut, and a woman, who had been in the act of stripping off her blouse, flinging herself into his arms. He had smiled, she had seen that much. But she had not stayed to see any more.

She had not trusted him. She had told him she loved him, but she had believed the very worst of him. Guilty tears sprang to her eyes. But she had been so insecure! She had never had much self-confidence, and what little she had, Frances had whittled away with her cutting little remarks.

'I'm so sorry,' she wept. 'All these wasted years…'

'It was not your fault. It was Frances Farrell at the back of it all, driving us apart! When I think of what she put you through…hiding you away when you were ill, then sending you off to Oakham Hall—' his face grew thunderous '—I could wring her blasted neck!'

Inadvertently, Cora's hand flew to her own throat. He looked stricken.

'I should not have said that! I'm sorry! So sorry. Hell, Cora, I cannot seem to do or say anything right with you! No wonder you don't want to marry me. Darling—' he grasped her hands in his, his expression pleading '—I am not a violent man. I have never struck a woman in anger. I am not like your father.'

When he saw her frown, he reminded her, 'You told me that your father beat your mother to death. I can understand why you find it hard to trust men, but I am nothing like him! I might speak intemperately, but—'

She reached up and laid her hands to his mouth, stopping the torrent of words. 'I have always known you are a far better person than him. But even he was not as bad as I imagined. He did not kill my mother. Not exactly.' She sighed. 'That scene I recalled, when I thought I was Mary, was the very last time he hit her. The time he went too far. Until then, whenever he lost his temper, she tried to pretend it had not happened. She would wear clothes that concealed her bruises. She was always determined to uphold his reputation in public. But that last time seemed to break her spirit. She went in on herself, and ceased carrying out her parish duties no matter how much he ranted and roared at her. And then, come winter, she took a cold, and it went to her lungs. She just gave up on life. And he knew it was his fault.' Her face went hard. 'But in his guilt, as in all else, he was out of control. Those last few months...' She shivered, and hung her head. 'When he died, all I felt was relief.'

'No wonder you were so afraid of men, while you were Mary. All you had ever known was violence... and—' his voice hitched '—betrayal. But couldn't you learn to love me again? Or at least—'

'I do love you,' she interjected. 'With all my heart.'

'Then...' He proffered the ring again.

'Kit,' she said with a frown, 'you will think I'm being really silly, but I don't want you to put that ring on my finger again.'

'Why not? If you love me? You were willing to be my mistress...when you thought you were Mary.' He speared his fingers through his hair again. 'Now you know who you are. It all started to go wrong when your memory came back.' His face darkened. 'I wish to God I had never brought you back here!'

'Kit, please just listen to me! I do want to marry you. So much. Last night I realised I would marry you even if you took a dozen mistresses. I cannot bear the thought of living without you!'

'Cora,' he grated, 'you don't know how I have longed to hear you say that.' He crushed her to him, kissing her in almost frenzied desperation. 'I have missed you so much,' he said, pulling back, and smoothing away the hair that had tumbled over her face.

'You are the only person who has ever really cared much for me. Me, not the position I could provide, or my wealth, or, latterly, my notoriety.' His dark eyes blazed with fervour. 'You loved me enough to follow me from your home land to this miserable barn of a place…it almost broke your heart when you saw me kissing another woman. Even when you forgot who *you* were, you fell in love with me all over again. You gifted me your virginity. Trusted me to take care of you when everyone else said I was some kind of demonic—' his face twisted '—murdering…'

She shook her head, and stroked his tortured face with her injured hand. 'Don't think about that any more. It is over now. We are together again.'

'What as?' he bit out. 'If you cannot bear to marry a man whose reputation is as tarnished as mine has become, if you wish to remain as my mistress…'

She shook her head again. 'I would be honoured to be your wife. But not…' She looked at the ring, glowing in his outstretched hand. 'Not with that ring. Is there…have you ever heard there was a curse on it?'

'A curse?' He looked at the ring, mystified.

Cora felt her cheeks grow warm, but she had to tell

him what was bothering her, even if he did think she was being overly fanciful.

'It seems to bring nothing but misery to those who covet it. Your father was a rotten husband to your mother. You would not have thought she would have any sentimental feelings about the ring that betrothed her to him, and yet she hung on to it, when he had sold everything else of value. She gave it to Frances to hide. Frances kept putting it on, and dreaming of becoming Lady Matthison and went completely mad…and I wore it for only seven days, and we both went through seven years of utter misery. I suppose it could all be coincidence, but…'

With a shrug, he tucked the ring into his pocket. 'The ring is of no consequence. If you do not like it, I shall buy you another. An emerald—' he smiled '—to match your eyes.'

The shadows Cora had sensed hovering in the corners dissipated. Sunlight flooded the room.

'Now,' he said, determination jutting his jaw, 'Miss Cora Montague, love of my life, will you please marry me? Now that I have dealt with the obstacles thrown up by—' he raised one hand, and began to count off on his fingers '—Robbie, and Frances, and Maggie, and Miss Winters, and Madame Pichot, and Lord Sandiford. And now that I have promised to burn the sofa, and buy you a ring that no other woman who wanted to be Lady Matthison has ever worn…' He paused, the light of challenge in his eyes. 'Come on, Cora, I know you want to. You promised me for ever.'

'I did.' She smiled, flinging her arms round his neck. 'I do.'

'Then nothing,' he growled, 'and nobody shall ever part us again.'

* * * * *

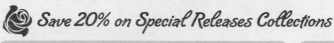